'*The writing is plain, powerful, and confident, and a terrific sense of foreboding informs the subtext. Wow.*'
– **Karen Karbo,** author of: *Trespassers Welcome Here* and *How Georgia Became O'Keeffe*

Praise for *Roberta's Woods*, also by Betty J. Cotter

'*This terrific look at the near future Bush domestic legacy is a wonderful suspense thriller that describes a future with immense energy shortfalls forcing difficult decisions to be made by individuals and government. Although Roberta is the star who holds the futuristic tale together, the support cast with their varying reactions to the crisis and how to "fix" it make Betty J. Cotter's bleak vision seem genuine.*'
– **Harriet Klausner,** literary critic

'*Cotter's competent debut imagines the Yankee frontier as recreated by a severe energy crisis, along with an unlikely heroine to navigate it ... Cotter's suspenseful vision of the near future features strong character development, sensual writing and an absorbing plot.*'
– **Publisher's Weekly**

PUBLISHER'S INFORMATION

Copyright©2012 Betty J. Cotter.

Swamp Yankee Publishing
475 Woodruff Avenue
Wakefield, RI 02879

Cover photo: Betty J. Cotter
Cover design: EbookBakery.com

ISBN 978-1-938517-08-2

THE WINTERS

A novel by Betty J. Cotter

ACKNOWLEDGEMENTS

This book was made possible by financial support from the R.I. State Council on the Arts, for which the author is grateful. Many other people provided guidance, advice, and assistance in the years it took to complete. I am grateful to John King, professor of oceanography at the University of Rhode Island, for sharing his research on South County's coastal ponds; any mistakes herein are not his, but solely the author's. Many people read the manuscript and provided editorial guidance, including members of the South County Writers Group; my agents, Jack and Joan Ryan; my sister, Andrea A. Thayer; and fellow graduates of the Vermont College of Fine Arts MFA program, Mark Lupinetti, Laurie Cannady, and James Pounds. I am grateful to my many writing friends, especially Tara Flynn, Marybeth Reilly McGreen, and Laura Kelly, for their support, advice, and friendship. To my writing students, thank you for letting me into your lives. Thank you to Michael Grossman of the eBook Bakery, who provided technical assistance and designed the cover. Mostly, I'm grateful to my husband, Tim, and children, Mary, Colby and Perry, for their unwavering faith and support.

In memory of my mother
Eleanor C. Thayer
1919-2012

CHAPTER ONE

On the morning that her father died, Joyce Winter woke to nothing.

She had shaken awake before her alarm sounded but could not decide what had startled her. She listened for the gurgle of kerosene draining into the firebox of the kitchen range, or kindling tumbling into the wood box, or her father's boots scuffing against the mat in the mudroom. The wind rattling the window glass was all she heard. The farmhouse, like a tired old heart, had stopped beating.

She got up and walked to the window, where a scrap of flannel – ripped from an old nightgown – plugged a small hole in the pane, but not enough to keep out a draft. Snow littered the ground like dirty laundry. It was that time before dawn when enough light burns on the horizon to cast the trees and buildings in black shadow, and in the milky sky she saw both the ghost of the moon and a thin outline of the sun's forehead lifting. There was the barn, gray fields beyond, and the Atlantic Ocean, a jagged line of blue. And that was all. She did not know what she expected to see, but the empty familiarity of the farm did nothing to reassure her.

Joyce's mother, Helen, was asleep in the next room, her breath faintly stirring the patchwork coverlet. Her father's side of the bed was taken down, a faint wrinkle still impressed in the sheets. Joyce stood at the door. The room smelled of damp wool and something faintly cloying, like perfume that has turned. On her mother's nightstand were her glasses, an overturned and tattered copy of "Walden," a composition notebook and a black pen. Her father did not have a nightstand. On his bureau were three familiar objects – a cracked leather wallet, a college class ring that he never wore, and a china saucer full of change.

Joyce wrapped her robe tighter around her and slunk downstairs. The kitchen was empty and the range was cold. The stove jug was missing, and her father's coat was gone from the peg in the hall. He had gone to get kerosene. With the back of her hand Joyce rubbed a circle in the frost on the window. From this view she could see clearly what had been eclipsed from upstairs. The jug was standing in the snow next to the barn, under the tap of the 55-gallon drum. Her father's boot prints led away from it, to the back of the barn. Something had distracted him, probably the animals, and he had wandered off. Her mother, she knew, wouldn't get up until her father brought her hot coffee; and Dale was gone now. Even when he was home her brother was little help, but sometimes when she begged him he would do the difficult chores, like fetch wood for the parlor stove or kerosene for the kitchen. For a moment she considered jumping back into bed and covering her head under the pile of blankets until someone else had heated the house. But her father was nowhere to be seen and her mother would never rise this early. She hated the thought of it but it had to be done. She threw on her coat over her robe and slipped into her boots without tying them.

Outside she called to her father twice but there was no answer. She felt vaguely uneasy but dismissed the feeling. Behind the barn it was hard to hear, and as her mother said, he was deaf as a post anyway. The wind was coming off the ocean, stirring up snow like dust devils that swirled around her ankles, and the wind tore at her hands as she held the kerosene jug to the spigot. The fuel came out in a rush, missing the lip of the jug and spilling onto her boots and legs. *Damn.* She would stink all day;

there was no getting the smell out. Either that or she'd burn the house down. Her classmates were still sleeping beneath electric blankets in bedrooms with central heating, their mothers starting coffee makers while their fathers put on suit coats and ties. Their breakfast tables looked like the TV commercials, where glasses of milk and orange juice stand sentinel at every place setting and lunch boxes are filled with miniature bags of potato chips and sandwiches in Baggies.

She screwed on the cap and cut off her thoughts. As she turned around, the old house stood before her, leaning into the wind. Two hundred years off the Atlantic Ocean had worn it down. The shingles were a dull, faded brown, and the central chimney listed toward the water like a jib on a sinking ship. Icicles gleamed in a jagged row of daggers from the eaves, and one gutter sagged off the side of the house. Another cascade dripped down the sides of the rain barrel. She wondered if there would be enough water this morning, or if she would have to chip ice from the barrel and melt it on the stove. So far the well had held out this winter, a relief after last year's drought, but last week the pipes had frozen and she had been stuck washing her hair in rainwater. Other girls bought shampoo that promised to get their hair rainwater clean. She had the real thing.

Her father had not returned. She hoisted the kerosene jug onto its cradle on the back of the stove, opened the damper and lit the range. Soon the flames had died back and the jug was making reassuring glug-glug noises. She hated lighting the stove, but it was easier when her mother wasn't around to fret about how much she'd opened the damper or whether the chimney was afire. She filled the coffeepot, put water on for oatmeal and toasted some bread. Once the kitchen had begun to warm and she had sat down to breakfast, the morning didn't seem too bad. She liked to pretend at times like this that she lived alone. This was her house in some indefinite time in the future. Her parents were gone – not dead, of course, but just gone, vanished from the scene for her convenience. She imagined herself living alone, a famous writer of independence and means. She made over the house in her mind. The peeling paint and rough pine floors were replaced by floral wallpaper and shiny hardwoods. Thick, lush fabrics and overstuffed upholstery transformed the living room, and the kitchen gleamed with oak cabinets and tile. Every surface of the house was new and clean. Upstairs, the master bedroom – the largest room in the house, which had been sealed since her grandmother died – had been reopened as Joyce's personal suite, with a chaise for lounging, a walk-in closet and deep pile carpeting. There she would take her breakfast, reading the New York Times and pondering which character to work on this morning. She would write in the mornings at a mahogany secretary. Maybe a maid would come in at noontime, to make her lunch and tidy up. Why not? She imagined a red sports car, an MG with leather interior, parked by the barn.

The cat, Peppermint, was walking in the snow, shaking off one black boot and one white boot as he stepped where lately the fantasy car had been. Joyce sighed and shifted her gaze toward the trees to the east and the thin strip of blue that was the ocean. In the south field she saw something move, then freeze. Coyote. It was small, barely bigger than a German shepherd, but its stiff tail and long ears gave it away. A kit, probably, newly weaned and looking for food. Maybe her father had seen it and gone for the shotgun. He probably had found another one of the hens gone. The coyotes must be hungry, with all this snow cover. The new year was only three weeks old, and already they had had two storms – big, dramatic episodes, especially the last one, which had ended with sleet and glazed every twig and bush with curtains of ice. It had brought a crystal beauty to the farm, but the glitter was gone now and all that remained were crunchy layers of snow and those icicle fangs hanging off the gutters.

Her mother would be looking for her coffee. Joyce had a passing thought of trying to find her father, but the prospect of putting on her boots and coat again stopped her. It would be easier to bring her mother the coffee. Her father wouldn't appreciate it if she came upon him suddenly; that's how people got their heads blown off. Besides, Monday was Helen Winter's deadline and she wouldn't want to sleep late. Her mother wrote a column for the local weekly, a cross between the Old Farmer's Almanac and the newspaper dispatches of 50 years ago – who was visiting whom and who had just bought a new car, preceded by a few lyrical paragraphs about life at the farm. It was called A Country Woman's Diary, and her mother took great pains over it. After breakfast Helen would leave the dishes, Joyce knew, and sit down to compose it on her Royal typewriter. She was a fine typist and not a bad writer, and her impeccable use of the English language compensated for her sometimes mawkish prose. Pouring the milk in her mother's coffee, Joyce imagined Helen would start her column with the weekend's snow and ice. It was a shame she hadn't been up to see the cat hopping in the drifts, and the coyote on the prowl; they were just the sort of observations she liked. Joyce thought she could bring them to her, along with the coffee, and it might make up for last night.

They had had an awful row. Joyce wasn't sure now what it had all been about. Her mother didn't like her tone. Her mother never liked her tone, and Joyce was so tired of talking to her and answering her stupid questions that she couldn't always keep the tone under control. It had been after supper, and Joyce was trying to finish her Spanish homework, which she had put off all weekend. Her mother wanted her to do the dishes. She said she'd do them later. And it went on from there, until Helen was screaming about how ungrateful Joyce was and how she never did anything around the house and how she, Helen, was tired of being everyone's servant. Joyce's father was in the recliner in the living room, asleep, or pretending to be, and Helen seemed to be talking to him more than to her. He never liked to get involved in their spats; he would do anything to avoid a fight with Helen, even if it meant leaving the house. So when Helen began to cry, twisting the dish towel in her hands like the neck of a chicken, Joyce knew better than to expect any paternal intervention. She took her homework upstairs and slammed her bedroom door. Her mother was crazed. No one in the world, she thought, had a mother as unstable as hers.

She put the coffee on a tray. That episode would never make it into A Country Woman's Diary. She smiled to herself, wishing she could write a real account of her mother's days. "The snow came thick and furious this weekend, and so did the invective." But there was no room for emotional truth in the two and a half pages her mother filed every Monday afternoon – that would get in the way of Helen Winter's carefully cultivated image as a Mayflower descendent and poet passing genteel days on her husband's ancestral farm. In the winter the column was all cozy nights by the woodstove and purring cats; nothing about the drafts, the unreliable plumbing or lack of central heating. To find out that the heavily mortgaged Winter farm was in danger of tax foreclosure her readers would have to turn the page, for the Legal Advertisements, and to learn that its only male heir – her brother, Dale – spent his days fishing and drinking they would have to turn to Police Beat. They might know that the Winter daughter made the honor roll, but not because Helen had mentioned it.

Joyce shook her head, trying to will away the bad thoughts. She would bring Helen the tray, and then wash up and get dressed. She always bathed the night before; she had no hair dryer, and it was too cold to go out with wet hair. If she hurried she could put on her makeup before Helen got up and noticed how much she was wearing. Camille would be pulling in soon to pick her up, and she didn't want her mother to notice that, either. Helen had never liked Camille. She had been dragged into the fight last night, too; Joyce was spending way too much time with that girl, didn't she have any other friends? More suitable friends? It might have been more of her mother's weirdness, the odd way her body stiffened and her smile went cold when anyone she did not know intimately invaded her private space. Or it might have been because Camille traced her ancestry back to a Narragansett Indian sachem instead of the Mayflower passenger manifest. Whatever the reason, Helen merely tolerated Joyce's friend on a good day – and after last night, just the sight of Camille might set her off again.

Joyce began to head up the stairs, balancing the tray with two hands. She heard the noise when she reached the fourth step, and there was a second delay between hearing and it realizing what it was, before the sharp retort translated in her brain. Somehow she knew, before the tray fell and her mother's coffee splashed brown waves onto the stair tread, that it had not been a coyote at the end of the bullet.

CHAPTER TWO

The last storm hit Winter Farm particularly hard.
The Atlantic Ocean took the dunes in great gulps,
and for a while we thought it would make a new
breach, but in the end only gullies remained where
the waves were driven onto the flats and back again.
– A Country Woman's Diary, January 1978

Helen Winter sat at her desk, fingers on the keys of her old black typewriter. Beneath the platen lay the paragraph she had written the day before Jim died. The storm had been the second one of the new year, a wild January squall that dumped almost a foot of snow and encased the trees in ice. The news of it was weeks old, yet the column seemed so full of portent she couldn't bear to rip it out of the roller. When she did, that old life, when she sat benignly before the window describing farm days as they unfolded, would be gone. She would be left with this new life in which she, not Jim or the children or the animals or the fields before her, was the center around which all revolved.

She had put the newspaper off for a month now. How could she write about raccoon tracks in the snow when all she could see was the trail of blood Jim had left when the paramedics had pulled him out of the woods? How could she pick up the threads of life on the farm, when it had been so lately visited by death? Anything she might write would seem artificial, a fantasy of what country life should be instead of what it really was. She could no longer grasp the patterns of her day that once had seemed so important.

Sometimes, when words wouldn't come, she would stare out the 12-paned window toward the barn and meadows beyond. The view was narrow, but wide enough so that something always appeared in her field of vision to spark an idea. But the days when she had to find inspiration out the window on deadline were rare. Most times she came to the hard-backed chair with a burning idea to start the column, which she then stitched together from scraps of paper she had scribbled on all week – notes about births and deaths and roast beef suppers, which she recorded with the matter-of-fact detachment of a true reporter.

Each of the farm's seasonal faces gave her material; the starkness of winter, the budding promise of spring, the explosion of green each summer, the muted reds and browns that scorched the landscape in autumn. She wrote about this world with romantic abandon and dressed it up with every adjective and metaphor she could think of, but the truth, which she hid from everyone except herself, was that she loved writing more than the whole flat, open, scraggly business of Winter Farm.

To this day she wasn't sure what she had expected to find when Jim brought her down to meet his folks, back in '49. She was a farm girl and knew about muddy fields and unsavory smells; she knew animals got you out of bed before dawn and the same fields that nourished crops one year could be seared by drought the next. But nothing could have prepared her for what she saw. Fields that, despite the stone walls that meandered through the woods, grew more rocks than potatoes and corn. The flatness of the terrain, as though God had taken his hand and reduced the hills to pancakes. How everything seemed barely hanging on against the ocean wind – the scrub pine, dune grass that clung to the sand, clumps of berries and rose hips. Even the apple and pear trees in the orchard were so crooked and gnarled she couldn't believe they had ever borne fruit. And overriding it all was the water, so close she feared at any moment the waves would crest the dunes and come after her – although it was silly, really, the house was so far inland. Still, on the first night she spent in the farmhouse, the ocean's roar kept her awake for hours.

How different home was. There was a feeling of safety to the landscape of Cooperstown, New York, nestled as it was in the mountains, and its fields were rolling and hummocked. The hills kept the sky and the vastness of the land at bay and made her world small and manageable. It was true thunder clouds rolled black over the mountains and every faded red barn was topped by a lightning rod; but even in the worst rain storm, when it seemed as if the sky itself would crack, she felt snug in her little maple bed under the eaves.

Sometimes the New York farm came to her in dreams. She saw the acres of hops and corn her father had patched together like squares on a quilt, the beech and aspen aflame on the hillsides, the winding dirt road that connected them to the rest of the world. Sometimes, walking across a room, she would catch a whiff of memory – a freshly ironed pillowcase, a jar of apricot preserves, or the rich, loamy smell of turned earth – that made her insides ache for home.

In New York there was no ocean, only Lake Otsego, which plunged 110 feet deep and hid secrets as big as a wrecked paddle-wheeler and as small as a young woman's diamond ring. She had been an innocent college senior who had given her heart to an English professor who found a student prettier and more talented than she. Jim Winter had been a 26-year-old veteran, returning to finish his studies at Cornell University on the GI Bill; smart and funny and irrepressible, he had made her forget she ever loved anyone else. Her parents weren't so sure. Somehow they never forgave him for spiriting their only daughter to Rhode Island, with its flat fields and damp, salty air.

Now this scrap of a farm, from which they had struggled to make a living for so many years, had claimed another victim, and somehow she was expected to go on. She could not remember where she had been going with this column that sat dusty and unfinished in her typewriter. She had started it confidently enough that Sunday, the day before her deadline, intending to bang out most of it the next morning. Now the column, like the rest of her life she had been so sure about, lay unfinished. In fact it seemed so cold and dead she wondered if she could ever return to it.

She had not heard Jim's gun go off, but she had heard the breakfast tray crashing on the stairs and awoke with a flash of annoyance, thinking he had dropped her coffee. But something in Joyce's sharp cry had made her realize that it was not the spilled cup that had upset her. And Joyce hadn't run back into the kitchen but out of the house. Helen knew because she heard the padding of her feet, Joyce screaming "Daddy!" and the door slam. Joyce had not stopped to put on her boots but had run out in her slippers.

Helen shook her head, trying to banish the memory, and looked out the window with a sort of desperation. Somehow she had to begin. She had to get past Jim's death – put it down in the column so she could move beyond it, return to that Country Woman's voice that had carried her along for so many years. She could do it directly, perhaps, by thanking all her neighbors who had brought casseroles and helped with the chores. Thank the ladies' club at the church, whose members had made the refreshments for the funeral. She would keep the tone simple, one neighbor to another; a Country Woman whose life has taken a tragic turn but who accepts that death is part of the cycle of life. A metaphor, perhaps, in the coyotes that Jim had felled with his gun . . .

She could see Jim in the woods. His gun dropped in the snow where it formed the spine of an angel. Then the red snow, as bright as the trail of a wounded deer. Something in the trees – pink up there, like insulation. He had tripped, hadn't he? Wasn't it possible? Dropped the gun, it went off . . . but when she repeated this to the police chief, twice, three times, each time he patiently shook his head. *No, Mrs. Winter. We can't rule it an accident.*

There was no way around it, then. No easy way to write about it, nothing to compare it to at all.

She could always continue on as though nothing had happened – start yet another January column, with musings on the constellations and the bone-chilling weather. Maybe her readers would find something between the lines that she couldn't come out and say. Perhaps that was the better way to handle it. After all, the paper's obituary had never once mentioned how Jim had died. That was the way things were done. No one would expect her to write about it. But she knew they would examine her column with a morbid curiosity. Her friends and neighbors, her regular readers, would read it as they always had and admit no untoward interest; but other people, people who otherwise never would have made it from beginning to end, would take in every word, wondering: What had happened in the Winter farmhouse? What was going through Helen's mind? *What had made him do it?*

The questions had begun the day of the funeral.

They had gathered at Loretta Winter's Victorian house by the sea, which stood at the head of a cornfield in the tiny village of Matunuck. Loretta was Jim's older sister, a buxom and domineering woman who ran all their lives in some measure. She had picked the minister for the service, and she had selected the music; Helen, numb, had silently gone along.

While the mourners ate, Helen slipped into the music room, a small study with an upright piano, a scratchy velveteen settee and an overstuffed armchair. From here Loretta scanned the yard for birds and made notes on their behavior and travels. Loretta was an ornithologist. She had recently retired as a professor of biology, but her days were still filled with birding trips, guided nature walks and symposia. This room had the best view of the birds that made Matunuck a rest stop on the Atlantic Flyway. From here Loretta watched mergansers, scaup, eider and gadwalls dip into a salt pond across the road. The room was small and dark, crammed with bric-a-brac and old issues of National Geographic piled on end tables, an arrangement that made navigation difficult. To some people it was claustrophobic; for Helen it was a refuge.

Sounds drifted in from the living room. The rustle of a stout woman's slip against a rayon skirt; the clank of spoons on saucers; coffee being poured. And below it all a buzz, waxing and waning in intensity, occasionally disgorging a phrase, a word, innocuous and incongruous, like "A&P" or "left last Saturday" or "fell on the ice, not bad you understand."

Then, coming at Helen through the door, a question, uttered in a nook where someone thought they had found a haven, a place to speak the truth:

"Why do you suppose he did it?"

Outside winter still ruled the landscape. The cornfields were white, Loretta's bird feeders were capped with cones of cream;

the cars scattered along the lane were the only color against this blank page. Out there, somewhere, were answers to their questions, but in this stuffy room where the sky was cracked plaster and the ground was a threadbare carpet, the only answers were inside, locked away from view.

Helen stood up and straightened her wool skirt, which had once been half of a suit and now was the only salvageable black item in her wardrobe. Her blouse, white with a shirred front, was hopelessly wrinkled, and her skirt was askew, the zipper drifting to the front. She had such a hard time staying presentable. On any other day her mussed clothes would have been cause for worry. How many parties had she endured silently in a corner, pretending to admire the host's artwork or lingering too long at the buffet table? But today no one was expecting her to look collected, and no one was looking for her. They were probably relieved the widow was out of earshot. No one knew what to say to her, and their strained attempts at sympathy only made Helen more uncomfortable.

At least they were in Loretta's house. In the beginning the family seemed to be hinting that Helen should invite everyone to the farm after the service. Loretta had put a stop to that. Jim's sister could be overbearing, even boorish, but she had the good sense to know that even on a good day Helen wasn't up for company, especially in that drafty old farmhouse that hadn't been papered or painted in 25 years. Loretta's house wasn't much better, but it had a genteel shabbiness about it. It had come down in the family somehow, a relic from when Captain James Winter was bringing home booty from the Far East and the Winters had more money and social standing. The stuffing might be coming out of the sofa cushions and water stains might have yellowed the wallpaper, but the spoon in your hand had the tarnish of real silver.

Helen walked across the room, where an ornate gold mirror caught her from the waist up. She had been attractive once. Not tall, but tall enough so a suit hung on her well and high heels gave her legs a comely shape. Dark hair that took a permanent, a certain symmetry of features that fit the dark lipstick and heavy makeup so popular in her day. But now her face looked sallow and worn. Cosmetics today were "natural," whatever that meant, all peachy and glossy, and clothes had lost that dramatic cut that once had made something of her figure. Polyester clothes and peach blush were supposed to have freed the seventies woman, but they had left Helen with nothing to hold herself together.

Behind her reflection the cornfields stretched back over the years, the same fields she had seen that first afternoon Jim had brought her to meet his family, almost 30 years ago. She had been shy and afraid, especially when his mother demanded, "Doesn't she talk?" But Jim had been there to steady the arm in her brown wool blazer, the rest of the Winters seemed to pay the woman no mind, and she had conquered it that time, buoyed by love and the other friendly faces.

"There you are."

Helen startled to see that in the periphery of her vision, just outside the mirror's reach, Ludlow Winter stood in front of the doorway, an old-fashioned glass in his right hand. He had parted and closed the pocket doors without a sound and had been watching her watch herself, for how long she didn't know.

Ludlow was Loretta's adopted son, a real estate agent who walked about his mother's house as though he were tagging her antiques for auction. Adopted son was the official version, although it was pretty much an unspoken truth in the family that Ludlow had been conceived the summer 37 years ago Loretta spent in the Appalachians. She had been down there studying the Swainson's warbler, a rather plain, rusty-capped songbird remarkable only for its rarity in that habitat, but she had stayed long after her sabbatical was up and brought back baby Ludlow – with a story about a poor family with 12 kids and no food on the table. Jim had told Helen they all suspected she had met a soldier down there, but Helen imagined instead a local swain who had helped Loretta look for her rare bird in the mountain thickets. With his square jaw and reddish hair, Ludlow had the look of an errant Hatfield or McCoy who had wandered in from a still in the mountains to find himself inexplicably in New England.

"You want a drink, or something?" He waved his glass at her.

"No, no, I'm fine." She walked back to the couch and sat down. Might as well get this over with. She had avoided Ludlow at the funeral home and during the procession, when she had slipped out of Loretta's Lincoln Continental at the last minute on the pretext that Dale and Joyce wanted her to ride with them.

"It's a sad day, Helen." He sat down on the couch, stretching his long legs and cradling the drink close to his heart. "I wish I had something to say. I keep going over and over it in my mind. I just can't figure it."

He was fishing. Let him fish. She had nothing to offer.

He crossed his bare ankles under the coffee table. Ludlow never wore socks, even in a blizzard. His arm was casually draped over the sofa back. "Leaves you in an awful fix."

"I'll get along." His arm was so close she could smell him, a mixture of the musty house and Old Spice after-shave. It was not, in truth, unpleasant, which made his closeness even more discomfiting. She leaned forward on the couch as though getting ready to rise. It was an empty threat; he knew she wouldn't come out of hiding.

"This may not seem the time to discuss it, Helen, but it has to be faced. You're in a tough situation." He put the drink down on the coffee table and leaned toward her, hands folded, gazing at her earnestly. "Even if Jim had insurance, no company's going to pay on a suicide. He didn't leave you with any financial cushion. Everyone knows you're behind on the taxes. The place needs work. And Joyce is headed to college, I presume. She's a smart girl."

She wondered if this, too, was the subject of whispers – if the question of why Jim did it was followed by what Helen would do now that he was gone. Ludlow certainly had given it some thought, but then, he would. It was, after all, a real estate opportunity.

"I don't see as Dale's been much help to you." He was continuing on, her silence giving him the opening he needed. She felt frozen to the seat: She should be outraged, she should tell him to stop, but she didn't know how. She wished he would just give up and go away. "You know Jim and I had many conversations about the farm. I made it very clear I was willing to help him out. Just the east woods alone would have given him enough to get back on his feet. Throw in a piece of the waterfront and your worries would be over, Helen. You could send Joyce to school, give Dale a little something for a business."

So there it was. She could imagine the trees gone, houses sprouted in their place. After all, it had happened before. When Jim's father died, Jim and his siblings had sold off the whole western parcel, 20 acres, to Jim's uncle, Tom Winter, who had filled the land with houses – row after row of two-bedroom ranches, lining narrow tar roads with names like Ladyslipper Lane and Elderberry Road. They called it Salt Marsh Acres, but there was no more salt marsh anywhere – or lady's slippers or elderberries, for that matter. From the window over the kitchen sink, as she washed dishes or made dinner, Helen could see the backs of the ranches, yellow and blue and white, their yards filled with plastic garbage cans and swing sets and webbed lawn chairs. It had been 10 years now and the brush had started to grow up again, but the thickets of bittersweet were not enough to block the shrill laughter of children or the acrid smell of grilling hot dogs. Still, the sale that spoiled her view had saved the farm, and she recognized that if Jim didn't.

He and Loretta had been the holdouts. Loretta had spent her life defending wild places, from the rainforests of the Amazon to the Australian bush, but that love of nature had started in the bogs and woods of the Winter Farm. She was the one who had convinced Jim's father to give 100 acres to the Audubon people back in the 1950s, and she was clamoring to do the same with the west parcel when Eddie and Clara, Jim's brother and sister, dug their heels in. (His baby brother, Russell, the one he loved the best, who would have sided with Jim no matter what, had died in the war.) They wanted to turn the old man's estate into cash, and if Jim and Loretta wouldn't go along they would force the sale of the whole farm. In the end Jim had too much to lose to stand on principle.

The pocket doors slid open again and Helen snapped to attention. Loretta stood there, hands folded over her ample crepe de chine bosom, frowning in disapproval. How much had she heard? She was glaring at her son, suspicious, but she also swept Helen into her gaze.

"Ludlow, put out the rest of the desserts. I want to talk to Helen for a moment." He looked back at her, as though to say something, but she was ushering him out of the room.

Loretta sat next to her in the impression Ludlow had made in the velveteen. Despite the bird walks and gardening, at 63 she was a heavy woman, and the springs squeaked beneath her. Loretta was built like a man, tall with a thick trunk and legs, but her bosom was like a shelf and she favored dresses over pants, even when walking in the woods. Today she wore a plain black shift dressed up with a goldfinch pin, and old-lady shoes, laced, with tiny air vents in the leather.

"I don't know what he was saying to you, but I hope you ignored it." It was Loretta's unique quality to believe that everyone else was a busybody and she alone possessed the wisdom to give advice. "There's a time for talking business and today isn't it."

Helen had always had a soft spot for Jim's older sister, even when she was at her most overbearing. "Thank you, Loretta."

"But there is something I want to talk to you about." Loretta sat up straighter, pointing her bosom at the fireplace. "You've had an awful blow. We all have. Who would have thought Jim, raised in a Christian household, could do such a thing? This isn't like Russell. Fate just reached out and took him. It was war, what could we do? But this was deliberate!"

She stopped a moment, overcome. Loretta still visited Russell's grave at least once a month, put fresh flowers there, kept it mowed. "But we can't sit around wringing our hands. It's done and it's a terrible thing. But you've got two children in there to raise. You've got the farm." Loretta took a breath, as though what she was about to say was difficult even for her. "Helen, I know you've had a tough time over the years. You took care of Mother all those years, and we appreciated it, of course we did. We knew how difficult she could be. But life has always been harder for you, hasn't it? I know you'd rather sit in here and look out that window than go back inside and talk to people. But you've got to get over that. You've got to fight it. We all need you. Dale and Joyce need you. I'm afraid for you, I am." Loretta's voice caught and Helen saw to her surprise that Jim's sister was crying. "Jim's not here any more to protect you. You can't shut yourself up in that house. I'll help you in any way I can, but you've got to meet me half way. You've just got to come out of your shell, that's all."

Now Helen, still waiting for inspiration to strike, shifted in the desk chair, trying to banish Loretta's voice from her head.

After 29 years of being sisters-in-law, they should understand each other, but too many secrets were in the way – information withheld, emotions hidden. Helen knew she was shy; she had never been good around people. Loretta was right about that. Helen was in hiding, a turtle retreating from the world, but Loretta knew only the what, not the why. And without the why nothing else made sense. If Helen told her, what would she say then? What counsel could she possibly have to offer?

Helen ripped out the old page of her column, tore it into tiny squares and watched them fall in tatters into the wastebasket. She rolled a fresh sheet into the typewriter, and each zizzt zizzt of the turning roller recoiled in her arm like the kick of a shotgun. She began typing furiously, unmindful of mistakes, only caring to fill up the page.

CHAPTER THREE

The small barn window was caked in film – years of motor oil and manure dust and mud – but through it Joyce could make out the outline of Ludlow Winter's new white Chrysler. It was quite a car, she thought, taking another hit off the roach and passing it to Dale. Quite a car.

"Who's that?" Dale asked, his breath tight.

"Ludlow."

"Come to pay his respects?"

"He already did that." There was nothing left of the joint; she stubbed the flame out on the windowsill and dropped the roach into a flowerpot. "Didn't you notice the two of them missing at Aunt Loretta's? Secreted away in the old music room?"

Dale nodded vaguely. He had been high on hash and coke and God knows what else during the funeral, and she doubted he remembered any of it. For a while he had even left Joyce on the couch, stuffed between miserable Aunt Clara and one of Loretta's chirpy birding friends, while he and some of their cousins took off to a seedy beachfront bar down the road from Loretta's. At least now, she thought, Dale's home, and she didn't mind getting high if it would keep him there. His beard was scraggly and his clothes faintly smelled, but he didn't ask stupid questions, like how she felt, and he didn't treat her with an embarrassed deference as though she were about to crack.

"Dale."

"Hmm?" He looked up at her, unguarded, and his face had that rare look she remembered from their childhood, open, patient, ready to throw a rope across the years that divided them.

"I don't know what, but she did something." Joyce lowered her voice although they were a hundred feet from the house. "She was nuts, the night before. Started screaming at me about drying the dishes. Had a complete crying fit, and he just sat in the chair like nothing was happening."

"So what? It was probably just more of her change of life kicking in. And you know how he hated it when she went off."

"This was different." Joyce could not explain how, but there was a measure of desperation in her mother's tantrum that she had not seen before, as though she were goading Jim Winter into responding. It was curious, but she had displayed more emotion that night over the dishes than she had at the funeral a few days later. In fact, Joyce realized now, she had not seen her mother cry at all. Yes, there had been histrionics in the chaos of that morning, when the paramedics and the State Police and every neighbor within a mile seemed to be milling about the place, but Helen's wails were dry-eyed and could have been for show. When the house had at last emptied, she merely sat at the kitchen table, staring out the window toward the woods.

"Dale, why?" Joyce rushed ahead, although she could see her brother's face had closed down and he was looking away, toward the dark corners where the hay baler sat under cobwebs. "There must be a reason. People don't just wake up and decide to shoot themselves. I mean, he was in the middle of getting kerosene."

Dale shrugged and his face stiffened, like a door closing. He turned his back to her and leaned against the ladder that led to the loft. "Ludlow must think he's won the lottery. How long has he waited for this? He knew Dad would throw him out on his ear. But now the little widow is all by herself, with no money in the bank and a big pile of bills."

She was smashing the roach in the base of the flowerpot, an alchemist working out some new cure with a mortar and pestle. She had gotten too close. Broken the pact.

"Maybe we should go in and help her," Joyce said, but even as she formed the words she knew she couldn't.

"Nah. She won't sell out, no matter how crazy she is. We couldn't get that lucky."

She felt a flash of irritation. "I don't know why you think it would be so lucky."

"I wouldn't turn it down if she came into some money. Maybe then I wouldn't have to haul my ass out to Georges Bank three weeks out of the month, slogging around in a hold full of flounder."

Joyce pressed her lips together. Her reflection in the windowpane looked just like her mother, prim and disapproving, and holding her tongue. Like it's doing us any good, since you drink it all up anyway, was what she wanted to say.

Dale gazed up at the hayloft, toward a pinpoint of light from the roof. "Do you think he's watching us?"

"If he is, he's having a heart attack."

"Oh, come on, Joycie. What did he do in this old barn? Smoked Camels when he was 12. He told us that. Probably bedded the old lady up there. If those old timbers could talk."

"You're disgusting."

"Don't tell me you haven't."

It was she who turned away now; she was too high to fool him, and the less he knew about that sort of thing the better. Somehow, when Tom was roofing the house last summer, she had figured they were the only ones who had ever rolled around in the hayloft. The thought that other Winters had been there before them took something away from the memory.

"Tom the carpenter," Dale went on. "Bang, bang, bang."

"Shut up, Dale." This was their usual level of discourse, bantering. Any other day she would have given it right back to him, but she didn't have the emotional energy today.

From the opposite window she could see the corner of the woodlot that Ludlow wanted so badly. How her father had loved the place. Sometimes she would wander out to the field, and he would stop what he was doing – lean on the post hole digger or shut off the tractor – and just gaze out over the sweep of the farm, from the oak and pine woods to the hay fields and the Atlantic Ocean beyond. And he would start talking, without her having to say a word or ask a question. "That over there," he would say, and pointing to the corn crib or a stretch of stone wall or the old outhouse, he would launch into a story about his boyhood on the farm or the first Winters who hewed a living out of the land. A beautiful place, he would imply, with its warm ocean breezes sweetening up the hay and corn, but an unforgiving one, with the ocean so close a Nor'easter or hurricane could send the tide roaring into the pond and onto the fields. Joyce would listen to her father as though she were in church, and afterward she would walk back toward the decrepit farmhouse and sagging barn with a strange feeling inside her, a pang somewhere between lovesick and homesick that she didn't know how to name.

She looked out the dirty barn window and wondered. Next to his family the Winter Farm was the only thing in the world her father cared about. He would have done almost anything to keep it, but she knew he would put the family first. Now Ludlow was snaking around her mother like a vulture around roadkill. Her father must have known that would happen.

If Dale would stay, if he could be relied upon, she felt certain her mother wouldn't have to sell. But he had made it clear he was only home while the *Linda Lee* was in port, and as soon as his captain called he would be on his way to Galilee. He could even keep fishing, she thought, if only he'd share his take. It would be tough, even then. All those things their father had done to scratch a living out of this place – who was going to do them? That woodlot Ludlow wanted had been a steady source of income. In the fall Jim Winter had brought out the cordwood, sawed it up on a rig and then seasoned it for a year. He delivered it to the cottages near the beach, where a woodstove can keep the heating bill down and take the salty chill out of the air. This time of year he would be doing odd jobs; plowing for the town, a little inside carpentry, minor engine repairs for his friends. He could do a bit of everything, she reflected, and when the demand for one skill fell off he turned to something else.

She looked at Dale, who was still leaning against the ladder, staring up. She loved him, as a sister loves a brother; he was reckless and self-centered and unreliable, and he drank and smoked and got high way too much, but she saw that as immaturity more than anything. Someday he would fill Jim Winter's shoes, but she doubted he knew that.

Dale was 26, but in some ways, he seemed to be the younger one. After high school he had drifted from one job to another before finally settling down on the *Linda Lee*. He had been on the boat for nearly a year, an eternity for him, and the fisherman's lifestyle seemed to suit him – smelly, dirty, rough work away from the eyes of virtually everyone, plenty of money on a strictly cash basis with time for a bender when they got into port.

Dale pushed himself away from the ladder. He was looking out the window again at Ludlow's car, a white Cordoba. "That's the car that guy from 'Fantasy Island' advertises . . . You could take a ride in it with that little short guy, what's-his-name, for your chauffeur."

"Herve Villechaize," Joyce said dully.

"No, no, his name on the show. Tattoo! 'De plane! De plane!'"

Joyce wasn't listening. Once Dale got on one of his pot-induced fantasies, all substance left the conversation.

"Ludlow's going to be in there forever," he said, suddenly sounding lucid. "Time enough for a ride."

Joyce couldn't imagine what Ludlow would do if he found Dale, with his greasy hands and sweat-stained jeans, sitting in the Cordoba's white leather bucket seat, or if he saw his precious new car bouncing down the farm's rutted dirt paths. "Instead of hijacking his car, why don't you go in the house and do something? He's getting ready to make off with half the farm."

Dale, the fantasy of driving Ludlow's car having spent his energy, the world's demands weighing on him, leaned on the sawhorse and lit a cigarette. His eyes looked red and far away; his voice, when he finally used it, was raspy and low, almost a whisper. "She should just sell him the whole God-damn thing. The old man's gone. Doesn't make any difference anymore."

Joyce wanted to shake him. "It does too make a difference. What would Dad have wanted? If we let the woods go that will only be the beginning. You know what happened next door. She sells out, pretty soon there'll be houses everywhere. So much for taking a walk. Forget fishing in the pond, Dale. So much for your free rent. And what about me? If Mom sells this place, she's going back to New York. Guess who she's taking with her."

Dale grabbed her arm, squeezed hard and pointed. Ludlow Winter had emerged from the kitchen door and was standing on the back steps. He pulled on his suede gloves, snapped his hands together in a muffled retort, pulled up the collar of his coat and stared off to the east, toward the woods he wanted so badly.

They watched silently as he got in the Chrysler, turned it

around and drove away.

The yellow Ford Maverick roared into the driveway and sprayed a shower of snow as it slid to a stop. Camille Evans flew out of the front seat, coat open, and tossed a half-smoked Virginia Slims into a dirty hump of snow.

"You made it," Joyce said, as Camille dashed into the mud room.

It had been snowing since morning, light flakes at first, but by noontime a serious blizzard was under way and they'd been dismissed early from school. The bus had struggled along its route, wheezing up and down hills and threading through mill villages to the seaside colonies south of Route 1. It had taken Joyce an hour to get home, nearly twice as long as normal, and she had been wondering when Camille was going to show up. She often dropped by after school and before her shift as a waitress at the bowling alley.

Camille Evans, Joyce's best friend, lived in a three-room house on King's Factory Road with her mother, stepfather and two brothers. The few times Joyce had visited Camille's home made her a little less ashamed of her own living arrangements. Camille's grandfather had built the Evans house out of a chicken coop and scrap lumber washed up by Hurricane Carol in 1954. Its uninsulated walls were covered by tar paper outside and cheap paneling inside, and the floors were a patchwork of linoleum scraps he had picked out of the dump. Camille's parents slept in one room and her stepbrothers in another, leaving the living room couch to her. She kept her clothes in an old trunk, probably dump-picked too, and other than that she had no real place to call her own, which was one reason she treasured her car. She had saved up $500 waitressing to buy it, and she worked a couple of shifts a week to keep herself in clothes and gas. The Maverick was also an escape from her stepfather, who, Joyce suspected, was responsible for the welts on Camille's arms and legs.

Joyce poured Camille a Coke. She drank the stuff morning, noon and night. "You still going to work?"

"Yes, damn it. The coffee shop never closes."

They sat at the kitchen table. Outside the snow was pounding down and the wind off the ocean was whirling it around;

the bottom half of the window was laced in ice. Camille's shift wouldn't start for an hour and she seemed in no hurry. That was fine with Joyce. Dale was gone. He had left Saturday night for the port, but Joyce couldn't believe they had gone out in this weather. She imagined Dale had helped stock the boat with food and ice yesterday and waited around until the captain called off the trip. He was probably sleeping it off now on the floor of somebody's living room.

Helen was in the next room clacking away at the typewriter. She was back writing that stupid column, where icicles always shone, sunlight was dappled and the hard brown earth lay like a Persian carpet. It made Joyce want to gag. She had been at it all day; Monday was her deadline.

"Did you see Pink Floyd this weekend?" While Joyce spoke, Camille looked outside, one hand idly palming her cigarette pack. "On Don Kirshner?"

Camille nodded absently. Sometimes Joyce felt so unsure of her. They were best friends, yet Camille always seemed on the verge of finding someone cooler and more daring to hang out with. Days like this made Joyce especially nervous, as though she had to keep Camille entertained and was doing a poor job of it.

Helen came into the kitchen wearing a faded floral duster with her hair in pink foam rollers. The lines around her mouth were slack, her eyelids puffy, but her whole face tightened when she saw Camille. He lips pinched together in disapproval and her body seemed to grow taut, as though it were ready to leap over something.

"Why hello, Camille." There was an edge to her voice as she said the young woman's name; it was the way she pronounced words she disapproved of – the way she would say "Jewish" or "Irish" or any other manner of person different from herself.

"'lo, Mrs. Winter." Camille's face had shut down, her response an automaton's. Joyce had seen it happen a million times in school, whenever Camille sensed someone was looking down at her.

Helen busied herself getting coffee. Outside the wind was knocking something against the house, but already the snow had drifted enough to muffle the sound. Joyce was having trouble breathing. The kitchen smelled of damp wool socks, coffee grounds and the sour dish cloth hanging over the faucet.

"My, it's coming down." Helen had sat between them and was slurping her coffee. "I hope we can get to Wakefield. I've got to deliver my column."

Joyce couldn't believe her mother was considering venturing out. Even from the window she could tell that the weather had ratcheted up a notch. She could no longer see the barn, and Camille's Maverick was barely visible under a crown of snow. Dale wasn't around to plow the driveway, a long, narrow road that stretched nearly a tenth of a mile to Old Post Road. She wondered if Camille would be able to get out.

"We don't have a choice," Helen said cheerily, downing the last of her coffee and heading upstairs to change. "We'll take the station wagon. It's always been good in snow."

That "we" was alarming and, sure enough, when her mother returned – dressed in a pair of wool slacks and one of Jim Winter's old flannel shirts – she confirmed it: Of course, Joyce would drive. She was a much better driver.

Her mother stayed inside while they cleared a path to the cars. Camille haphazardly brushed off the Maverick with her sleeve, put a finger and thumb to her mouth and winked at Joyce. She had a joint in her pocket, but Joyce waved her off. There was no way she was going to get high and drive her mother to Wakefield in a snowstorm. Camille, rebuffed, didn't even say goodbye before getting into her car. Then it wouldn't start.

Joyce was miffed as well. Camille was always having these fits of temper when Joyce wouldn't do exactly what she wanted to do. Most of the time she went along with her, but Camille would keep pushing her to do something more outrageous. It was as though she wanted to prove, once and for all, that Joyce wasn't up to hanging out with her.

Joyce was tempted to leave Camille behind, but the only solution was to give her a ride to work, and when she offered Camille wordlessly joined them. Helen sat in front and Camille settled into the back seat of the black Chevy Biscayne. The wagon had been her father's car. He used it to go fishing or deliver a chain saw or a small load of wood, and it smelled of him – a faint pine woods aroma that knocked the wind out of Joyce as soon as she sat down. He had taught her to drive in this car. If she could drive this, he'd said, she could drive anything. It had a column shift and a notoriously fickle clutch.

"Well, this is sort of fun," her mother was saying. "An adventure."

Joyce, keeping the wagon at a crawl and squinting to see out the windshield, said nothing. The only sound from the back was her father's tackle box clattering against a spare tire.

Up ahead, the driveway funneled through a break in the stone wall, and then the open fields narrowed to a grove of white pine and hemlock. Joyce felt a bump as they hit this section of the driveway, full of washed-out gravel holes. Her mother began reciting "Snowbound."

"All day the gusty north-wind bore/The loosening drift its breadth before," she was saying in a sing-song voice. Outside the wind followed them like a freight train in a tunnel, but it was not loud enough to drown out Helen.

"Mother! Please!" Joyce turned down the blower on the heater, which was sputtering out lukewarm air. "I can't concentrate with you chanting over there."

"Well! I thought it would be festive, a little poem."

They had come to the end of the drive and Joyce, not daring to stop for fear of getting stuck, wheeled the car in a slow arc onto Old Post Road, which had been plowed but barely showed it. She felt the back wheels slip and then slide back. All that heavy stuff her father had put in the hatch was keeping them anchored to the road.

"This would have been a good day to work on your applications, Joyce."

"What applications?" Joyce knew full well what. For months they had been arguing about where she would go to college. Joyce wanted to go to URI, with Camille, who had gotten a full scholarship to the nursing program. Her mother had other ideas. In some vicarious reliving of her youth, she saw Joyce enrolling at Cornell, closer to Helen's childhood home in Cooperstown.

"Your essay for Cornell is due at the end of the month."

Joyce looked in the rear-view mirror and saw the alarmed look on Camille's face. Well, let her be pissed, she thought. She was sick of Camille – and her mother – planning out her life for her.

"I'll type it up for you, if you want." Her mother leaned her arm back on the seat. "How is your mother, Camille?" She emphasized the word "mother," as though it held some loaded secret.

"She's fine," came the voice from the back seat, edged with wariness.

"Is she still working at Ladd?"

Camille's mother had been an aide at Ladd School, an institution for the mentally retarded, but she hadn't worked in years, and Helen certainly knew that. Joyce tightened her hands on the steering wheel.

"She's disabled, Mrs. Winter. She can't work."

"Disabled?" Her tone cast suspicion on the whole word.

"Yes, Mrs. Winter." Camille sighed, and Joyce thought her mother must be getting to her; trained at the hand of an abusive parent, her friend rarely let emotion show. "She had polio. Quite a few years ago. Her right leg drags. She isn't strong enough to lift the patients." Camille spoke in short, staccato sentences, like a mother answering a pestering child.

Joyce breathed out slowly, and she noticed fog forming on the inside of the windshield. She jacked the defroster to high. The car was staying on the road but she knew somewhere up here Old Post Road merged onto the highway, and she feared the traffic island was going to come upon them any minute.

"Polio. I'd quite forgotten. And how about Hamilton? I hope he's supporting her."

"He works as a roofer. In good weather. He's laid off right now, but he's been working under the table at a machine shop."

"Your mother was a beautiful woman in her day." Helen had picked up the line of conversation with enthusiasm. Christ, Joyce thought, why did I stop her inane poetry recital? "I remember the first time I met her, at a dance at the Atlantic Hotel. She had her hair pinned up in a twist, quite a daring hairdo then, and a pink dress in that new Chanel style, long you know, quite a change from the war. Her waist was so slim. She was dancing with a friend of Jim's. I didn't even realize she was a Negro."

Joyce inhaled sharply. "Mother, for God's sake, don't use that word." Dead ahead, out of the fog of snow, came the Route 1 sign, completely shrouded in white. She jerked the wheel as hard as she dared and, like a track at a car wash, the curb guided her back onto the road.

"What? What have I said out of the way?"

"It's all right," Camille said quickly, as much to Joyce as her mother. "She isn't Negro, or black, Mrs. Winter. She's a Narragansett Indian."

"I suppose. Joyce, you'd better slow down, the roads are pretty slick." Helen leaned back on the seat to look at Camille. "She was light-skinned, you see, was my point. Back then, she could pass. That was what we called it. No one knew she was Negro, or Indian, or whatever you call it. It wasn't like it is now. There was no 'black power,' believe me. Women like Marian were glad to be able to pass. It made their lives a lot easier. She was dancing with a white boy. She looked only a little exotic, Italian maybe. I hadn't a clue."

The swirling snow was mixed with blowing sand. Joyce couldn't hear it or see it, but she sensed a plow up ahead, and she followed the tracks it had cleared, which were almost immediately washed over in white.

"You're getting a little close to that plow, Joyce." Her mother returned her attention to Camille, as though they were having a friendly conversation. "Joyce tells me you're going to URI to study nursing."

Joyce looked in the rearview mirror and saw Camille wrapping her scarf around her neck in a pantomime of strangling herself. "I've been accepted through early admissions."

"Isn't that nice. Joyce here needs to get going on her applications. URI, I think, is just a little too close to home. I went to Cornell, you know. That's where I met – " Helen stopped, as though she'd forgotten someone's name. "That's where I met Joyce's father."

The car was having more and more difficulty plowing through the snow, which was building up on the pavement and drifting across the hood and windshield. Joyce could no longer say with absolute certainty if the station wagon was on the road, in the breakdown lane or in the median. She had lost sight of the snowplow and it no longer was leaving a trail to follow. The white view through her wipers was hypnotic; little tornadoes of snowflakes that kept swirling and swirling until her head ached. She knew suddenly that she would have to turn around, whether her mother liked it or not, but before she could say it aloud, the car turned on its own, spinning in an 180-degree arc and coming to rest against a small mountain on the side of the road.

CHAPTER FOUR

Long after we have packed away our bathing suits,
the moon jelly is still drifting on the currents, wait-
ing for their larvae to be shaken off and attach them-
selves to the ocean bottom, where they will ride out
the worst of the winter gales. The adult jellyfish die
by October, but this summer's generation is out there
now, moving and swaying with violent currents, wait-
ing for warmer temperatures so they can break off
into swimming saucers, ready to begin the cycle anew.

– A Country Woman's Diary, Feb. 16, 1978

It was fortuitous that the plow had stopped to help them, and it was convenient when it turned out they were less than a mile from Loretta's house in Matunuck. But packed into the steamy cab of the Mack truck, sandwiched between Joyce and the beefy-chested plow driver, Helen had begun to feel a slow, icy panic slither under her coat and up her neck. She was missing her deadline, they would have to stay in Matunuck over- night and there was no way to get rid of that churlish Camille. The blizzard was yet another thing beyond her control.

Loretta slapped her back to reality. Loretta had a way of doing that. In her presence Helen often felt like she'd been caught sleepwalking, that she was drifting around in a somno- lent haze that Loretta felt it her personal duty to dissolve. Her sharp voice could prick a balloon, and her looming profile in a doorway blocked the light and whatever images appeared in the mind's eye. She liked to get to the point. She didn't have any ap- preciation for people who didn't.

"You're not going anywhere, not tonight and probably not tomorrow, either." She had come up behind Helen, who stood behind a parted curtain in the parlor, squinting to see something in the maelstrom of blowing snow that obscured the road. "Town plows already have given up trying to keep that road clear. They don't call it the Drift Road for nothing."

"We certainly hate to impose on you."

"You're not imposing, Helen." Loretta looked at her in disapproval. "What is the matter with you? Good heavens, you're family, and besides that, I'd take in a total stranger on a night like tonight. Thank God you were close by. People die in weather like this."

Helen turned back toward the window. Yes, people die in weather like this. If only she could be so lucky. Jim had taken the easy way out. No more living, no more nerves scraped raw by the daily exchange of human intercourse, no more doubt or guilt or fear. She could picture him, asleep under the thickening blanket of snow, his face placid, his hands folded neatly on his chest, as they were on the day of the funeral. This day, this storm – which would have seen him up at dawn to plow out neighbor after neighbor, drift after drift – was dead to him. He did not have to wonder if Dale was at the bottom of the briny Atlantic; he did not have to spend the night under Loretta's roof, dodging her stern gaze; he did not have to baby-sit two teenage girls. He had nothing left to do in this world.

"There's one good thing," Loretta was saying. "Ludlow will be home soon. He's just down the street, checking on the rentals. If anything comes up, God help us, he can take care of it. That certainly eases my mind."

Helen wondered how on earth she was going to get through the night.

On a good day she didn't particularly care for visiting Loretta, never mind sleeping beneath her roof. It wasn't a personal antipathy that drove that feeling so much as a deep-seated aversion to the different smells and tastes of someone else's house – sleeping beneath the chenille bedspread and heavy wool blankets in one of the upstairs bedrooms, eating Loretta's cooking – which wasn't so bad, mind you, but leaned a little too much toward boiled vegetables for Helen's taste – and, worst of all, wearing another woman's bathrobe and nightclothes, which would smell like the mothballs at the bottom of a steamer trunk. This was the first night she had spent away from home since Jim's accident. She had not yet changed the case on his pillow, and at night she burrowed her head in the fabric, still faintly rich with his smell. Without her there, she feared, the sense of him would disappear forever.

Then there were the girls. At any moment one of them – probably Camille – would say or do something that would shock Loretta or at least unleash some embarrassing exchange that Helen would hear about later. It was bad enough she had had to endure Joyce's temper in the car. The girl was so touchy; Helen had been making such an effort to include Camille, to make the harrowing trip seem like an adventure, something normal, and all she got from Joyce was sass. As soon as the power cut out, the girls began to complain – that the kerosene lamp stank; they were missing their favorite show on TV; and that the only source of music in the house was a small portable radio in the kitchen, which Loretta insisted on keeping tuned to an all-news station. And Loretta, who was not used to having teenagers around the house, particularly of the female variety, assumed they would help make dinner, wash the dishes and make up the beds. Helen was the one who would have to make sure they did so without grumbling.

As if all that wasn't bad enough, now she had to wait for Ludlow. It was one thing to deal with him on her turf. When he came to the farm, she had no problem being firm. No, Ludlow, I don't need anything. No, I don't need a loan. No, I'm not interested in selling. It wasn't like that day in the parlor, during the funeral, when she was caught unawares. Last time she had seen his car pull up, she'd had time to collect herself, think of a way to get rid of him. She had not weakened, and he had left shortly; though she knew the encounter was only an early volley in what was sure to be a persistent campaign.

Loretta made hamburger pie with green beans and tomato soup, and the girls ate it, though none too enthusiastically, and afterwards they washed the dishes, standing at the sink with the radio newly tuned to some hard rock station and whispering to each other about God-knows-what. Camille's jeans were so tight that Helen could nearly count the tines of the comb stuck in her back pocket. At least Joyce's corduroy pants were cut more generously, although she had taken to wearing her makeup heavy and matted, as though trying to match her friend's dark complexion. She would have looked so much prettier without it, but you couldn't tell an 18-year-old girl that. Some day she would figure it out for herself.

Loretta was in the music room, sitting in front of the fire, her back to the rattling windows. There was nothing to do but join her. It was the sort of evening Helen would have enjoyed, had she been in her own home, by her own fire. How ironic that she had thought of "Snowbound" this morning, for now she was Whittier's "not unfeared, half welcome guest," wasn't she? "Unmarked by time, yet not young." Sitting by the fire while a blizzard raged, the guest who had broken the family circle, the woman whose mental state was so unpredictable it was used to excuse her inability to find a husband. Well, Helen had found one, she had just been powerless to keep him.

"You know, I've been thinking about your dilemma, Helen." Loretta was finishing up her Indian pudding, and she scraped the spoon on the bowl. "I don't see how you're going to hang on to the farm. If you want to pay the taxes and have enough money to live, you're going to have to find a job."

A gust hit the windows in the parlor, and from where they sat in the next room the glass sounded as though it were about to shatter. Helen dug her nails into the chair's upholstery. "I can't work. There's nothing I'm qualified to do."

"Don't be ridiculous. You're an educated woman. There are plenty of things you could do."

"I'm not going to work." If she repeated it enough, Loretta would drop the subject.

"You have a degree from Cornell. You could teach. You're an excellent typist; you'd make a fine secretary. You probably could secure a position at the paper, if you were interested."

"I'm not." This was a nightmare. Where had Loretta gotten the idea she should work? It was all she could do to write a column once a week and get it delivered on time. The idea of having to meet and deal with strangers every day would send her into a panic. No, it just wasn't possible.

"You'll have to do something," Loretta said after a pause. "I doubt if the insurance is going to pay, considering the way Jim died. You'll get some Social Security, I suppose, but that won't keep the farm going."

"I'll manage," Helen said coldly. She liked Loretta, she really did, but it was maddening how she tried to run other people's lives. It was just like her to bring up such a loaded subject when Helen was trapped. Of course Loretta assumed Helen would do anything to avoid selling out. Even Ludlow had no idea how tempted she was by his offer. Helen had learned from Jim to keep her cards close to her heart; and now that act of self-preservation was paying off. Loretta thought she would go to work, debase herself just to keep the muddy old place; Ludlow was using the water-on-rock method, drilling into her how ill-equipped she was to manage a farm, how few assets she had, how many liabilities. The only thing she could do was wait them out.

Ludlow came home after Helen had gone to bed. By the time she was dressed in the morning he had left again, to help shovel out some of the beach cottages. She passed the day in a suspended dread. The wind was still howling and the snow falling, and it seemed the storm would never end. She imagined the house completely buried in white, only its chimney top exposed, suffocating its occupants until they struggled to crawl their way out of the drifts. Even now the snow pellets were so thick the windows seemed wrapped in gauze.

Loretta had taken the girls up to the attic, where they found trunks of Civil War ball gowns and wedding dresses, boxes of photographs and stereopticons, ice skates and fishing boots, lawn furniture and croquet sets, chipped dishes and encyclopedias with frayed bindings. Hearing them from the foot of the staircase, giggling and carrying on, Helen felt a stab of what was almost jealousy. If she had suggested such a diversion, the girls would have reacted with scorn, yet here they were having a great time, and they all seemed to be enjoying each other's company – Loretta was laughing like a teenage girl and Camille and Joyce sounded positively giddy.

They came bounding back down the stairs, their arms stacked with scrapbooks. Loretta had always been a great one for starting scrapbooks, on any imaginable theme – dried flowers snipped from the garden, recipes clipped from magazines, pictures of birds, newspaper clippings (poetry, dress patterns, obituaries), stories about people she admired (Helen Keller, John James Audubon). Helen remembered helping her fill them years ago, when she and Jim were engaged, using that flour-and-water paste that would turn to lumpy mold if you didn't get the right consistency. Helen kept notebooks with poems and diary entries and occasionally sketches from nature; anything else seemed somehow second hand and not very appealing.

"God! Look at that dress!" Joyce was squealing. She and Camille had brought the scrapbooks down to the kitchen table, where they were slowly flipping through pages of yellowed bridal announcements. Helen looked over their heads, vaguely recognizing some of the women – acquaintances of Loretta's, people from church, and Jim's sister, Clara, in a pillbox wedding hat.

Loretta heaved a larger scrapbook on the table, its gilt pages overstuffed with loose paper. "My trip below the equator," she announced. "Panama, Brazil, Argentina, around Cape Horn, Chile, Easter Island, the Galapagos. The birds! The flowers! You can't even imagine."

Camille was asking Loretta questions about South America. When were you there? Where did you stay? How much did it cost? – and Loretta was answering her in professorial detail, showing off each photograph and keepsake. She pointed to the cobbled, narrow streets of La Paz, to villages nestled high in the Andes, glass and concrete apartment buildings in the modern cities of Rio de Janeiro and Montevideo.

"This book doesn't do it justice, these are just snapshots," Loretta said. "If the power would come back on I'd show you my slides. Kodachrome. Stunning, really."

Helen exchanged a look with Joyce. They had seen these slides a million times. They *were* stunning – Loretta was a fair photographer – but they were such a microcosm that it was hard to get a feel for where you were. It was birds, after all, that Loretta was interested in, and her slides were filled with them – colorful macaws and tiny wrens and yellow flashes of goldfinch. Occasionally the monotony would be broken by a butterfly garden or some tourist attraction, like the monoliths of Easter Island, but mostly the slides were of interest only to birdwatchers.

Helen sat next to Joyce, who was reading Helen and Jim's wedding announcement. Looking at the faded photograph, Helen could barely recognize her younger self – smiling primly, her hair cut short like Audrey Hepburn's. If she closed her eyes she could remember the moment in the studio, a few weeks before the wedding. Unfinished, the gown was fixed with pins in the back that stabbed into her skin; she had had such a time with that peplum waist, she hadn't gotten it right until two days before the wedding. It was hot in the studio, the photographer was curt, she was afraid to smile (she wanted to look demure), but when it was over she was too happy to care.

"I didn't know you went to Niagara Falls." Joyce had come to the end of the wedding write-up. "I thought you went to Canada."

In her ignorance of geography Joyce had picked up on a secret only she and Jim shared. "Niagara Falls, the town, is in New York, but the bigger falls is over the line, in Canada." She did not add that they had spent one night in a tacky motel with heart-shaped pillows and then decided, spur of the moment, to ditch the honeymoon capital and drive to Toronto. They had taken in shows, ate at glamorous restaurants and walked the streets hand-in-hand; most important, they had told no one, mailing all their postcards from Niagara Falls on the way home and bringing home the requisite ash trays and souvenir pillows. Toronto was the only time alone together they ever had, because after the honeymoon they came home to the farm, to live with Jim's mother.

"I would love to go to South America," Camille said. She almost sighed as she spoke. "And not just on a tour, but to live there, to speak Spanish all the time. My father was Spanish, you know."

Helen had never heard Camille mention a father. Spanish? What lies had Marian been filling her with? She was no more Spanish than a Spanish onion. Helen supposed when you had to invent a father you might as well go all out.

"Things were different then. I was there in the thirties," Loretta said. "The politics down there has complicated matters."

Helen noticed that Joyce had yet to look up. She was reading her own birth announcement. It told so little, that paragraph; that Joyce was born at the local hospital, what she'd weighed, and who her parents were. It said nothing about the three months before she was born, when Helen had fled to New York to stay with her parents. The Richmonds hadn't really known what to do when their only daughter had shown up, six months pregnant and with Dale in tow, and announced she wasn't going home. Her mother said it was foolishness, she should go home to her husband. Helen's father, who secretly adored having Dale follow him everywhere, shushed his wife and let her stay. As for Helen, she wasn't about to go home when her husband was carrying on with that woman. She had figured running away to New York would bring him to his senses. He kept her guessing until the very end; it was Christmas Eve, and she was five days shy of delivery, when he came to take her home. Helen had already registered at the Cooperstown hospital. She never knew if it was the prospect of not seeing his daughter's birth or missing Christmas with Dale that forced his hand. She was certain he hadn't come to New York for her.

Joyce turned the page. "Hey. Who's this? Who's Susan?"

Helen, shaken from her reverie, reached over, grabbed the scrapbook and slammed it shut, holding the thick, unwieldy thing behind her back as though it had never been there on the table at all.

Joyce seemed too startled to speak. Then the back door burst open and in came Ludlow, stomping his boots on the doormat and bringing in a cloud of frosty air. They were too busy then to talk about Cuba or wedding dresses or Niagara Falls. Helen kept the scrapbook beneath her elbow. Ludlow had saved her.

Ludlow was in an expansive mood. The storm, he pronounced, had been the worst damn disaster they could expect to live through, yet they were very lucky, because they had suffered no property damage. The roofs were holding up under heavy piles of snow, the gale had loosened a few shingles but that was all. Even the plumbing in the vacant cottages had withstood the wind and cold. But they were going to have a helluva time getting everyone dug out.

"The highway is just littered with cars and trucks. They can't get them out of there. It might be the end of the week before we get mail."

He had changed out of his sodden clothes into a sweatshirt and pants and poured himself a brandy. The girls were upstairs, trying to get better reception out of the portable radio, and Loretta was starting dinner – spaghetti squash pulled from the rapidly thawing contents of the freezer. Helen sat in the living room with Ludlow, listening politely. She felt as though all the blood had drained out of her head. She could have used a brandy too, if she was the type. She had put the scrapbook on top of the piano, under a pile of National Geographics.

"I saw Mom brought out the South America book. Are we going to have slides later?"

Helen did not reply. She didn't like the way he said it. He was Loretta's son, for God's sake; she didn't want to join him in a conspiracy to make fun of the poor woman.

He took a swig of brandy. "I'd bet you're dying to get home." Something about the way he said it, the way he said everything, was too familiar.

"Not necessarily." She felt another stab of loyalty to Loretta. "But I think the girls are. They don't want to go back to school, mind you, but they miss the trappings of civilization, like hair dryers and stereos."

"You could go home tomorrow and not have power." He cleared his throat. "I hope you've thought about our talk, Helen."

She looked at him again and said nothing. Ludlow represented a way out, but she despised him too much to take it; and besides, he was trying to cheat her blind. That was his favorite tactic – find someone so low, so vulnerable they would take anything for their property, then sit back and watch his investment appreciate. He knew exactly what that lot was worth and he was offering her 50 cents on the dollar. In fact, his offer wouldn't pay the back taxes.

"You know, Helen, Mother tells me you're looking for a job." He smiled; it was his way of letting her know he had the upper hand and there was nothing she could do about it. "I've got a terrible problem at the office. I've got agents going full bore every day. Property is selling again, and listings are up. But I've got this receptionist who can't spell her way out of a paper bag. Nice girl, don't get me wrong, good with people, but dumb as a post. I've got my mother calling me up every day complaining about our ads. This word spelled wrong, that house isn't a Colonial; you know how she can be. And we're way behind in our paperwork."

"I'm not looking for a job." I know what your game is, she thought: If I don't sell, I'll have to work for you.

"Now hear me out. No working with the public; you'd be in the back, just typing, spiffing up our ad copy, helping me out, you know. What do you say? I'll pay you well, Helen, and not just because you're family. I know you can do it."

What a salesman, Helen thought. He was selling her on this job just the way he was selling her on the idea of giving up part of the farm. He made it sound so easy, so matter of fact. He knew what she was afraid of, what she hated to do; he knew she was a good typist, he knew she could write copy that would meet Loretta's exacting standards. He also knew the prospect of working scared her to death. It was a tease, and either way he scored. If she didn't take it, she would be under even more pressure to sell; if she did, he would control another aspect of her life.

She watched the snow scratch against the window and wondered when it would stop.

CHAPTER FIVE

▲

For weeks after the blizzard, Joyce spent every afternoon after school in her bedroom, spinning a rotating set of the darkest albums she owned, and a new artist Camille had turned her on to, Graham Parker, who sang about love and loss in a sharp, cynical style. Outside it was snowy, dirty and cold, and inside she was stuck in neutral, unable to find the energy to do more than eat, study and sleep. This should have been one of the best times of her life, but somehow senior year had passed her by. At school everyone else was caught up in making plans – getting letters from colleges in the mail, enlisting in the military, making prom dates, getting summer jobs. Joyce went through the motions, but more and more she did so alone.

She had applied to URI, Rhode Island College, two state schools in Massachusetts and, at her mother's insistence, Cornell. Her mother filled out each application for Joyce, and in the box that said "father," Helen typed in all capital letters, "DECEASED." Joyce wondered if her mother thought that might score her points.

She stayed after school one day for a student newspaper meeting, but when two junior girls – dressed similarly in pink hip-hugging pants and blue sweaters with cowl-neck collars – began to whisper in the back of the room, she decided not to go back. Instead she found a part-time job shelving books at the village library, a small shingled bungalow next to the church where the librarian still stamped due dates by hand and where gilt-edged editions of Dickens and Hardy nestled up to the crinkly covers of Agatha Christie and Alex Haley. After her two-hour shift she went home, did her homework and played side after side of the most depressing and mystical music she could find.

Things were different between Joyce and Camille. Joyce could not pinpoint how or when it had happened, but she felt it those three days they were snowed in at Aunt Loretta's, with Camille rhapsodizing about going to South America and finding her father. She and Loretta had gotten quite chummy – she had sent Camille on her way with a stack of National Geographics – and Loretta's warmth toward her friend had made Joyce realize that her mother didn't like Camille at all, which she had always known but never thought about too much. Loretta liked Camille, saw something in her, and instead of vindicating their friendship this observation struck a profound chord of jealousy in Joyce. Camille's curiosity and interest, in itself so surprising, made Joyce long to be different. She had no father to search for; she could not imagine traveling to South America, speaking Spanish every day and fitting in; and these feelings made her realize that Camille, although she still professed to be her friend, had left her behind.

In fact, Camille had a bewitching effect on everyone except her mother. Dale showed up on the last day they were snowed in at Aunt Loretta's, and it was typical of Camille that after she had been sugary sweet to Loretta, going on and on about South America, she could without compunction sneak out of the house the following evening with Dale to get drunk at the Sea Shanty. They had invited Joyce but she had been too timid to go along, or maybe she sensed the invitation wasn't sincere. From the back porch she watched the two of them wade off through snow drifts, Camille bumming a cigarette off her brother and Dale, in a stage whisper, doing Monty Python imitations.

In school a week later Camille related she had gotten served at the Sea Shanty but after a couple of beers they had decided to walk home and get high, during which trip they found themselves wandering through the deserted trailer park at the end of the Drift Road, where they had a long, involved adventure half-believing they had landed in a parallel universe that served as a junkyard for Earth. Joyce could just picture this – Dale was an avid reader of Ray Bradbury – and she wondered what it was about Camille that made everyone who spent time with her believe that she was deeply, sincerely interested in every word they said.

Everyone, that is, except Joyce's mother.

In school as well Camille seemed more distant. She had been accepted into one course at URI through some special minority program, and she was released early every Tuesday and Thursday. Camille began to eat lunch with a boy who was taking automotive at the vo-tech next door and offered to work on her car. Her visits to Joyce's house had become more infrequent, and often when Joyce called, Marian told her in a weary voice that Camille was out.

It puzzled her, how Camille could have drifted away now, when so many other times she had feared it. For so long she had been a good and loyal friend. In the church at her father's funeral, Joyce had twisted around and seen, sitting alone in a rear pew, straight-backed and serene, Camille. Finding her there had calmed Joyce enough to get through the service. Camille had not come back to Loretta's house afterward – they both knew it would have been awkward – but Camille sought her out in the church parking lot, gave her a hard, unabashed hug, and that was enough.

Their friendship, Joyce saw now, had been borne out of class necessity. It was hard being a smart girl of limited means. Joyce had always felt it: She never had the same kinds of clothes, the latest shoes or sandals, or any of the tributes to teen consumption – the flavored lip gloss, the hand-tooled leather shoulder bags, the white, woven bracelets that soon became gray with dirt. She did not know these things existed until they started to show up, spreading through the school population like a discriminatory germ, somehow fading away by the time she had convinced her mother how badly she needed whatever it was. There was the matter of the Winter house, too; it embarrassed her to bring people home. Girls who lived in tidy ranch houses with modern furniture, who slept in white canopy beds with a princess phone on the night table, these girls had no appreciation for a house with a history. All they saw was the kitchen wallpaper curling at the seams and the tufts of dingy stuffing exploding from the easy chair. The wide, expansive fields that meandered down to the ocean interested Joyce but not her peers, who couldn't understand why the Winters didn't just tear the house down and build a new one right on the water.

Then there was talk – there was always talk – and it filtered down to Joyce from the girls' parents, weird, cryptic allusions to her mother not being right and her father's shiftlessness (which Joyce never could understand, because it seemed to her he worked harder than anyone she knew) and, when she countered that her family came from one of the oldest blood lines in town, her pseudo-friends laughed at the idea anyone would care about such a thing.

If Joyce and her family were poor, if they lived on the edge, it was still a middle class edge they clung to, on the basis of their proud family history and a prosperous past. Camille was not middle class. For one thing, she was an Indian, and it didn't matter what they were taught in school about the Indian movement or the standoff at Wounded Knee, in this tiny corner of Rhode Island in 1978, the Narragansetts were not popular – partly out of prejudice, but also because they were pressing a land claim that had put dozens of people's real estate titles in jeopardy. And not only was she an Indian, Camille was truly poor. That shack on Kings Factory Road made the dilapidated Winter farmhouse look respectable.

Joyce and Camille had been thrown together by circumstance, but their friendship had been fertilized by the attraction of their strong personalities. Camille told Joyce she was smart and an independent thinker, that she had a real mind, praise Joyce gobbled up, but what fascinated Joyce was Camille's utter disinterest in everyone else. Camille didn't care what the tennis-playing blonde girls in polo shirts thought; she didn't want to live in their Monopoly houses, as she called them, and she didn't want to join their cheerleading squads or sell pencils and pens with them during lunch. She did not care about them in the least.

So it seemed impossible to Joyce that this friendship, which had been their conspiracy against the world, would start to sputter out like a flame splashed with water. For someone like Camille, who seemed not to care about anything, what would it mean to no longer have Joyce as a best friend? Nothing, probably. For Joyce losing Camille would be, on the heels of her father's death, another unfathomable loss.

Through the rest of February and March, as the earth began throwing off the snow in fits and starts of muddy, crusty
undulations, Joyce took to walking about the farm. The ground
was still squishy in places, the grass barely showing a stubble
of green, but she didn't care. To walk, to be in motion, was the
goal; while listening to music had quieted the storm in her head
for a while, now it was the simple act of exercise that helped her
push everything out of her mind. She had a long route for the
days when she didn't work after school. She started at the north-
ern end of the field, passing briskly by the cemetery (she could
not linger there), to the dirt road that divided the property from
north to south, through the dunes and onto the rocky beach,
where a cold slap of air hit her as soon as she scrambled down
the dune face. Then she was on the beach, heading west, the soft
sand slowing her down but stretching the tendons in the backs
of her legs; she walked as far as she could – sometimes a mile,
the sun already sinking in front of her, turning the sky shades of
apricot and dusty rose. Then, exhausted, she would turn back,
searching for the dune break that marked the farm's property
line, and head home by the salt pond and the orchard.

Her muscles, in her calves and feet and knees, knew every
inch of the farm and the beach beyond. They knew the gnarly
tree root in the dirt road that, when the earth was dry, could
catch the toe of a shoe and send you flying. They knew where
the high tide had reached by the rise and fall of the dampened
sand. They knew the Russian olive that would scratch her face
and catch her arm if she didn't twist away. They knew the gravel
part of the path to avoid so she wouldn't scare the scaup and
white-winged scauters off the pond, the ducks her father refused to let anyone shoot though his hunting friends teased him
unrelentingly.

When she did this, when she walked to the point of fatigue,
she could sleep at night. When she didn't, she would awake at
1 or 2 o'clock and lie there, her head frantically racing from image to image. The insomnia always started with a dream, and
her dreams were on the same theme – the ocean had risen up,
was coming to get her, cresting over the dunes, filling up the salt
pond, engulfing the house, they would all drown, they would die.
Sometimes she was on the beach when it happened. Sometimes
she was upstairs, in her grandmother's bedroom, watching the

tide inch ever higher. Sometimes the ocean was bubbling under chunks of ice; sometimes it was green and frothy; sometimes it was white and crested and filled with debris probable and improbable – boat timbers, lobster pots, a Coke machine, rakes and hammers and saws. But always her dream image was the briny Atlantic, coming to claim her at last, to drown its prodigal daughter. She never thought about her father, saw him dead, remembered the shot. All of her dreams and the waking horror that followed were filled not with blood but salt water.

The worst part of Joyce's growing isolation was the people who were trying to drag her out of it. One afternoon in February her guidance counselor, a tall, ex-hippie with corkscrew locks and nerdy black glasses, pulled her out of social studies and tried to have a talk with her. He was concerned about her. He understood how devastating it must be to lose a parent. He wanted to do whatever he could for her. Joyce looked around his office, which was barely big enough for his desk and two chairs, and made a game out of counting the items with smiley faces on them – a pack of note cards, a sign that read, "Pick a career that will bring a lifetime of happiness!," an alarm clock, a dish for holding paper clips. She brightly told him that she was fine, really, she had a wonderful, supportive family, many friends, and she was eager to make a new start in college next fall. When she returned to class she noticed that her fingernails had tattooed bloody half-moons into her palms.

One Saturday at the post office, the pastor of the Pawcatuck Valley Baptist Church cornered her while she was struggling with the combination to the Winter box, which was worse than her locker at school. She desperately turned the knob, hoping for the tumbler to release, and after Reverend Greene had gently stepped in and opened it for her, she had to listen to his plea that she return to church. And bring her mother, the poor woman, who needed to accept God's grace and seek comfort in His home. She could get away only by lying that yes, certainly, they would come soon.

She didn't tell her mother any of this, because Helen Winter was oblivious to her daughter's pain, and even if she had not been, her mother had established that they would not be talking about her father, not now or anytime soon. In fact, the widow Winter seemed to be on a mission to rid all signs of her husband from the house. One day when Joyce was looking for an extension cord (after having moved her stereo farther from the plug in her bedroom), she stumbled on boxes of her father's books in the barn. Another time she carried the garbage out to the burn barrel to discover a mound of freshly torched paper; on the top, barely singed, was a canceled check signed in her father's cramped, hurried hand.

On the Saturday before Easter, a cold, drizzly morning, Joyce was halfway through her walk, about to turn from the field to the dirt trail that led to the beach, when she happened to glance to the east, toward the Audubon land, and in the distance saw an older woman with binoculars around her neck headed straight for her. Joyce quickly put her head down and turned toward the dunes, but Aunt Loretta had an eye for spotting creatures who tried to fade into their natural surroundings.

"Hold up there!" Loretta, aided by a gnarled walking stick and despite two layers of sweatshirts and a black flannel skirt, soon was upon her. Her chest heaving but speaking slowly, as not to scare this specimen she had overtaken, Loretta opened up her notebook and pointed out a hastily drawn sketch of what to Joyce's untrained eye looked like an oriole.

"An American redstart. *Setophaga ruticilla*. Very early for him to be this far north."

Joyce said something polite. Loretta was eyeing her more closely now, as though to make another sketch. "I found what I came for," the old woman replied, which Joyce realized could be taken two ways. "Come back to my house. Too damned cold to be out here anyway."

Loretta brought Joyce back to her car, parked in the gravel lot at the entrance to the Audubon land, and soon they were standing on Loretta's glassed-in porch, which was warm and steamy as a greenhouse. The sun was pouring in on rows of empty seed cups Loretta had set out on planks held up by saw-horses. Loretta brought out potting soil and a box full of seeds, some half opened from seasons previous, and in an assembly line they began stuffing the seeds – pumpkin, tomato, pepper, chard, lettuce, radish, zinnia, marigold, cosmos – into the cups of dirt. Joyce went through the mechanical motions of planting, but she felt like her brain was on fire.

"Your grandfather always loved this time of year," Loretta

said, breaking the silence. She stopped working, gazing across the street at the fallow cornfield and the lip of ocean beyond. "He wasn't happy until he could get his fingers back in the soil. All winter long he would mope around the house. Then the seed catalogs would come, and that would lift his spirits; and finally the hardware store would begin to get in its spring stock, and he'd be down there every other day, looking at the harrows and mowing machines and fencing. But on the day when he could finally work the soil, oh, he was a happy man. And so was your grandmother, because that meant he was finally out of her hair."

Joyce had not heard much about her grandfather. She knew he'd died young, only 48, while her grandmother had lived on into old age almost out of spite. His name was a respected one among the state's farmers and politicians; he had served in the state legislature and on the Town Council. She imagined him to be more pleasant than her grandmother, who had made them all so miserable with her constant carping and her extended stays in bed.

"I wish you'd known him, Joyce." Loretta reached over and hugged her around the waist, her ample body folding into her like a huge pillow. Joyce stiffened and tried not to show it. "Come on. I'll show you a picture."

They walked into the kitchen, washed their hands in the cast iron sink, and Joyce followed Aunt Loretta up the stairs into the bedroom she had shared with Camille when they were snowbound – iron twin beds, a mahogany highboy and a vanity with a big round mirror, just as they'd left it, only now Camille's bed was covered with boxes and a pile of scrapbooks. Including the one Joyce had been looking at the day Ludlow came home and interrupted her inopportune question.

"I was just sorting through this stuff yesterday." Loretta opened a box and a musty smell escaped like a genie. "All these old pictures, I really should do something with them. Get them into albums."

Joyce leaned casually against the bed and her fingers grazed the scrapbook's binding, the one with the brown cover, the one that held some sort of secret. But it was on the bottom of the pile. She would never get a look at it.

"There. That's your grandfather." Loretta produced a warped black and white photo, small with crinkled edges, of a man in overalls standing next to a tractor. If it were not for the receding hairline and the ancient Farm-All tractor, Joyce would have sworn the man was her father. "He loved the land. Look at that smile. Didn't care much for getting into his suit and traveling up to the city, but he did it, for years. Because it was important, he said, to contribute something."

Joyce held the picture Loretta proffered. Staring into the dark, snapping eyes of her grandfather, noticing the black-and-white sweep of the land behind him, she felt that same homesick feeling in her gut that her father inspired when he talked about the farm.

"Do you think she's going to sell?"

"Who? Your mother?" Loretta stopped for a moment, considering. "I don't know. I hope she doesn't have to. I always thought someday the rest of that east woods should go to Audubon. But that doesn't pay the bills, I suppose."

"Can't you help her? Ludlow is pressuring her. He came to the house."

Loretta raised a brow. "Really?"

"Dale and I were outside. She won't talk about it, but I know that's why he was there."

Loretta pursed her lips and slapped the photo against her wrist. "You don't know that for sure, and you shouldn't speculate."

Joyce felt rebuked. She had gone too far. Of course, Ludlow was Aunt Loretta's son, and she would defend him. She wished she had just shut up. The day had been starting to feel like it looked, that bright April sun that washes every bare twig with color, but now it had gone dark again, and Joyce felt worse than when she walked the dunes. No matter how tangled her emotions, no matter how they drifted up unbidden like stinky seaweed, at least on the beach no one was there to put them in further disarray. She turned away, so Loretta could not see the flush of red on her face. It was too bad, because she liked Aunt Loretta; she liked her house of knick-knacks and books; she liked her overflowing scrapbooks and her amateur sketches of sea birds; she liked the patient way she answered Joyce's questions about the moldering antiques that filled the house. But she could turn sometimes, flashing from gentle to brusque in a fingersnap.

"Are you worried about it?" Loretta was trying to make amends, reaching for her, but Joyce rushed out of the room, down the stairs and out of the house.

CHAPTER SIX

The yuccas look like they belong in Arizona, not Rhode Island, and I have no idea how they got here. Because they like the sandiest, poorest soil imaginable and never need to be pruned, fed or watered, they have become so firmly entrenched I couldn't get rid of them if I wanted to. Still, every year we remark on how odd and out of place the yuccas look, though their roots are by now so deep and knotty they are as firmly fixed as a tree's.
– A Country Woman's Diary, April 7, 1978

Helen had been loathe to do it, but she had burned all of Jim's papers except the most important, watching his cramped, angular script turn to black inside the burn barrel. If she hadn't, Joyce would have been into them, sifting through each one for some kind of souvenir. Helen had packed Jim's clothes away in bags for the Salvation Army, keeping only the most precious in one bureau drawer – his Cornell sweatshirt, its neckline and cuffs frayed; her favorite flannel shirt, a blackwatch plaid; and a pair of red-checked pajamas she had given him years ago that he had never worn. His pillowcase was still on the bed, the scent that was once so strong now reduced to a faint after-note.

There had been other things, the stuff of secrets – old letters, diaries, photographs – that she had boxed away and hidden where she was convinced Joyce would never find them. Standing at her bedroom door, Helen hoped the room looked as it should and not too clean and spare; she didn't want Joyce to sense something was missing. That was why she'd left the saucer of change and Jim's wallet on the bureau, carefully dusting around them. There was no telling what that girl would be into while she was gone.

At the top of the stairs, Helen opened up old Mother Winter's room. She kept it locked but Joyce had been breaking into it, she was sure, because she kept finding fingerprints in the dust. She couldn't imagine what Joyce thought she would find inside. Helen had many reasons for keeping the room shuttered, but sometimes she wondered if maybe it was as simple as hating the sight and smell of it. In the early years of her marriage she had dreamed of the day when the old woman would be dead and they could claim the master bedroom for their own. But when that time finally came she could not banish the musty, old-woman smell from the mattress or rug or draperies, and when she was in the room all she could hear was Martha's shrill voice demanding attention.

Now, standing beside the oak four-poster bed, she wondered if it wasn't time to sweep away Martha Winter the way she had banished her husband. Jim hadn't been in the ground three months and she had managed it: gritted her teeth and sifted through everything he owned and consigned most of it to the dust heap. It was anger that had pushed her along, a cold fury that grew each day as she thought about what Jim had done and why, and the fix he had left her in. Surely she could summon up some of that rage against that old harpy she had waited on for so many years. But Martha Winter's ghost had faded, and whatever unease the room held no longer had anything to do with an old invalid who rang a bell each time she wanted her covers turned. Helen walked across the room and raised the shade, so rotten it nearly split in her hands as it flapped up. She had not looked out this window in years, decades, and yet the view was the same as the last time she had stood here, April 10, 1956. To the east, the apple and peach trees, still stark in the early spring, raising branches like bony fingers to the sky; in the center a lazy path of worn gravel and dirt, choked with oak leaves; and beyond it all the salt pond, blinking at her in the sunlight. The old sickness rose in her throat, and she pressed her nose to the wavy glass as though she could will herself outside, down there by the pond, within an arm's reach of a girl's desperate hand instead of up here, tending to Martha's strident complaints about her lukewarm lunch.

But it was no use. She could shut up the room, she could open it up; she could leave it to the dust balls or scrub it within an inch of her life. The essential facts would be the same, inexorable, immutable, fixed in time. She could not change what happened. She had tried to tell Jim that so many times. Did he take her resignation as a lack of atonement? Were his sins expiated by hers? She would never know, because he had ended the conversation he refused to have in life. His death was the last word.

But she no longer had to worry about the bedroom, or the window, or the view. For now she wouldn't think about the pond and the spirits that misted above its tiny whitecaps. Tomorrow she was going to New York, where the family would gather around her and she would have time to think through what she was going to do.

Helen bowed her head and, her lips moving but her throat silenced, recited the Lord's prayer.

From the moment she invited them in, Helen could see that Fran and Peter Kennedy made a strange couple. Fran was tall and lithe, with the build of an athlete and her hair cut in a practical feathery bob. Peter, who introduced himself by stressing that he was "Peter, not Pete," was shorter than his wife, a squarely built man with flirtatious eyes and a smile that always seemed to be fighting its way out from under his moustache. Fran kept ducking her head when she talked, reminding Helen of the cormorants who dove for eelgrass in the salt pond. Fran looked around the room as though she had never seen a kitchen before, and she spoke to her husband as though Helen weren't sitting at the table with them. She made Helen self-conscious of the pilly cardigan she had pulled on when they drove up.

Helen was not sure what she'd expected when they had telephoned her that morning, after Joyce left for school. A couple from New Jersey, who loved to vacation in South County, with two children. Fran, on the phone, had sounded like she was applying for a job. She talked quickly and breathlessly. Helen had pictured her – shorter, yes, with a round, pleasant face, like an apple, not tall and angular with such sharp cheekbones. She had no idea how they knew to call her or what, exactly, they wanted, but she gathered they were looking for property. She supposed they could come over. What would it hurt to listen?

"Peter, look at that clock! It's an Avery!" Fran said, pointing to the grandfather clock in the living room. Helen hated that clock: It lost time every third day. "What a quaint place you have, Mrs. Winter."

Helen began to feel uneasy. She had heard about people like the Kennedys coming into a house, staking it out and then coming back later to steal antiques. Their volubility made her nervous. Peter Kennedy touched her elbow every time he said something, as though she were a blind woman who needed steering around the room, and Fran talked to her as though she were deaf. She supposed they thought she was some backwards Yankee who needed to be humored.

"Maybe you'd like to see the farm," Helen offered. This visit had been a mistake; they weren't serious about buying land, they were sight-seers having fun at her expense. One tramp down to the dunes would tire them out and send them scurrying back to their motel room.

But the Kennedys were enthusiastic. In their LL Bean duck shoes they matched Helen's stride down the old driftway, stopping every few feet to ask a question or exclaim at the view. "What do you grow? What's that building, the leaning one? Who owns that property over there?" They peppered her with questions until they reached the dunes, where they stopped and took in the sweep of the ocean. It was one of those early April days that carry the taste of summer – still bracing, but with the sun gleaming off the water, the wind at last softer and Block Island shining like a tropical paradise to the south. Even Helen stopped to drink it all in, closing her eyes while the sun burned reddish yellow into her eyelids and the ocean roared in her ears. She could feel her feet sinking. Maybe she did have roots here – maybe, like the dune grass, she could bend with the storms and stay fixed in the sand.

"This is it, Peter. This is what we've been searching for." Fran was whispering to her husband, bending down until their heads touched, side to side. "Oh God, the view."

"There isn't another place like this from Boston to Washington," Peter murmured.

"We'll build a big wrap-around deck where we'll have drinks

every night and watch the sunset." Fran was rocking back and forth, as though trying to gain purchase in the shifting dunes. "At dusk we'll jump into the water and take a swim, just like in the movies. We'll buy a telescope and watch the boats go by. We'll have cocktail parties."

While their imaginary guests chattered on the deck, clinking ice in imaginary drinks, Helen walked discreetly away and sat on a piece of ship's timber that had washed up over the winter. There was more debris farther down the beach – a wooden lobster pot, an orange buoy and an empty bleach bottle. The ocean yielded these things up as though they had meaning, which of course they did not. They were the random collections of churning water and stinging wind, and while some people would prize such detritus, putting rounded edges of green and blue beach glass in their pockets and dragging driftwood to their cars, Helen saw it for what it was – trash. A winter's worth of ocean-borne garbage, no more worth saving than the cigarette butts and Old Milwaukee cans left on Post Road by the retreating snow.

She tried to picture the Kennedys in the rambling house of their imagination, but she could not. She supposed they thought this April day was cold; she wondered what they would do when the October gales came or when the snow roared off the ocean like stinging pellets of sand in a desert storm. But of course, they would not be here then; their house would be closed up, its walls of glass shuttered against the wailing wind.

Helen's thoughts lurched back and forth like the incoming high tide. Part of her mind, rushing forward, executed the sale with a pen stroke of rationality. What was it to her if they wanted a piece of this paradise? What did it matter in the long run? They had money and they were willing to spend it. She could pay off the back taxes and all she would sacrifice would be a little privacy in the summer – sharing the right-of-way with the Kennedys and putting up with a speck of a house on the horizon. Maybe she'd have a little money left over to put off working. It made good business sense. She had to do something. She wasn't about to set out corn and potatoes this spring, and Dale certainly wasn't making a move to take over.

But another part of her retreated an inch or two, sucking back all the ground she had gained. The family would give her a hard time, of that she was certain. Dale and Joyce would have something to say about it. Joyce walked these dunes in all kinds of weather, and Dale liked to hunt in the east woods when he wasn't out fishing. Was it fair to divide the place up so soon, with Jim dead only a few months? Loretta would get after her, too. Her sister-in-law had always wanted Jim to donate the east woods to Audubon, that and the cedar swamp. A rare habitat, eastern woodlands, kettle ponds, swamp; Loretta would rattle off the land's features along with the names of birds that called it home. No, it would not be easy facing the kids or her sister-in-law with the news.

But what did they expect her to do? Loretta wanted her to work for Ludlow. Ha! She could not imagine a worse match of employer and employee. Even if she sold the land, sooner or later she would have to get a job, but at least this would give her a chance to find something she could cope with. If she had the guts to go through with it. Like the tide, the progress of her emotions was hard to read. Tides make a line in the sand that is soon erased. Backward – fear, guilt; forward – self-interest, hope. She wondered how those periwinkles lived in the inter-tidal zone, where they could shrivel to the point of near-death before the next tide swept in and overwhelmed them with wa-ter. At some point they must wither and die before the waves come back, before life returns.

It was not as though she did not have some feeling for the land. Of course she did. She had lived here 29 years, seven more than in Cooperstown. It was her home now. She had written about the beach and its many moods countless times in her column – from the gales of fall, when the ocean frothed over the dune line, to the summer days when the sand was so hot it turned the soles of her feet white. In good weather she came down here almost every day, and the ocean was always a differ-ent shade – from the palest pea green to the deepest azure. It seemed the stories it churned up were endless, too, but like the trash from the bottom of the ocean, she had lost all interest in whatever they were trying to tell her.

The Kennedys were ready to go. The wife had chapped cheeks from the wind, and the husband kept clapping his un-gloved hands together. They were soft and white, the hands of a man who spends his days in heated offices pushing but-tons on a calculator and telephone. Helen took the lead down the path like a tugboat dragging a heavy cargo. There were no whispers behind her, and she heard an oriole on the edge of the east woods singing them home. The question rang in her head: What was the right thing to do? The Kennedys seemed to sense the enormity of what they asked. Back at the car Fran and Peter one at a time solemnly shook her hand. "You have a lot of thinking to do," Peter Kennedy said.

The way to New York was not one road but many, a patchwork of highway stitched together with switchback exits, toll booths and long stretches of macadam. Helen left early, before Joyce was awake, so as to avoid the traffic that would snarl the interstates later in the day. She carried with her one suitcase, a cooler with lunch and a map, although she had driven the route dozens of times. Helen Winter, her true baggage unseen, was going home, whatever that meant.

CHAPTER SEVEN

▲

The farmhouse seemed bigger now, more open, as the wind picked up the lace curtains in the living room and set them down again, blew its way around corners and down hallways, lifted up doilies and peeked into doors, like a ghost freed of its crypt.

Helen had finally left for New York. Dale was fishing, due in two days. For the first time in as long as she could remember, Joyce was alone.

She walked into the living room, still keeping an eye toward the window. Her mother's desk, cleared of work and bills, was neater than usual. A yellowed plastic cover lay over the typewriter. On the blotter a wooden tray held a stack of blank paper, and in an orange juice can – which Joyce had covered in wallpaper remnants long ago, for a Brownie project – were a ballpoint pen and two yellow pencils.

She tried the drawers of the old cherry desk. Either stuck in the humidity or locked. What she needed was her mother's letter opener – reed thin, sturdy, with a sharp point – but that, too, must be locked up. She gave the drawers one more tug. They all stopped at the same point.

She walked to the bookcase. Her grandfather had built it, along one and a half walls, and it reached from floor to the ceiling, a good nine feet high. The lower shelves were a mishmash of contemporary stuff – her mother's gardening books, thick dictionaries and almanacs, Reader's Digest condensed books, Phyllis Whitney thrillers, her grandmother's threadbare cookbooks. Higher up the books got older and mustier, 19th-century collections of Longfellow and Whittier, small volumes with gilt edges and cracked spines. Up there, she knew, her mother wouldn't venture; even standing on tiptoe she could see that Helen rarely dusted beyond the two lower shelves.

The bottom shelf, then.

Her mother had a habit of sticking things in books – newspaper clippings, jottings, old photos. Joyce had once seen her pull a $50 bill from the middle of a Jacquelyn Susann novel. It was the randomness of it as a hiding place that appealed to Helen. She knew that *they* knew that the house was full of too many books of too many pages to give up her secrets easily. And then, too, she was always around. There was precious little opportunity for snooping. Until now.

Joyce pulled a volume from the end of the first shelf. A Rodale organic gardening book, its paper cover splintered from heavy use. The pages were full of clippings. A yellowed newspaper advice column on how to get rid of slugs. A receipt from the A&P, apparently used as a bookmark, with "5 gal." written on the bottom, as though she had been taking note of some formula. Other junk – a magazine ad for a rototiller, a real bookmark with a cardinal at the top, and a brittle yellow maple leaf.

Joyce put the book back and tried another. An hour later, her knees aching and her hands grimy with dust, she gave up in disgust. She hadn't even found money, and certainly not what she was looking for.

Whatever that was.

She walked around the room, taking note of the furnishings that were almost too familiar – trying to find a drawer, a cabinet in the wall, an old piece of crockery that might prove worthy of searching. Her instincts told her the living room was the center of something, a likely place for her mother to stash away correspondence or evidence of the things she kept hidden. The kitchen might be the heart of the house, but the expansive living room, with its bookcases and stone hearth and lumpy chairs, was the center of Helen's world. It was, after all, where she wrote. That alone gave it a sort of intimacy, branded it as her room even though they all had gathered there over the years . . . her father in the brown upholstered armchair, she and Dale on the faded oriental carpet to do homework or play Monopoly;

company forced to sit on the stiff-backed horsehair sofa. No, this was Helen's room, where she read and copied recipes and signed report cards and made out checks and did the crossword puzzle. She might spend time in her bedroom, in the kitchen and the mudroom and the hall, but this was where she lived.

Joyce gave one last look out the window and climbed the stairs.

Her mother and father had shared the worst bedroom in the house – narrow and cramped, it faced the development of one-story ranch houses instead of the fields or the ocean. It was big enough only for a double bed, a highboy and a wooden wardrobe. There was no closet, and only one window let in light. At one time it probably had been a nursery or maid's room, if Captain Winter had ever had such a thing. Today the only good use for it would be as a guest room, a place to tuck a couple of twin beds in case of unexpected company. But for some reason Helen and Jim had chosen it as their own, and even Joyce's room, with its broken window pane stuffed with rags, was more commodious.

Joyce stopped at the head of the stairs, briefly considered turning the knob to her grandmother's room, but superstition outweighed curiosity. She even hesitated at her mother's threshold. What was she snooping for, anyway? Confessions in a journal? Unpaid bills? An empty pill bottle? She could not say, yet she slinked into the room, resting her hands on the blue bedspread. The room was spare, unlived in, with so many of her mother's belongings gone with her. No slippers on the scatter rug. The bureau still held her father's wallet, keys and ring, but her mother's nightstand was dusted and bare. She walked to the wardrobe, turned the key until the doors fell open. She knew then what she had expected to find – her father's clothes, lined up neatly on wire hangers – but they were gone, the hangers clinking together from the inrush of air.

So she had gotten rid of them all. Taken them to the Salvation Army or, more likely, with her to Cooperstown, for some uncle or cousin of like build to wear. Her mother wasn't sentimental about much, at least not about things that belonged to other people. She had swept that wardrobe clean, pulling out every pair of pants and each flannel shirt, the scuffed pair of work boots, the shiny black dress shoes (worn only to church and funerals, both rare occasions) and the old brown slippers. Not even a belt hung from the nail.

She had been looking for something, not the absence of something, and the sight of her father's hangers standing unused jabbed at her more than any reminder of him could have. How could her mother do it . . . how could she take it all away so soon, as though it had never existed? Joyce closed her eyes and saw her father's green work shirts, the wrinkles never entirely free of sawdust and hay spears, and she could smell the essence of him in the faded cotton broadcloth. To fold all that up and stuff into a bag, why, she could never do it. Better to lock it away in the wardrobe, the way they had locked away Grandma's life after she had gone. At least then you knew it was there if you needed it. At least then you didn't have to fold it up and stuff it away for someone else; at least then you didn't have to give it away, another burial to suffer through.

She sat on the bed, making a wrinkle in the smoothed lines of chenille. Outside she heard a faint thud, like wood being chopped or a door slammed shut. If she was going to search she best get about it, and quickly. She opened the drawer of the nightstand. It was shallow but wide, and stuffed with the detritus of bedroom living: pens without caps, a bottle of children's aspirin (how long since that had been needed in the middle of the night?), loose change, nail clippers, a gold lipstick case. She flattened her hand against the mess, moving it around, looking under this and that, not really wanting to touch any of it. The second layer was mostly old snapshots, their edges curling, perhaps sandwiched together in the hope they would be flattened (but why not use a book then?). She flipped through them idly. Days at Watchaug Pond, picnics in old roadside parks, games of croquet at family reunions. They presented a black-and-white world that no longer existed, when her mother was young and relaxed, her brow unlined, her dark hair a little shorter and more tightly curled, her legs tanned and shapely; her father seemed so different too, his hair in a butch cut, his stomach flat, his eyes still sparkling with life. What had happened to them? She didn't remember these times, this couple, although probably Dale did – he had lived a different life from hers, he had come first and so many years before. It couldn't have been just Dale who had changed them. Of course, he had been difficult, still was; he had fallen out of a tree when he was 12 and cracked his head open, then crashed the car when he was 16, breaking his leg and frightening Helen half to death. Joyce had been only eight, but she remembered the strain in her mother's face, the crying jags, and her father's white-lipped anger.

But in these photos all that was ahead of them. Her father had his arm around her mother's shoulder (and they were beautiful shoulders too, rounded, not bony like some women's), and Helen was looking up at him, her lips slightly parted and curled (as though about to say something? Caught at the beginning of a laugh?). The date on the photograph's border said 1955 – Dale would have been four, but she didn't see him in this picture, though they were at the beach, and surely he was there. She reached in for another stack. Christmas snow, a herd of cows, Dale in a Roy Rogers outfit. Then – yes – more pictures at the pond, people sitting at the picnic tables, her aunts eating watermelon, a little girl toddling into the water. She stopped a moment, trying to place the blond curls and chubby legs. One of her cousins, probably, but who? She flipped over another picture. The girl was between Jim and Helen now, holding their hands as they lifted her over the lapping waves. Dale was next to them, his face screwed up into a howl as though the water were too cold.

She put the pictures back, but for some reason she kept the last two, tucking them into the front pocket of her jeans. Dale would know who the little girl was, not that it mattered. Oddly, it bothered her to see her parents having so much fun with a little girl who wasn't theirs and – well, to tell the truth – wasn't *her*. She couldn't remember ever having that much fun at Watchaug; in her mind's eye she saw Helen sitting on their blanket, yelling at her to be careful, to wait an hour after eating lunch before going in again, not to swallow any of that *nasty* water . . . Who was this carefree woman taking such joy in a day at the beach? It sure as hell wasn't the mother she knew.

Joyce smoothed the bedspread and closed the door. She felt no closer to answers now than before she had started looking. She didn't even know what the questions were. She went into her bedroom to look for a book, a hiding place of her own to keep them.

Dale was upstairs in the loft of the barn, where he was setting up his stereo. He had faced the speakers out the loft doors and was threading wires up and down the ladder, muttering to himself through the screwdriver wedged between his teeth. It seemed like he had dragged his entire record collection up to the loft, crate after crate of LPs standing ready to entertain. Dale's taste ran a small gamut from Southern rock to heavy metal, from cracker bands like Lynyrd Skynrd to serious head music like Robin Trower's and Ted Nugent's. Joyce flipped through his LPs looking for something remotely to her taste.

"You won't find any of that fairy Fleetwood Mac in there," he said, unsnarling an extension cord.

"God, Dale, they are not fairies." They had had this discussion many times, and sometimes Joyce thought he teased her about her favorite bands just to have something to talk about. "I don't care who or what you play, as long as Ma doesn't find out. You know she'll find a way to blame me."

"Why is that?" He looked up then, flashing a smile of mischief and delight. "Don't worry. I've got the situation firmly under control. Nobody'll be in the house. I rented a port-a-potty and put it behind the barn. We'll be outside howling at the moon, and Helen will never have any idea."

Another possibility was that Helen would find out and not care, which Joyce found even more maddening. You never could predict when she would explode or when she would just shrug something off.

"You better hope she has a good time in Cooperstown, Jimmy D." Dale's real name was James Dale Jr., and Joyce liked to call him Jimmy in a playful way. This was the first time she'd done so since their father died.

"Relax. Nothing's going to happen. Helen's not going to find out and, even if she does, so what? We had a few people over. Big deal."

"Watch that 'we.'"

"OK. I had a few friends over. Hand me that wire." He was behind a speaker plugging things in, and it came alive with a deep hum when he made contact. "So what do you think prompted this holiday? I mean, I can't remember the last time she went home. Must be years."

Joyce had her theories. It would be just like Helen to enlist

Gramp and Gram's help in convincing Joyce to go to Cornell. She had been accepted at URI, the bill had even arrived in the mail, but Joyce sensed her mother hadn't given up the fight. Next thing she knew, her mother would come up with some Cooperstown money to sweeten the pot. The irony was that if Joyce had wanted to go to Cornell, Helen never would have consented to it. Going to college out of state only made sense because it was her idea.

"She probably just wants to get away." Joyce almost added "from us," and was thinking "from you," but stopped short.

"I'm surprised she left Jailbait behind." He grinned, showing teeth that were gray from tobacco. "She usually doesn't like to let you out of her sight."

"I'm eighteen, asshole, and I think she's got more to worry about from you than from me."

"Not so, little sister. This party will be a tribute to the safe and peaceful use of intoxicants, with no property damage and only the slightest risk of neurological malfunction."

The other speaker came alive then and Joyce hastened down the ladder, where she found two notes posted on the barn's clapboards, scrawled in heavy slashes of black marker. "RULES. Keep cars off the lawn. House off limits! No smoking in the barn!!" In the driveway in front of the barn Dale had set up a volleyball net, and next to the house he had placed their father's ancient charcoal grill. He had told Joyce the menu – burgers, hot dogs and watermelon – but she found the main course in the lee of the barn doors, where he had rolled two kegs. That, and a few dimes of pot he kept hidden in the top drawer of his bureau beneath his rolled-up, slightly gray briefs.

She wanted to go back up the ladder, grab him by the arm and ask him about the pictures she had found. The birth notice for someone named Susan Winter. She had guessed all that it meant, but at the same time it seemed impossible. If she could put these questions into words she might have climbed the ladder again, but something stopped her; something that hummed beneath her consciousness louder than the reverb from Dale's speakers.

People were arriving, mostly Dale's fishermen friends and their girlfriends, and he was waving them to the field next to the barn, putting dishes of proffered food on two tables he had made out of 2-by-4s and sawhorses and delegating various party tasks to his friends. One was manning the kegs, passing out plastic cups and collecting donations, and another was in the loft, apparently playing DJ. In the middle of it all was Dale, his dirty blond ponytail flopping behind him, looking like a tramp who'd been pressed into service as a traffic cop.

Joyce was trying to stay away from the whole scene, mostly because she didn't know any of Dale's friends but also because she wanted to be able to say truthfully that she'd had nothing to do with the party. For the first time in weeks Camille had come over. They sat on the small section of stone wall that jutted out at the end of the orchard. Camille was cradling a plastic cup of beer, but Joyce sat empty handed; she hated the bitter taste on her tongue.

Camille was in a quiet, almost sullen mood. She was dressed in a pair of yellow twill shorts and a short-sleeved top with a little hood hanging down her neck. The color reminded Joyce of the jonquils that sprung up in the fields every year of their own bidding, and it made Camille's skin seem darker than usual. With her waitressing money Camille was always buying clothes. Joyce wanted to compliment her on them but knew her friend hated compliments. If Joyce said something nice about her, she would immediately contradict her, as though she had no taste. Fashion for Camille was a fruitless search for perfection.

Camille asked about Helen, and Joyce told her how her mother had left the day before, and then blurted out what she had found – or rather, not found – in her father's room.

"She went on this cleaning spree a couple of days ago and took everything out of his closet. I mean everything – clothes, hangers and all, boxes of old shoes, anything she could find."

"Maybe she'll give it to the tribe," she said, deadpan.

Joyce felt her cheeks flush. "No, she'll give it to the Salvation Army, but she'll write it a note on it telling them not to send the clothes to South Providence." She felt disloyal as soon as she'd said it.

Camille obliged by twisting her mouth into a smile, but Joyce noticed her eyes were on the volleyball game. The party must have been satisfactorily under way, because Dale was finally having a beer, which he held in one hand while trying to spike the volleyball with the other. He had kicked up the music a notch, to Aerosmith, and was keeping a nervous eye on the opening to the loft, where his buddy was stacking the turntable.

"Maybe we should play the next game. They look like they could use some help."

Joyce was not athletic, and the last thing she wanted to do was be humiliated in front of Dale's fishing friends. "I can't wait for fall," she said instead. "We'll move into Merrow together and we'll be able to hang out whenever we want. You know, we should go shopping pretty soon, get some stuff for the room, shades, bedspreads, that kind of stuff."

Camille looked over at her then. Joyce could tell she was turning something over in her mind, weighing what to say and how to say it. Sadness was a gravity that kept Joyce rooted to the stone wall. This afternoon was not going the way she had intended.

"Joyce, I'm not going to URI in the fall. I won't be able to room with you at Merrow Hall. I've deferred admission to the spring."

"What? But why?" Joyce had images of Hammond, or her mother, doing something to keep Camille down. How could she be so calm about it?

"I'm going away at the end of the summer. I'm going down South, to New Orleans and maybe even South America. I'm going to find my father."

A shard of rock on the wall shifted and Joyce felt herself wobble. It was true Camille had once seen a letter to her mother, with a return address from New Orleans, but Joyce had always thought the connection a wishful one. Now Camille was heading down there as though she had an invitation. How Joyce had pitied her friend all these years when she had no father. Now Camille was going off to find hers, and Joyce's was gone for good.

"Do you even know where he is?" Joyce knew she sounded petulant, but she couldn't help it. They had had everything worked out.

"Don't be a bonehead. I have a good idea. The last time my mother heard from him, he was working on a shrimp boat out of Baton Rouge. I'll go down there, make some inquiries. And I think he was born in Brazil."

On the volleyball court a great cheer erupted as a burly fisherman with a black beard and a generous gut spiked the ball for a winning point.

"Who am I supposed to room with?" Joyce demanded. After all the crap she had gone through to enroll at URI, refusing to apply to Cornell, all the arguments with her mother, all the tension. For nothing.

"Residential Life will pair you up with somebody, and you'll make new friends. You know, it's probably for the best. We can't hang out together for the rest of our lives."

Of course not. What had she been thinking? That friendships outlasted changes in your life? That you could grow up but still be friends?

Joyce said none of this. She got up and stalked off toward the barn. It smelled like hay, axle grease and stale beer. Through the cracked window she could see a tall, thin guy taking a piss behind the barn, urine arcing like a fountain before him. Behind the kegs a long-haired woman in a halter top and cutoffs was passing a joint to a red-headed fisherman wearing a T-shirt that said, "Keep on truckin'." So much for Dale's rules.

She snaked by the barn, underneath the opening to the loft. The hook that was used to lift hay bales swung there, issuing a rusty creak in the wind, listing left and right like a dead man's body. She passed the volleyball game and kept going, toward the field and down the dirt path. The hooting and laughing fell away until she could hear the ocean, a muffled swell, and a phoebe calling its name in the east woods. The gate to the cemetery was rutted in the grass; she squeezed by it, down the rows of unmarked fieldstones, past Captain Winter's stone monument and around the back corner, where sprigs of grass were just sprouting on a hump of earth for which no marker had been laid. Her legs collapsed. Joyce sank down until her back was up against someone else's gravestone, and waited for the dark.

BOOK II

CHAPTER EIGHT

▲

Joyce could not pinpoint when she'd stopped talking to her mother. It was a gradual shutting down, a stream that trickles dry rather than a faucet abruptly turned off. It would have been easy to blame it on the Kennedy episode, but that had been years ago, back when she thought reasonable arguments and impassioned speeches would penetrate Helen's cool detachment. No, it was everything that came afterward that choked off the flow, dried up the last bit of hope that they could have some sort of relationship. The backhoes had come and the Kennedy house had begun to take shape, braced walls of plywood and two-by-fours that looked like a good stiff wind would topple them, but they stood fast, and before she knew it roofers were nailing on shingles, and painters in their white coveralls were swaying on scaffolding, and it was done – a long expanse of gables and porches and pediments that looked more like a pavilion than a house. There was no sense in arguing then; the house was up, most of the east farm was gone, and she would never walk on those dunes again.

It was what happened after that, and after that. The east side was gone but now her mother had all this money, nearly $75,000 according to Loretta, an unheard of amount, enough to make them rich. And what had she done with it? Given it to Dale to buy a boat. Oh, not all of it; Joyce's share had been four years at URI (and what had that cost? $1,000 a year?) and a used car that Helen had picked out for her, a red AMC Hornet that was the ugliest thing Joyce had ever seen. She refused to drive it, just kept using her father's old station wagon, even though its springs were gone and the windows wouldn't roll down, until finally she traded the Hornet in (for half of what her mother had paid for it) and got enough money for a down payment on a new Datsun. Meanwhile Dale had gone to Alabama, where a boat yard was fashioning a 75-foot steel-hulled fishing boat with a state-of-the-art freezer compartment, so he could stay out even longer, and the latest Loran navigational system, so he could operate the boat drunk or sober with minimal chance of colliding with somebody.

But it wasn't all about the money. Sometimes Joyce thought that it was her mother who had pulled away from her. For years now she had been having imagined conversations with Helen, in which daughter asked mother all the questions that burned in her head and mother replied in a soft and reassuring voice, a voice Joyce hadn't heard since she was a child, sick on the couch or in tears over some drama on the playground. These days she would walk into the living room where her mother sat hunched over the typewriter and she would start the conversation – even choke out the first words of a difficult question – and Helen wouldn't hear her, would go on typing until finally, distracted, she would startle and snap at Joyce: Couldn't she see she was writing? Didn't she know this was Monday, her deadline day? Why did she always pick the worst time to interrupt?

It wasn't even that she needed the answers, because she had figured out most of them herself, but she needed to hear them from her mother, needed to hear Helen make it all real by admitting, explaining, amplifying. She had kept the crinkly-edged photo of the little girl, Susan. Her older sister. She had drowned in the pond when she was 4. Dale finally had told her. While she tried to grasp the secret, Dale insisted she keep it; she must never, ever speak about it; it would kill Helen, did she understand? She thought Dale was being melodramatic, because he had been there to witness it, see the pain when it was raw. Joyce thought she knew her mother better than that. This was the woman who had said, when Joyce's grandmother died: "It's for the best." What she meant was, it was better for Helen. She wondered if losing the girl, Susan, had been better for all of them, too.

So it was pointless to try to figure out how it had started. Her mother wouldn't talk to her about anything meaningful, and finally Joyce gave up. As much as she loved the farm, she moved away as soon as she could scrape enough money together, renting a tiny beach cottage the winter after she graduated. Weeks, then months went by and she would only occasionally stop in at home, using as an excuse her busy schedule. When she did visit, Helen spent the whole time talking about Dale. Had Joyce heard from her brother? Did she ever see him out at any of the drinking spots, the Sea Shanty, the Harbor Lights? (That Joyce might be there seemed to concern Helen not at all.) Did she ever hear any gossip at the Point about him? Did she think he would take care of the boat?

Her mother seemed completely disinterested in what Joyce was doing. The fact was she had gotten a job that should have fascinated Helen. At URI she had majored in history almost by default; she was only mildly interested in most of the courses she had to take, like European Conflicts and the Age of Exploration, but the major seemed to be the only way to get at what she really wanted to study – which was the history all about her, from the arrowheads the plow turned up every spring to the dilapidated mill villages she drove through on her way to campus. When the department chairman had sent her up to Providence to intern with the Historical Preservation Commission, a light turned on. People actually wrote about and studied these things and got paid for it. The internship had not been much; mostly she had been a glorified secretary to its president, an eccentric but brilliant society lady named Alexandra Duffy who was credited with saving most of the houses on Providence's East Side from the wrecking ball. Tall, with silvery hair piled atop her head and given to wearing suits with big pieces of jewelry like broaches and cameos, Miss Duffy – as everyone called her although she was nearly 80 – had taken a shine to Joyce. It certainly wasn't her typing, which was only adequate, that caused Miss Duffy to notice her out of all the interns who paraded in and out of the office each semester. Maybe it was the way Joyce listened when she spoke and sometimes even wrote down what she said. Maybe it was Joyce's habit of straightening out the files when she had a free moment, spreading old photographs reverently on her desk and easing them into plastic sleeves. Whatever the reason, Miss Duffy saw something in Joyce Winter, and when the commission received a federal grant to inventory all the old houses in the southern part of the state, she hired Joyce for the project.

Miss Duffy did not sugar-coat the job. This was field work of the worst sort – hours on the road photographing old houses and then long days in libraries and town halls comparing what you found to the historic record. Every detail had to be accurate and verifiable. The goal was to provide a certified list of historic resources, which, in turn, could be used to apply for further grant money. On Joyce's work might depend the future restoration of entire villages. Did she understand the importance of it? To Joyce that seemed like a rhetorical question, although it scared her a little when Miss Duffy lifted one of her penciled eyebrows. Of course she understood, but she was trying not to sound too eager. That she was getting paid to do this, although it was only $180 a week, seemed like some kind of miracle.

But when Joyce told her mother about the job, expecting that she would at least express relief that her daughter was able to support herself, she did not get the reaction she expected.

"Is that really what you want to do all day? Drive around taking pictures of old houses?"

Helen was digging in the flower bed next to the house. Joyce wished her mother would wipe the dirt off her hands, put the trowel away and invite her in for a soda, but Helen seemed intent on finishing her weeding. She was craning her neck around to look at Joyce, who stood next to her, arms folded.

"Mother, this is a very important job. The future of entire villages could depend on it."

Helen turned away and began tugging at a piece of crabgrass. "What are you going to do when the grant runs out? You'll have to find another job."

"It will help me get another job. Alexandra Duffy is one of the most influential preservationists in New England. I'm sure if I do well she'll recommend me for something else."

"If this is so important, why doesn't she do it?"

"Mother! She has other things to do! She runs the organization. She testifies before the legislature. Besides, she's an old woman. She can't go tramping around South County looking for houses." Joyce felt sweat trickling on her neck. The sun was climbing; it must have been 80 degrees already, but her mother seemed oblivious.

"Well, fine, if that's what you want. Hand me that little shovel, will you?"

It was no use; her mother had no concept of what Joyce was doing and didn't want to understand. Joyce had been so full of news about her job that she had ignored the little bell that went off in her head as soon as she turned down the farm's driveway. Each time she reached out to her mother she thought maybe Helen would surprise her this time, and each time her expectations were dashed. In Psychology 101 she had learned about the rats who kept pressing the wrong bar for food, even when they were starving. They called it learned helplessness.

"Mother, I'm going to take a walk on the beach." She didn't stop to hear her reply. It was hot down here by the house, but maybe a breeze would be stirring on the water; in any case, a walk would calm her down, what little walk was left. As she passed through the orchard she looked out at the Kennedys' house. Their Jeep Cherokee was in the driveway; they were here all the time now that school was out. She imagined them sitting on that long columned porch, having lunch, watching the kids playing in the sand. They had two: a boy, 7, whose screams sometimes traveled across the field, and a girl, 10, who was tall and dark like her mother and liked to do cartwheels in the sand, her legs two enormous sticks rotating in the air. Joyce did not know them as well as her mother did. She would wave and say hello as she passed by on the beach, and once she had encountered the husband on his way back from a sunset walk, and he had stood too close to her as they talked, cutting off her air. She did not trust him. Joyce had this sudden, unbidden revelation: *He cheats on her* – although she knew nothing to substantiate it. Fran Kennedy did not like her; when she did speak to Joyce there was always an undertone of sarcasm. Maybe that was why Joyce suspected Peter Kennedy had a wandering eye. Women whose husbands cheated have to distrust every woman they meet, because they never know who is going to be the next quarry.

The pond glimmered in the heat, and as she walked closer she heard, then saw, a pontoon boat making its way from the Salt Marsh Acres launch. She stopped, wondering. The pond was closed to motorized vessels; this fact was posted on all sides of the pond and prominently at the launch, where the Salt Marsh

Acres people occasionally set a canoe or kayak into the water. (Mostly they kept power boats on trailers for the bigger pond to the west; they weren't the type to enjoy quiet recreation.) They certainly didn't look like Salt Marsh Acres people. State coastal officials, maybe; they used to slip into the pond every spring, to addle the swans' eggs, until her mother raised a fuss. Now what the hell were they up to?

Maybe she told her mother just to stir up trouble, to see her aggravated; whatever the reason, the story had the desired effect. Helen was livid. It was bad enough they had to endure those low-class Salt Marsh Acres neighbors of theirs, who left beer cans on the shoreline and fishing line for the ducks to get tangled up in. Couldn't those state people read? The state officials had posted the ban on motorized vessels themselves! Was their no end, she wanted to know, to what the government would do if left to its own devices?

Joyce thought no more about it, but a few days later her mother called with a name. Michael Avery. URI Graduate School of Oceanography. "Loretta says he's doing some work on the pond. I want you to find out what's going on."

Embarrassed, but with no one but herself to blame, Joyce now had to call up this Michael Avery and ask him what he was doing on the pond. She figured they would have a curt conversation and that would be all, but he invited her to join him and his crew on the boat. So she could see what it was all about.

Avery was not what she expected – short, dark and bear-like, with thick hair, a moustache and a square frame. His assistant, Clark, was taller, with dirty blond hair and a curly beard, and his skin was already florid with sunburn. They had two other crew members, but Avery and Clark seemed to be the ones most engaged in the research. Avery explained it thus: they first trolled the pond with a sonar device, to find the optimal place for gathering samples. They then would insert a syringe-like device into the mud and suck up five to eight feet worth of pond detritus – "Layers of history, you might say." They were studying the displacement of sand in past hurricanes.

"Otherwise known as Clark's only hope for a Ph.D.," Avery said after giving a tour of the boat. The two of them erupted into laughter. Clark, unabashedly staring at her T-shirt, hadn't said a word since she came aboard.

"We'll take these samples back to the lab, and, eventually we may be able to determine just how much these storms have altered the beach – and how much damage they could do in the future," Avery said.

Clark was smiling idiotically. She wondered if he was stoned or just shy around women.

"My father could tell you how many times the pond had breached, at least back to the 1600s, because our ancestors kept records," she offered.

"Where is your father? We'd like to talk to him."

"He's dead." She hadn't meant to say it so abruptly, but maybe she had.

"I'm sorry to hear that." He stole a look at Clark, who was busying himself with what they called the moon pool, glass doors that opened to give a view of the pond bottom. "Your mother shouldn't be so upset about us," he added. "What we're doing won't harm the environment."

"My mother doesn't like people on the pond." She had not thought of this before, not made the connection, but as she spoke it was coming to her. "My sister drowned here when she was four. I think this is a sort of sacred place for her. She doesn't want it disturbed."

Michael Avery was finally speechless. He seemed to be waiting for the next revelation, but she quickly changed the subject, steering the conversation back to his research.

"What are you looking for, exactly?" She imagined layers of fossils, like the cutouts in a science book labeled with dates and eras: Pleistocene, Mesozoic, Cenozoic. She wondered if they would come up with human bones, arrowheads, tomahawk shards, like the pieces that clinked against her father's plow in the spring.

But their views were microscopic: They were looking at dirt, and within that dirt pollen and fossils would provide the clues to date the soil. In the most recent layers, it was a substance of man that would date their samples – cesium 137 marked the years 1950 to 1964, when hydrogen bombs were still being tested. The presence of ragweed was indicative of the coming of the Europeans and their cultivation of wheat. Radiocarbon dating was used for the oldest samples.

Michael Avery's eyes glinted like mica as he described his

research. He might be Clark's major professor, supervising his doctoral research, but it was clear how much this project meant to him, too.

"We suspect the major hurricanes, like the '38 storm, deposited sand way up here." He pointed toward the head of the pond. "These samples will go back five hundred, maybe seven hundred years, and give us a good timeline on some of the storms that aren't in the historical record."

She liked the idea of it – digging down into the earth beneath the pond, finding the past still there, waiting to be discovered – but she wondered what good it would do.

"If you find something, what then? Can you protect the area? Keep people from building houses like that?" She jerked her thumb toward the Kennedys'. She imagined a wave crashing over the mansion, breaking it up, floating pieces out to sea.

He laughed. "You Swamp Yankees. You're all alike. You'd like to build a moat around South County." She could tell by his tone he was flirting with her, but he turned serious as he eyed the flag that flapped from the Kennedy front porch. "You don't need us to stop something like that. Mother Nature will take care of it in due time."

That was how it began. She ate lunch with them, sitting Indian-style on the hard-packed sand on the Salt Marsh Acres shore, and before she knew it she and Avery were making plans to take his skiff onto Point Judith Pond the next day. It turned out to be a June day in July: warm but not hot, a cooling breeze rippling up the pond from the ocean, the sky the smoky blue of blueberries. They rowed, they drifted, then turned on the tiny outboard; and the rhythm of water against wood felt ancient, comforting, tantalizing. They pulled the boat onto a wooded island, and it was only later that she noticed the welts on her legs where the mosquitoes had feasted on her skin.

Joyce thought she could happily spend the rest of her days listening to Michael Avery talk, he knew so much and had seen so many places – the Mediterranean, the Arctic, Africa – yet it was not the stories that drew her to him, it was the spaces between the stories, the pauses, the listening. She told him about it all – her father's suicide, her difficult mother, the sister she never knew, her crazy, drunken brother. He listened with his eyes and his soul, and his arms kept her secrets safe, so she could let them out one at a time, a valve releasing steam.

He had secrets of his own to tell. He was divorced, for one thing. They had been young, he was in grad school; he was away on a ship taking core samples and she was sampling the man next door. An old story, and believable, except when Joyce held Michael's hand sometimes she could feel a bump, like a callus, where his ring had been, though the finger was as tan as the rest of him. No children, thank God; isn't that what people always said? "Well, when they're young, and there's no children . . ." As though it didn't count, somehow. There had been girlfriends since, including three years with a secretary in his department, but he didn't want to marry her and she wanted to get married. Another old story.

There was his age, for another thing. He was 34, hardly ancient, but older than she, and his every frame of reference seemed different. "When I was in grad school" started many a conversation, which didn't bother Joyce until one day she figured out that she was 12 at the time – 1971, years ago, but he talked as though it were yesterday. And the third thing – she actually enumerated these doubts on her fingers at night when they were apart, trying to slow down her dreams, which were in hyper-speed – was that he was going away. A two-month trip to the North Atlantic, an impossible time when you're 22 years old and in love.

CHAPTER NINE

When I first moved to South County, in 1949, we had an old swamp maple in the yard that was over a hundred years old. It stood straight and tall and every year blossomed with leaves. It was the picture of health. Meanwhile, all around it we were losing trees, mostly to Dutch elm disease. We thanked God for that maple, which seemed impervious to insects, weather and blight. And then one day a rogue wind came off the water, an early summer gale, and ripped it right out of the ground. We ran outside in amazement. It had been extracted, roots and all. Jim got out the chain saw, and that was when we uncovered its secret: the whole core was stained the color of whiskey. The tree that had stood so sturdily for so long, taller than any of its brothers, was rotting from the inside out.
– A Country Woman's Diary, July 14, 1983

On the morning of her first day working for Ludlow, Helen threw up her breakfast. After that there was nothing to do but get up from the cold tile floor, splash her face, reapply her makeup and leave the house. When she'd had morning sickness, mostly with Susan, she had at least felt a purpose to it; now she felt empty, as though the only thing growing inside her were her own cells, multiplying crazily and without purpose. In the mirror, she almost did look pregnant. She wore a paisley dress with a cinch belt, which she had picked up at the thrift store, and maroon high heels that pinched. Even in pantyhose her legs were pasty, swollen, like dough running over a bowl, and the dress, despite the shoulder pads that had suddenly come back into vogue, did nothing to hide her plumpness.

It would have to do – she had nothing else to wear.

Ludlow's office was in a converted house at the head of the Beach Road. The sign above the porch read "Winter Coastal Homes," which Helen had always thought an odd name, as though the only houses he sold were for people who liked to winter on the coast. Of course, the exact opposite was true. The majority of Ludlow's clients were buying beach property for summer homes, which they then rented in the winter, cheap, to college students and poor families who couldn't afford year-round housing. The sign was of engraved wood, and instead of some coastal icon, like a lighthouse or an anchor, it featured a carving of Ludlow's head.

The driveway's quahog shells crackled as Helen pulled in and parked. She sat for a moment, the motor cut, trying to slow her breathing. She was difficult to understand when she was nervous, and being out of breath only made things worse. She rehearsed what she would say: "I'm the new employee. Is Ludlow available?" Her mouth, still mucky from sickness, moved in slow motion as she pantomimed the words.

The first floor had been gutted, lined with indoor-outdoor carpet and filled with two rows of desks against each inside wall. The walls were covered with paneling, but one side of the big room was lined with windows, and French doors led to what Helen assumed was Ludlow's office. Most of the desks were empty. The receptionist, who faced the side door, was a petite brunette who couldn't be much older than Joyce. Her hair was teased into an extravagant bouffant, and her long nails gleamed pinkly, like the inside of a shell. Helen croaked out her introduction and the girl said nothing, merely looked at her indifferently and picked up the intercom to buzz Ludlow. Then she pointed to the French doors.

The morning paper was spread on Ludlow's desk, and on it a doughnut and a large takeout cup of coffee. "Now this is what I'm talking about," he said as Helen sank into a wooden chair. He was jabbing a powder-covered finger at the pages, his eyes blazing. "Look at this. They're going through with it. Nobody will be able to build a house in this town."

Helen tried to read the paper, but he had it lifted toward him, obscuring the headline. "Large-lot zoning. What an asinine idea. So only the rich people will be able to afford houses.

The market's going to dry up like a whore going through the change." He ranted for a few more minutes, then stopped suddenly, tipping a box of doughnuts toward her. "Breakfast?"

"No thanks." Helen's stomach contracted.

He looked as though he were noticing her for the first time. "Helen! I knew I'd get you to work for me one of these days! But if you'd followed my advice, you probably wouldn't have had to. Should never have accepted that first offer from the Kennedys. Look what property's done since. What you'd get for that land? Fifty? Seventy-five? It's worth well over hundred, maybe even a hundred-fifty today. Waterfront, Helen. You should have held out. They would have paid more. I could tell by looking at them."

Held out? But when he had tried to buy the land, he told her the market was going to collapse any day. "It doesn't matter now, does it?" If she were going to walk out, she should do it now. But she stayed in the hard chair that had no arms; she kept her hands in her lap.

"Shouldn't have given all that money to Dale. I know he's your son and all, but he's never going to pay it back and you know it. Well! Let's get you started!" He clapped his hands, a faint dust of powder rising, then snowing onto the newspaper.

Helen's first task was to type up that week's listings for the newspapers. The agents, who slowly drifted in after a busy weekend of open houses and showings, filled out forms on the properties, and it was her job to translate them into English, keeping them to a minimum number of words. She soon learned that "BR" meant bedroom, "LR" living room, and so forth, and that none of the real estate agents knew much about the houses they were representing. Anything built after 1950 was classified as a ranch, unless it was two-story, in which case it was considered a colonial, even though neither description was accurate. Loretta was right; the agents couldn't spell, either. Helen tried to translate the listings into at least serviceable English. One of her early efforts read:

"Gambrel-roofed colonial in desirable neighborhood features four bedrooms, family room, fireplace, and full, finished basement. This property has a perennial flower garden, a swimming pool and paved driveway. $52,000."

Ludlow did not appreciate her complete sentences. "Helen!

You're trying to sell this house, not put people to sleep!" He took an envelope off his desk and scrawled:

"Bring the kids! Four-bed sparkler in Eden Estates! Pool, just in time for summer! Won't last at $52,000!"

"That doesn't make any sense," Helen said, deciphering his scrawl. "Of course they'll bring the kids, if they have them; but what if they don't, and they want a large house?"

"Trust me, Helen," he said. "Exclamation marks. Pizzazz. We're selling houses, not writing term papers."

She spent the rest of the morning throwing in indiscriminate punctuation, which seemed to please Ludlow, and after lunch she began more tedious work, typing up sales agreements and correspondence. The typewriter was a Selectric, with a correction ribbon, which diminished her pride; she had never even used correction fluid with her manual. She could hear Holly, the receptionist, type a line or two, swear under her breath and hit the back space button; then the phone would ring and she would be a new, suddenly perky self, but Helen knew she couldn't do what Holly was doing, not even for a minute.

The office had a rhythm from which Helen felt excluded. The agents wandered in and out, talked on the phone, gathered at the coffeemaker, laughed, told little stories about their customers. Occasionally they would bring in a prospect, as customers were called out of earshot, and the office hum would be muffled for a time, while an earnest young couple looked through listing books or sat close to an agent's desk, putting dollar figures on their future. Ludlow never emerged from his office for these visits, but when men in suits and polished wing tips showed up, Holly would usher them right in. Then Ludlow's booming laugh and the visitors' deep, rich voices would float through the office like clouds of cigar smoke. Helen would try to pick out their words, while she typed up forms – "YOUR SIGNATURE ACKNOWLEDGES THAT YOU HAVE BEEN INFORMED OF ALL LAWS AND REGULATIONS UNDER THE U.S. HOUSING AND URBAN DEVELOPMENT ACT" – but the pieces that came to her wafted away too soon to mean anything.

Although she worked only three days – Mondays, Tuesdays, Wednesdays – Helen strained under the artificial schedule that work forced upon her. In the world of the real estate office, time was marked by deals and phone calls and showings; morning was time for coffee, doughnuts, a quick look at the newspaper, buyers were wooed over lunch, and showings sometimes stretched into the evenings. She watched this go on from her small metal desk with its typewriter apron, occasionally looking up at her view – a bulletin board on a paneled wall, a calendar "From Your Friends at Cole Construction" pinned to it – and wondered what she was missing at home, what flashes of cardinal or goldfinch were flitting at the birdfeeder, what shades the sky and ocean were trading, if anything was greening in the garden.

Inside the office, the natural world rarely intruded. Light came from fluorescent tubes overhead that winked on and off without warning. The air was stirred by the clanking air-conditioner in the window, which occasionally paused like an old man trying to get up steps, exhaling, coughing, then moving again. At the height of the day, when the sun finally made it to the western side of the building and light began to pour in, Holly would close the shades. If an agent tarried too long at the door, she would bark at them to hurry up and close it, they were letting the cool air out. Before the day was over Holly carefully dusted the plastic leaves of the ficus tree in the corner.

"You should get some windowboxes," Helen suggested to her one day. It was Wednesday morning, when Ludlow and the agents toured all the new listings in the area, and they were alone. "Would brighten up the porch."

"Ludlow would never go along with it. He hates flowers. Says they die every fall anyway and they're a waste of money."

Helen did not have an economic argument to defend geraniums. She went back to her sales agreement.

For a while she was afraid that she, too, was being poisoned by the freon-cooled air, that soon she would lose touch with everything that was important to her. She was having trouble focusing on her column, it was true. Fewer days to observe and blunted senses were giving her a sort of naturalist's writing block. All those hours typing people's names, plat and lot numbers, metes and bounds had turned her fingers into a typist's, not a writer's, and when she sat down on Sunday evenings to write "A Country Woman's Diary" she found herself wishing the paper had blank lines, empty spaces where you could plug in the right words and be done with it.

One afternoon in August the air changed. It had been heavy and hot for most of the week, muggy in the way that only the Rhode Island shore can get, and for once Helen was glad for the air-conditioner, which was wheezing more than usual but still spitting cold air. She felt it first in her fingertips, a zip of electricity that gave her a shock when she opened the metal filing cabinet next to her desk. Ludlow was out and Holly was unabashedly reading a book, a paperback the cover of which featured a buxom, long-haired woman on horseback. Only one agent, Sylvia, was in the office; she had been on the phone for a half-hour with a client whose house she couldn't sell, and she kept rolling her eyes at Helen, as though Helen could hear both sides of the conversation. Helen tried to get Holly's attention, snapping her fingers, but Holly was lost in the love-making of her cleft-chinned hero.

Helen walked to the window and raised the shade, where past the parking lot she saw the gathering darkness – billows of clouds, black and murky as the pond's bottom, rolling up from the beach. She walked out the door, across the crushed shells of the driveway, where she looked across the street to the potato fields – there Mr. Lillibridge was riding his harvester, trying to beat the storm, and the sky was still faintly blue above him. From the galloping horde she could see waterspouts, three of them, dipping down and up again, mini-tornadoes that could be harmless as a horse's tail or as dangerous as a whip, it was impossible to tell. She wanted to shout to Mr. Lillibridge, yell at him to look behind, but he would never hear her above the roar of the combine, and he probably already knew; he would get into the barn just as the hail fell.

She dashed back into the office, out of breath, yelling about the storm; and just as she did the lights cut and the air-conditioner whined to a stop. Sylvia and Holly looked at her, their mouths opening just as the thunder exploded. They had not noticed her leave. It amazed them, how she knew these things, but they didn't see much value in it. The power was out but it would come back on eventually.

She took lunch every day outdoors on a bench next to the porch – a tuna sandwich in waxed paper, an apple, iced tea in a thermos – and then she walked down the Post Road, though it had no sidewalks and she kicked up dust in the weeds as she went. Sometimes she saw things. A flash of yellow in an olive bush; a goldfinch. Crumpled lottery tickets. The carcass of a squirrel or a woodchuck that had been hit and then tossed to the roadside. Clumps of flowers stubbornly growing beside asphalt, Queen Anne's lace or goldenrod or tiger lilies. She walked slowly, looking for signs of the natural world. Even the ants who made their golden hills gave a pinch of hope.

As she walked, she thought about the family, as though she had been called before each one, asked to account for the other. Joyce was always there in her head accusing her of something. She had made it no secret that she disapproved of the boat. Even Loretta – and Loretta had so much common sense, and a son to boot – Loretta questioned it. Each to his own needs. Isn't that what her parents had taught her? Her brother, George, wasn't as smart as she was; he never would have made it through Cornell; so they gave him the farm, just gave it to him. And she had been plenty miffed at the time. But now she understood. She had had a husband. That was the way they thought back then. Joyce, of course, wasn't close to getting married, she hoped, but she didn't need her mother's help on any account. Joyce could take care of herself. She had been always been self-contained, that one. Barely shed a tear when her father died. Not cold, no, she wouldn't go so far as to say that, although the word had crossed her mind a time or two. But Joyce was self-sufficient. She didn't need a handout; but Dale did. If she hadn't bought him that boat, sooner or later he would have ended up dead. She believed that.

Jim. She imagined him in heaven, looking down at her, a speck moving slowly down the road. In the beginning, soon after his death, she had seen him pale, lost, casting about in the clouds for some footing. But now she thought of him like an angry god, bitter, judgmental, ready to fling lightning bolts at her. She talked to him, muttered, the way crazy people talk to God. "I couldn't help it," she would find herself saying aloud. "I had to sell. It was your fault. You left a mess behind." On her walks these thoughts came out as disjointed mumblings, answers to questions no one was asking. "Would you have? Imagine. Rock and a hard place."

On the south side of the road stretched the Lillibridge Farm.

First came a field of potatoes that wended away toward the horizon and the beach. Then the potato barns, one-story structures, built into hills and with double doors that you could drive right through. Finally, behind a curtain of overgrown forsythia and maple trees, was the Lillibridge house, a bungalow they had thrown up after the hurricane destroyed the original farmhouse. It had a porch where, some days, Helen would see Mr. Lillibridge sitting in a rocker, his feet against the railing, his knife making its way through a fresh cantaloupe.

Her legs unwound and her mind, after her daily tiff with Jim, relaxed on these walks, until she passed Mr. Lillibridge's house. She never knew what to do or what to say. Sometimes she gave him a stiff wave, and he nodded in return, his knife saluting against the bill of his John Deere cap. Other times she said something inane, something she had actually rehearsed, such as, "Nice day, isn't it, Mr. Lillibridge?" or, "You're smart to stay out of the sun today," and he would reply, but he mumbled so that she could only pretend to understand what he said. She felt bad that she didn't have more to say to him. Mr. Lillibridge was a decent man. His wife had died of cancer about 10 years ago. His only son lived in the West, Montana or somewhere, and his daughter, a nurse, hardly ever visited him. One day Helen had seen a map unfolded on Ludlow's desk. She recognized the rectangle of land as Mr. Lillibridge's. Ludlow had drawn a red border around it.

She wanted to stop and chat with Mr. Lillibridge. She wanted to explain to him why she had sold part of the farm; he might understand. She wanted to give him advice. But the dust choked in her throat when she tried to say anything more.

Days off – she had so few of them, it seemed – she lived to work in the gardens. They were getting ahead of her. She hoed beans, weeded the cutting garden, deadheaded the pansies and petunias and marigolds that flocked in little beds next to the foundation. Everything was getting ahead of her. The natural world, unobserved, not only held its secrets, it ran rampant; cutworms dined on peppers, tomato worms fed on Big Beauties, mealy bugs chewed lacy holes in the squash leaves. Nature kept Helen so busy she had no time to write, no time to drop the hoe or rake for the pen. The back of her neck was bandanna red because she was always kneeling, away from the sun, head to the earth, looking down.

And on those days when she had almost caught up, when only a general tidying was keeping her from a good book and a glass of iced tea, Fran Kennedy would slink up. She was the weed that appeared overnight, tall, stubborn, leaves glossy, roots inextricable. Helen could chop her head off and she would be back the next day, serpentine, erect, her chin pointed to the sun. This, she seemed to say, was her preferred environment, not the palatial house in the sand her husband had built. She longed for the shabby farmhouse like a lilac rooted next to a cellar hole. Only she could not admit this to herself. At least, that was Helen's guess.

Helen was not a talker, but after a while she learned how to entertain Fran. They would walk into the house. Helen would offer her a lemonade, and Fran would say thank you. Then Helen would catch her eye roving. Maybe it was the teacups in the corner cupboard, the ones with blue flowerets on the rims, or the yellowware bowls nested inside each other. She would bring them over, tell Fran where they came from, to whom they'd belonged, how old they were. Fran, her coltish legs tucked beneath her, would touch the object reverently. Sometimes she even wrote down what Helen said in a tiny spiral-bound notebook she kept in her back pocket. "I've been going to antique shops and flea markets," she would say. "I'm trying to learn what things are worth, how old they are." She had lips that made a wide smile. Her teeth were perfectly straight. She wore sleeveless shells in colors of the sea, aquamarine, turquoise, pale sand.

She hardly ever brought the children. If they were with her, Helen knew this was a quick stop, a don't-invite-me-in visit, usually an excuse to bring her something – banana bread, the children's school pictures (she guessed she was supposed to want them, so she said thank you), some clams they had dug in the flats of Point Judith Pond. This felt like a debt Fran was paying off for her friendship. Helen had no friends so, she supposed, her friendship probably was a rare thing, a valuable thing.

In Fran's mind, Helen figured, she was the strange farmer's widow who lived next door, a character to be described in letters home or phone conversations, her shyness turned into some characteristic Yankee reserve. If only she knew that Helen was no more a native than Fran Kennedy. They both, in fact, were New Yorkers.

At the Cooperstown farm, all was white and gray: aluminum siding, fieldstone walls, split-rail fencing, the sides of cows.

Up to the moment Helen walked in the kitchen, creaky from the five-hour drive, her nerves jagged from too much coffee, she knew why she had come. But as her mother stood silently wiping her hands on a dish towel and her father scurried off to the barn, the vision of her purpose left as quickly as it had come. Alice Richmond was old – thin and gray, like the raggedy head of a mop, and tired to the bone. At 75, she had an excuse, but Helen was not seeing the lines on her mother's face or the drag in her gait, but her eyes, which had not aged at all, still a sharp, censorious blue.

Her brother George, who lived about a half-mile down the road in a modern raised ranch, worked the farm now, and he stopped in for coffee in the morning and afternoon. She had not realized how frail her father was: Stooped over, he walked at an impressive pace, but the stretch from barn to house winded him. George was running the farm – ordering the feed and other supplies, arranging for veterinary visits, negotiating with the co-op – while her parents did enough so it seemed they were still in charge. Her father was up for the milking at 5, although machines did the work now. Her mother signed the checks, but George kept the books and did the taxes. Alice's frailty was more subtle: She still mopped the floors and cooked the meals, but Helen noticed that her mother no longer read the paper, and her sewing basket lay untouched. When Helen volunteered to do the shopping, she did not protest, which was alarming. Alice had never trusted anyone to do the marketing.

Helen tried to keep busy. When she realized that what she had imagined – coming home to a warm bed, a shoulder, hot meals and a family's love – was a fantasy, she knew she would have to do everything in her power to hide it. She longed to stay abed, but she forced herself to get up with her parents before first light. She longed to linger at the dinner table, chatting with her father or George, but she rushed up to help her mother with the dishes. She longed to talk to them all, but she kept her mouth shut. Once she tried to hug Alice, but the old woman shook her off, surprised, and said, "What's the matter with you? Are you coming down with something?"

The night before she left, her father took her out into the barn. The water that leaked down the thick stone walls and froze, the hard-packed earthen floor and the pungent smell of manure combined for a sharp childhood memory, and she stopped at the door, trying to place it. She had spent time enough here as a child – she had milked cows, mucked stalls, oiled harnesses, candled eggs, done whatever needed to be done, although she couldn't imagine doing it now. Her father was shuffling his feet, sending dust motes into the light cast by the kerosene lantern. The cows made lowing noises and seemed disturbed to find a stranger in their midst.

"Take this," he said, and pressed a wad of bills into Helen's hands. She should have known. That was her father's way of showing affection – giving her money. And Alice wouldn't have approved, so he had to go outside to do it. The bills felt fresh, like the pages of a paperback when you first open it. Three fifties and two hundreds. The money sat there, flat in her hand. She was too proud to put it in her pocket but not so proud that she would give it back.

He hawked and spat; he was chewing tobacco again, another habit that had to be hidden from Alice. "I wish we could do more."

George, the only son, was getting the farm, and she knew that what she was getting probably amounted to not much more than she held in her palm.

"Bring Dale up next time," he said, seeming to have forgotten she had a daughter, and he snuffed out the lantern and headed back to the house.

CHAPTER TEN

▲

Armed with her notebook, camera and state ID, Joyce had begun traveling the back roads of South County, looking for old houses that might interest Alexandra Duffy. The job had sounded ideal in the beginning, but it boiled down to driving around alone, often getting lost, sometimes finding nothing after hours of aimless searching. It kept her occupied, though. Everyone else, it seemed, was on some journey that she couldn't take. Michael was steaming toward the Black Sea on the university research ship, embarked on a three-month study of sediment and oxygen levels. Dale was on his way home from Birmingham in the new boat, bringing her up the Eastern Seaboard with a retired merchant marine he had met in Alabama. Even Loretta was traveling, on one of her group tours with the Plant Society to Australia. Meanwhile, Joyce was driving in tighter and tighter circles, looking for any piece of the past that would have some meaning.

When she had started the job, every day had been an adventure, with the goal having something to report to Michael at the end. But Michael was gone and she didn't even have a home of her own any more. She had lost her cottage for the summer. Michael was living with Clark and she certainly couldn't stay there while he was gone. Her closest friend from college, Althea Cappolino, was still living with her Italian grandmother in Westerly while she eked out a living as a first-year teacher. So Joyce had moved back to the farm, and there was nobody there she wanted to talk to.

In the beginning she hit the town halls every morning, although they weren't much help. If you didn't know the owner of the property you were searching for, it was virtually impossible to find its deed; but if she had known the owner she wouldn't need the deed, she could open up the phone book. Instead she flipped through deed book after deed book, looking for property that could be traced back to the 1700s or earlier. Records were spotty – in one town most had been destroyed by a fire in the early 1900s – and the older the deed, the more difficult it was to decipher. The ink was brown and faded, the old clerks' handwriting often slanted, and many times they had used the English conventions, using "f" to denote "s," and Latin expressions. The paper crumbled to the touch and smelled musty, like the Winters' attic.

She was driving through Richmond on a late afternoon in July when the road turned from asphalt to dirt and the trees came in thick on both sides, nearly making a bower. A farm had been here once, maybe as recently as 50 years ago. She had learned the signs. The forest was new growth and it was lined with tumbling-down stone walls. The grassy paths that veered off from the main road had the look of recent use, probably by hunters. No gunfire today, only the cackle of blue jays and the loud chit-chit of the squirrels. She drove on, the car kicking up a fine trail of dust; she wondered if the road led somewhere or narrowed to a dead-end, empty clearing, as another trail in Exeter had last week. She had been following all the right signs that day, too, but the house had burned years ago and never been rebuilt. That had been the fate of so many of these houses Alexandra Duffy sought.

The dirt trail humped over a culvert and began to wind downhill. Joyce felt her throat constrict with thirst. All that dust, but she could not bear to roll up the windows in this heat. If this road didn't pan out all she had to show for the week was a Colonial on Barber Road that already was listed in a book the town historical society had published 10 years before. The lines of the house were straight but it looked deserted. A clerk at Town Hall had told her the family that owned it, the Peckhams, also had houses in Newport and Florida. She took too many pictures and long, unnecessary notes.

Down another curve and the road narrowed. Up ahead, behind a wall of overgrown wild roses and bittersweet, she caught sight of the shingled side of a sagging Cape Cod. She stopped in a skid of gravel and cut the engine. The road went on, how far she couldn't tell; across from the house was an historic cemetery, its neatly mowed grass sharply contrasting with the veil of growth surrounding the farm.

As Joyce stepped out of the car, she was overwhelmed with the scent of concord grapes, which sagged from wild vines on both sides of the road. The mailbox was rusted and she couldn't read a name or a number, although a bent flag was raised to indicate the presence of outgoing mail. She walked toward the drive, her camera bouncing on her hip. From what she could see the house was a typical Cape Cod, with one primary story and a second story tucked under the eaves, and 12-over-12 windowpanes. An older example, to be sure, probably early to mid-1700s, but otherwise unremarkable – were it not for the thick, off-center chimney. She stood at the edge of the driveway, craning her neck up at it. If she wasn't mistaken this Cape had been fashioned out of a much older cabin. If that chimney was original, this house had been expanded from a 17th-century stone-ender, a design found almost exclusively in Rhode Island and a rare quarry.

She heard the sound of wood chopping. Joyce took some tentative steps into the driveway, past a red pickup and around the corner of a lilac bush. She saw a man with scraggly gray hair, in a flannel shirt and jeans, bent over chopping kindling and tossing it into a pile. She was about to speak when a tiny black mongrel stirred from beneath the bush and began barking up a racket.

"Good God!" The man turned around and became a woman, a stooped, gray-haired, chicken-necked woman with thick-set hands and the fire of God of her eyes. "No trespassing! Didn't you see the sign? No trespassing!"

Joyce had not seen any "no trespassing" signs, but she was not completely surprised by the woman's outburst. She had been chased off a few properties already. Old houses in the middle of the woods often were home to people who didn't want to be found, especially by the government.

Joyce held out her laminated badge. "Joyce Winter, Historical Preservation Commission. I'm merely doing an architectural survey – ”

"I said, No trespassing!" The woman clutched her ax. "I'll call the police."

"I work for the state Historical Preservation Commission," Joyce said, her voice clipped. "I'm interested in your house, that's all."

"It ain't for sale!" The woman's high-pitched voice had set the dog to barking anew.

"I don't want to buy it." If the house hadn't been a possible stone-ender she would have given up. Her hands felt awkwardly full, as she tried to balance her notebook, pen and camera. "We're compiling a record of old houses, that's all."

"Why? So you can tax the be-Jesus out of me, that's why. Why don't you go back to Providence where you come from?"

The back of her neck was sweaty; she had to go to the bathroom; and the day, by all rights, was nearly over. But something told Joyce to keep the conversation going.

"I'm not from Providence. I'm from South County. My father was James Winter, of Winter Farm in the Green Hill section. His father was James Winter Sr. He was in the Senate –"

"I'll be goddamned." The woman threw the ax and it landed with a thump in the chopping block. "I remember Senator Winter. Used to haul cedar out of the swamp for us. Married Martha Naylor, disagreeable woman, if I do say so. She lived over to Westerly way."

Joyce stood there, wondering whether to be insulted. Suddenly the woman grabbed her arm and steered her toward the house. "What in God's name are you doing, scaring the life out of a soul like that? I could've blown your head off. Now get in the house with me and tell me what all this is about."

Her name, Joyce soon learned, was Lydia Franklin, and she was the last line of Franklins to live in the house, which had been built in the late 1600s. As Joyce suspected, it had first been a cabin, "back when Indians roamed all through here," as Lydia put it, and the chimney was part of the original house. But Lydia didn't much want to talk about the provenance of her home or the James family. They had built the house, which through marriage to the Franklins and male primogeniture, had ended up in the hands of Lydia, who had never married and was glad of it, by the Lord Jesus.

She did let on that much, but Lydia was much more concerned about her tax bill, which, seeing the state badge, she was convinced Joyce somehow could remedy.

"Terrible. Almost a thousand dollars this past June, and I can't pay it. They think because I've got all this land, see, I'm a rich woman." She snorted. "They want the land, that's the angle. They figure they'll just keep upping my taxes until I can't pay, and then they'll have a tax sale and quicker than you can say Jack Robinson I'll be in a nursing home and my whole place'll be gone."

Joyce looked around the dark room where they had settled. At one end was a large cookstove, the word "Gibson" on its oven door and a vase of dried yarrow atop the cast-iron burners. In the corner they sat on a lumpy maroon sofa with crocheted antimacassars on the arms. Next to a window was a gate-leg table with a hurricane lamp atop it. Gazing around the room, she saw no outlets, lamps or other evidence of electricity, and that was when she realized there had been no light poles on the road. The room was reasonably clean, but the ceiling plaster was etched with cracks and wallpaper was falling off the wall, half peeled, like gauze unspooling from a wound.

Freed of her suspicion of Joyce, Lydia Franklin was a talker. Joyce guessed the woman to be about 75, but was proved wrong when Lydia pronounced her birthdate – June 30, 1895, in this very house, that front bedroom. She was in fact 87 years old. Aside from the white hair, a pure color the likes of which Joyce had seen only on the underbelly of a cat, and a few wrinkles on her thin face, Lydia did not betray her age. Her eyes were brown but sharp, and she wore no glasses. She had on a pair of men's jeans and, despite the heat, a flannel shirt the sleeves of which she had cut off and hemmed. Her figure had sunk in the way an old woman's will, the breasts and stomach becoming one shelf, but she was petite and agile for her age. In her rambling way she confided that she still rose every morning at 5 o'clock to milk her 10 head of cattle, feed the chickens and put the horses out to pasture. She had a pair of Morgans that she still rode almost every day – thus, the jeans – and a palomino she boarded.

Joyce asked to use the bathroom. Lydia took her out the back door and pointed to a shingled privy partly hidden by green lilac leaves. Inside she found walls covered with pages from a farm catalog, a roll of toilet paper hanging off a long nail and a broom in the corner. A musty, earthen smell came from the two holes. The crescent moon in the wall was filled with real glass, and through it came the sky, blue and cloudless.

She had hated giving up her beach cottage.

It was tiny – a kitchenette, a living room that was really an enclosed porch, a bedroom she could barely turn around in – but it had been hers alone. She had bought a set of cracked china at a yard sale and stocked up on Rubbermaid accessories. Otherwise it came furnished, with a green cotton-covered sofa, a lumpy double bed and a scratched bureau. After she and Michael started dating, they spent most nights at his house, a two-story affair on stilts that faced the pond. He could not stand her bed; it gave him a back ache, and he claimed the bathroom smelled musty. She scrubbed the sink until her wrists ached to no avail. Michael was particular about things. It always took him longer than her to get ready to go out. He had to shower, shave, trim his beard, re-iron his shirt (she never got it crisp enough), and they were often late, sometimes losing their dinner reservations. His idea of time was that it should serve him, not the other way around. When he was picking her up, she soon learned, seven o'clock meant 7:30 or later.

Clark was sanguine about his peculiarities. When Michael was spraying down the phone with Windex or polishing his glasses, Clark would catch Joyce's eye and wink, just once, quick enough so he didn't get caught. Clark was no slob either, but he seemed to float through life with an ease that eluded his roommate. All of his belongings were outdoors: a kayak, a canoe, a surfboard, a bicycle – and thus easier to keep track of. His bedroom, from what she had seen of it, was as spare as a hotel room. Joyce wondered if he had a storage locker, because she had not seen him bring so much as a paperback into the house. He dressed the same all the time, in long surfer shorts and a T-shirt from some event, such as a road race or triathlon. He seemed unburdened by material cares.

Michael Avery, on the other hand, was a slave to his possessions. Everything he owned seemed to need polishing, adjusting, lubricating. His telescopes (he owned two, trained toward the sky above the pond), camera equipment (which looked professional) and binoculars were kept carefully capped and encased when not in use. He detailed his own car, a VW Sirocco with leather seats. Joyce could not find a stray crumb or hair in his house. If he took out bread, he would refasten the loaf bag with a vigorous twist and put it in the bread drawer before beginning to make sandwiches.

"When you're on board, putting things back where they belong can mean the difference between a successful mission and a flubbed one, sometimes even life and death," he had told her once, after she had put his scissors in the cutlery drawer by mistake. "It's all about paying attention." That had been the start of their first argument.

After the stress of staying in Michael's house, coming back to her cottage was often a relief. She had places for her own things, too, but if she wanted to leave the newspaper on the kitchen table, she did, and there was no one to complain about it. In a way she was glad he hated to stay at her place. It gave her a refuge when his personality began to overwhelm her. Sometimes Michael was a high tide that she floated upon, and he carried her to islands she never would have seen otherwise. But he had an undertow that could be dangerous when ignored.

Living back at the farm, with all its dust, disorder and unfinished business, Joyce concentrated on making it through the summer. She bought a black composition notebook in which she wrote down snatches of dreams, letters to Michael Avery (which she didn't send) and, sometimes, titles for stories she knew she would never write. Somewhere between high school and college she had dropped the fantasy of becoming a writer. Wrapped up in Alexandra Duffy's ideas about history, she toyed with the idea of enrolling in graduate school or applying for a fellowship. The truth was she did not really know what she wanted to do, or who she wanted to be.

She had taken a second job on the weekends, to earn more money and get away from Helen. All day Saturdays and on Sunday afternoons, she worked in the tourist information center on Route 1, dispensing maps, directions and advice. The center was little more than a converted fair booth with a counter, a chair and a filing cabinet. At night a garage door was pulled down over the front and locked. A port-o-john in back of the dusty parking lot completed the set-up. From the counter Joyce could see the traffic stream by on the divided highway, and some days she watched with dread as the cars slowed to a stop. Often the gravel parking lot was nearly full before she had unfolded the garage door and opened for the day. The hours went by fast and the sign-in book on the counter filled quickly, as tourists came from all over the country and the world. One weekend she counted signatures from 15 states and five countries – Great Britain, New Zealand, Spain, Japan and Germany.

She could divide the tourists into types – the families with school-age children, who arrived in station wagons crammed with lawn chairs and luggage; the senior citizens, who maneuvered their lumbering RVs into awkward parking spots and then had trouble backing out of them; and the active young couples, with kayaks on top of their cars and bicycles on the back, who asked arcane questions about the area's hiking trails and camp sites and rolled their eyes if she didn't know the answers. Most of the tourists, however, were easy to please. "Do you have a rest room?" was the most popular question, followed by "How do we get to the beach?"

She knew soon there'd be a bite in the air, the tips of the maple trees on Post Road would begin to flame and the tourist season would wind down. Still, she hated the lines of people at the shack. She hated when they talked to each other instead of her. When they marveled aloud at how quaint the tourist shack was, or how rutted Route 1 had become (sometimes they were repeat visitors), or whined that the town didn't have a supermarket, or a McDonald's or a pharmacy or a department store. But most of all she hated it when, despite their complaints, they picked up the free real estate circulars on the counter and asked her about the school system. When they asked why property was still so cheap here compared to – and she could fill in the blanks – New York, New Jersey, Washington, D.C. If it was true that the town had no streetlights. What the tax rate was. Whether it was a town friendly to – fill in the blank – children, seniors, artists, surfers, motorcycle riders, alternative lifestyles (code for gays or pot smokers), Jews, Catholics, Democrats, Republicans, unions, the NRA, the ACLU, developers, conservationists or even, one newly retired gentleman had asked her, ultralights.

No matter what her answers, Joyce knew she could not dissuade any of them. They were like Fran Kennedy – bewitched by a place they didn't understand, but determined to lay some kind of claim to it and make it as much like home as they could.

CHAPTER ELEVEN

*No bird will work harder for its food than the sea
gull – diving into the water, picking out a clam, soar-
ing as high as 40 feet before dropping the shell to
rocks below. If the descent does not crack open the
shell, it will try again, and again, until another bird
swipes the clam or it is successful. But given the opportunity, the sea gull is a freeloader. It hangs around
the beach in late afternoon, waiting for an opportunity to pick at leftover hot dog rolls or potato chips.
It knows every restaurant back alley, every dump,
every picnic grove. So is the sea gull a lazy scaven-
ger, living off our trash? Or is he a noble bird with
a keen instinct for survival? I would say that, depending on his circumstances, he is a little of both.*
– A Country Woman's Diary, July 21, 1983

The port was a place where Helen wouldn't drive. It was far
too busy and confusing, with knots of people crossing the
road, beeping fish trucks, one-way streets, and bicyclists
zipping in and out of traffic. Everyone was frantically trying
to get somewhere – the out-of-state drivers late for the ferry,
the wholesalers rushing out to New York or Boston, the Coast
Guard ensigns racing to the boathouse. Negotiating all that, and
finding a parking space, and fitting into it, overwhelmed Helen.
That was why she had asked Loretta for a ride.

The traffic did not bother Loretta a bit. They were already
stuck on the Escape Road, a wide straightaway that had been
built after the Hurricane of 1938, which had taught the powers-
that-be the wisdom of having more than one way out of the Point.

Loretta lurched along in her new cherry red Cadillac, talking to Helen and slamming on the brakes at the last minute when the car in front of her inched to a stop. Riding with Loretta was only slightly less stressful than driving. Jim's sister was one of those highly intelligent people who had supreme powers of concentration – except when she got behind the wheel, which she considered such a mundane chore as to be worth only a fraction of her attention. Over the years she had collected more than her share of traffic tickets, and last time, if Ludlow hadn't called a favor with a state legislator, she would have lost her license.

She talked to Helen about their gardens – Did she have tomatoes yet? Really? How many? – the weather (muggy, though the Cadillac had air conditioning), her trip to Australia (cockatoos, parrots, and masked boobies), and everything out the window save the traffic ahead (clammers on the flats, look at that heron, and you can see the fishing fleet).

Helen crossed her legs. The Cadillac was too cold, and she had to pee. The traffic crawled along, the car bucking as Loretta reacted at the last minute. "This is a quite a day," Loretta said. "I hope I don't get seasick."

Helen already felt green. "Yes," she said vaguely. "I'm sure you'll do fine." They were going out on Dale's boat for the Blessing of the Fleet. It was a big event every year, one ordinarily she would have stayed far away from, but he had practically begged her to come. He had decorated the new fishing boat with a pirate's theme. All the boats in Point Judith, from the tiniest skiff to the island ferries, loaded up with passengers and festooned their decks for the big parade up the Harbor of Refuge, where the Bishop blessed their coming days at sea. There would probably be a lot of drinking. But Helen was superstitious, and she couldn't tell Dale not to participate, and she couldn't stay home, either. That would be like watching a boat sail off into the horizon. You just didn't do it and sleep at night.

Dale had reserved spaces for them in the state lot, and Loretta asked the attendant to back the car in for her. They were early, but already the port was a jumble of pedestrians, vendors hawking balloons, motorcycles, even a couple of TV camera crews. Loretta, walking like the Queen Mary steaming into New York harbor, led Helen to a tiny doughnut shop so she could use the bathroom, then bought two iced coffees. It was too early to get on the boat, they decided. They would walk down to the jetty and watch the preparations.

She and Jim had come here so many times when the kids – that is, Dale and Susan – were little. On Saturday nights they would buy greasy bags of clam cakes and cardboard cups of clear chowder, then sit on the rocks that lined the Harbor of Refuge. They had to keep an eye on Dale; he liked to scamper along the hunks of granite, and Helen was always afraid he would slip into the water, or jam his leg in a crack, or get bitten by the well-fed harbor rats that slipped in and out of the crevices. Susan was not like that. She sat on a curbstone next to Helen, chubby legs before her like a table, and nibbled at a clam cake. No, she did not have to worry about Susan.

What Dale wanted was the sea gulls. He threw nuggets of clam cake dough on the rocks, and when they landed he gave chase. No matter how many times Jim and Helen told him not to, the game became an endless cycle of advance and retreat. The herring gulls were unfazed. They would scarf up what they could, circle in the air awhile, then return for more. They knew soon the blond boy would disappear with his big people and they would have the clam cake leftovers to themselves, even if they had to rummage through a garbage can to find them.

"That gull's been eating somebody's hamburger," Dale complained one evening, when he had no more crumbs to hand out. "He's got ketchup on his lip."

Jim and Helen laughed, a sound that soared with the gulls. "Dale, he was born with that ketchup stain," Jim finally explained. Dale frowned and went skipping back from rock to rock. He did not like being laughed at.

The ferry had just left, sending Dale's boat rocking at its berth. It was almost their turn. Helen clutched a squat plastic cup, the kind with a wide mouth, that was filled with ginger ale and melted ice. After the iced coffee she was not thirsty, and she did not want to have to use the bathroom again anytime soon, but everyone held drinks of some kind, and holding the cup gave her something to do with her hands.

Loretta had abandoned her. Wherever they went, Loretta was always spotting someone she knew, and now she was on the starboard side, talking with a tanned couple that Helen recognized as having visited Ludlow's office recently. Cottagers, probably. Dale had given her a quick tour topside, but there were too many people and too many things to do for him to entertain his mother. Even Joyce, who you would think would have something to say to her mother, was spending most of her time at the bow, cuddled up with that new boyfriend of hers. Helen put one elbow on the rail and looked back toward the water, feigning interest in the line of boats forming ahead of them. She took a sip of warm ginger ale. She imagined her bladder filling again, drip by drip.

Then they were under way. She watched Dale in the pilot house, the concentration in his face, locks of hair tumbling onto his forehead, as he turned the wheel first this way, then that, backing the fishing boat away from the pier. The twin diesel engines made a muffled roar, and the smell of fuel hung rich in the air. There was no turning back now.

She had not been mistaken about Dale. This, after all, was what he needed. No one had any faith in Dale. They had told her she was throwing her money away; that he would lose the boat because of his drinking; that he needed to work his way up to captain, not have a boat handed to him. But she understood her only son. If you placed faith in him, he would work hard to live up to that faith. If you didn't, if you assumed he was going to fail, he would live up – or down – to your expectations. The money she had given him was an investment, in her son as well as the boat.

And it had worked. He was not drinking. The boat consumed his time – from preparations for each trip, the long days at sea, the time spent unloading, and then turning around and doing it again. He looked better. He had gained a little weight in his face, but his body was lean and his chest had lost that white flabbiness of the drunk. He did seem to have a cold, though. He was always sniffling. She would talk to him about that. He needed to take care of his health.

Joyce was different. She did not need, nor would she take, a handout from her mother. Joyce had a steely inner strength that could only have come from Martha Winter. She would have her own way no matter what. She had a fuse that burned long and silent, just like old Martha; she would nurse a grudge forever if that's what it took. Helen supposed her daughter was still angry about Jim's death. Blamed her. Now she was sulking about the boat, all the money Helen had given Dale. Well, let her sulk. Joyce wouldn't have taken the money. She was going to have the farm someday; that was what she really wanted. Each to their own nature. That was the one rule of parenting Helen followed faithfully. You could not treat your children the same, because they were different. Deep down, Dale was still the five-year-old boy trying to impress his mother. So you had to appeal to that in his nature. And Joyce was still a stubborn two-year-old who refused to do anything asked of her. She would do it her way. So they were different, and you gave them what they needed and let God take care of the rest.

Joyce, she supposed, was doing well, though it was difficult to determine behind her sullen mask. When she had asked to move home for the summer, Helen had imagined it would be nice to have company again. She thought now that Joyce was an adult they would be friends – not in the odd way Frances Kennedy was her friend, but like Loretta, who knew her and accepted her for what she was. But Joyce barely talked to her, and when she did it was in an accusatory tone, which she remembered all too well from Joyce's teenage years. She realized she knew little about her daughter's life. It was Loretta, in fact, who had told her all about Joyce's drives into the country, the old people she had met, the houses she was finding. Loretta talked about it as though it was some great accomplishment. Helen wondered what she was missing. And this man she had met – Helen rather liked him, but she didn't think it would last. After the infatuation wore off, he would become someone else to thwart that quiet intractability of hers. He was older than Joyce, for one thing, and he was always off on that URI ship for weeks at a time. He had just returned and Joyce was hanging on him, her arm around his shoulders while they talked to a member of Dale's crew. Her cheeks were flushed, her hair, trimmed short and curvy, was blowing into her face as they made their way slowly up the channel. How many moments Helen and Jim had had like that – but alone, not on parade for the whole world to see.

To this day she could not remember how they had managed it – an entire day without old Mother Winter, a day away from the farm at the height of summer, an unheard-of luxury. It had been late July, Helen remembered that much. The haying was done and the early corn had yet to come in. Even so there must have been plenty of other things that needed doing on a summer Saturday; vegetables to be picked, beans to be hoed, late fall crops to be sown. Probably one of the farmhands was doubling up on the chores. As for the other matter, Martha, they had decided to leave her alone, and although Helen could not remember whether it had been Jim's idea or hers, she did remember that Martha didn't like it one bit. Almost from the moment Helen had arrived at Winter Farm the old woman had been bedridden, and she wasted no opportunity in telling anyone who would listen that she was an invalid, although she was vague on the details. The embarrassing truth was that Martha had trouble controlling her bodily functions, which was why she stayed in her bedroom at the top of the stairs, which conveniently opened into a tiny bathroom. Sometimes she made it; sometimes she didn't, and Helen would find her sodden or soiled underwear under the bed, in the hamper, even stuffed under the bathmat. She was not convinced the woman even had a medical condition. Jim said it was "nerves," or some sort of "women's trouble," speaking in that code all Swamp Yankees used when they wanted to avoid the cold medical truth. But Helen doubted her mother-in-law had anything seriously wrong with her. What goes in goes out, and Martha, who had no teeth and refused to be fitted for a false set, drank copious amounts of prune juice and lemon water and ate only vegetables that had been boiled and mashed to a pulp. Anyone on that diet might find themselves rushing to the toilet, Helen thought.

But Martha stayed in bed, where she ate, read, wrote letters and mostly complained. She kept a tiny brass bell on her nightstand that she rang dozens of times a day. In the beginning Helen, trying to be a dutiful daughter-in-law, ran herself ragged up and down the stairs all day. But after Dale and then Susan, she quickly learned to distinguish between the tinny petulance of a "want" and the insistent gong of a "need." And on this July Saturday in 1955, she was determined that Martha wasn't going to ruin their outing, not this time.

She had prepared Martha's lunch ahead – a cold salad, iced tea, Jell-O – and packed it in a picnic hamper so Martha wouldn't have to leave her room. She had changed her sheets, tidied up the bedroom, brought her some new books from the library. Still Martha complained. "Suppose I fall? I'm prone to falls." You've never fallen, Helen reminded her, and there's no reason to think you will now. She moved the rug so she wouldn't trip. As Helen cheerfully ignored her fears, Martha upped the ante. "I can't even get to a phone to call the police. The house could burn down and I'd be a sitting duck." Helen stretched the cord and moved the phone extension to her nightstand. "I'm feeling poorly. I think I might take a stroke. It's this terrible heat. I'm going to have a stroke and you'll come home to find me dead."

That was when something snapped in Helen. The whiny, petulant voice, the sour smell of Martha's room, her yellowed toenails poking out of the bed sheet – she had to get away from it, all of it, now. She walked over to Martha and put her face close to hers. "If you should die while we're gone, I'd be the happiest woman in the world." She stepped back, smiled, then walked quickly out of the room, her sandals clicking on the hardwood floor.

Loretta raised the binoculars and pointed toward the Gap, where the fishing fleet entered and exited the Harbor of Refuge. "Cormorants," she said to the blonde cottager, who fingered a gold chain hanging around her neck. Helen followed Loretta's gaze. The black birds clustered on the rocks that formed the jetty, fanning their wings like bats. "Double-crested."

On the coast these birds were like robins, almost as common as sea gulls, but the blonde watched politely as they craned their long necks into the water, grabbed tufts of slimy eelgrass and gulped them down. They shook their wings as the diesel engines came closer but seemed unfazed by all the boat traffic. Centuries ago the only sounds had been the paddle of Indians' dugouts, but these birds lived with the sounds of the harbor every day, the ferries shuttling back and forth, the fishing charters, the tiny lobster skiffs heading to check their pots, the pleasure boats that sped up as soon as they passed the no-wake zone. After a while the noise became like the clouds and the sea, just another element.

They had gone to Watchaug Pond that day like a normal family. They had waded in with Susan and Dale, splashing, holding each one aloft, trying to teach them to swim. Dale was almost there, he could dog-paddle, but Susan was too young, the water at her ankles made her giggle but anything above her waist, near her chest and she froze, holding hands up to Jim, demanding that he hold her. They picnicked under the trees: deviled eggs, ham sandwiches, watermelon. They only left when Susan began to whine (she was tired, she had missed her nap) and the mosquitoes and wasps had become too thick around the picnic table.

She had said nothing to Jim about his mother, but as they drove home it was back again, her intemperate comment – her honest comment, almost a confession, she really did wish the old bag would die – like a lump of fried dough in her stomach. Martha would tell. That was what really troubled her, the idea that she would tell Jim; what would he say? He loved his mother. He knew nothing of the day-in, day-out reality of cleaning up after her, listening to her harpy comments, being tethered to the house. She would tell and she would either have to lie (Martha was growing senile, perhaps?) or admit that she, the woman he loved, secretly wished his mother dead.

She opened Martha's door with trepidation. Suppose the woman really was dead? Suppose God, in some perverted way of punishing her, had struck the old woman down? Suppose Helen had made it happen? It was more likely that Martha, left to her own vindictive devices, would find a down-to-earth way to punish her – making some vile mess on the bed that she would have to clean up, for example.

But when she walked in, there was Martha, alive and alert, sitting up in bed reading a book (Agatha Christie, one of the library books Helen had checked out for her), her face glowing pinkly. She had given herself a bath. She was wearing a quilted blue bed jacket with satin ribbons; a Mother's Day present she had claimed to dislike, for nobody had any taste anymore, these clothes today were so vulgar. She was smiling, Martha was, her eyes fairly twinkling; and the sight of her, so perky, so clean, so seemingly content, struck a different kind of fear in Helen's heart. She would not give Helen the satisfaction of dropping dead. She would not let go of this leverage by telling Jim. She would exact her revenge some other time.

The boat had left the harbor, swung around and into its place in line. They were about midway in the procession, between a couple of fishing charters, and the vessels idled noisily, their engines chugging. Helen turned and emptied her cup of ginger ale overboard. The wind washed it back over the side, where it made a white trail that soon disappeared in the foam washing against the hull. Guilty, she wondered if she had been seen; but she turned around to find that the party – her family, Dale's crew, total strangers – was entangled in tiny, busy groups that did not include her. She felt dismay, yet, at the same time, relief that she did not have to talk brightly or try to remember any-one's name. Loretta, her sister-in-law Clara, Jim's nephews and nieces, her son or daughter – someone, you would think, would turn suddenly, nudge her arm, draw her in to their conversa-tion. But the boat began to steam forward and, beyond the red, white and blue balloons of the *Glenda Anne* ahead of them, she could just make out the Bishop on the rocks. He was waving the sleeves of his black cassock like a cormorant drying his wings, bestowing his forgiveness on those who had sinned.

But no, that wasn't right. The Bishop was here to bless the boats, not forgive; he was casting prayers to the wind with the abandon of a child tossing out his last clam cake. *May you find safe harbors*. Something like that. *Smooth sailing. Protection from the storm-tossed waves of life*. Helen had no idea what a Roman Catholic priest would say to protect a boat when, truly, none of them was safe, they all were taking their chances on the tides, the tempests, the deep and rocky waters.

They were back inside the harbor now, waiting to pass. The boat gurgled as its engines strained; the party chatter dulled as the Bishop drew near. Helen realized she had waded in too deep. This idea became fixed in her mind with such sudden clarity that she wondered that all of the fishing boat's occupants did not turn to her and see her for what she was – a cold and stupid sinner, one who had hidden her true nature from no one so much as herself. Her husband had seen her for who she was; her daughter and son certainly did; and Susan, she had paid the ultimate price for her mother's venal nature. She wondered if the Bishop, too, would see. They were coming upon him. If he blessed the boat and she was on it, would that doom her son and his crew to the same fate as Susan's? Suddenly her thoughts, so disconnected and dark, gathered in one painful urge. She roused herself, stepped away from the rail, rushed across the deck – slick now from the spray they had encountered outside the Gap – and made for the head below. Her bladder was dangerously full; her head burned red with shame as she hurried. She found the first step but the second step slipped away, and all was black, the Bishop's dark wings engulfing her.

CHAPTER TWELVE

▲

Joyce was sitting in the hospital cafeteria, trying to choke down a blueberry muffin and bitter orange juice from a plastic bottle. The cafeteria's narrow, ceiling-to-floor windows overlooked the salt pond and a cluster of marinas across the highway, but Joyce sat with her back to the view. Without her contacts in she couldn't see anything anyway. It was daylight but she had no concept of what time it was. The cafeteria was nearly deserted.

Across the room, a nurse was staring at her. At least, Joyce thought she was a nurse; she wore an aquamarine smock, white pants and clogs. She was old enough to remember the days when nurses wore white uniforms and caps. Just this morning – was it today? Or yesterday? – she had asked a housekeeper about her mother's pain medication, and received a blank stare in response. The woman did not speak English. When the nurse arrived, she was wearing a pink uniform that looked like she should be working first shift at Howard Johnson's.

Joyce capped her orange juice bottle and absently shook the pulp settled on the bottom. The woman was still staring at her. Joyce looked away. She was too tired to go home but didn't have the energy to go back to her mother's room. Dale was leaving the port tonight. He already had stayed in an extra day, but time was money, he reminded her. Michael was presenting at a conference today in Boston but had promised to meet her at the hospital tonight. She supposed she could go home, but that would leave her mother alone. Even Aunt Loretta, who had been at the hospital for the first 24 hours, had given up and gone home. Everyone was exhausted.

The woman across the room got up, balled up her trash and threw it in a bin. She was tall and dark, with her hair pinned around her head in braids. Joyce looked away and took a last swig of orange juice pulp. The woman brushed past her. She wondered if she was one of the nurses who had attended to her mother in the first hours after the accident. There had been so many of them, all telling her something slightly different, that their faces had blurred together. All she clearly remembered was the sight of her mother on the bed, tubes snaking into her arms and nose and, swaddling her head, a gauze bandage flushed with blood.

"We think she may have had a slight stroke." This was the neurologist they had dragged in off the golf course and who looked none too happy to be there. Whenever he spoke to Joyce – for Dale, ashen at the sight of blood, had not made it past the waiting room – he took an accusatory tone, as if she were somehow responsible for Helen's injuries. "There is no doubt she has a severe concussion from the impact, but there's some evidence of damage preceding the fall."

"That's why she fell? She had a stroke?"

"I didn't say she had a stroke," he snapped. "I said she *may* have had one. We have no idea why she fell."

Later, when Helen had been moved from the Emergency Room to the Intensive Care Unit, they all took turns trying to convince Joyce to go home. Loretta, whose hair was windblown from the water and whose pink jacket had a ketchup stain on the lapel, offered to drive her. Joyce had ridden in the ambulance with her mother and now, she realized, her car was down at the port in one of the state lots, where it was stuck until tomorrow morning when the attendants would unlock the gate. Loretta squeezed her into a tense embrace. "There's nothing you can do here. You look about ready to collapse. I know I am."

Dale, hovering behind Loretta with his hands jammed into the front pockets of his jean shorts, looked at Joyce with his ashen face and sniffed. "Go," he said. "I'll stay. Go." There's something wrong with him, Joyce thought suddenly, but she was too exhausted to wonder what it was.

"She'll be in and out of consciousness for another day," said a nurse in a blue-checked smock, adjusting a dial on the IV pole. "You might as well go home and get some sleep. We'll call you if – anything happens."

But Joyce refused to leave. She had the feeling that, if she stepped out of the hospital, she would never see her mother again. So Loretta stayed with her, and Dale fell asleep on an orange vinyl couch in the waiting room.

The thing was, she had seen and heard it all. Her mother running, suddenly, toward the stairs. A ping noise as Helen's foot stumbled on the rung, then the terrible thud as she landed below decks. Through the balloons popping and vessel horns blasting and diesel engines growling, above the din of people laughing and toasting and yelling to shore, she had heard every second of her mother's accident, as if she were watching a stop-motion recording of it, as if every line and mast of the boat had hummed with its sound. Later they had told it was her screams, not her mother's collapse, that had brought them running. She had pointed, unable to get the words out, and Dale had been the first one to peer below, the first to see Helen crumbled in blood that puddled like fish guts in the hold.

Although he had a microphone, Joyce's screams drowned out all sound of the Bishop blessing Dale's boat.

On the second day Helen was still not speaking, although she seemed aware of their presence. The neurologist used the word "incident" instead of "stroke," as though Joyce could no longer be trusted with medical terms. He squeezed Helen's hands when he examined her. Joyce could not tell if her mother reacted. "Have you been here this whole time?" he asked Joyce, taking note of her jeans and T-shirt, which, she realized, had been slept in for two days. "You should go home and get some sleep," he continued, not waiting for her to answer. "You're not doing your mother any good just sitting there."

Joyce wondered if perhaps this doctor had guessed some things about her relationship with Helen. She wondered if perhaps his animosity was not misplaced.

On the second day her mother began to have visitors. The first was Fran Kennedy. She came in, nervous as a plover skittering across the beach, dressed in a black knit workout outfit – she was either headed for, or coming back from, the gym. Helen was sleeping, so Fran spoke to Joyce in a high, exaggerated whisper. She sat in the other vinyl seat and soon her left foot and calf had entwined themselves around the chair leg. She earlier had sent a bouquet – lilies, chrysanthemums, stock, babies' breath, tiny white roses; it must have cost her a fortune, and Joyce thought a much prettier, more honest arrangement could have been had of the wildflowers in the farm fields that Fran and her husband now owned. But Joyce smiled tightly and thanked her. Her mother would have expected her to.

"I've been worried sick since I heard. You must be devastated." Fran looked at her with those bright brown eyes that looked made up with mascara and shadow but weren't. All this emotional drama was her stock in trade. She felt everything so deeply, so sincerely, and she was practically imploring Joyce to share the depths of her despair. Joyce had a sudden impulse to laugh that she squelched with difficulty. The sight of Fran, leaning forward with such intensity, recalled to mind what Dale had said about her: "That woman needs a good swift dick."

"Your mother, your poor mother, she's been working too hard, you know." Fran shook her head. They were in agreement, the head shaking seemed to imply. "Working for Ludlow, that pig, beg your pardon; I know he's your cousin but he takes such advantage of her. Then all that gardening, and her writing – none of us can even imagine what all that takes out of her. She's such a sensitive person."

Joyce thought her mother had a pretty good life. Worked three days, off four; plenty of time to putter around the garden and write, and what was her mother's writing if not another form of puttering? She murmured something noncommittal. She wished her mother would wake up and take over. She was getting a headache herself listening to Fran prattle.

"What do the doctors think?" Fran lowered her voice. You can tell me, the tone said. Don't tell anyone else, but please tell me.

"Possible stroke; they aren't sure. Could just be the effects of the fractured skull." She did not add that her mother wasn't speaking and possibly had paralysis in the right arm; her good arm, her writing arm. "We should know more in a few days."

"Oh, Joyce, Joyce, that's terrible. Stroke." Fran leaned forward, put a hand on Joyce's knee. "If you need anything, anything at all, call me. Really. Your mother and I, we're pretty good friends, you know. I can't tell you what it means to me to have her living next door. She's been a life-saver. Truly. Truly."

Ordinarily Joyce would have done the polite, expected thing and said of course we'll call on you and then, of course, done nothing of the sort. But her annoyance with Fran gave her a perverse sense of justification. She wants to help, let her help. "Actually, there are some things you can do. Stop by the newspaper office on Main Street. Explain to them why my mother didn't have her column in this week. Tell them they can reprise her old ones as long as necessary. Then go to the unemployment office and see if you can get the paperwork so Mother can get paid while she's sick." Fran Kennedy had frantically rifled through her purse, pulled out a grocery list and begun taking notes on the back of it. "Finally, go to the post office and ask for her mail. Tell them I sent you. You can put it on the kitchen table. No, it's all right. The door's never locked."

Fran reached for both her hands. "Joyce, thank you for calling on me in your time of need. I won't disappoint you. It feels good to be able to do something." She stood up, gathering the bulky soft leather folds of her purse. "I'll get right on it."

Later that day a man came into the room. He looked familiar. Maybe it was just that, with his pressed green pants, blue checked shirt and John Deere hat, he reminded Joyce of her father on the rare occasions when he had dressed up. Except this man was older, and thinner, than Jim Winter. Beneath the cap his hair had started to gray. He had the lobbing gait of many farmers she knew – they walked almost hunched over, from years of bending, stooping, stretching. This man also had a slight limp.

He took off his hat and introduced himself. She saw that his right hand trembled when he held it out to shake hers. His name was Percy Lillibridge, but everybody called him Dub. Joyce knew him now. He owned a farm near Charlestown Beach, a potato farm. He had been leasing the last field they had left to grow hay. She wondered if he were here because something was wrong at home, but no, of course not, he wanted to see her mother. He talked to Joyce but he looked at Helen, who was dopey from the pain medication dripping into her arm. The oxygen tube was out and she breathed noisily through her mouth, something rattling inside there. Mr. Lillibridge watched Helen, transfixed. He seemed afraid to go near her. After a long time Joyce realized he wanted to talk to her mother, to sit next to her, but he would do neither while she was there. She excused herself and headed for the coffee shop.

At night Helen continued to sleep, and Joyce curled her legs under her in the wide vinyl chair, lapsing into fitful dreams. Sometimes, at the end of third shift or the beginning of first, a figure would enter the room, cover her in a waffle-weave blanket, and then walk away, not saying a word.

When Joyce couldn't sleep she tried to talk to her mother, whispering low so no one in the hallway would hear. *Mother. I'm not ready for you to go yet, Mother.*

That was true. Although she had stopped trying to reach her mother before the accident, although she did not talk to her about even mundane things, yet it was true she was not ready to give up on her entirely. She still held out hope that something in their disparate natures would be reconciled. Despite the difficulties they had had, which were compounded by her father's death, Joyce deep down loved her mother, and she wanted her mother's love in return.

Mother, hear me. Please get well. Mother.

Back from the cafeteria, the orange juice still sour on her tongue, Joyce stood at the door to her mother's room. Helen lay under the covers, her face as thin as a chewed pencil. Beneath her eyes were purple shadows; her head was still wrapped, but the bandage, at least, was white. Mr. Lillibridge was gone. A nurse stood next to her mother's bed, staring down at her, but she was not holding her wrist for a pulse, pumping the bulb of the blood pressure machine, adjusting her IV drip. She was simply looking down at Helen. A nurse in an aquamarine smock, with thick, dark hair framing a thin-boned face. She looked up at Joyce. Her eyes were rich brown, like the soil on the farm.

Joyce squinted and took another step forward. Yes. The nurse from the coffee shop. It was Camille.

CHAPTER THIRTEEN

I used to bring the children down to the beach to see what would wash up. The rocks would be covered in periwinkles, their shells in varying stages of wet – from dried-up to submerged – and the children could not understand how they survived between tides. The common European periwinkle (Littorina littorea) found on the Atlantic can survive up to 42 days out of water. The animal, a snail really, withdraws into its shell, tightly closing its horny operculum and thus keeping its gills saturated. They do not have the ability, or the desire, to migrate far, so in this way they wait for the shifting tides to come back to them.
– A Country Woman's Diary, Aug. 18, 1976; reprinted Aug. 4, 1983

Helen awoke in the oak four-poster bed in the south-facing bedroom. It was the biggest bedroom in the house, the one with the fireplace and marble mantel, the adjacent tiny bathroom, a highboy and chest of drawers, a rocking chair with a cane seat, long, lacy curtains that kissed the floor.

Martha's room.

At first, she thought it was another dream, like the ones she had had in the hospital. Martha was calling her, yelling while she rang that damned brass bell. Something was wrong with her lunch. Toast! She had wanted crisp toast, a little butter melting on it like a vernal pool, topped by a soft-boiled egg, perfect at the midpoint between uncooked and congealed. And what had she gotten! Helen, tramping up the stairs (her feet like lead boots), saying, yes, Mother Winter, what is it, yes, I'll get you new toast . . . something ominous in the woman's smile, like the animated babies she sometimes dreamt about too – their eyes, mouths alive with an adult intelligence, an almost evil sagacity. The old woman was still in bed, but Helen, somehow, was the invalid. And now here she was, in Martha's bedroom, a sheet up to her chin.

That smell: Someone had been up here, cleaning, but they had not been able to banish it. A mixture of Evening in Paris, stale urine, an old lady's sweat, feather bedding (But had they changed the mattress? This one felt hard, new, not at all like the saggy one on which Martha had slept), cold cream, rotting lace (the curtains had been in tatters; these floated free and white like a ghost's nightgown), cracked rubber (the hot water bottle, the feet of the commode that had eventually become necessary) . . .She could smell all of it, even though, she noticed as she blinked and focused, everything was new or polished, brushed, swept clean.

She wanted to scream. In this bed, on the other side; Martha had exacted her revenge. She remembered the priest now with his billowing black cassock, the rows of boats bedecked with green, orange, red and blue balloons. That was all she could remember, that and the fleeting sight of her family and loved ones, talking to her in a sort of gibberish she couldn't understand. Now they had put her in this room, in this bed. She tried to move but her body felt stiff, frozen, like in a dream where danger is coming but you can't move out of its way.

Gradually she became aware of what was wrong. Her head hurt, worse than a headache, a splitting pain centered just above her forehead. With her left hand she felt a gauze pad up there and stubble where her hair had been. They had shaved her head. And her right hand. Lightning bolts went up her arm when she tried to flex her fingers. She had crushed the delicate bones that run from the wrist to the fingertips. At first, Joyce told her, they thought she had had a stroke. Now they assumed it was nerve damage from the fall. Her hand was held fast by a splint; the wrist was wound in gauze. The doctor – an osteopath, not the neurosurgeon – had said her hand would heal, eventually. She might notice some stiffness, have some minor permanent damage.

Minor damage. Would she be able to write? Type? Why couldn't she have injured her ankle, her elbow, her knee – anything but her right hand and her head, the centers of her creativity, her expression, her livelihood. Her right arm was propped on a pillow outside the blanket, an object outside of herself. She stared at it, willing it to mend. Helen could not think of getting out of this bed and this room – this invalid's room – if her hand was crippled, her mind less than sharp. Yet she had to get out of here. The odor – of death, decay, bitterness – was choking her.

They bought her a window air conditioner, like the one at work, only smaller. It hummed – loudly – but it did not wheeze or rattle like Ludlow's model. She thought it kept the room too cool, and said so. Joyce pressed her lips together, exasperated. "It's about a hundred downstairs." Then Joyce decided they should move the furniture around, so Helen would have a view of the windows instead of the old dresser. Joyce had bought a bird feeder, which affixed outside the window glass with suction cups, and filled it with sunflower seeds. She insisted they should turn her bed around so Helen could see the birds without craning her neck. No, no, no, Helen said, but again Joyce just thought she was being difficult. She moved Helen into her old room – blessed old bed, dresser, wardrobe! View of nothing but those houses next door! Who knew it could be so precious? – while Michael Avery and his roommate moved her furniture around. She could hear the ball-and-claw feet of the bureau scraping on the hardwood floor. Somehow she had to get out of this bed and this terrible state of dependency.

For one thing, no one ever stayed. They came to visit – Fran, Loretta, Clara, even Ludlow – but no one wanted to hang around. They can smell it too, she thought. She wondered if the odor had seeped into her skin. She wondered if she, like Martha, were giving off a sour sickroom smell. She remembered herself, 25 years ago, and how quickly she ran out of this room, away from her mother-in-law. It was as though, if she had stayed too long, she wouldn't have been able to leave.

For another thing, she was left out. Life was happening beyond that door (which Joyce insisted on keeping shut, because of the air conditioner) and it was happening without her; without her knowledge, her consent, her blessing. She heard, detected glimpses of it. Joyce and Loretta were doing something to the house. But what! She heard vacuuming, furniture being moved (downstairs this time), the screen door slamming, windows raised and lowered, equipment roaring, like a skill saw. She smelled strong chemical odors; perhaps paint or cleaning fluids. The phone rang hour upon hour. She listened on the extension (Had Martha done this too? How had she not known?). Always Michael Avery. Meet me here for a drink, there for dinner. Joyce meekly going along. Not meekly, exactly, but agreeably – so unlike the Joyce she knew. Helen's heart constricted with envy. A warm summer night, a loose cotton dress (and she had had pretty ones, with sprigged rose prints, tiny buttons up the back), rides with the car windows down, and dinner on the deck of a restaurant. She wondered if she would ever enjoy a summer night again, or if she would be like Martha, doomed to spend the rest of her life eavesdropping on everyone else.

There was the matter of Mr. Lillibridge. He had come to the hospital – this much she remembered – and he had been to visit her twice since she came home. Joyce wasn't going to let him upstairs. He had insisted, in that slow but firm way he had of talking, and Joyce had come in the room to ask her, "You don't want to see that old farmer, do you? Lillibridge?" and Helen had said, of course, yes, but help me cover my hair (she was wearing a scarf, to hide the stubble) and give me my robe. He had come in the room, cap in hand, and sat in the rocking chair. The motion of it seemed to calm him. He told her about his farm. It was dry, the height of summer, and he was irrigating every day. And the corn he had planted on her property – her piece, he called it – was up above his waist, doing very well, but not quite ready for harvest. She fell easily into the rhythm of his speech, watching him rock, back and forth, like the tide. Finally he stopped and looked right at her.

"You're going to get out of that bed, now."

Right now? She was confused. What was he saying?

"Not right now. 'ventually. You're going to get out of that bed. Going to get better. Maybe not til fall, but soon. When you do, we'll go out. I'll buy you dinner."

She was speechless. She imagined watching him eat, the fork going in and out of his mouth like his jackknife slicing through melon, the same lazy rhythm of the rocking chair. She could see herself, sitting across from him, her right hand gripping a sweating glass of iced tea, holding it fast, not dropping it. Everything working again.

I'd like that, she told him, surprising herself.

Then came the day that Joyce and Loretta helped her downstairs.

She truly was better. The bandages were off her head. Her hair was coming back like a cygnet's downy fuzz, flat and brown, mousier than before. The headaches were infrequent. As for her hand – well, she could not hold a fork, so she doubted she could hold a pen; but she could almost touch her fingertips, her thumb to the center of her palm. The flourish of her palm's marriage M that had once looked so promising was now nothing more than wrinkles, and the backs of her hands were dotted with liver spots, but she no longer cared how anything looked, so long as it worked.

They helped her walk – she was lightheaded, dizzy from the weeks in bed – to the living room, where she sank into Jim's old arm chair. How different everything seemed downstairs. Yes, Joyce had been busy. The living room, like Martha's old room, had been scrubbed to a fare-thee-well. The old floors gleamed, and the woodwork had been painted. Something else, she couldn't put her finger on: The quality of light was different. She turned and craned her neck toward the windows. The curtains were new; more gauzy lace. But that was not the difference. Her desk was gone. In its place was a white window seat, with pillows of blue and orange corduroy. The bookcases had been repainted to match. But no desk.

Joyce! She could not help crying out. But Joyce was smiling, as though she had done something of which to be proud.

"It was supposed to be a surprise. We're having it refinished. A present from Dale and me. Don't worry, it will fit here, see?"

A square indentation in the window boxes. Her place for writing changed, messed with. What was it the young people said? Karma. Altering her karma, that mysterious ingredient that helped her get the ideas into words and the words onto paper in some meaningful order. It wasn't bad enough she had shattered her right hand – "there are no accidents," they said that, too – but now the place she dreamed of, that she most would want undisturbed, was not only altered, it was gone. How could she imagine returning to her writing desk when it was in somebody's antiques shop, getting stripped down? And all her belongings, her books (thesaurus, dictionary, nature guides), the contents of those three sticky drawers (letters, bills, notebooks she had been keeping for years, pencils as sharp as arrows) – all moved, gone from their rightful places. How had they even gotten into the drawers? Jimmied them open?

It was all too much. Her arms were damp with sweat. The headache that had lately gone, that seared the top of her head in two, was replaced by a dull throb in her left temple. She wondered, perversely, if Joyce had done all this on purpose, if she had just been waiting for some moment of weakness before she took over the house.

Her gardens needed tending, and she could not trust anyone else to take care of them. Joyce insisted she was watering "the garden" every night, but this only made Helen more nervous, for there was more than one garden, there were many, and her use of the singular implied neglect. The kitchen garden, with herbs and a few tomato plants, was near the back door, on the north side of the house. The cutting garden – with its zinnias, cosmos, sunflowers, black-eyed Susans, coreopsis, strawflower, glads, dahlias – was on the south side, just outside the orchard's shade. Beyond the barn was "the garden" to which Joyce probably referred, her vegetable plot, with its rows of neatly planted greens and squash and beans. In other clumps throughout the yard were the various perennials that would be coming into their own, the hollyhocks, phlox, hydrangea, larkspur, peonies, sweet William. When Helen complained, Joyce asked Loretta to come over and weed, but that only made Helen more fretful. Loretta was an aggressive, ruthless weeder: She yanked and pulled, often dispensing with late-planted seedlings or wildflowers that Helen would have left alone. Queen Anne's lace, for example, which grew wild next to the barn – Helen had a soft spot for it, sometimes even gathering it into bunches for bouquets. Loretta extracted it by the roots and threw it in the burn barrel (never the compost heap, that would only start the cycle all over again). She was the same way with birds; an avowed environmentalist Loretta was, but if she'd owned a shotgun there would be a lot fewer starlings and English sparrows in the world. That was how they differed. To Helen there were no good plants and bad plants, no good or bad creatures. So when Loretta visited, Helen sat in her bedroom, where the roar of the air conditioner covered every outdoor sound, and wondered what had become of the plants she had nurtured into bloom.

Just as Helen thought she would go crazy if she did not get back on her feet, two things happened to distract her. Both emanated from the Kennedy compound, as Joyce, with a bitter sarcasm, called what was now Fran and Peter Kennedy's side of the farm.

The first arrived on the wind. Helen was downstairs lying on the couch, where – now that she could walk around for spells during the day – she was spending more and more of her time. What came was the unmistakable rank odor of rotting shellfish, the same aroma that wafted through the docks of Galilee and around the parking lot of the fish market.

She got up, with difficulty, for her ankle and right hand were still weak and with her left arm she barely had enough strength to push herself off the sofa. But she managed somehow, using a cane, and when she staggered to the kitchen window she saw the source of the smell: a dump truck unloading quahog shells along the right-of-way they shared with the Kennedys, and a bulldozer following close behind, crushing them down.

"Oh, for God's sake." She actually said it aloud, although Joyce was at work and she was alone. Even she, the New Yorker, would never dream of using dead shellfish – for as much as they were supposed to be "clean," a little meat always clung to the shells – to pave her driveway. The sea gulls would be hanging around for days, crapping everywhere and squawking over the pickings, before the shells had dried out and the smell disappeared. Helen sank into a kitchen chair. It was too hot to close the windows, but she was tempted.

As if carried by the same ill wind, Fran Kennedy showed up the next afternoon. She was wearing a bathing suit, a coral-colored, one-piece affair with a plunging neckline that looked like it was leftover from the Miss America pageant, and a beach towel bunched around her waist. Helen, who had nearly fallen as she struggled off the couch to answer Fran's insistent knock, snapped at her as soon as opened the door. "I don't want visitors. I'm convalescing."

The look on Fran's face stopped her. The woman's eyes were sunken, the skin beneath them the brownish-gray of kelp, and she was shivering in the bathing suit, although the day was torrid. Helen had kept her hand on the doorknob, hoping to close it again quickly, but confronted by Fran's face – sapped by some unnamed emotion – she felt a rush of guilt.

"Fran. I- I'm sorry, where's my manners? It just takes so long to get up and answer the door – and that awful smell, it's making me nauseous."

Fran helped her back to the couch. Damn this woman, Helen thought. She wanted to hate her, she really did, but how could you hate someone who held no ill will toward anyone, least of all you? Fran doted on her every word, for some crazy reason. Now she would have to repay the favor.

"I'm sorry about the shells, they were Peter's idea." Fran was sitting on the ottoman across from Helen. "I just had to talk to you. The most awful thing. Oh." She put her head down, then brought it back up, her hair flipping back from her face. "It's Peter. I don't know what to do. I just don't know what to do."

It developed that Peter Kennedy, on his many two-week sales trips, was cheating on his wife. Fran, left for longer and longer spells with the children, and her suspicions aroused by the coldness her husband displayed at home, had done some detective work. An examination of their credit card and phone bills had told most of the story, which Peter had helpfully filled in when confronted.

Helen sighed. She was not used to this generation, in which confiding one's troubles seemed to have become a national pastime. She did not know this woman that well. In fact, she barely knew her at all, she was more an acquaintance than a friend, a neighbor with whom she shared a sort of grudging companionship. Yet Fran felt compelled – yes, that was the word, it was confession fueled by need – to divulge her most personal secrets. Helen had never discussed Jim's infidelity with anyone, not even Loretta, although probably her parents had guessed it, that long ago winter in New York. She could not imagine discussing it with anyone now, but wasn't that why Fran was here? It was almost as though she detected in Helen a kindred spirit.

She must have other friends, women she worked out with at the health club, close friends back in New Jersey; she even had two sisters, one in Maryland, one in Florida. Surely they talked by phone? Wrote letters? Yet here Fran was, tears carving gullies through her cheeks, her body shaking with humiliation, hurt and anger, and she was looking for comfort from Helen, who felt ill-equipped to offer her anything.

"Do you still love him?" It was an abrupt, rude, get-to-the-bottom question, and Helen knew she sounded impatient, even irritated.

"Yeesss," Fran sobbed, dropping her face back into her hands.

Helen sat quietly, thinking. It was hard to draw parallels between Peter Kennedy, who had probably been cheating on his wife for years and not gotten caught, who saw it as a game of opportunity, and Jim, her Jim, who had turned from her in anger and grief and then fallen in love with someone else. She almost wondered if Fran was better off. Peter certainly wasn't worth crying over, and in good time she would figure that out if she had any sense. But Jim. He had been a good man, but flawed. He had loved her once. Maybe he never stopped. His infidelity had been one strand in a Gordian knot of guilt, blame, retribution, sorrow, regret. You could follow it, in twists and tangled turns, to that January morning five years ago when he had cut it, snapped it in two, ending one pain and igniting another. What could she tell Fran Kennedy of any of this? No one knew, only she and Jim and one other person. Whatever wisdom she had gained would die with her. That was how she had always imagined it.

Fran wiped her face with the back of her hands, then found the Kleenex on the coffee table and blew her nose. "This was supposed to be our second chance, this house. Get away from New Jersey. This has been going on for a long time. It's a woman he works with. A sales director. She doesn't have children. She doesn't get tired. She wears suits and has her hair done in New York and plays golf with the other salesmen . . ." Fran's voice drifted off, as though wistful.

Helen looked at Fran's bathing suit, no bigger than a size 8, her wavy blunt-cut hair, her manicured fingernails. Fran was an attractive woman. Yes, she had children, but she also had

a babysitter and a cleaning service and a health club membership. She wondered why she got tired. Maybe it was the ennui of
the unimportant. She had nothing to do – she didn't even garden, leaving that to the landscaping company that came once
a week, its large, noisy mowers and trimmers scaring the birds
and kicking up puffs of sand and dust.

"Where are your children?" Helen blurted. An image of the
girl and boy wandering toward the pond came to her, unbidden.
She could feel her heart punching the inside of her chest. This,
after all, was the lesson she should pass on.

"With Casey," Fran said, oblivious to Helen's tone. Casey
was the Kennedys' live-in babysitter, a college girl with blonde
hair down the middle of her back and a golden tan. Joyce had
spotted her sunning herself below the dunes.

"Go home and take care of them," Helen said. "Forget about
Peter. He's not going to change. But your children need *you*, not
some nymphet who's tanning herself all the time. Go home and
be a mother."

For a week now the sun had been obscured by haze, a combination of muggy August weather and the pollution that wafted east from New York City's freeways and the power plants of
Ohio. The sky was milky, the air thick and moist. Helen thought
longingly of the hills of New York, where the sky was either
the color of hydrangeas, or black with coming thunder. Good
weather, or time to run for cover; none of these smoggy, oppres-
sive skies that hung over everything like feather pillows, threatening to smother you.

That December in Cooperstown, where she had run after
learning of Jim's affair, her mother said almost the same thing
she said to Fran: "You have a baby on the way. Go home and be
a mother." Her words had stung. Only Helen's father, getting
her out to the barn on some pretext, had told her he cared. *You
will always have a home here with us*, he had said. But two women
could not live in the same house without one of them being miserable. Helen had learned that from Martha. And her mother
had made it plain that she wasn't about to take her back in. This
said while she made brother George his favorite breakfast, hash
and eggs. George was not yet married and needed someone to
look after him.

She stewed over Fran. She had been too harsh with her, but she believed and felt the words as she said them. How, then, to reconcile the deep hatred she still felt for her mother, the hurt that cut to the quick and had never gone away? Today she could not deny the wisdom of what her mother had said; it was the tone, the utter dismissal, that she could not forgive. Yet she had just done the same thing to Fran Kennedy, sent her away as though she, not the errant husband, were guilty of something.

CHAPTER FOURTEEN

▲

The first thing that struck Joyce was Camille's voice. It had changed, so radically in fact that when Camille first spoke to her she thought she must be mistaken, this was not her old friend. The physical changes were not so startling; you expected, after five years, a new hairdo (short and full, turned under), an older face (more angular, all the baby fat gone, the eyes sharper), even perhaps, different mannerisms, an adult air. But the voice. Where the teenage Camille had spoken richly, roughly, like a brook over rocks, her words now came out in a smooth, slightly higher pitched tone, with all traces of the throaty laugh gone. She had married – so she told Joyce in their first conversation, back at the coffee shop. Her husband, Eric Robinson, was older by about eight years. A lawyer, he worked in Providence for a social service agency, making far less money than he would have as a private litigator. Camille mentioned this fact several times. She and Eric had met in New Orleans (and here she made no mention of why she had gone there or what she had found), where he was in law school at Tulane and she studied nursing. Back in Rhode Island (again, no explanation of the move), they had bought an old mill house in Wakefield, near the river, which they were in the process of remodeling. This inspired much talk about hardwood flooring, mantels and paint colors. After this exhaustive monologue Joyce felt she could have built the house from scratch, but she could not fathom the emotional architecture of this woman who had once been her closest friend.

And after their long, one-way conversation, after her coffee had turned cold and bitter, Joyce wondered what to think. Camille had made some sort of peace with herself and her heritage, what little she knew of it. It was not something she wanted to discuss – that much was clear. She had either given up on the search for her father, or her mother had told her the truth, and she had learned to accept whatever no-account bastard had sired her. Hamilton, her stepfather, was dead, killed in a bar fight in a beachfront honky-tonk. Joyce had read this in the Westerly newspaper. Marian, according to Aunt Loretta, was so crippled she was bed-ridden. Camille didn't mention either parent. It was as though she had been born, silky voiced and respectable, down in New Orleans, and whatever had happened before no longer mattered.

Joyce knew better, and she would have forgiven Camille if she hadn't spoken to her at all, for who wants to be reminded of their past? After Camille's carefully worded and too cheerful account of her life, Joyce figured that would be the end of it, for obviously they had nothing in common. When Camille invited her to dinner, she assumed it was one of those social niceties, like "we must get together sometime." She could not have been more surprised when, two weeks later, Camille phoned and asked her to come over that Saturday.

The house was typical of the older mill houses on the town's side streets. Joyce recognized its vernacular architecture from her work with Alexandra Duffy. One and a half stories with a sharp roof line, it was identical to its cousins on either side – facing the street were a door and two windows on the first floor and one window on the second; inside, she knew, would be three rooms downstairs, two bedrooms up. The front yard was a tiny quilt of grass, a cracked sidewalk and two squat yew bushes under the windows. The neighborhood had not always been the best, but it was coming back, fueled by the housing boom, and the other houses were neatly kept although modest. In the muggy early evening, when the only sounds were frogs keeping a snare drum beat by the river, it had an air of calm suburban domesticity.

Joyce sat in her Datsun for a few minutes while the engine idled. What on earth would they talk about, after all this time?

Why was Camille reaching out to her when she had so cleanly, and quickly, ended their friendship years before? She picked up the hostess gift she had bought, a bottle of white wine; it felt heavy, like a weapon. It was not too late to put the car into gear and leave. The trouble with meetings like this was, you had to decide who'd you be and how much you'd disclose: how happy you were, how successful, what your ambitions were and what (if any) regrets you dared mention. That she could walk into Camille's house and be honest never crossed Joyce's mind. Honesty implied vulnerability. Honesty would be saying: You severed our friendship, and it hurt. Honesty was more than a simple invitation to dinner could bear, especially when it included Camille's husband, a stranger.

In the sky over the river, white thunderheads gathered. Thunder rumbled, but it was not dark enough yet to see any lightning strikes. Joyce cut the motor, gathered the folds of her yellow sundress and climbed out of the car. Whoever she was today, she was not going to be late.

Although tiny, the interior of the Robinson house was spare and modern, giving a feel of space. The living room furniture was a blond wood with beige cushions. Carved African statuary rested on the mantel and in the corners. The only remotely romantic element was a painting above the sofa, of the steamboat Natchez plying the Mississippi River – a souvenir, Joyce supposed, of their years in New Orleans.

They had expanded the house out the back, adding a dining room, and built a patio that overlooked the river. It was here Joyce and Camille sipped wine while Eric Robinson manned the grill. He was tall, with skin the color of cinnamon and sharp, handsome features. She would have guessed he hailed from somewhere exotic, like the French West Indies, but Camille said he was from New Jersey and had moved to New Orleans to attend law school. Joyce did not ask any questions. A conversation about anyone's heritage was risky with Camille in the room.

She had evolved from an edgy, sarcastic teenager into a tall, serene goddess. Her skin flowed like caramel, unblemished, golden. She wore a sleeveless shift of brown geometric patterns; her bare legs cascaded down to leather sandals. Joyce was not sure about the serenity. It was that voice again – slower, more modulated, like that of a TV anchorwoman who has been bullied out of her accent. It spoke of a calm, even personality, but it was like an alien's voice, not Camille's at all, and her eyes smoldered. Joyce could not decide if she was content or a simmering cauldron about to boil over.

"Eric has a new client," Camille said, pouring herself another glass of wine. "You might say members of the family."

Her husband glanced over her with a tight smile. "Let's not talk business."

"The Narragansetts. Another group that can't afford to pay his fee."

Joyce shifted in the wrought-iron chair. It was digging into her back.

"Just some consulting work," he said, flipping a burger. "They have a law firm that represented them in the land claim. And I wouldn't worry about the fee. They just became the first tribe in the nation to be federally recognized. At some point they'll receive the reparations that are due them. And you would be one of the first people to benefit."

Joyce felt like she was eavesdropping on a private conversation. She tried to make sense of it. She did not always read the paper and had followed the tribe's recent successes only superficially. She had heard her mother complaining about all the land the Narragansetts had won back, 1,800 acres, and how the threat of the lawsuit had stifled real estate deals in town for several years. She knew about this federal recognition, too, but to her mind neither development had really changed anything. All the Indians she knew still lived in poverty in tiny houses on what was now tribal land. That included Camille's mother.

The burgers done, Eric served them with salad, sliced tomatoes and pinches of mint. They ate quietly while the river rippled by, carrying a mallard or two between the cattails and purple loosestrife. They talked of nothing; the food, Eric's garden, the thunderclouds that hovered but wouldn't strike. Then Eric cleared the plates and disappeared in the house, and Camille led Joyce to the Adirondack chairs that overlooked the river.

"We sit out here at night, when it's not too buggy. It's quite peaceful." That voice again. Where was the Camille she had known? Where was the sarcasm, the fire, the wild pitch of her voice, always so unpredictable?

"It's very nice," Joyce offered, not knowing what else to say.

"My mother's crippled." Just like that Camille came out with it, keeping her eyes leveled on the water, as though she were talking to herself. "Not the polio. Rheumatoid arthritis. Some days she can barely get out of bed, do the dishes, take care of the house. She's in pain almost all the time."

Joyce murmured that she was sorry, and she truly was. She had always like Marian. No matter how poor and mean the family's existence, Mrs. Evans had always welcomed Joyce into her home, asked about her mother, offered her something to eat or drink, taken a moment to talk to her in a way that noticed and cared. No, it was not right, or fair, that Marian Evans should continue to suffer, in a house and a body that were not worthy of her, now that she had finally gotten free of Hamilton.

"I came into your room one night," Camille continued. "I knew your mother was in the hospital, you know. I was working in Pediatrics but I had heard about the accident. Then one day I saw you in the coffee shop. I wasn't going to say anything. I didn't know what to say. I figured after all this time you were probably pretty angry with me, and, to tell the truth, I wasn't sure I had anything to say to you, either. It just seemed like we didn't have anything in common anymore, ever since that summer when I left. I know I should have answered your letters, but what could I say? 'Gee, I'm broke, but having a wonderful time'? 'Gee, I'm glad I didn't go to URI! It's so much more fun working in a strip club'? But then I saw you there, with your mother. You were asleep in the chair, all twisted up like a pretzel, and your mother was pale and bruised, her arm all banged up."

"You were the one who covered me with the blanket," Joyce said, and Camille turned to look at her for the first time.

"You looked cold," she said, and then laughed. The voice had changed but the laughter had not; it still soared, throaty and uninhibited, so loud she spooked a great blue heron that had been lurking in the reeds. The bird took off with its heavy, majestic wings, beating so slowly it barely cleared the water.

"You see, you became real to me again," she said. "You and your mother. We had something in common."

Joyce crawled into the cold side of Michael Avery's bed, curling up against his solid, square, hairy torso. It was late and she had awoken him; his hands reached for her automatically, running down her back and the curves of her behind. She wanted to give in to the moment – they had had so little time together since her mother's accident. She had begged Aunt Loretta to stay with Helen, so she could have a night off, and certainly the dinner at Camille's was not the only reason. But her mind was still in Camille's backyard, listening and trying to find a connection after all these years.

"What's the matter? Didn't you have a good time?" Michael propped up on his elbow and turned on the bedside lamp. His voice was slightly irritated but no longer groggy.

Joyce was still turning the evening over in her mind, like the rocks from the beach she had once put in a gem tumbler she'd gotten for Christmas. All she had ended up with then were smaller beach stones – they had been more brilliant and interesting back at the beach, before she'd tried to make them into something.

"Her mother's sick." That was one thing. "She and her husband, they seemed a little at odds, but it was hard to tell." That was another. "Her voice – her whole persona – I can't explain it, but it seemed sort of fake. Like she had adopted this new personality. She wasn't the Camille I used to know."

"Well, she grew up. You probably seem different to her, too." Resigned that there would be no sex until Joyce got all this out of her system, Avery groaned, hauled himself out of bed and stalked into the kitchen. Joyce followed him to the barstools at the counter. Michael rooted around in the freezer for his favorite midnight snack, ice cream, and came up with a pint of chocolate cherry-fudge, which he set on the counter alongside two spoons. For a while they silently dipped into the cardboard container.

"So are you still friends? Or not? That's what you have to decide."

Michael was so good at getting to the point. Plus he hated long, protracted discussions, as much as Joyce loved them. She wanted to pick the problem apart from every angle. He wanted to come up with the answer so they could get back to bed.

"I don't know. It was weird." She dived for the last frozen cherry before he could get to it. "At first, it was like we were strangers. Her husband was nice enough. But I kept thinking, what do I have in common with her anymore? She's married. She's working this intense nursing job. She could be anybody."

"And then?" He had backed off the pint, giving her the last of it.

"Well, then, after we ate, her husband disappeared into the house, I guess on purpose, and she started opening up, telling me all this stuff about New Orleans, about her mother, etcetera."

"New Orleans?"

She explained about Camille's quest to find her father. "So it was kind of like old times, you know, she was sharing all this personal stuff, and when she talked about her mother she sounded a little more like herself."

"What about her father? Did she ever find him?"

That was the strangest thing. Joyce had never dared ask, and Camille hadn't said.

Michael was home for a long stretch now. Except for a symposium out West in October, he would be spending the academic year on campus, teaching, advising, and working on a major research paper for a scientific journal. The traveling over for now, they were settling in as a couple. Joyce had a shelf in his medicine cabinet. Half her clothes seemed to be at his house, and she kept a sweatshirt in his closet for the cooler evenings when they would sit on the deck and watch the pond. The rough edges of their first year together seemed to have smoothed over. They no longer fought about the little things (knife on the left or right side of the plate? Napkin folded in a triangle or rectangle? These things mattered more to him than they did to her, and she found it was easy to concede them) or the big ones (How much time should they spend together? Could they keep their opposite-sex friends? How committed were they?). An understanding of long-term plans seemed to have evolved between them, so that when Joyce's September-to-June rental became available again, they agreed it would be easier for her to stay at the farm. The idea being that when Helen got back on her feet, Joyce would move in with Avery, and eventually they would marry.

Sometimes it seemed, though, that an impenetrable gulf loomed between their intentions and the execution of them. Michael thought Joyce needed to work on her career. What exactly that meant she wasn't sure, although she did have a difficult time defending her job with Historical Preservation. The grant expired in October and the agency had not renewed its funding; Joyce would be out of a job in a few months. She had completed the survey in the spring and now she was meticulously preparing a report for Alexandra Duffy, complete with maps, photographs and indexing. Still, something about it seemed unfinished. She tried to explain this once to Miss Duffy, who rapped a sharp pencil on her blotter while Joyce spoke. It was just that in the lists and photos and footnotes, the gist of what she had discovered seemed to have been lost. She told her about Lydia Franklin, the old woman living in the stone-ender with no plumbing or electricity.

"She's afraid she'll lose her house. The town's going to take it for taxes, and some developer will buy it, and all the land around it will be subdivided."

"That's the problem. These people don't have any money, they can't take care of anything. The house is probably falling in."

Joyce tried again, telling her about another man she had met in Exeter whose children had convinced him to turn over the deed to his house. When he died, they would inherit 75 acres of prime farmland, but they had already found a buyer for it – a man whose stock in trade was raised ranch houses on quarter-acre lots. The house had been in the family since the 1700s.

But Miss Duffy seemed interested in preserving architecture, not people's lives. "We aren't a social service agency," she snapped, stabbing the pencil back into her bun. "As long as they aren't tearing the house down, it's none of our affair."

Joyce had related some of this to Michael, and in her frustration he heard the yearning for a new calling. He suggested she go back to school. No one, he assured her, could do anything today without a master's degree. Then she could give up that awful job at the tourism shack, as he called it, and do something more worthy of her intellect. She could get an assistantship at the university, maybe even study for a doctorate. The time to act was now, while she was young, before she – they – had children.

Unsure what path to take, Joyce stood still. Sometimes on the beach she would stand at the sea's edge while the tide swept out, sucking away the water, leaving behind porous mounds of collapsing sand. In the same way her world was shifting, and sooner or later it would force her to move, to step back, to decide.

CHAPTER FIFTEEN

It is August, the autumnal equinox is a month away, and we go along harvesting our tomatoes and corn and admiring the zinnias' sunny gold faces. But the orb weaver knows. At my kitchen window once again she has spun her web, right on time, a wagon-wheel death trap to catch wayward gnats, mosquitoes, even other spiders. Seeing her has jolted me awake; the change of seasons already has begun.
–A Country Woman's Diary, Aug. 28, 1975, reprinted Aug. 25, 1983

The doctor said it would be good for her to get out. Helen still used a cane, but barely leaned on it; and while she could not type or write with a pen, keeping her out of work, she could grasp things again, like doorknobs and pot handles, which meant she no longer needed Loretta or Joyce to baby-sit her all day. Save for a nap each afternoon on the couch, she was on her feet. Yes, the doctor said it would be good for her to get out, so she was going to the cemetery to visit Susan's grave.

They had never bought a marker for their daughter's burial place. They could not afford it. But one day Helen had found a rounded piece of pink quartzite on the beach and lugged it, with much difficulty, up to the graveyard, where Jim embedded it in a hole near the stub of metal that marked the site. In the sun flecks of silver shone on its surface, and the shade of pink reminded Helen of a smocked dress Susan had worn her last summer. The grave was off in the northwest corner of the family plot, away from Martha and her husband, James Sr., with their stone of square granite, and Jim, with his simple tablet, but in the same row with the oldest graves there, the weathered field stones that had no markings at all.

Before she left the yard Helen gathered some flowers for Susan. Not the riotous blooms in her annual garden, the zinnias and dahlias and cosmos, but the flowers that her little girl had always been drawn to: the leggy Queen Anne's lace, buttercups ("Do you like butter?," asked as they were held under a tiny chin), tiny purple asters, the rooster tails with which she and Dale had fought to the last grain of pollen. Weeds at a little girl's eye level, easy to hold in stubby hands and bring to Mother.

Picking the flowers, with all the bending it required, made Helen's right leg stiff, so she leaned on the cane as she walked toward the graveyard. She could not remember the last time she had been to the cemetery or, especially, to Susan's grave. Poor girl whose innocence and curiosity had set in motion so many things beyond her understanding. Some people visit graves out of guilt; Helen had stayed away from her daughter's for the same reason. Now, since the accident, she had no more reason to avoid Susan. The doctor had said getting out would be good for her.

When she thought about her accident, she thought of getting struck by lightning. A bolt that, in an instant, had changed everything. She was not sure if it was the moment of being struck down or the agonizing weeks afterward, in the hospital and then Martha's bed, that had made the difference. The one was God's retribution; the other, her own penance. Whatever the reason, she had emerged on the other side scarred but also healed. She felt like a burn victim whose skin had grown back, or an asthmatic who can breathe again.

She realized she had avoided thinking about her daughter all these years, had shoved her into a corner much like the cemetery parcel they had chosen, as far away from everyone else as possible. So terrible, when she had loved Susan the best. Mothers weren't supposed to have favorites, but inevitably there was one child who tore at you in a way the others did not, whose flesh was more of your flesh. That had been Susan. Blonde, almost white hair, trusting brown eyes (a sign her hair, like Joyce's, would have turned brunette eventually), a heart-shaped face, a tiny cleft in the chin; adding up to a girl who was pretty, but in a real way, not like the little girls whose mothers entered them into pageants and put ribbons in their pigtails.

She had been always been good. Obedient. Patient, except when she was tired. Helen had been fixing her a grilled cheese for lunch. It was early April, but unseasonably warm, that first warm day that makes you hope for the summer that seems so far away. Helen had opened two kitchen windows, and a breeze was rocking the curtains, ruffling the paper on which Susan painted. She was making circles with a rubber stamp, in reds and yellows that jumped off the page; they reminded Helen of beach balls. Rushing, rushing, Helen flipped Susan's sandwich, paged through a cookbook for a recipe – salmon loaf; the canned salmon had been expensive, but she had a craving – and plotted out her afternoon. A walk with Susan, Susan's nap and then, if Martha cooperated, an hour to write. But she had to plan dinner first, and she had promised Jim she would write out some checks. He was gone for the day, to Connecticut to look at a used tractor; at least, that was where he said he was. It had never occurred to Helen until this moment that she had not kept track of his whereabouts back then at all, because she had no reason to be suspicious. She had always assumed the wandering started later. After Susan.

Then the bell started ringing. Insistently, three rings, pause, then four. *Damn.* She almost burned Susan's grilled cheese. She had fed Martha, adjusted her pillows, brought her a book – what did she want now? Dale had eaten earlier, and now he was in the dirt driveway pushing around yellow construction toys. She helped Susan wash her hands and left her at the table, happily nibbling the edges of her sandwich. She had not given a thought to the unhooked screen door – and why should she have? Dale was outside. She wouldn't lock him out.

Helen paused on the Kennedys' right of way. The quahog shells had been flattened by the big tires of their Jeep Cherokee, which seemed to go up and down the driveway a dozen times a day, and their odor was gone, bleached clean by the sun. Still, the shells were hard to walk on, especially with the cane, and she rested a moment, letting the sea breeze cool her brow. A moment, but not too long. The doctor had said she needed to get out.

By mid-September she could drive again. No work yet; her fingers were not healed enough to type, and the doctor had extended her disability for another month. To her surprise, Helen was growing restless at home. She decided one Wednesday morning – when she knew Ludlow would be out of the office – to visit her co-workers, who had sent her flowers, a card, and a fruit basket in the previous weeks. As much as this idea surprised her, the reception she received was unexpected as well. Even Holly, who was struggling with her two-finger typing when Helen walked in, seemed glad to see her. *I can't wait until you get back*, she said. *Ludlow's making me do all your crap.* From Holly that was practically an endearment. Only two agents were in the office – Sylvia, a tall, silver-haired woman who was Ludlow's best producer and who rarely went on the Wednesday morning tour, and a thin, nervous young man in a suit whom Helen had never met. Apparently business was so good Ludlow was hiring agents. The young man, whose name was Ed Appleton, shook her hand, and Sylvia enveloped her in a hug. Helen was startled by this familiarity; the crisp cotton of Sylvia's teal suit scratching her cheek, the smell of Sylvia's shampoo like cocoa beans.

"Helen, we've missed you! Ludlow doesn't know what to do without you. We are so busy. Let me look at you." Sylvia held her at arm's length, her fingers lightly on Helen's shoulders. "You look wonderful. I was so afraid for you when I saw you at the hospital."

"You came to the hospital?" This was not the first time someone had told her this and she couldn't recall their visit.

"The next day. We were sick about it." Sylvia leaned against her desk and waved for her to sit down in the chair in front of it, where clients usually sat. "I think it was Ludlow's mother who told us. Loretta?" Helen nodded. "I couldn't believe it. When you didn't come into work Monday, there was this pall over the place. I thought, 'Who's going to tell us the weather? And who'll bring us zucchini?'"

Helen smiled. As a matter of fact, she did have some in the car. They laughed, and even Holly joined in.

"Well, you have to come back soon. We're selling houses so fast we can't keep up. I just turned over a Cape in Green Hill in two days. Five thousand over asking price. It's crazy." She lowered her voice. "If I were you I'd ask Ludlow for a raise. He'd pay anything to get you back, and he's making a killing right now."

When Helen left it was about 10:30. She had thought, in the back of her mind, of stopping in to see Mr. Lillibridge, but it was too early for him to be on his porch, and she had no idea where to find him if he was working outside. She sat at the wheel of the car, poised to pull out of the parking lot, indecisive as to whether to turn right or left. Would he think it forward of her to visit? Yet he had visited her, several times, in the hospital and at home. His was one of the few faces she remembered. What would she say to him if she did visit? Would it be awkward? Would he ask her what she wanted? And what did she want?

She stared across the road, straining to see if he was out on the tractor, but all she saw was rows of potato plants, shimmering green in the hazy sun. In the ditch between the road and the field, tiny orange flags vibrated as if to the rumbling of an unseen train. She had been looking at them all this time but not seeing them. Not understanding.

It couldn't be. There must be some explanation – perhaps the town was about to do work, to soften the intersection with the Beach Road, and they had taken a slice of Mr. Lillibridge's land. Or perhaps they were surveying, getting ready to repave the road. God knows it needed it, as full of ruts and patches as it was. The flags could not mean what she thought they meant.

She turned right and headed toward Mr. Lillibridge's house. An urge to find him had overtaken her. The awkwardness she had felt a moment ago was gone, replaced by concern and disbelief. They were, after all, friends, and friends must stick together. He would not think she was forward to visit under such circumstances. After all, she had been through it. She had succumbed, too.

He was not on the porch, and although she was fully prepared to look in the barn or even walk out to the fields if necessary, she saw right away that his black Cadillac was gone. He must have headed into town. Deflated, Helen started the engine and began to back out of the driveway. Then he came running out the side door, waving at her to wait.

"Cadillac's in the shop. Don't be leaving on my account."

She had not realized it before, but he was a handsome man without his hat. His head, with its closely cut crop of hair, had a fine, oval shape, and his eyes were as blue as the ocean. He took care of himself, too. Just now, although she had caught him unawares, he was freshly shaven, and his green checked shirt was ironed. As he leaned into her car window, she caught a smell of Old Spice. He had not been working, then.

She stumbled out an apology. She hated people who dropped in on folks uninvited. But, like the ladies at Winter Coastal Homes, he seemed delighted to see her, and he practically pulled her out of the car and up the steps.

Mr. Lillibridge's home was modest but, like the man, it was neat, clean and orderly. He brought her into the kitchen and they sat down at a red Formica table. The seats were vinyl and its upholstery matched the table's speckled pattern. He had been having coffee, and wordlessly he poured her a cup.

"I came over because – ," she started, and then stopped. Why did she need an excuse? Surely to Mr. Lillibridge she could tell the truth. "I wanted to see you, but I thought it was too early in the day, that you'd be out in the fields."

"Here I am. Having a coffee break. Just got back from the bank." He was beaming.

"Then I saw the surveyor's flags. Around your potato fields."

His face darkened. He stirred his coffee, making a clanging sound. "It's true," he said finally. "This is my last year growing potatoes. I signed a sales agreement with Ludlow Winter. He's going to develop the whole shebang."

So it was worse than she thought. Now, suddenly, she realized how Joyce had felt when she learned about the east field. But at least she hadn't sold everything. Just enough to get by. She had done what she had to do.

"Mr. Lillibridge, I am so sorry. Truly."

He sighed and spooned more sugar in his coffee. "Helen, if I have to beg you, I will. Please do not call me 'Mr. Lillibridge.'"

The problem was, if she did not call him by his last name, she would have to call him by his first name, which was Percy, and she had never, ever heard anyone call him that. He was universally known as Dub, for what reason she did not know. Still, she felt silly saying "Dub."

"But what will you do? Where will you go?"

"I don't know. For the first time in my life, I'll have money. But what difference does it make? I won't have the one thing I want, which is this place, but I just can't seem to hang on to it.

The town's going to take it anyway if I don't sell. I can't make a go of it and pay the taxes."

Helen shook her head. As they spoke, her tax bill sat on the kitchen table, nestled in a napkin holder with her other bills. With the money gone from selling the Kennedy lot, she was having more and more trouble paying it, and every year the first of September loomed like an impossible deadline. She had been thinking of asking Ludlow for a raise even before Sylvia suggested it.

"You've got to have some place to live, uh, Dub," she said. "Can't you at least hang on to the house, maybe a couple of acres?"

"It's going to be hard. Looking out the window every day while they toss up another hundred ranch houses. Watching all that good, fertile soil covered in lawns and pavement."

"You can still farm what's left of my place. If the lease is too high, maybe we can work something out." More than her salary, it was the lease income that was keeping her going, but she couldn't think of that now. They had to stick together.

He stood up and cleared their coffee cups, looking out the window as he replied. "I told you so, Helen."

"Told me?"

"That you would be up and around in no time."

Helen was beginning to get her footing. For a long time it had been as though she were standing in the sand, watching the tide wash out around her, marooned by the ebb and flow. Now she could put one foot in front of another. She was on higher ground, and with this feeling of solid earth under her, she began to look ahead, much as a walker keeps both eyes on the horizon. There was a sense of movement, progression, linear time.

She began to make plans. She knew now that she would be returning to work. Not only was her hand stronger, if not fully healed, but she could picture herself back at the real estate office; indeed, she almost looked forward to it. Besides work, her days would be shaped by other contingencies. For too long the newspaper had been reprinting her old columns and, although no one had complained, her words from years past seemed insufficient to describe the changing landscape of the South Shore. So many of the vistas and natural features she had written about were in danger of disappearing or, worse, already had vanished. She felt strongly that she must campaign to save what could be saved of this fair place. Her words would need to be braver and stronger. At a time when her hands were weak, her mind would have to be sharp, her vision clear. The newspaper might not like it. Her editor, a man in his 50s who wore rumpled dress shirts and propped his glasses atop his balding head, did not like to make waves. She could envision Mason Dudley telling her to tone it down or, worse, letting her go. But suddenly, her eyes trained on the future, it did not matter. She only knew she could not go back to the way things were before.

And there was the matter of Joyce and Dale. She had lost track of them somehow, along the way. Like the walker on the shore who stares back and sees only his own footprints, she had forgotten she was still sharing life with her children, even if they were grown. Helen could see now that giving Dale all that money had been an excuse to get out of parenting. She had given him the tools to make his own way, hadn't she? She didn't need to worry anymore, then, did she? But she wondered just how he was doing. She hardly ever saw him. And Joyce, well, even this summer, sharing the house, Joyce providing so much care, they had barely talked. She sensed something tense and buttoned up in her daughter; her whole self seemed coiled, ready to strike. Joyce was angry, still so angry, despite all the things going right for her – the job, her boyfriend, her fierce independence. They confounded Helen, both of them did. But she would have to try to reach them somehow.

Feeling up to a longer trip, Helen drove into Wakefield. She had in mind buying a dress, or maybe two – clothes for the fall that she could wear to work. She had a favorite store in town, a thrift shop called Twice as Nice, located in the basement of an old mill by the river. Racks were crowded into a long room below a high ceiling of pipes and valves, and the store had a musty smell that penetrated the clothes. This did not deter Helen. The odor was easily removed by washing the clothes and hanging them out to dry, and the woman who ran it, Natalie, was one of the few clerks who made Helen comfortable. She did not make meaningless chit-chat or follow Helen around the store; yet she always said hello and smiled, recognizing her. Natalie was always well dressed in the top pickings of her inventory – bright-colored jackets offset by paisley scarves, crisply tailored pants, sleeveless silk shirts. Walking into the store, seeing Natalie folding clothes on the counter or chatting with a customer, gave Helen a peaceful feeling. The store was so unlike the chain department stores where everyone shopped now, with their long aisles, racks and racks of merchandise and glaring fluorescent lights. Sometimes Joyce dragged her into one; as soon as she entered, she felt as though a boot was weighing down her chest. Walking in circles among the racks made her head spin, and inevitably some impatient shopper was behind her, trying to get by. Joyce, whipping through the hangers, would look back at her in disgust. What was she doing, anyway?

But in Natalie's store there were no squealing shopping carts, no lights that turned your skin green, no knots of shoppers wrestling you for access to a sales rack. In fact, it was rather dark in the old mill room, with its tiny cellar-like windows and walls of stone. But Helen found it familiar and comforting, like a rabbit warren. She quickly found a long rack of fall dresses and began sifting through it. Flattering styles finally had returned; the shoulder pads and long skirts reminded her of the 1940s, yet now the fabrics were so much more forgiving – most of them could be thrown in the washer. She savored the colors and textures. Red-and-black checked flannels, soft gray wools, plaid jumpers and skirts. Feeling greedy, she slung four dresses over her arm and headed to the dressing room.

The woman in the mirror was not remarkably pretty and certainly was not young, but Helen regarded herself with a new affection. She was 56, and it showed in the lines that rayed from her eyes and the parentheses that sheltered her mouth. Yet she saw something new in this image that she rather liked. Her face had a high color; her eyes glittered; the overall impression was weathered and worn, but in a good way, like beach glass that has lost its sharp edges to the pounding of the sea.

With difficulty she began inching into the dresses she had chosen. Her right hand was sensitive still, and the fingers clung together like a palsy victim's as she threaded them through the sleeve.

"It's a shame." Outside the dressing room two women were chatting as they shopped, their conversation punctuated by hangers scraping along a bar.

"That's what they get. Drug addicts. Money's too tempting."

Helen had decided the first dress was too short and was zipping up a green checked shirtwaist that reminded her of fall.

"But seizing somebody's property. When you're innocent until proven guilty."

"Innocent my foot. They caught them red-handed."

The green dress was a yes, and she would take this black-watch plaid jumper, too. Now for the red wool skirt. It had such a nice flair, with its pleats and belt.

"All of it, under the hold," the same woman was continuing on, her voice growing louder as she proceeded down the rack. "Those fishing boats make for good cover."

The skirt was so tight she could not zip it up. Helen snapped it back on the hanger quickly. The women's voices, like some Muzak tape gone beserk, were giving her a headache. She would pay for the two dresses and leave. She had wanted to look for a new purse, but not today. Some other day. When the shop wasn't so crowded.

Helen sat in the mill parking lot for what seemed like a half-hour. A fishing boat had been seized in the port because the captain was smuggling drugs. That's what they did these days, the federal authorities. They took the property and didn't give it back. It was a policy she had always wholeheartedly endorsed.

She rolled down the window. Although the day was cooler, even breezy, sweat dripped down the back of her neck. She could not remember the last time she had read a daily newspaper. She received her weekly in the mail, two days after it was published; it came on Saturdays. Today was Wednesday. The paper hadn't even been printed yet. And when was the last time she had watched the TV news? She hated TV, always had. Occasionally she tuned in the radio, the news out of Providence, but most of the time she left it off. Too many ads, too many loud drumbeats. She started the engine and began hurriedly switching from station to station, but it was twenty past the hour and she would have to wait 40 minutes to catch the next broadcast.

She took a tissue out of her purse and began blotting the back of her neck. A fishing boat. The women hadn't even said what port it was from; it could be Stonington or Gloucester or

New Bedford for all she knew. And even if it was Galilee, what were the odds it was Dale's? There must be 40 vessels in the port. It could be anyone. Anywhere.

She felt light-headed. She hadn't had lunch and it was nearly noon. She rooted around in her purse and found a hard candy, its wrapper dusty, the candy sticky, but she popped it into her mouth anyway. She could not go home yet. That was all she felt certain of. She would drive down to the port herself and find out what was going on. As soon as she saw Dale, or as soon as she heard news of his whereabouts, everything would be fine.

Although it was only Wednesday, beach traffic clogged the roads to the port, and it took Helen twice as long to reach Galilee. She circled twice before finally finding a parking space near the Dutch Inn. She tried to remember where Dale's boat, the *Diana*, was berthed. That day of the Blessing seemed so long ago, and it was all a blur, especially because Loretta had been in charge – driving, parking, herding her to the dock. She headed vaguely toward the State Pier. Rows of draggers were in port, and their black hulls and raised nets looked too alike to differentiate.

She bought a hot dog from the man on the sidewalk, a balding vendor in shorts and a T-shirt. The odor of the steam table sickened her as he handed her the bun. "Looking for something?" he asked, as she stared off toward the docks.

"The *Diana*. Is she in port?"

"Derrick Houston's boat? The freezer-catcher?"

She stared back at him blankly. "Yes, the freezer-catcher, but it's Dale Winter's. He had it built last year."

The man was wiping the steel surfaces of his cart and pacing. "Yes, Dale Winter's, but really it belongs to Houston. He sold the majority interest to Houston just last month, and Houston captains it for him. Winter don't go out no more, just lays back and lets the money roll in. If you ask me he wasn't cut out for fishing. Lazy son-of-a-bitch."

"That lazy son-of-a-bitch happens to be my son." She did not recognize the clipped voice that had suddenly emerged from her. "You wouldn't happen to know the *Diana's* whereabouts, would you? I heard today that some fishing boat was seized for drugs."

He looked up, startled. "That would be the *Georgia May* out of New Bedford. Heard it on the news this morning." She had begun to walk away, her cane clicking on the concrete sidewalk, but he was still talking. "Didn't mean nothing about your son. Just some people aren't cut out for the business, that's all."

Now Helen knew she would have to take someone into her confidence. Someone who could help her deal with Dale. He had sold a majority interest in the boat – for what? It had to be worth close to what he had paid for it. That, combined with his share of the take, would run into tens of thousands a year. And what was he doing it with it, she wondered. He lived in a sublet condominium and drove a used pickup truck. She had never seen him with extravagant clothes; he did not travel; and as for girlfriends, he did not date the sort you lavished money on.

She rifled through the people whose confidence she could trust. To talk to Joyce was inviting trouble. Any conversation about Dale would just trigger the old feelings of competition and bitterness. Joyce probably knew something about Dale, but she doubted she would share it. Then there was Loretta. She would barge into the situation, all booming voice and scolding tone, but like a sea gull squawking, all the noise wouldn't amount to much. She cast around her. There was Mr. Lillibridge. Even in her mind she couldn't bring herself to think of him as Dub. He had trusted her with his personal financial troubles, and he seemed the sort to listen and not condemn. Yet what did he know about mother-child relations? He was virtually estranged from his daughter. Then there was Fran Kennedy. She had been thinking a lot about Fran, who had not been by to visit since that disastrous afternoon when she had come to Helen for help and Helen had driven her out of the house, chiding her to go home and take care of her children. Although deep down she still felt the rightness of her outburst, as time passed Helen had begun to feel weaker and weaker about its execution. Fran, in her own dippy, clingy way, had been her friend. Fran had cared for her when no one else did. And Helen had rewarded that friendship by turning her away when she most needed help. Still, she couldn't go to Fran now and ask for help, after the way she had treated her.

And there was Ludlow.

As much as she despised him – for his fatuous nature, his greed, his opportunism – there was something steely and resolute about Ludlow. He got his own way. He didn't get bogged down in feelings and sentiment when he went after something. He just took it. Bad qualities for a human being, but for a businessman, especially in this booming shoreline town, they were indispensable. There were two problems here: One, her son, true to his nature, had fouled up after being given every opportunity in the world at honest work. Two, he had made a great deal of money off her investment and he had hid that fact from her. Deep down, she could not honestly say which infuriated her more: that her son was floundering as a human being, or that he had a bad head for business.

It was all the more galling when she thought of what she had sacrificed to buy him that boat. Half the farm gone and developed, and a daughter who rarely spoke more than superficialities to her. When it meant Dale's livelihood she had let it go. There was no one left to work the farm anyway, and Joyce, in time, would get over her spite. Now she wondered. Looking out her kitchen window, seeing the quahog shell-covered driveway and, in the distance, the profile of the Kennedys' mammoth oceanfront house, she felt unmoored. Thinking of Joyce, Helen not only drifted, but she could see no land in sight.

CHAPTER SIXTEEN

▲

Joyce sat on the bare twin mattress in her old bedroom on the farm. She was leaving home for good. It was not as though she had not moved out before – when she went to college, and in and out of the house as she rented her winter cottage on the beach. Each time she had left parts of herself behind, as if knowing the move away from home was only temporary. This time she did not carry the illusion that she would ever return. She was moving in with Michael, and in five months they would be married.

She glanced around the room. The floor was covered in boxes she had obtained at the liquor store in Wakefield. Grand Marnier, with its neat cardboard dividers, was stuffed with breakables nested in tissue paper. Here were wrapped carefully all the knickknacks she had acquired over the years, at county fairs, secondhand shops and summer carnivals, alongside the few valuables she owned – her grandmother's silver comb and brush set and the tiny antique glass bottles Loretta had given her. Martini & Rossi, deep and wide, and Bartles & James held a lifetime's accumulation of books, from the yellow-bound Nancy Drew to weathered paperback copies of Walt Whitman's poems, *The Rubaiyat* by Omar Khayyam, her children's encyclopedia set. Finally, Four Roses had become the repository for all her notebooks, nearly a dozen in all, carefully layered and sealed away.

The boxes were not coming with her. Camille was coming by after lunch, and together they would carry them to the Robinsons', where they would find a new home in the attic crawl-space. Michael did not like a lot of stuff lying around. He especially hated books, an odd stance for a professor, but a product of his antipathy to dust. He owned two barrister's bookcases that were already full of his most cherished textbooks and his own collection of Hardy Boys, and Joyce knew she would not be getting any shelf space in this relationship. Yet, she could not keep her belongings at home anymore either. It would have been a sign she could not make a commitment, as though she had left one foot at home in case things didn't work out. That was no way to start a relationship.

She was actually looking forward to today. Her college friend Althea, the teacher, was coming over to help out too, and it would be the first time she had brought the two together. She was slightly anxious about this bridging of her two lives. Although on the surface they had little more in common than Joyce herself, Camille and Althea were important people to her, and she hoped they liked each other. If they didn't, it was going to be a long afternoon.

She walked over to her desk, now empty, and sat in the ladderback chair to look out the window. It was Labor Day weekend, and the weather was more August than September, with a milky, overcast sky and humidity that made even the tree branches seem to sag. The ocean, what she could see of it around the Kennedys' house, was gray. She would be glad when this season was over and a cold fall wind cleaned away all memory of this last summer on the farm. It had not been a good one. Her mother's fall in July and the weeks of recuperation had taken their toll on both of them. For a while she had wondered if her mother would ever be able to live alone again. She imagined herself stuck here for years, waiting on Helen as she grew increasingly cranky and frail. But her mother seemed to have finally rebounded. She was driving again and talking about going back to work. She no longer needed help cooking or caring for herself, although some nights late she still called to Joyce, asking for her pain pills or demanding that she check to make sure the doors were locked. She could tell Helen was fearful of what lay ahead after this weekend, when she would be truly alone.

Dale had not helped much. His drinking was getting worse. One night the police called, saying they had him in custody for disorderly conduct, and Joyce found him at the police station so drunk he did not recognize her when she came to bail him out. She had paid the bail and driven him home, and their mother had never been the wiser. But with the matter of the boat he had not been so lucky. Helen had finally found out, through some street vendor of all things, that Dale had sold a majority share to his captain. Joyce had never seen her so furious, but when all was said and done nothing much changed. Dale stayed in his apartment, sleeping during the day and snorting cocaine at night, and Joyce tried to keep as much of the truth from their mother as possible. She did not have in mind protecting either one of them; she just knew that the more contact those two had, the worse it was for her, always stuck in the middle.

She walked back to the bed, lay back on the mattress and stared at the ceiling. One long crack widened from south to north, paint flaking on either side of it. She had imagined it to be many things in her life: The Amazon, the Nile, a snake slithering in the grass. Now it was a metaphor for everything that was wrong with the house and, in turn, the family. A great divide that kept son from mother, daughter from mother, father from them all. She had never known a time when the crack wasn't there. When she had slept in a crib it must have been there, and even before, when this room belonged to – whom? Dale? Or Susan, the sister she would never know?

Camille was late, but Althea was on time. Her grandmother had sent food – potato salad, plum tomatoes, Italian cold cuts, fresh-baked grinder rolls. It was a tradition that had begun in their college days where her care packages of Italian pastry had fueled many a long night of cramming.

Joyce peered in the box and inhaled. It smelled like an Italian bakery. "Mama Cappolino comes through again."

"She wanted me to wait until her gravy was done, but I told her it would have to wait until another day." Gravy was the colloquial expression for spaghetti sauce. Joyce could imagine Althea's grandmother, Mama Cappolino, stirring the bubbling sauce in her immaculate kitchen, the sleeves of her housedress rolled up. "Where's Camille?"

"Late." Joyce said, her mouth full of an Italian cookie. "The boxes are packed, almost. I just have a couple more things to deal with. Really what I need help with is the lifting."

"Are you sure you want to do this?" Althea regarded her with dramatic eyes. They were deep set, brown, and generously set off by eye-liner. Her personality was deep, too, almost soulful. Joyce had sat up with her friend many a night talking Althea's problems to death. Every decision was preceded by a painful and slow process of reflection, doubt and hesitation. She had been talking about moving out of her grandparents' now for two years and was no closer to breaking the news to them than when she had graduated from college. Joyce was convinced Althea had lost two boyfriends because of it. Now Joyce had made a decision of her own, and Althea was applying the same deliberation to her friend's problems that she exercised so exhaustively on her own.

"You know, I had a funny dream last night." Joyce began unpacking the food onto the kitchen table. Althea loved to hear other people's dreams; this was sure to distract her. "I was standing by a car at the pond, Watchaug Pond, and suddenly a white bear came out of the woods, chasing me. It was terrifying. I managed to get into the car and shut the door just in time, but I was still frightened, and half convinced the bear was going to break through the glass."

"A white bear," Althea mused. She had stopped pouring her diet Coke and was looking out the window, as though the answer might be found outside. "The bear symbolizes the mother. It can be a protective or menacing figure, depending on whether you cross it. I would say you are trying to get away from your mother by running away, but you're afraid that you can't really elude what's chasing you."

Her interpretation was so dead-on that Joyce sat down, defeated. There was no distracting Althea. She was, Joyce reflected, probably the person who knew her best. "What about the color? White?" she said finally.

"I don't know. It's supposed to symbolize goodness, purity, and so forth. Maybe your mind is trying to tell you that this powerful figure you are trying to get away from has good intentions."

"I doubt it."

"Has she said anything yet? About you moving out?"

That was the surprising thing; Helen had had little reaction when Joyce finally screwed up enough nerve to disclose her plans. "No. I think she's so preoccupied with going back to work, and worrying about Dale, that she doesn't have the energy to lay her usual guilt trip on me."

"I think your mother will miss you very much, but she doesn't know how to tell you."

Joyce did not have time to reflect on that, because Camille walked in carrying more empty boxes. There was a flurry of greetings and then they set to making Italian grinders. Whereas years ago she would have hesitated to introduce Camille to anyone as sensitive as Althea, the new Camille seemed to warm to her immediately. Funny, she thought, that six years ago Camille had been her roommate of choice, and Althea had become her roommate by chance. They were such an odd couple – Camille, tall and lithe, her hair braided and her face bare of makeup; Althea, shorter than Joyce, with ripples of long golden hair and a body of soft curves – that Joyce almost laughed seeing them together. It was odd that one person could have two friends who were so strikingly different.

It was Althea who had talked her into getting a teaching job. Next week she was starting work as a seventh-grade history teacher at her old high school. It was time to move on. She had to get through Labor Day weekend at the tourist shack, but she was done with the Preservation Commission. The agency had published her 152-page report, "Historical Houses in Coastal Rhode Island," but Alexandra Duffy had taken a red pencil to her conclusion. "The eighteenth- and nineteenth-century houses of Washington County are threatened by neglect, over-development, owners' ignorance and the ravages of nature. What termites, powder beetles, and hurricanes do not render useless, man will surely destroy by a policy of allowing wholesale subdividing of land; over-taxing the landowners who can least afford it; and failing to value the heritage of self-sufficiency left us by our ancestors." She had gone on in this vein for a number of paragraphs, prompting Miss Duffy to write in the margin: "Get off your high horse!" It was just as well. Increasingly she had not been able to reconcile her work with the other reports being produced out of the Providence office, long, detailed treatises about cornices and porticoes that exalted the architecture of the rich at the expense of the vernacular. The day she left the Providence office, carrying three copies of the softbound report, the rest of the print run still sat in four boxes in the office of Alexandra Duffy, who had not yet bothered to open them.

Althea had told her about the high school job, and she had easily obtained a temporary teaching certificate. Michael had not been crazy about it; he was still pushing her to enroll in graduate school. But for Joyce the job had several attractions. For one thing, she would be teaching in the same school as Althea, at her alma mater, which made her feel a little at ease. The class itself held a certain appeal as well, for it was designed with a local history component mixed with the standard curriculum, which spanned the discovery of America to the Industrial Revolution. With field trips and guest speakers, she was supposed to give these 12- and 13-year-olds a sense of the history in their own backyard. Once again, she had found a job that she felt not only interested in, but destined to perform.

Labor Day weekend, and Joyce was back at the tourist shack, passing out brochures, giving directions, pointing the way to the port-a-john. They had a bank of about 25 pamphlets to choose from, neatly stacked in a display nailed together by one of the retired volunteers. The most popular brochures were for attractions beyond their area – Cape Cod, Newport, Edaville Railroad – but she also had to replenish "beaches" and "hiking trails" fairly regularly. "Museums" and "historical trails," however, were growing faded by the sun. Some of the retirees asked about them, but families with children would open the brochures and quickly put them back. In the hot weather the youngsters were too antsy to file through a house where Ben Franklin had stayed or a shed full of 19th-century farm implements. The parents were looking for something more exciting – something with color, with movement, and a fully stocked gift shop at the end. Many had already visited Mystic Seaport, and that was enough history for one trip.

"So what are your students like?"

Joyce and Michael were sitting on the deck, trying to catch the last of the late summer light. The salt marsh mosquitoes were feasting on her ankles, but Michael sat by with impunity.

"Like?" She had been thinking of something else, something

Althea had said.

"You know. Interested, smart, or bored, rude, typical teenagers."

She thought about it for a minute. "They're still poised between grade school and junior high school. The girls are all wearing those big haircuts, teased and spiky, and Flashdance t-shirts, which makes the boys sort of giggly. A few kids have already paired off. But most of them look awkward, like a butterfly that just climbed out of its cocoon."

"A wonderful image." He put his finger on the tip of her nose. "But what I meant was, what are they like as students."

"Students! I'm lucky if I can get them to be quiet. They have no interest in American history, and when I talk about local history, they roll their eyes. But they like the field trips, because it gets them out of school." They already had taken two – to the Great Swamp Monument, where the Narragansett Indians were attacked by the colonists during King Philip's War, and to Smith's Castle, the outpost where the soldiers had dragged back their dead. "I suppose they aren't bad kids. But I think a lot of what I'm talking about is lost on them."

"That's your job, you know. Make it interesting."

Michael was irritating but right. These seventh-graders she was trying to teach not only knew nothing about their hometown, some of them had been here such a short time they knew little about Rhode Island itself. Many of their fathers worked at the submarine plant in Groton, Conn., or had settled here after the Navy base closed in the 1970s. They lived in houses like the development next to the farm – one-story ranches or newer Garrison colonials, houses that were sprouting in the blueberry fields and scrub pine forests with alarming regularity. She recognized a few names – Browning, Burdick, Richmond, Potter, Stanton – but for the most part her classes were a mishmash. Not of race or religion; all but one student in her five sections was white, and they were mostly Catholic. They were, however, of varying nationalities, Polish, German, Irish, French, Italian, Portuguese. She thought it might be fun at the end of the year to have a potluck.

She was not sure how to reach them, or if she could reach them. But she had a clue when one of them, a skinny girl with blonde hair that she crimped to resemble Madonna's, raised her hand and asked if the Indians were extinct.

"No," she said, "they are not. And next week, you will meet a full-blooded Narragansett."

It had been a stupid thing to say, a slight stretch of the truth, and she had not known if Camille would even say yes. If she didn't, then what would she do? But Camille seemed actually excited about the idea.

She agreed to speak to two sections on a Thursday morning in October. Joyce had grounded the classes in the basics of European contact and indigenous peoples, and she hoped they wouldn't embarrass her too much. She settled in the back of the room in one of the junior high-sized chairs, nervously scanning the room for signs of trouble – notes being passed, furtive whisperings. But then Camille began to talk, and for 45 minutes no one moved.

First she told them about her family's history. How her mother's mother had been a tribal princess and a renowned storyteller. How everyone in the family had an Indian as well as a Christian name, and hers was Laughing Thunder. She described the splint baskets her mother and grandmother wove, and said one was in the Smithsonian Institution in Washington, D.C. She told them Indian words for the places they lived, and the long words came off her tongue like a log rolling downhill.

Then she told about going to school. How she wore beads in her hair, and in third grade the boy sitting behind her tugged at her braids and called her a "stupid Injun." How in sixth grade the principal sent her home because she had insisted to her teacher that the Great Swamp Fight wasn't a fight at all, but a massacre of women and children. How in junior high, in the very school where they now sat, she and two of her cousins were expelled for holding a sit-in during the Wounded Knee standoff in South Dakota.

Joyce listened to Camille's voice, so deep and authoritative, and wondered where she had been while all this had gone on. She remembered the Wounded Knee incident – the local paper had even covered it, which incensed the school administration even more; but Camille had never spoken of her culture, or the divide between what she was taught at home and what was gospel at school. Joyce wondered how she could have been so oblivious.

When she was finished a silence hung over the room. Finally the Madonna lookalike raised her hand. "Is it true you're a full-blooded Indian?"

Joyce wanted to hide. What had she said, in her moment of exaggeration? Why had she been thinking?

"No, it is not true," Camille said, her eyes sweeping over her audience. "My mother is three-quarters Narragansett and one-quarter Pequot. I never knew my father, but I know he wasn't an Indian. My father was white."

Michael Avery, having been a bachelor for so many years, had a tight routine that governed his leisure time.

On Saturday mornings, from 9:30 to 11 o'clock, he played racquetball at a local sports club. He then bought a bran muffin and orange juice, drove home, read the paper and showered, before moving on to his outdoor exercise of the day – a trip in his kayak, a hike in the wildlife refuge or a jog along the Post Road. Sunday mornings he spent reading the New York Times at a breakfast place in Wakefield, where he always ordered two eggs, sunnyside up, with unbuttered toast, bacon and a side order of hash. If the weather was good on a Sunday afternoon he might find some chore around the yard; but typically Sundays were spent in his den, a bedroom he had converted into an office, where he did most of his professional writing – articles for peer-reviewed journals, reviews of scientific books and the draft of a book he tentatively titled "On the Trail of Hurricanes."

Joyce, upon moving in, began to insert herself gently in the spaces between his preordained activities. They shared brunch and the paper on Sundays, and occasionally she convinced him to stay home, where they ate pancakes on the deck. She eagerly joined him for the kayaking and hiking; although she would never be a jogger, she sometimes loped along beside him for a mile or two. But his life, still so separate from hers, left her with time that had to be filled. On Saturday mornings, when he was on the squash court, she cleaned house, vacuuming, washing the floors, dusting the rustic pine furniture. Michael had a Filipino cleaning woman, the wife of one of his graduate students, who came on Thursdays, but after Joyce moved in, he got rid of her. "Women don't like other women cleaning their houses," he said authoritatively. Joyce did not mind the housework – it made the place feel a little more like it was hers, too – but the house was difficult to keep clean. Its only charm was the location and the view; the construction was cheap, with paneled walls, a thin commercial-grade carpet and white linoleum that showed the dirt. Slowly she was getting rid of the uglier manifestations of his single existence. The brown-checked, quilted bedspread and brown draperies she had replaced with a green ivy pattern, and she had found a pair of crystal-base lamps at a yard sale that lightened up the décor of the bedroom. She found that introducing such changes was best done slowly and with little fanfare. If she asked Michael what he thought, his automatic reaction was No, he did not want to redo such-and-such, and that was that. But if a new object appeared in place of an old one, he grumbled at first and allowed later that maybe it was an improvement after all.

Some nights, when Michael was working late, she would pull out the box of decorating magazines she had brought with her. They had been the subject of their first living-together argument. Seeing the magazines, stacked in the box marked Grand Marnier, Michael had assumed they were trash and put them down in the basement, next to his tied-up newspapers. It was only happenstance that led Joyce to discover them before Garbage Day.

"I'm saving these," she said, dumping the box at his feet in the living room, still huffing from lugging them upstairs.

"You're saving a bunch of old magazines?" Michael subscribed to National Geographic, Scientific American and Time, the current issues of which were always fanned on his coffee table, with last month's editions consigned immediately to the trash heap. "What do you want with a bunch of moldy old magazines?"

"They weren't moldy when I moved in, and if they're moldy now it's because somebody stuck them in the BASEMENT."

"You're not going to junk up my house with a box of magazines."

The argument degenerated from there. From her indignity at the phrase "my house," instead of "our house," to her inability to articulate why she enjoyed leafing through the familiar pages of Country Home and Country Living, Joyce grew so furious that she did not speak to him for the rest of the night. They made up, tentatively, the next morning, and he pretended not to notice when she hid the magazines under their bed.

So it was only when Michael was gone that she took them out, gazing longingly at elegant Greek revival and Colonial interiors, Laura Ashley fabrics, antique highboys and four-poster beds. She fantasized about the day when Michael would agree that, yes, his house was not really practical for a couple anymore, especially not if they wanted to raise a family, and they should buy one of these sturdy old houses. One with a fireplace and an elaborate porch, and a kitchen with tall beadboard cupboards and a window over the sink, instead of the Formica-and-particle-board tomb she was forced to cook in now.

In late October Michael left for Seattle for two weeks, to an annual convention of a professional society of which he was a director, to be followed by a series of meetings with oceanography researchers at the University of Washington. Joyce had longed to go with him, but he had not invited her and it was obvious she would not be able to take time off from teaching. She tried to approach his absence positively: a good time to put more of her stamp on the house, get ahead on correcting papers, reconnect with her friends.

Joyce still thought of the house as Michael's, and when he was gone, she looked for the secrets he must be keeping in the places he had not shared. There was his study: A bedroom, really, it contained a closet with sliding doors, behind which hung rows of gray and black suits, wool blazers, a couple of winter coats – his off-season wardrobe. The shoes were lined up, polished black wingtips and caramel-colored moccasins, as though he had just stepped out of them, and the ties suspended on the door were sorted by color and pattern. The rest of the room was crammed with the business of academia. Three bookcases sagging with volumes, a large mahogany desk piled with paper, a metal filing cabinet with a dent in the side. For all of Michael's punctiliousness, the room had a shabby air.

She opened the drawers. Unlike her mother, Michael never locked anything. Because he never dreamed she would snoop? Or because he had nothing to hide? The top drawer was a pile of bills, their due dates neatly written on the envelopes. Joyce knew little about Michael's financial position. Every month she wrote him a check for her half of the household expenses, and she took his word for the figure he quoted her. She slipped a finger into the top envelope, a credit card bill, and then put it back without looking inside. She could not decide if she was having a crisis of conscience or she simply didn't want to stumble on something she was better off not knowing.

Althea came over on a Friday night with Chinese food. They had invited Camille, but she had begged off – she was pregnant and feeling too tired after work to go out at night. After her appearance in Joyce's classroom, Joyce had regarded her friend with even more trepidation. They had still been spending time together, shopping for baby clothes and occasionally taking in a movie, but Joyce treaded lightly around her.

"This stupid girl asked her if she was full blooded, and it was all my fault," she told Althea, who was helping herself to more rice. "And then she said that about her father being white. I couldn't tell if she was trying to shock them, or it was true."

"You said she doesn't know who her father is, that it could have been anybody."

"That's what I thought. She went looking for him down South and came back with nothing. Maybe she finally put two and two together, that her mother was too ashamed to admit she didn't know who her father was, and it was obvious he was light-skinned because she is."

Althea's eyes filled. "It must be awful not knowing who your father is." Her parents had divorced, messily, and both her parents had remarried, outside of the church. Unable to reconcile with either of them, she lived with her grandmother, a bastion of Old World conservatism. "You should talk to her about it. She probably needs to talk about it."

But Camille wasn't like Althea. She didn't talk everything out; she was private, she had secrets, and this was beyond Althea's understanding. "I don't want to talk to her about it now. She's so happy about the baby, so why bring it up? I just hope she isn't mad at me."

Althea cracked open her fortune cookie and a thin slip of paper slipped onto the table. "Four, seven, sixteen, eighteen," she read, and then flipped it over. "Your beauty is rivaled only by your goodness."

"That fortune has your name on it, Althea." Joyce broke her cookie open and popped half of it into her mouth, tasting vanilla. "Ten, seventeen, twenty-five, forty-two. My age is in there, anyway. 'All is not as it seems.' Well, that's creepy."

"Don't play those numbers," Althea said somberly.

Joyce laughed and ate the rest of the cookie. "Maybe I should. Maybe things are really better than they seem."

CHAPTER SEVENTEEN

I sat on a cove at Beavertail Point on a bright au-
tumn day and watched the sea trying to reclaim the
land. The waves work on the rocks, sliding in, pulling
out, chipping away at them a sliver of granite at a
time. The ocean roars, the tide comes in; for a stopped
heartbeat, the water is suspended, gurgling like blood
around the edges. Then the process starts anew, in
and out, as it has for all time. The key to erosion is
not only its infinitesimal pace but its relentlessness.

There are other forces, working with the patience
of water, that are trying to take our land. They must
be stopped at any cost.
– A Country Woman's Diary, Oct. 10, 1985

oretta had invited Helen on a birding trip. It was one
of the van tours that she guided every fall to catch the
fall migrants stopping by the shore on their way south –
not just the Canada geese that mark their familiar V overhead,
but ducks like the lesser scaup and canvasback, hawks that skip
along the shoreline, like the sharp-shinned and Cooper's, and
the magnificent osprey finally leaving their large, untidy nests
atop light poles. This trip was to Jamestown, an island between
Narragansett and Newport, but Loretta had a whole series of
excursions planned this fall up and down the coast.

Helen was not crazy about going, because she thought the
people Loretta attracted to these trips were a little odd. Their
knowledge of birds was fanatical, and the equipment they carried – spotting scopes with tripods – seemed this side of un-

necessary. Even Loretta, who had made a career out of watching birds, only brought binoculars, because she did not want to be bothered carrying anything else. They also seemed to have nothing else to talk about but birds – it was as though the whole palette of nature, from bottle-green dragonflies to wispy milkweed seeds, was eclipsed from view, and the only thing they could see was a tiny gadwall about 100 yards away.

But Loretta genuinely seemed to want Helen along, and so she packed a small bag lunch, found her binoculars and Peterson's and drove to the commuter lot where the van was picking everyone up. It was a glorious autumn day: the sky as blue as an old medicine bottle, the air sharp and frosty, the trees in the full explosion of their color. She breathed in and shed some of her nerves: It was good to be alive. She was proud of herself – this was a trip she would not have taken six months ago; even the drive down Route 1 was an adventure that was unprecedented.

Loretta left the driving to a young man she had hired from the university, and Helen was relieved when she sat with her in the first row of seats. Loretta was fanning herself with the itinerary as she plopped down next to her. She had her hair covered with a blue bandanna, and her brow was dotted with sweat.

"I can't imagine what makes me so hot, I'm too old to be sweating this way. I'm glad everyone was on time." She looked over at Helen as though just seeing her there. "I believe this is the first time you've joined us! You're in for a treat today. Last year this was one of our best trips."

Helen murmured something to be polite, and then looked out the window at the next lane of traffic. She tried not to think of the things she could be doing on this glorious Saturday, from raking leaves to putting the perennials to bed. "I'm not as much of a birdwatcher as these people," she admitted.

"I wanted to get you out of the house. Ludlow tells me you're back to work."

"Two days a week. He's pushing for three."

"Let 'im push. He's lucky to have you for two. He's so busy I hardly ever see him anymore. He's moved out to that condo, and he's got some development he's talking about building. The Beach Road."

The van turned a corner, and Helen felt her stomach lurch. "That's Mr. Lillibridge's land. I wish he didn't have to sell. It's an awful shame, Loretta. Those have been potato fields for 50 years. It's a beautiful vista, almost down to the water. It's not going to be so pretty to look at when he gets done with it."

Loretta sighed and wiped her brow with a Kleenex. "It's his money. I can't tell him anything." She shifted in her seat, the vinyl making a wet, smacking noise. "You know how it is. Look at Dale. I saw him at the fish market the other day, flirting with some young thing behind the counter." She lowered her voice. "He looked awful."

Helen sneaked a glance behind her, where an older couple sat reading. "He's drinking all the time," she said, lowering her voice. "I'm afraid he's lost the boat. I think he might be into drugs. Joyce knows, but I can't get her to tell me a thing."

Helen had tried to confront Dale but talking to him was like riding a tractor around a field, endlessly circling. And Joyce had said: "You're the one who gave him that money. I could have told you the boat was a bad idea."

"That surprises me," Loretta said. "Not the part about Dale, unfortunately. But Joyce doesn't strike me as the type to look the other way if her brother's in trouble."

"Well, she's almost as bad as he is! She never comes to visit me, she hardly talks to me when she does, she's living with this boyfriend of hers – " With effort Helen stopped. Loretta didn't need to know any of this.

"Helen, maybe it's time you talked to Joyce."

"Don't be silly. I talk to her all the time."

"To her? Or at her?" Loretta squeezed her hand. "I don't mean that the way it sounds. But if you want a better relationship with your daughter, you're going to have to put some effort into it."

They were coming over the rickety Jamestown Bridge, and the van's tires were weaving and humming as they passed over the grate at the top. Helen gripped the back of the driver's seat. She had always hated this bridge. It seemed like at any moment it would collapse, sending them flying into the water. She closed her eyes to the deep blue of the bay and the sailboats that were cutting through the waves, and said a silent prayer.

After more than an hour trooping through a salt marsh and then a stop at Mackerel Cove, they drove to Beavertail to have lunch. The point was so named because it fanned out like a beaver's tail, dividing the west and east passages of Narragansett Bay. At the promontory stood a granite lighthouse attached to a white keeper's station. Leading up to it was a narrow road that snaked through parking areas and grassy overlooks. They stopped at a parking lot close to the lighthouse and spread out on the grass to eat.

Helen used one of the port-a-potties that lined the field, and, while Loretta was distracted answering a question about the afternoon's last stop, made a beeline for one of the many paths leading to the rocks. Large and jagged, these pieces of granite had been left behind by a glacier to take the brunt of wind and waves pounding up the bay. Helen carefully stepped down the narrow path, overgrown with rose hips and purple clover and stunted Queen Anne's lace, wondering why she had left her cane at home. Pride, mostly, and a growing conviction that she didn't need it. If she fell onto the rocks, she would surely break a leg; if she fell into the water, she would drown, her body pummeled by the rocks. In any case, it would be precious minutes, maybe even hours before they discovered where she had wandered off to. She tried not to think about it. Better to keep moving, slowly and carefully, to the triangle-shaped rock below her. She gained it at last and sat, exhausted not from the physical effort, but the mental strain. So much of life was the mental strain, she thought.

Narragansett on the other side of the bay did not look so far away. The water seemed to have a skin, like pudding, and she felt as though she could step on it and walk all the way across. The view was tempting in this way, and the sound of the waves' ceaseless murmur was hypnotizing. If she could be lulled into these fantasies, what about a three-year-old girl, standing at a pond's edge, setting one foot out, tentatively, as though to see if the water would bear weight? At what age did we learn that we could not walk on water, that to do so would be a miracle, and that the time for miracles had passed?

Her sigh was drowned by the bay's roar. She clasped her arms around her knees and rocked, slowly, stretching her back like a cat. She could bring Joyce to the water's edge, try to explain after all these years, but forgiveness was never guaranteed. She could say: *A moment's inattention. That was all it took, and my little girl, so precious to me, was gone.* But there would be questions, Joyce was always full of questions. She would have to come up with answers. She would have to put Susan into words, define her, describe her, and that would be the ultimate end: She would have to grieve all over again.

She didn't owe Joyce anything, did she? It seemed inconceivable she could owe anyone anything. She had already paid the ultimate price.

Perhaps it was watching the waves eating away at the rocks on Beavertail, and feeling the chips of granite crumble in her hands, like rotten teeth. Maybe it was going back to work and listening to Ludlow on the phone, hour after hour, with brokers and builders and zoning lawyers, cursing, cajoling, bellowing. Maybe it was just that something in her had shifted, that day when she fell, and now she walked straighter and faster. Or maybe it was just the way autumn worked on her soul, sending shafts of light through yellow leaves and illuminating every landscape that was dear to her eyes.

Whatever it was, Helen sat at her Royal manual typewriter the following Sunday and typed her column out in lines of black pica fury. The carbon smeared, she was typing so fast and pressing so hard on the keys. The paper moved and the last line drifted uphill. She didn't care. She was weary of Ludlow and his blueprints and his leather Italian loafers and the university class ring he twirled on his pinkie when he talked. She was weary of little yellow surveyor's flags and for-sale signs and percolation pipes diving out of the ground like submarine periscopes. She was weary of reading the newspaper, with its endless 48-point headlines, with words like "plan" and "mull" and "zoners." She was weary, finally, of typing up deeds and mortgages like a well-trained Marionette, as though she were a party to it all, and in a way of course she was, because she was earning her living off the developers and real estate agents and newcomers.

The fire left her as soon as she folded the column into thirds and placed it into a blank business-sized envelope and dropped it off at the newspaper office, which she ducked into shyly as always, leaving her submission in the wire tray on the front counter and barely nodding to the receptionist, Emily, whom she'd known for 20 years now.

She drove home, kicked off her shoes and opened a can of chicken vegetable soup, too tired to tidy up her desk and cover up the typewriter.

Helen had decided that she must do something about Fran Kennedy.

It had been almost two months since Fran had come into her house, in a damp swimsuit, to confess her husband's infidelity, only to have Helen drive her off with a tirade about watching her children. Helen still had not sorted out that afternoon and her snippy response. All she knew was that she had expected Fran, after a brief period of hurt feelings, to resume her visits to the Winter kitchen. This did not happen. She had not seen Fran to speak to her since, and whenever the Jeep Cherokee flew down the driveway, Fran kept her eyes on the road and did not return Helen's wave. She knew Fran was home, she had seen her in the distance puttering in her backyard, but she was unsure of her status with Peter. He had bought himself a new car, a black BMW, but it had not been in the drive for some weeks. That could be a sales trip or the symptom of something more dire. Whatever it was, Helen found herself curious, and worried, about how Fran was making out. At first she did not understand these feelings and brushed them aside. Eventually she realized that she was, indeed, sorry for hurting Fran, and the sentiments stirring in her were of compassion and friendship. Fran Kennedy had been annoying and persistent and even a little odd; but Fran Kennedy, for all her faults, had been her friend.

Now she had to figure out what to do about this predicament. She had ignored the situation, hoping her feelings about it would disappear, but whenever she walked outdoors or worked in the garden, the towering house on the coast stood in the distance, never far from her field of vision. This was what she hated about these casual friendships: once they took root, they grew like weeds, and you had to learn to live with them, appreciate their reckless beauty, or resolve yourself to endless and fruitless attempts at eradication. Now, with Fran, it was too late. Even if Fran Kennedy sold the house and moved tomorrow, she had burrowed so far into Helen's life she wouldn't be able to forget her. She would always be wondering: What happened to that

Kennedy woman? Did she ever get rid of that cad of a husband?

Whom does she talk to, now that she's home alone and not stopping by here every day for a cup of tea?

She thought about walking over there, but it didn't seem like enough. You didn't just pop in on a neighbor and say, "Gee, I'm sorry I gave you the business, but I didn't mean it, you know." Maybe if she brought something with her. Something Fran really wanted – something she had always admired. She walked around the kitchen, her eyes darting from teacups to yellowware bowls to the cast-iron spider on the back of the stove. There must be something here that would do the trick.

Her column came out in the paper on Thursday, and the reaction was immediate.

Loretta called to congratulate her. She had finally written something worth reading, she said, meaning it as a compliment.

The pastor of the Baptist church, always looking for a excuse to lure her back into the fold, said he admired her courage.

Ludlow, his voice booming in the receiver, told her not to damn well bother coming to work next week, or ever, and Didn't she know what side her bread was buttered on? And didn't she believe in economic development? What was she, some kind of communist?

An anonymous caller, a woman with a sarcastic, flat voice, said there was no room in this town for people who were anti-progress and (she took a breath, like the drag of a cigarette, before issuing the final blow:) really, she should learn not to split her infinitives.

Shortly after that Mason Dudley, the editor of the paper, asked her to come into the office, please, as soon as possible. Friday morning would be good.

Helen had never been summoned to the newspaper office before but, then, she had never been fired before, either, or received crank phone calls, or felt everyone's eyes upon her when she walked into the post office. She was used to scurrying along like a crab at ebb tide, looking for the next moist, cozy rock to shelter under. On any other day, at any other time, a request from Mr. Dudley to come to his office – that inner sanctum littered with piles of newspapers, mail and unread reports on everything from sea level rise to bridge improvement projects

– would be a much-anticipated event. She had not been inside that office, although she had glimpsed it from the open door, in years. Any other time, the idea that Mr. Dudley might be upset with her would make such a summons even more urgent. But Helen had come to a decision before Mr. Dudley or any of the other column readers had begun calling her. On Friday she was going to visit Fran Kennedy.

"It will have to be in the afternoon," she told Mr. Dudley, more firmly than she intended. "I have an appointment before lunch."

He mumbled something about lunch, and Helen had the panicked thought that he might have misinterpreted her to be holding out for a free meal. "Later on," she said, talking more loudly than she had intended. "Two or later. Please."

So the appointment, although it would interfere with Mr. Dudley's Friday afternoon golf game, was scheduled.

She could not go to Fran Kennedy's empty handed, so she baked a loaf of zucchini bread and found a book that Fran had eyed once, months before. When she knocked on the breezeway door of the palatial house, she shifted her tribute from one hand to another, waiting for Fran to appear. For a moment she imagined her inside, refusing to answer the door or acknowledge her presence, but then Fran came bounding up from the basement, out of breath, and startled to see Helen standing there.

Fran took the proffered gifts and led Helen into a long, wide living room that ran nearly the length of the house. A wall of windows let in the ocean, which was so close it felt like they were on a boat. They sat, on the edge of facing blue-willow-print sofas, separated by a square coffee table that was bigger than Helen's dinette set.

"Gift from the Sea." Fran started thumbing through it, avoiding Helen's gaze. "'Purposeful giving is not as apt to deplete one's resources,'" she read aloud, opening to a random page. Helen looked down at her sneakers; they were damp from the grass.

"I thought you might like it," she said finally, trying to think of more to say. Wasn't the gift enough? Did she have to say it aloud? "I remember you admiring it one day." It was a hardcover edition, a nice one actually, and she hated to give it up, but sacrifice seemed to be called for.

"Yes. Well." Fran's eyes, when she finally looked up, were hard. "I'll take good care of it. Keep it away from the children." Did she imagine the emphasis on that last word?

A pain was spreading at Helen's right temple, over and under her eye. The headaches had started since her fall. They felt like someone was squeezing her jaw bone with a pair of pliers. She put her hand to her face, as though covering it would stop the jabbing, and willed herself to stop clenching her back molars. "The moon shell," she said. "That's the chapter on the moon shell. I think you will – what's the expression? – identify with it."

"I am not a solitary shell, if that's what you mean. Peter is away in New Jersey, closing a deal on some property we sold there, but he'll be back this weekend."

"Fran, for God's sake, I'm sorry." There; she'd said it; and if it had come out mean and begrudging, at least it had come out: an apology. "I know I said some nasty things to you. I don't know what came over me. I'm sorry. Truly. Sorry."

Fran stood up and smiled, stretching her arms to the ceiling like a child about to do a cartwheel. "Helen! Oh, Helen, I've missed you!" And she enveloped her in a hug that did not feel anywhere near as uncomfortable as she expected.

She had not planned it (had she?) but she told Fran about the column, the reactions of surprise and outrage, and her appointment that afternoon with Mr. Dudley. Fran listened thoughtfully, and then she said something that Helen had not expected, especially given that Frances Kennedy, owner of the biggest monstrosity on the South Shore, could be forgiven for taking a little umbrage at Helen's literary outburst. "I hope you're not going to tone down your column just because it makes some people uncomfortable."

That, of course, was just what she was planning to do; in fact, she had hoped to forestall any scolding by Mr. Dudley by promising to never, ever write about anything more than dahlias and dragonflies again. But the more she thought about it, the more she realized Fran was right. The column she had written Sunday had been no aberration. She had been writing it, albeit in code, for the past 20 years. She'd just finally found the courage to say what she meant. This was no time to turn back.

Mr. Dudley, returning from the Rotary Club luncheon, kept her waiting for 10 minutes. Helen had dressed in her finest warm weather suit: It was the color of jonquils and cut sharply, with a cigarette skirt that cleared her knees, and it was only ten years old. In his usual vague way, Mr. Dudley swept some papers away and offered her a seat.

"Helen, this column." He leaned back in his chair, put his hands behind his head, but then the phone rang and he snatched it up, seemingly relieved. What ensued was a long conversation about a police beat item that may or may not have contained a mistake. Helen looked around the office, which suffered for want of tidying. An editorial award hung, askew, behind Mr. Dudley's head. On his bookshelf sat two copies of the United Press International stylebook, a dictionary, a world almanac, and a book of quotations, along with a crumpled paper lunch bag and a tiny brass lion, from the Lions Club.

"I've had a lot of complaints," he said, hanging up the phone, "that I didn't anticipate. The truth is I didn't read your column until it was in print; Gracie just sends them directly to typesetting."

All those years, she had imagined him opening the envelope each week, and carefully going over each line, occasionally making a blue mark with his non-repro pen.

"What I'm saying is, you can't sneak stuff like that into your column. That's not what it's all about. It's a nature thing, for God's sake. People want to know about the goldenrod and the geese, they don't want to be preached at."

"There won't be any more goldenrod and geese if things keep going the way they are."

His face reddened. "Oh, wave your banner! I'm telling you I don't want any more of this political crap in your column. I've got the whole Rotary Club on my back about it. The real estate people are going nuts! Do you know how much they spend with me every year? If this paper's going to take a stand on development, I'll be the one to do it in an editorial, I won't be giving the job to my nature writer. Understood?"

"No." Helen could not remember the last time she had used that word, but it sent a jazzy tingle all the way to her toes. "No,

I don't understand. I don't understand why the editor of our newspaper is worried about what the Rotary Club – a bunch of businessmen – thinks about saving, or ruining, our town. I don't understand how a few real estate agents can buy off an independent publication such as yours. I think you've got your priorities backwards."

She stood up, and rushed on before he could speak. "Mr. Dudley, you've lived here all your life. I'm a transplant. I'm not the one who should be leading this rally. It should be you. But if you don't care to, then I don't care to write for you anymore, either."

She walked out of his office and wound her way through the warren of cubbyholes and desks, the eyes of everyone in the newsroom upon her. She had kept her composure, had said exactly what she wanted to say, but when she climbed into the car and fumbled the key into the ignition, she exploded into tears.

CHAPTER EIGHTEEN

▲

Forks scraped against plates, ceiling fans thumped and a wooden screen door slammed, and slammed again. It was the dinner hour at Snuffy's restaurant in Watch Hill, a casual diner-type establishment run by a genial Italian man who called nearly all his customers by their first names. Joyce pressed her backbone against the wooden booth and waited for Camille. It seemed she was always waiting for Camille, and since the birth of her daughter, Skye, Camille had become even more time-challenged. Joyce fingered the heavy plastic protecting her menu. There was no need to look; she would get the usual, an eggplant parmesan grinder, and Camille would order a big plate of spaghetti and meatballs. They had been coming here for several years, since Althea had introduced them to the down-home restaurant where Watch Hill millionaires mixed with the seaside resort's working class. A shame Althea couldn't be here tonight, but she had a date, her third with the same man, and it was finally starting to look serious.

"Oh God, I'm sorry." Camille plopped down in the booth, out of breath, wedging Skye's baby carrier into the seat beside her. She was wearing gray sweatpants and a T-shirt and Joyce thought, but was not sure, she saw a tiny dot of spit-up on her left shoulder. Skye, fat-cheeked at four months, was wearing pink, as usual: a jumpsuit with an orange giraffe on pink terrycloth. She was bubbling at the mouth.

"I had to stop and feed her." She turned to the waitress. "Iced tea, please, no sugar. Then, of course, her diaper needed changing. Everything I do these days is absurdly temporary."

Joyce smiled and dangled Skye's plastic keys in front of her grasping hands. Camille's complaints were not really complaints, they were more explanations, even celebrations. The baby had softened Camille so that her new voice, that light confection Joyce found so hard to get used to, seemed finally to fit her personality.

Although the place was nearly full, their food came quickly, and Skye, her appetite satisfied, amused herself by watching the fans twirling above. But it was as though Camille, finally able to turn her attention to Joyce, remembered she was not happy at all.

"Eric's driving me crazy with this tribe business," she said, tucking into her spaghetti. He was advising the tribe on several land disputes, in which Indian bones had been found on property that was about to be developed. Camille, however, had no interest in the subject, preferring her husband go out and make some money. "All these night meetings. He's at the Town Council every other thing. It's all he talks about. He gets all offended when I tell him I don't care."

"Why don't you?" She knew she shouldn't say it. Getting along with Camille often was an exercise in restraint.

"Why don't I? It's just stupid. There are Indian bones everywhere. They're probably under your house. They're probably under my house."

Maybe Camille was right, but there was something about Eric Robinson's attempt to preserve the native culture that struck a chord in Joyce. It was one thing when those bones were left alone. It was quite another when they turned up in some developer's backhoe.

"We used to find arrowheads in the fields, every spring when my father plowed," Joyce said, staring past Camille, her head foggy with the image of it. "When I was a kid I would try to imagine what it was like before the white man came, before our house was built and the fields were plowed."

Camille abruptly changed the subject. "My mother's been asking for you. She wants you to come see her."

"How is she?"

"Better. Not great, but better. She's still living alone, still driving. She loves Skye. She's been watching her so I can work a couple of shifts during the week. But she insists that once the baby starts walking, she won't be able to take care of her."

"The polio?" Marian's arthritis was in remission, thanks to cortisone shots.

"Yeah. She wouldn't be able to catch her if she started running toward the road. It's too bad because it does Mom so much good to watch her."

Marian had such a good heart, Joyce reflected. Her own mother had told her more than once not to expect free babysitting services if she and Michael decided to start a family. Typical, Joyce thought, of her to volunteer such a negative comment before she even had been asked.

"I'll go see her soon. I'll bring some of her favorite candy."

Camille laughed. "Peppermint Patties. Good thing she doesn't have diabetes." She wiped Skye's mouth with a napkin. "So. Wedding plans."

"Coming along. Invitations, flowers, cake ordered." She felt a stiffness between them. Camille was still irritated she didn't take her side in the dispute with Eric. Why did Camille always expect her to agree on everything? It didn't help that Joyce had asked Althea to be her maid of honor and Camille to be her bridesmaid, although she felt the decision was right. Still, she hated the defensive way it made her feel. She told Camille she had enough responsibilities with the new baby, but that wasn't the reason. The truth was, deep down, she still had not let go of the hurt of Camille's rejection eight years ago.

"How's your mother taking it?"

Another sore spot. "Same as before. She doesn't understand why we won't get married in the church; thinks it's barbaric to have a wedding on the beach; and wants to make sure none of the wedding guests will be going anywhere near the house."

Camille shook her head. "Now you know why Eric and I eloped."

"At least you had an excuse, being out of state. We have no such luck. It doesn't help that she has nothing else to focus on. She's not even writing for the paper anymore since that disastrous column. She sits in the house all day and broods."

"Maybe she'll come around." Dessert arrived and Camille spooned up her ice cream. "Hey, her only daughter's getting married. When she wakes up to that fact, she'll be showing up at your fittings and inviting relatives you've never heard of."

Joyce smiled. Somehow she doubted it.

She had a million things to do before July 22, 1986 – invitations to mail and favors to order (candy shaped like seashells), people to meet with (photographer, band leader, cake decorator), tables and chairs to rent – but in late June she found time to visit Marian Evans.

Camille's mother was invited to the wedding, and Joyce decided that the invitation provided her the perfect excuse to drop by. They had arrived just the week before: on the outer card was a painting, "On the Beach" by Winslow Homer, and the lettering inside was decidedly old-fashioned – she'd had the font copied from a 19th-century hotel menu in one of Aunt Loretta's scrapbooks.

"Beautiful," Marian pronounced it, reaching over to grasp Joyce's hand. "But I can't see as how I could go. Camille's going to need me to watch Skye."

"The baby will be there, too. And you don't have to worry about getting around. We're giving people rides back and forth to the beach. After the ceremony, you can sit under the trees in the orchard."

Marian got up from the table and limped over to the sink. She dragged her right leg behind her, as though it were made of wood. Marian had been frail as long as Joyce had known her, but there was something about her whole being that seemed older. It was hard to pin down what it was: She was still a striking woman, even though her hair was gray, and her face was unlined despite years of poverty and illness. No, it was something else in her manner, almost as though she had grown older simply by becoming a grandmother.

The shack in which she lived was still a shack, but Camille and her sons had paid to have it made livable: the kerosene stove was gone, and in its place electric baseboard heating; the cracked plaster walls were covered with knotty pine plywood; and fresh linoleum had been laid over the rotting wood floors. Now that Hamilton was gone, Marian also had finally been able to put her stamp on the ugly little cottage, setting African violets on the windowsills and hanging fresh white curtains on the windows. Something about the house had not changed, however; it still carried a smell, however faint, of smoking bacon grease and damp wool blankets.

Marian returned to the table with a Bible, opened it to a bookmarked page and took out a yellow maple leaf. "This came from your place a long time ago. I thought you might like to have it."

Joyce thanked her and set the desiccated leaf carefully on the table. She was afraid to touch its edges, they were so brittle.

"How is your mom?"

Joyce told her about how Helen had lost both jobs and had been crankily inconsolable ever since. "She needs to get out again. Working was good for her. But she's too proud to ask for either her column or her job with Ludlow back, so instead of doing anything about it she moons around the house all day. She keeps calling me up fretting about the most insignificant things, like getting her chimney cleaned in the middle of summer."

Marian frowned. "That's odd. She's probably lonely. Thank God I have little Skye, she makes life worth living. She sits in my lap all day, just as sunny as can be. But I keep telling Camille, pretty soon she'll be walking and I don't know what I'll do then. I could never catch her."

"There are ways, Mrs. Evans. Baby gates, fences."

"Gates can open when they aren't supposed to. I don't think that little tyke is going to know the meaning of 'baby proof.' She's got that devilish look in her eye. Just like her mother – she wore me ragged. Once she slipped out the back door, and I like to died looking for her. But she was sitting on that big old rock on the hill, piling up acorns like she was grocery shopping." Marian Evans laughed, revealing straight but yellowed teeth. "So I know what I'm in for."

Joyce wondered if her mother would ever embrace grandparenthood as eagerly as Mrs. Evans. She tried to imagine Helen Winter jostling a baby in her lap or giving it a bottle. She couldn't. How on Earth had her mother taken care of her own children? But Helen had had a helpful husband, which Marian had not. She had latched on to Hamilton Evans to raise Camille, and it had been the worst mistake of her life.

"Tell Camille that story," Marian was saying. "She just hates to be reminded what a gadabout she was."

Joyce, pulling the Peppermint Patties out of her bag, wanted to ask Mrs. Evans about Camille's father. Who was he? What had happened to him? Had she, or had she not, told Camille the truth about the man? But Marian was talking about some amusing episode in her daughter's childhood and there seemed no polite way to pry into family secrets.

"I'll try to make your wedding," Marian said as she was leaving. "I'll just have to see how I feel."

Every few months, when Michael was away, she made it a point to visit Lydia Franklin, the old woman who lived in the stone-ender in Richmond. The first time she'd come back with the Historical Preservation report, an excuse to see the old woman again, but after that they were friends, and now Lydia seemed to count on her visits. Joyce wasn't sure why she was drawn to the feisty woman living alone with her kerosene lamps and wood stove, but something settled in her as soon as she entered the tiny, neatly swept house. She had tried to explain it to Michael once, but he was skeptical. "She sounds like some crazy old lady to me," was all he said. After that she'd stopped talking to him about Lydia. In fact, no one knew about their friendship, not even Althea and Camille. It was as though Lydia belonged to a part of herself too deep, too secret to share with anyone else.

Sometimes Lydia told her stories about the past – about walking to school with nothing but a cold potato in her lunch box, about her mother, who fed them boiled dandelion greens when there was nothing else to eat, about her brothers, who went into the woods to work before they were 10 years old.

"Now there's only me that's left," she would say, rocking in her chair. "When I'm gone, my stories will die with me."

Aunt Loretta had planned a bridal shower for Joyce later in the month, at her house in Matunuck. "But I told her you didn't need one, since you already seem to have set up housekeeping," Helen told Joyce one night on the phone. "I couldn't imagine anything you might need."

Joyce, furious yet speechless, made up an excuse to get off the phone.

Michael was not around for most of the wedding preparations, which was just as well. He had his assignment – booking the honeymoon – and Joyce would just as soon plan the wedding details herself. He had concentrated his traveling in the late spring and early summer so he could take the rest of the semester break off for their honeymoon. He had picked the destination – South America – and the itinerary. Joyce, bothered only by the prospect of malaria shots, found his choice enchanting, and he had woven picturesque stories about the cities they would visit, from La Paz to Buenos Aries.

"Remember when you wanted to go to South America, back in high school?" she asked Camille.

But Camille claimed not to remember. New Orleans was far enough south for her, she said.

As her wedding day approached, Joyce felt an immense relief, as though she were finally crossing into adulthood. College, moving out of her mother's house, none of these passages seemed as final or as affirming as declaring a lifelong commitment. The act of changing her name suddenly took on a powerful importance. No longer would she be a Winter. She would be, from now on, Joyce Avery. It was like escaping the grasp of something she had been fleeing all her life. She thought of it in this way: *Once I am Joyce Avery, then . . . I can make my own decisions and no one will question them. I can move, anonymously, through bank transactions and credit card purchases and voting lines without anyone saying again, "You're a Winter, are you? Aren't you Jim's daughter?" Or worse, when people said: "Isn't your mother the one that wrote that column for the newspaper?" No, she could lie. She was an Avery. Her husband was a university professor. A nationally known researcher. She was a school teacher. No, she did not live on the old Winter place, she was not sister to that drunk fisherman Dale Winter, her father did not commit suicide, her mother was not the laughingstock of the community. She was simply Joyce Avery.*

But first, there was the big day to be gotten through, and so many things could go wrong.

Things were still a little off-kilter between her and Camille, and between Camille and Althea, but she knew she could count on her friends to behave themselves. After all, what was more important than a woman's wedding day? Even if Camille had eloped she recognized this truth, and although Althea was not even close to being engaged she carried a pure moral vision of marriage in her head and would never do anything to violate it.

She was not so secure, however, about the other side of the wedding aisle. (Not an aisle, really, but a sheet of white to be unrolled on the sand.) Michael's best man was Clark, who was as reliable as rain, but the groomsman – the man who would be escorting Camille down the makeshift train unfurled on the beach and helping to seat their guests in rented folding chairs – was Dale, and she could only pray that he would show up on time and sober. If he got drunk during the reception, so be it. They just had to get him through the ceremony.

Her mother was the other wild card. Besides foiling Joyce's shower, she had threatened several times not to attend the ceremony at all for reasons Joyce couldn't understand. What was the matter with her mother? She had wanted veto power over the guest list, for example, and when Joyce refused to share the list with her, she had suggested that maybe Joyce should rent a hall instead of using her mother's property. She had asked, repeatedly, what the plans were in case of rain, and was the tent they were renting really big enough for everybody on that invitation list – which, although she had not seen it, she knew to be long? On other occasions her excuse for not attending was that she had nothing to wear and, since the taxes on the property were due a few weeks after the wedding, she was too poor to buy anything. When Joyce – who was paying for the wedding herself – offered to buy her mother's dress, Helen grew peevish and said it didn't matter how much money she had, she would never be able to find a dress that would flatter her middle-aged figure. Finally Joyce, thinking her mother was really just being shy, suggested Mr. Lillibridge could be Helen's escort. This sent Helen into a rage; she said Mr. Lillibridge was coming as her friend, not her date, and she would thank Joyce to mind her own business.

Joyce was counting on Aunt Loretta to keep her mother in line. She knew Helen, for all her flustering, would never say anything out of the way in public; she was too reserved, and she cared too much about appearances. Loretta could probably help her pick out a dress and coax her out on the day of the ceremony.

"I don't understand what's the matter with her," Joyce said, stopping by Loretta's one afternoon. Loretta was doing the flowers, to be hand-picked from her garden and Helen's, and they were going over the arrangements. "She seems determined to ruin this day for me. You would think she would be *happy*. And she even likes Michael, I know she does."

Loretta, who had been jotting down notes about the table displays, stopped with pen in mid-air. "I think this is a difficult time for your mother. Don't be so hard on her."

"Difficult for her? What about me? She's making my life a living hell."

Loretta appeared not to be listening. "When a woman goes to a wedding, she thinks back to her own – if she's had one," she added pointedly. "I'm sure what to you is the happiest moment of your life is bringing up a lot of memories for Helen. She was married on the farm, too, you know. She was about your age."

"Oh . . ."

"And Mother gave her a terrible time."

That hardly seemed fair. That should make her mother, if anything, want to be more accommodating, not less. What was she so angry about? "I wish you'd talk to her. Every time I talk to her, we get in a fight."

Loretta resumed writing her list – cosmos, starflower, zinnias. "If you two would start talking to each other, it would save me a lot of aggravation."

The crisis with Dale, it turned out, happened not during the wedding but two weeks before, in the wee hours of a Sunday. Joyce was wakened at 2:45 a.m. by a phone that had been ringing for some time to hear a bleary, only vaguely familiar voice in the receiver. Dale was making his one phone call, from the cell block of a police station in Newport. He had been arrested not only for DWI but also damaging property, after he struck a stone wall and drove over the well manicured lawns of three estates off Bellevue Avenue in the city's oldest, most prosperous section.

Michael was in Washington, D.C., at a conference sponsored by the National Oceanic and Atmospheric Administration, so Joyce drove alone over the foggy Jamestown and Newport bridges, bailed out her brother and drove him home to Point Judith, where with some difficulty she dragged Dale up the stairs to his condominium and pushed him onto the unmade bed.

He was conscious, actually, muttering and raving things she didn't understand, occasionally yelling at her (he thought she was a police officer, evidently), until she smacked her hand, hard, against the left side of his face. It occurred to Joyce that not only did he not know who she was or where he was, he had no idea what he'd done. The idea that only a few hours before – when he was probably more intoxicated – he had been behind the wheel of his Ford pickup was frightening indeed. What if he had made it onto the Newport Bridge in that state? Driving onto the lawns of some of Newport's finer Victorian mansions was probably the best thing that could have happened to him, considering.

"Next time, what if you hit a person?" she yelled, caught in the futility of trying to have an intelligent conversation with a drunk. "What if you kill somebody? What if you kill yourself?"

"Sister, I was sure trying," he said, and then passed out.

Their mother didn't need to know. If she was in a state now over the wedding – and Joyce reflected that Aunt Loretta was probably right, all the plans were probably bringing up memories of her father that were better left undredged – finding out about Dale's arrest would send her over the edge. So Joyce did what she did best: She fixed things. She took Dale to his court hearing, two days before the wedding, convinced the judge that he could be trusted not to drive or drink (he was supposed to go to a detox center, but the judge agreed to postpone his committal until after the wedding), helped him buy a suit and get a haircut, persuaded Michael to let him move in so she could watch him for the next two days ("I guess we really will have to wait until our wedding night," he groused), and barely had time to pack for her honeymoon.

Dale padded around the house in his stocking feet, chain smoking Kools and drinking cup after cup of coffee. (She finally put her wedding dress in the back of Michael's car to keep it away from the cigarette smoke.) He looked gaunt and pale; his hair had started falling out in tufts, as though he suffered from arsenic poisoning. His left hand shook when he struck a match. He had lost so much weight that he continually was hiking up the waistline of his Levi's as he paced around the living room.

"When did you say he was going to Edgehill?" Michael asked

her one night in bed.

"The Monday after the wedding."

"And who's going to watch him until then? As a matter of fact, who's watching him right now?"

"I locked up the liquor cabinet. I hid the car keys. Unless he wants to walk 10 miles to the package store, he's out of luck."

"Your brother's an alcoholic. He'd walk 100 miles if he thought there was a drink at the end of the road." Michael, who looked down at Dale because he drank only beer, did not consider his Scotch habit any cause for worry.

Joyce, exhausted, found herself wishing it were all over with – Dale's detox, her wedding, the honeymoon. When would life get back to normal?

CHAPTER NINETEEN

Brown recluse spider in the basement. Saw her be-
fore she saw me, or I wouldn't be writing this now.
Have to stay out of there. Dark, with that swinging light
bulb that leaves the corners black; dirt floor, bugs,
mites, roaches; canning jars with putrid food still lin-
ing the sagging stairs. Martha's territory, what she al-
ways called the cellar. Keep the door closed. Stuff old
clothes under it. No need to go down there anyway.
– Journal of Helen Winter, Oct. 7, 1986

To live alone like this, to be the last one in a rambling, creaking, crooked-floor house, meant people had left you behind. Your husband – and not fighting it, but embracing gun powder and metal and velocity, leaving of his own will, deciding death was better than life with you – he was the first to go. And the children, who are supposed to leave the nest, gone, but dragging themselves back to see you as though it were an effort, a torture. Your baby girl, who left before she had really lived.

Someone had to be to blame for this. As Helen looked around, she found so many culprits; it seemed like everyone she knew, at one time or another, had had a hand in tearing her life apart. It was curious then that the overriding emotion she felt was not fury. It was guilt, at all that she had done and not done, and fear; that she would be found out, and that the past would return to haunt her once again.

Something had happened to Dale, right before the wedding. No one would tell her. It was clear, though, that he was on the wagon, and he seemed to be sticking to sobriety this time. Talking of AA meetings. Appearing at the house clean shaven, his clothes laundered if rumpled, but his eyes retaining a red, haunted look. Joyce was evasive. "The important thing, Mother, is that he's not drinking," was all she would say. Dale had lived with Joyce and Michael for a time, too, although Helen wasn't quite sure why, and he left as soon as they returned from their honeymoon. He didn't ask to move home, so she assumed he had a place, although he was vague on his address. As for the boat, she couldn't get many answers on that, either, only the sense that there had been more trouble and it was all lost, granted to the captain perhaps, a debt that had to be paid.

That Joyce. Always so ready to ask questions, but not one to answer them. Where had she learned that from? Well. Helen wondered if she really wanted to know, after all.

This was the truth: Joyce was not talking to *her*. Two weeks after she and Michael Avery got back from their honeymoon, and no phone call, no just-dropping-by, no little something brought back from an open air market (A silver bracelet? A shawl woven in the Andes? Helen had idly imagined these gifts, seen Joyce picking through the colorful street wares, thinking of her mother). When she finally did stop by, with packets of photos and that slinky, dark-eyed look of sex and indolence, Joyce brought her husband with her and he did most of the talking. All about their trip, Bolivia, Rio de Janeiro. Helen listened politely and poured more iced tea. Joyce played with the drapery cord and looked away.

Since then they had barely seen each other. Sometimes two to three weeks would pass before Joyce would stop by, and she always seemed to be on the way somewhere else. Meeting that Italian girl for an early dinner. Visiting Camille's new baby – a boy this time – *Forrest*. What a preposterous name. Helen had hoped over the years that the friendship with Camille would peter out, that Joyce would outgrow her, but she still seemed enthralled, talked about her all the time, Camille this, Camille that; Camille's collecting African art, Camille's husband represents the poor, they have this darling house! Her little Italian friend wasn't much better, but at least she treated Helen with deference. Silly girl, always asking Helen about her dreams, but earnest; and Joyce had had the good sense to reward her loyalty, asking her to be maid of honor. Camille, the bridesmaid in violet shantung silk, carried her pregnant belly like a beach ball underneath; she wore heels so she towered over the bride and she sashayed around as though her girth were only a balloon that could be popped. She gave a champagne toast and kicked off her shoes to dance barefoot to the loud, jarring music. She tossed her arm over Dale's shoulder, her plastic glass tipping within his peripheral vision. Camille's husband, Eric Robinson, stood stiffly to one side, his hands in the pockets of his rented pants. And there was Marian Evans, dressed like some Southern belle in layers of yellow ruffles, throwing her head back and laughing at something Ludlow Winter had said, then touching his sleeve, and laughing again, her voice carrying over the rock music like a warbler's pure note.

The mother of the bride watched from the doorway, then turned around, went inside the house and closed the door.

"You embarrassed me, Mother. You disappeared in the middle of the ceremony, you missed the toast, the dancing, everything." Joyce's voice on the phone, finally venting her anger. "I don't see why you couldn't act normal for one day out of my life, a day that meant so much to me."

Act normal. As though to be normal, she would have to put on an act. "I had a headache. All that loud music."

"You didn't have a headache. That's a lie. You don't get headaches. Isn't that what you always told Dad? Whenever he got one of his headaches, you would say you couldn't understand it, you'd never had a headache in your life."

"Maybe it was the champagne." She had not had any champagne, although she was sure Joyce didn't know that. And she was wrong about the headaches, but why get into it? "I think you're making too much of this. You had a beautiful wedding. Why ruin it, going over and over things that don't matter? You're just looking for something to be mad about."

"I'm not looking for something to be mad about! And if I were, I wouldn't have to look far!" Silence, and for a moment Helen thought her daughter had hung up, but then came a heavy sigh. "Everyone was asking for you. That poor Mr. Lillibridge, if he wasn't so shy he would have followed you into the house."

"Dub? He was asking for me?"

"Of course he was. You're practically the only person he knew, and we invited him because of you." Helen had a sudden picture of Dub Lillibridge sitting alone at a table, playing with his napkin. He had not called her since the wedding. "And Mrs. Evans. She hadn't seen you in years. She told me three times how much she had wanted to see you, and to make sure I sent her regards."

The reason she had retreated to the house in the first place. She could just hear Marian now, in that mellifluous voice, practically singing her name: "Tell Helen how much I regret we didn't see her." Frowning. Concerned. "I barely know the woman," she snapped. "I can't imagine she lost any sleep over it."

"That's not what she told me. She said how much she had always admired you, how much she missed your column. She was telling Camille that she thought you were very brave to write that last piece, and she thought the paper was wrong to fire you. She said no one would ever know you weren't a native, that you always stuck up for what was right."

"A lot she knows about what's right and wrong." A dumb thing to say; she had to cover it, and quickly. "I haven't got time to go over this, it's too silly. I'm sorry I disappeared during the reception. Now can't we just forget it?"

She needed to keep busy, but with no job to go to or column to write, it was becoming increasingly difficult to fill the days. Helen had never been much of a housekeeper. She had always been more interested in watching the orb weaver on the barn window or raking leaves or mulching the garden than in keeping the house neat and tidy. What housework she did had been the necessary sort, the laundry, the cooking, the bed-changing, and now that she was the only one home those chores took less and less time. Maybe, all these years she had spent on the farm she had been miscast; maybe she really should have been working. Certainly she had never realized how much that column had meant to her. She had assumed Mr. Dudley would break down eventually and ask her back. Mr. Dudley, who surely had been getting complaints from readers in her absence and whose paper, since her firing, was dominated by the dreary, gray tone of news flatly reported and examined. No more literary color in it, she thought, no sense of what mattered, only facts, gloomy facts, strung together in a haphazard order by reporters barely Joyce's age who had no idea what was really happening: they only knew dates, meetings, arrests, resolutions. But Mr. Dudley did not call, and when she saw Emily, the newspaper's front desk clerk, in the supermarket one afternoon, the woman avoided her eyes and pretended to be engrossed in a stack of canned tomatoes.

So when Ludlow Winter appeared at her door one dreary fall afternoon, she had to assume it was because he needed her in the office.

Helen had been making a meatloaf. Fixing dinner in the middle of the day was one way she coped. Cooking gave her a sense of purpose, even though it all seemed so fruitless – you cooked, you ate, you cleaned up, and you started all over again the next day, as though your labor had been for naught.

"Well, Helen." Slapping his knees, as though he were about to get started on a big project. "I'm concerned about you. I see you're still unemployed."

Helen had her back to him. She was chopping red pepper and onion into fine squares on the old wooden cutting board, which was so worn that pieces of wood pulp seemed to get into everything she cooked. "Yes, I'm afraid I am." This must be his lead-in, but she didn't want to seem too eager. Let him go through the excruciating process of asking.

"Things haven't slowed down since you left. The Beach Road development is selling like gangbusters . . . people can't get enough of those houses . . . inexpensive raised ranches, fenced yards, walk to the beach! The families love 'em! And the retirees – what an investment." He paused, as though he had lost track of what he was about to say. "It's not enough, though. We need more land. People need places to live. Families moving down here from the city, from Connecticut. This is the place they want to be."

"I don't see why you have to put a house up on every square inch of South County." Not the most politic thing to say, but she couldn't help it. How Ludlow could go on and on.

"We all know how you feel about development, Helen." He barked a laugh that was hollow and too loud. "Good God, that piece in the paper! Was I some pissed off! But after all it didn't accomplish anything, did it, but cause you a parcel of trouble."

The butter in the skillet was sizzling. Helen, her eyes smarting from the onion, scraped the chopped vegetables into the pan and rummaged through the refrigerator, hoping she had enough ketchup. "The office must be busy, especially with Holly pregnant," she hinted. Sylvia, the only agent she had been truly friendly with, had called her with that news.

"I hired a temp." He waved his hand dismissively. "Now, as I was saying. I could help you out of your situation. There's a piece of land I know you can spare. That skinny lot down by the Audubon land. Thought you sold that to those New Jersey people, but I went down to Town Hall to check it out. There's a sizeable portion there with frontage on Post Road. I could get sixteen, twenty houses on there, if you see where I'm going with this."

"The cedar swamp? Beyond the woods? You couldn't build there. It's too wet." So that was what he wanted.

"Oh, Jesus, Helen. That swamp's just a tiny piece of that land, you know that."

"Ludlow, you know you need a wetlands permit, and Coastal permission too." She couldn't believe what she was hearing. The swamp was practically on top of the land Loretta had donated to Audubon. It wasn't all strictly wet, that was true, but in rainy times it was. "There's lady's slipper in there," she said, talking more to herself than Ludlow. "And I've seen pitcher plant."

"Oh! 'Pitcher plant!' Call the Nature Conservancy!" His voice had taken on a mocking whine. "Can't build here, we might have to kill a flower! Can't build there, some endangered bug might die. Save the beetles! Save the dragonflies! Save the plovers! Now, the plovers – example A, Helen, of a species that deserves to die. Stupid birds build their nests right out in the open, defenseless against coyotes, even a bad spring storm'll kill their eggs. That's why they're going extinct! So what do we do – we help them survive! Completely going against what Nature intended."

Helen's mind reeled. How had he moved from the damp woods to the dunes? She thought of the tiny piping plovers that skittered along the beach each spring. The federal government had closed one beach to protect them, and now they were nesting from Watch Hill to Narragansett. She loved to hide behind the dunes and watch them pick tiny bugs out of the sand.

She turned back to the stove. The onions were brown, translucent. Another minute and they would be burning.

"Anyway, I was saying. I'll give you a fair price."

"A fair price? You're serious?" She whirled around again, her face flushed from the stove. He was dressed too casually for the office – khaki pants and a flannel shirt – and in place of his dress loafers he had on a pair of LL Bean boots, muddy on the bottom. That bastard had been walking the property just now. The condition of his footwear confirmed her suspicions: even in the dry fall, parts of that land were wet.

"Forty thousand. That's four thousand an acre."

She was mixing the ground beef, by hand, into the sautéed vegetables, beaten egg, ketchup and bread crumbs, and she could feel the meat griming under her fingernails. It was a nasty business, but sometimes cooking required getting your hands dirty. "You want to buy ten acres? That's almost up to the cemetery. That's not just the swamp, that's the east woods, too."

"It's a fair price, Helen."

"That butts up against the cemetery," she repeated. "These people's backyards are going to face the family cemetery."

"Forty thousand. You wouldn't have to worry about finding a job, would you?"

The quarterly tax bill was looming and she had no idea how she was going to pay it. In fact, she was in arrears on the August payment. Ludlow probably knew that, too, if he had been nosing around Town Hall.

If she sold him the land, she would be helping him destroy the very Nature she treasured. She would be carving another piece off the old farm. All that would be left would be the pond, the barn, the house and a small field. Yet if she didn't, she might eventually lose the farm anyway, when she couldn't pay the taxes.

She turned away from him and put the meatloaf in the oven, then busied herself with clearing up the dishes, soaking the frying pan. "There must be other land you could buy."

"Next to a bird sanctuary? With a water view? Even with the Kennedys' house there, the upper lots will have a view clear across to Block Island – just like you do."

The pan was still hot from the stove and it sizzled in the sink.

"What about the Kennedys? I can't imagine they'd be too keen on this. Or Audubon. Or your mother, for that matter."

"Helen, let me worry about that."

Outside, it had begun to rain, large needles of water that streamed down the windowpanes. The gutters on this side of the house were bad. The window sash was rotten, too, and the rain was seeping in the seam of the storm window. Helen shifted her weight from one foot to the other and the floor groaned; it was hollowed out from generations of women who had stood there washing dishes, and the joists underneath had termite damage. She had covered the spot with one of Martha's old rag rugs.

Helen let Ludlow out of the house. She took off her apron, hung it on a hook and washed her hands. She scrubbed with the nailbrush, its bristles scratching open the skin at her fingertips, but still a thin line of meatloaf mix stayed under there, eluding her efforts. No matter how hard she washed, some dirt always remained, until her skin absorbed it, another drop of poison in a clear pond.

Every month Loretta took her to the DAR luncheon in Kingston. The Daughters of the American Revolution had been meeting at the Babcock Inn for at least 60 years, in a small dining alcove known as the Washington Room, which commemorated George Washington's visit to the village during the Revolution. Helen sat squeezed between two dowagers with flag pins on their lapels. Loretta, the treasurer, spent most of the meeting in and out of her chair, making speeches to the ladies, imploring them to pay up their dues if they hadn't already.

Helen followed along like a child at church. DAR was like that; she did not have to think about what she was doing, and so, inexplicably, she had time to think. She put her hand over her heart and bowed her head. What was the right thing to do? How could she rail against development and then turn around and sell off her land? To Ludlow, of all people.

She mouthed the flag's creed and her allegiance to the United States of America, one nation, under God. What a fraud this all was. The DAR ladies, smelling of mothballs and old wool suits, each month knitted mittens for veterans and traded genealogies. Meanwhile, no one spoke of the real threat to their traditions and heritage: the old houses they were having trouble keeping up, the children who wanted to sell out, the declining membership that, eventually, would spell the end of the Daughters and all they stood for.

Helen listened dutifully to the speaker, a thin, WASP-ish man from a museum in Providence who described its collection of silver from the Revolution. Working her way through salad and soup, chicken breast and mashed potatoes, her mind drifted. She did not care about old silver, and she did not care, either, about news from their sister chapters or the national office in Washington. "Club women," her mother had always dismissed them. Loretta seemed to find fellowship at these meetings, but they left Helen cold. Sometimes she thought there was no group, anywhere, to which she belonged.

When Loretta had said the final goodbye – she was always the last to leave – and they had gathered their coats from the musty cloakroom and settled into her Cadillac, Helen at last had her alone.

"Ludlow came to see me the other day." She pressed her hands against the cherry red vinyl of the front seat. Loretta was passing somebody on the right, veering the car into a pot hole. "He apparently has plans to build a development next to the Audubon land. He wants to buy ten acres from me."

Loretta's face, trained straight ahead, showed no trace of surprise, although Helen noticed the speedometer was creeping up to fifty.

"Twenty houses." She looked over, but Loretta said nothing, keeping her gaze straight ahead. "All right on top of each other."

"Land's pretty wet. Twenty is an optimistic figure." Loretta's lips were pursed, and she turned on the radio to a blast of Tchaikovsky.

"That land is more than wet. It's part swamp. Jim used to haul out cedar from it every year. I've seen lady's slipper there." Helen cast about in her mind, trying to come up with birds she'd heard on the land, but she couldn't think of any.

"What are you going to do?"

The thing was, she didn't know. She was needling Loretta, hoping that some of this conversation would make its way back to Ludlow. Yet part of her hoped that Loretta, even if she tried, couldn't persuade her son to withdraw the offer. Short of getting another job, Ludlow's forty thousand was Helen's only op-tion – or maybe not.

"Somebody else might want to buy it," Helen said. "To protect it."

Loretta huffed. "I doubt it. It's too small for Audubon to be interested. It's nothing but an old cedar swamp. You can find those all over South County. Not that it doesn't mean something to the Winters," she added. "But I would say if somebody wants to give you cash on the barrel head for that old swamp, wet or not, you should take it before he changes his mind."

Helen said nothing. They drove along Ministerial Road until it ended at Route 1, a divided concrete highway that separated the hills from the sea. Cars whizzed by as Loretta waited for an opening. It seemed like everyone these days was in a hurry to get somewhere.

Despite Joyce and Dale's efforts to clean and paint, the house needed attention. Like anything neglected for years, the old colonial had settled further and further into its state of shabby disrepair as though sinking into itself. The gutters were only the most obvious symptom of a general structural and decorative malaise. Years of wind and salt had softened the clapboards to a faded gray that was quite striking, like the white or gray hair of a fine, distinguished elderly woman, but the weathering was a sign of deeper problems in the bones of the house. It was the interior condition, demoralizing but not terminal, that bothered Helen the most. Cracked paint and water stains on the ceilings, buckling floorboards, wallpaper peeling off like tree bark – it was shameful, really, how they had lived all these years. At least when Jim had been alive he had made basic repairs, keeping the roof shingled, the gutters clear, but since his death she had let the house go completely, too poor and too distracted to keep up appearances.

Helen had gotten it into her head that new wallpaper would make a difference. Her mother had been like that: Whenever Alice Richmond had a setback, she would start tearing up the house, painting and scraping and buying rolls of rose or lilac or ivy. For days the house would be in an uproar, sawhorses in the dining room, the laundry piling up, the kitchen heavy with the smell of paste. Helen's father would hide in the barn or take a protracted trip into town, usually with George. Somehow she always was left behind to follow her mother around with strips of pasted wallpaper while Alice barked orders about matching patterns and borders.

Helen had never been good at papering, but she knew someone who was: Loretta. She was like Alice, competent in that way domineering women sometimes are. Loretta had never had a husband to wallpaper her hall or paint her ceiling, and she was too cheap to pay someone to do it. Loretta would throw on a paint-stained sweat shirt and a pair of Ludlow's old dungarees, and before you knew it she would be running a roller over freshly papered walls.

"I've got two leftover double rolls." Loretta said on the phone, and Helen could hear rustling in the background. "From when I did the music room last year." Helen pictured it: A repeating pattern of goldfinches and cardinals on a tree branch.

"I already picked something out," she lied. "I'm picking it up next week."

That, she figured, gave her time to lay her hands on something suitable. When Loretta came over – carrying the double rolls of Audubon birds, just in case – Helen quickly pulled out a muted green stripe with trailing honeysuckle, and they set to work.

Her bedroom had not been papered since they were married. They ripped off sheets of what had been a textured peach, browned by dirt and sunlight. Underneath, the walls of the house revealed themselves, plaster-lath construction that had been liberally patched over the years. They scraped and sanded; the skin on Helen's hands cracked and bled. It was November and cold upstairs, where the heat did not survive the long journey from the furnace to the second-story hall.

Loretta did most of the work. Despite her girth, she moved like a man, swinging her arms high and wide and cutting with a carpenter's precision. Her strokes were quick and even as she lathered on the adhesive. Helen stood by, keeping the wallpaper paste mixed, holding sheets for cutting. She would not have been able to do this, she realized, if it hadn't been for her sister-in-law.

"You could put that bird print in the hall," Loretta was saying. "I'll bet you there's enough, you could go all the way from the downstairs landing to Joyce's room."

"Mmm." Even if she could stomach the Audubon paper, Helen wasn't sure she was ready to do more. This was a big enough step, redecorating this room that had not been touched since Jim died. She had cleaned today, before Loretta arrived, and found a sales receipt under the bed from January 1978. Jim had bought a bottle of aspirin and a newspaper at the little convenience store up the street, just days before his suicide.

"You could paint the walls, I suppose, but I never liked the look of paint. Shows up all the flaws in the plaster." Loretta grunted as she lifted a sheet to the wall. "Give me a hand here."

Even now, eight years later, it hurt finding that piece of paper under the bed, an insignificant castoff of his life, carelessly dropped to the floor, probably out of his pants pocket. He was always swallowing aspirin, four, five at a time. Claimed he had headaches. The night before he died, he had said: *You're giving me a goddamn headache.* Part of her, bitter, had always thought he deserved those headaches. Now the pain came to her, squeezing her temples, blinding her at odd moments.

"Are you going to put up a border? Room would look nice with a border. Maybe yellow flowers, to match the honeysuckle." Loretta dropped a plumb line from the ceiling. "Jesus, Mary and Joseph, there isn't a straight wall in this house."

It was true: You dropped a penny, it rolled to the corner. Everything disappeared under the bed. Nothing was even, no lines matched up; the house was like a dirt road, with bumps and hills and pot holes, a world with its own elevations. That was probably why old Mother Winter had chosen the textured peach paper; it was so easy to match, you'd never know the wall varied as much as two inches from one end of the room to another. Even if she had been crazy, Martha Winter knew something. She had learned to live with the old house by the sea, like a sailor who leans into the wind instead of standing up hard against it.

"Hark! Your doorbell's ringing," Loretta announced, wiping her hand on a rag.

Helen stopped mixing paste and listened, subtracting out the wind chimes that were making a racket and the distant roar of the surf. Loretta was right: Someone was ringing the front-door bell, which she hadn't heard in years. Since the subdivision took away part of their front yard, they had let the brush grow up so much Helen couldn't believe anyone could find the front door, let alone make their way to it. But from the window she looked down to see a figure standing there, a black woman in a wool coat and a muffler circling her neck. Leaning on a cane in the harsh November wind. Marian Evans.

"Aren't you going to answer it?"

"Jehovah's Witnesses." If she had been alone, Helen would have let the doorbell ring all day. But the only thing worse than facing Marian Evans was having Loretta find out it was Marian Evans. She dashed down the stairs. She would get rid of her, that was all.

The door, glued to the frame by cobwebs and years of disuse, opened with a sickening thud. Marian stood there, about to ring the bell again. Her face was soft, smooth, an inscrutable moon. Gone were the fancy wedding clothes. Helen spotted a tiny moth hole above the top button of her green coat. Her hair was held back by two bobby pins.

"Helen. I'm so sorry to disturb you." She made a motion with a cane, as though about to walk in.

Helen stepped outside and shut the door. She had not stood on the front portico in years. The stone wall that divided Winter land from Salt Marsh Acres was completely covered in brush and ivy, but she could still make out the backs of ranch houses and cheap prefabricated sheds.

"Loretta's upstairs papering my bedroom. You know how nosy she is, she'll want to know why you're here."

"Walk me to my car. I'm so slow, we can have a good talk." Marian tried a smile, then turned away. Although it was November, the grass could have used one last mowing, which made her progress all the more difficult. "Helen, I don't expect you to be my friend. But life and circumstance have bound us together, haven't they?"

Helen had walked out without a coat, but she still felt sick with sweat. Something was warring inside her. The urge to be quiet, polite, passive, was running into a concrete wall of rage. She wondered what Marian would do if she kicked that cane out of her hand and struck her with it. Terrible images filled her mind. Blood. Bruises. She heard cracking bones, she imagined pleading and whimpering.

"I brought you something." Marian had reached the car.

With difficulty she balanced the cane in one hand and opened the passenger door with the other. Helen would not help her. If she stumbled, she would not steady her; if she fell, she would not pick her up.

Marian handed her a large manila envelope that was soft and yellowed from years of use. "This isn't mine. It belongs to you, and you should have it."

The package lay flat in Helen's outstretched hands. Three-cent stamps of Queen Elizabeth, in blue, red and purple, covered the surface like the stickers on a steamship trunk. Scrawled across one corner she read: *Keep this for me.*

She would not open it in front of Marian Evans. She would not give her the satisfaction. In fact, she would not open it at all. She would hide it somewhere, bury it deep away. Burn it.

"Why are you doing this?"

Marian dragged herself around to the driver's side of the car and leaned against the opened door. "My mother was a wise woman. She said hate was like acid. If you're not careful, it will eat away at you until there's nothing left."

Her dreams grew longer, more vivid. They centered around the house. It was as though ripping out the wallpaper, taking the walls down to the paint, had exposed something dark and alive; the house was animate, it was talking to her. The doors vibrated like the back of an animal; the curtains moved in a whisper; creatures appeared, out of context, in cupboards and hallways. But every dream had one common thread rushing through it: the sea.

Sometimes it bubbled beneath the floorboards. It would start in the cellar; she would open the door, and find dirty water pouring up the stairs, washing over her feet. It would rise; she dashed up the stairs to Martha's room; the water, like a snake, was slithering down the hallway, making for the door. She struggled with the window, but it was stuck, or she rattled the door knob of the bathroom, but it fell off in her hand . . . It seemed no matter how hard Helen fought to get away, she ended up trapped, preparing to drown.

Other dreams started at some landscape she did not recognize, but always with the same result. A broken-down hotel at the edge of the sea. She stood on its porch, feeling safe, but soon a tidal wave rose up to engulf her. A pleasant spit of land that curved out along the shoreline, until the waters washed away her connection to the land. When not drowning, she was marooned, caught by the sea's whim and left to die.

"When are you going to see that friend of yours again? Andrea?"

"*Althea*, Mother." Joyce's voice on the phone was annoyed. "I don't know. Why? What do you care?"

"Well, I thought if you were going to see her, you could bring her over here."

"Althea? What do you want to see her for?"

"I don't know, I thought it would be nice if you invited her over here once in a while, that's all." She swallowed. "I haven't seen her since the wedding."

Silence. "So, tell me about this dream."

Helen tried to laugh, go along with the joke. "Oh, it's nothing."

"If it was nothing you wouldn't be asking for Althea."

She stood at the cellar door, holding the envelope.

She could dig a hole and bury it, but what would be the point? She could guess what was inside. And years from now, if Joyce stumbled upon the lumpy old manila envelope, she would not be around when she learned the truth. Marian had been right to bring it over, because if Joyce or Camille found it at Marian's, then the trouble would start.

Damn it.

What *was* in the envelope? She couldn't assume she knew. She could be carrying a stick of dynamite. Secrets she could only guess at. Hurts too horrible to imagine.

Still: Would Marian bring it over just to hurt her? After all these years? And make some stupid speech about burying the hatchet?

The envelope grew heavier as she stood on the stairs. Her back, curved to avoid the rafters, had begun to ache. The cellar smelled like rotten potatoes. She took the envelope and, aiming it like a Frisbee, tossed it toward the dirt floor. Let the spiders have it.

Joyce had insisted on having Thanksgiving. "It's too much

work for you, Mother." Helen suspected darker motives, but she went along. It was only when she walked in and found Joyce's living room crowded with young people that panic overtook her. Clark, Michael Avery's best man, and some girl she had never met. Dale with some girl who had a butterfly tattoo on her wrist. Althea. And Camille and her husband, baby, and two-year-old girl, who was already wailing and running about the house.

But no Marian.

She had imagined just the family – Dale, Joyce, Michael. It was awkward enough having a son-in-law. But what were all these people doing here on Thanksgiving? Didn't they have a home to go to?

Helen said as much to her daughter in the kitchen, while Joyce stirred gravy she had poured from a jar. She said it nicely, of course. Merely inquiring.

"*Mother.*" There it was again, that tone. Helen had heard some mothers and daughters became the best of friends after the rocky shoals of adolescence had been navigated. But Joyce was still talking to her as though she were in high school and railing at an early curfew.

"I don't understand, that's all. Why isn't Camille with her mother? And I thought Althea had a big Italian family – "

"Mrs. Evans was invited, but she wasn't feeling well. I think they're going over there for dessert. And Althea doesn't have much family anymore, since her grandmother died last month. Her parents are divorced and they hate each other."

"I see." Marian had stayed away because Helen was going to be there. She didn't know whether to be angry or relieved. "Who's that girl with your brother?"

Joyce stopped rifling through the cupboards and looked at her oddly. "That's his girlfriend, Mother. Monica. You met her at the wedding."

She must look different. Helen could not for the life of her remember meeting a girlfriend of Dale's.

Camille had grown into a beautiful woman, if you liked the type. Tall, but not lanky. Stood up straight. Her cheekbones were high, her brown eyes deep set, and her skin was even lighter than Marian's. Like a cup of coffee cut with too much milk. Something nervous about her, edgy; she had trouble sitting still. She was dressed up, a silky shirt over matching brown trousers, and leather high-heeled boots; she'd always loved the clothes. Helen could imagine a cigarette caught in her long, thin fingers. She didn't look like anybody's mother.

For years, she had watched Camille for some sign, but none had come. Except for her height and a certain sharpness to her features, Camille Evans was her mother's child. Neither her face nor her personality betrayed anything else. The anger was the most mysterious ingredient of all. Marian was calm, almost placid; that was how Hamilton had gotten away with knocking her around all those years. No, Helen did not understand Camille's anger. She even seemed annoyed at Eric, whom Helen found to be unfailingly polite and deferential to his fiery wife. Although there was something in him, too, that seemed to defy crossing, as though even a gentle, long-suffering husband had his limits.

"We should just sell our house and trade up. I bet we'd double our investment." Camille was sitting on the arm of Eric's chair, her legs crossed, twirling an ankle.

"You have done a beautiful job with that house." Michael was sitting on the sofa across from them.

"It's too small. Especially since Forrest was born. I'm constantly tripping over toys and diaper bags and their playpen . . ."

Eric, holding the baby in his lap, said nothing.

"And I'm not crazy about being next to the river, now that I have two of them to watch."

"You could build a fence," Michael suggested.

"A fence would be cheaper than a new house." Eric looked like the baby had just filled its diaper and he didn't want to change it. "We can't trade up as long as Camille's only working part time."

"Let's not forget all your pro bono work." Camille snatched up the baby and headed for the kitchen. "The only lawyer I know who's living in a one-bathroom house," she added, almost to herself.

Helen was still back at the river, with those two children playing on its banks.

After dinner Helen volunteered to help Althea do the dishes. Like her, Althea seemed lonely and uncomfortable in the large group. She had barely said a word at dinner. Thanksgiving was a difficult day to be away from family, Helen reflected, wondering how different Althea's holidays must have been when she was growing up in that big Italian household.

"I've been having strange dreams," Helen ventured, taking a wet plate from Althea's rubber-gloved hands.

Althea asked her to describe them, and she did: The water in all its frightening forms, whether drowning her by the shore or filling up the house. Narrated, they lost some of their power, so that Helen despaired if she had captured their menace at all.

Althea ran some knives under hot water. "Water is the unconscious. It is sweeping you away, overwhelming you."

"The unconscious?" That could mean anything. All dreams were about the unconscious. Helen felt cheated, somehow, by Althea's answer.

"I can only give you generalities. You know, in your heart, what your dreams are about."

Helen had a history of making the wrong decisions. It seemed the information she needed was always up ahead, just out of her vision, waiting around a sharp corner to trip her up. She was magnetized by whatever made the most noise, while a silent clue stood nearby, unseen, only to be recalled later, regretfully. It had been that way with Jim. He took her out of herself, and the possibility that he loved her was almost as intoxicating as the knowledge that it was true. He was not just any farmer; he was intelligent, a war hero, and funny, charismatic, mischievous. So unlike the stolid farm boys of Cooperstown and the villages surrounding the farm. At 26 James Winter already had fought in Europe, led men in battle as a second lieutenant, and lost his brother to the war. God might as well have been shining a spotlight on him: "Marry this man!" It was her mother, with one of her typical icy comments, who seemed to know what was coming. "You're too plain for him," Alice Richmond had said.

Noise was always distracting her, coming from every quarter. Martha with that bell, the clapper banging its brass head first to one side, then the other. *Pay attention to me.* And the little girl, propped up on a pillow in the kitchen chair, eating her grilled cheese sandwich, and the little boy, pushing dirt around the yard with his Tonka truck, were silent, for once not demanding any attention at all. Again, all arrows telling her what to do, only it was the wrong thing. The Devil leading her astray. *Pay attention to me*.

And now Ludlow, with his demands and his temptations, pacing around her kitchen, banging his hand flat on the table, gesturing wildly, his words drawing a picture of her future. If only she knew where the silent clues were hiding, the message that would tell her what was coming next. It was as though she already knew she would do it and regret it later. This was the story of her life.

"I didn't know you had another daughter."

Like a child, Fran Kennedy was sitting cross-legged on the maroon rug in the living room, paging through Helen's old photo albums. Her hair was gathered in a tight, perky ponytail and she was wearing Navy blue sweats; she had come over to help Helen clean out the attic. Another chore that had been delayed for too long, and in the intervening years the crawl space above Joyce's bedroom had become the repository for everything that needed to be put away but was too good for the dank cellar. Old clothes. White iron bed frames, their paint flaking, their metal rusting, only one grade below what was in use on the second floor. And the albums of black-and-white snapshots taken with Jim's old Brownie camera; Fran had seized upon these immediately. Since she was the one navigating the narrow pull-down stairs, Helen could not tell her what to bring down and what to leave alone.

"Susan." From the couch above where Fran sat, Helen saw Susan, chubby-cheeked, sitting in her lap at the old picnic table they used to keep next to the barn. "She drowned in the pond when she was four."

"The pond here? The salt pond? Oh, Helen. That must have been terrible for you."

"I was taking care of old Mother Winter then. Jim's mother. She was forever demanding this, demanding that. There really wasn't much wrong with her, she had just decided to take to her bed. She used to ring her bell at the worst times. I was feeding Susan lunch." She could smell the cheese burning, hear the milk being poured into a glass. "She was ringing and ringing, so I left Susan and went upstairs. While I was gone Susan opened the

screen latch, went outside, walked right by Dale, who was playing in the dirt, and wandered down to the pond. By the time I
came downstairs it was too late."

Fran's hand had flown to her own chest, as though to keep
something inside. "Good God."

"It was April. Jim was down to Matunuck, plowing some
cornfields he rented from Loretta. I called her to go down there
and bring him home, and then I had to tell him. I don't think he
ever forgave me. After that, you know, things were not the same
between us."

Fran looked back at the picture, and then at Helen. As
though she were watching this drama play out from above,
Helen saw herself as calm and self-assured. The words piling
up made each subsequent revelation easier than the last. Fran
was her victim, helplessly sitting on the floor, weighed down by
Helen's life pasted into the black corners of the photo album.
She must have been thinking about her own troubles, but she
met Helen's story with only sympathy, not the cruel recrimina-
tion that Helen had thrown at her, that day she confessed her
husband's infidelity.

"She's buried in the cemetery, isn't she? The rock where you
leave the buttercups?"

Helen pictured the stone, its pink mica glistening in the autumn rain. Only brown oak leaves adorned it now. That had
been the hardest thing, leaving her baby to the wormy earth and
the ravages of the weather. You got used to it, though. You could
get used to anything.

"Joyce doesn't know, and she doesn't need to know. So
please don't speak of this to anyone."

Fran shut the album, put it in the cardboard box and carried
it back upstairs.

She hadn't really told Fran anything. Susan was the beginning of the story; there was so much more to it. Yet she wondered why she had confided in Fran, why suddenly it was as
though a faucet had begun to drip in her head, loosened by
years of rust and disuse. Even if Fran had not stumbled on the
picture of Susan, even if she had not figured out the blonde tod-
dler was not Joyce, Helen thought she would have found a way
to talk about her lost daughter. That frightened her more than

what she had actually said.

She blamed the house. All these months since she'd stopped working, Helen had been alone inside almost every day, and her secrets were bulging behind the walls, pressing to get out. That was the real reason she had asked Loretta to paper her bedroom, and why she had asked Fran to help her clean out the attic. It was like trying to flush thoughts from your head. If she could change the way things looked, if she could empty out the trash of accumulated years, it would be like erasing memories. She could make a clean start. But if she did nothing, the hold the house exerted over her would intensify, until there was no hope of purging the past.

Money. The house needed it – gutters, roof, clapboards, sills, joists. If the house had a skeleton, it was arthritic, the bones sagging and breaking under the pressure of the years. Like an old woman with a dowager's hump, it was leaning forward, almost listing in the wind. The timbers and posts – heavy, thick, hand-hewn – that had held it up all these years were no more than sawdust.

At least, that was what Dale contended. He poked a jackknife in a cellar beam to prove his point, and the evidence of powder post beetles sifted out in the form of a fine sand of digested wood. Some of it floated in the air before falling to the dirt floor, to join centuries of dust, insect leavings and general filth. Helen shuddered. She wasn't sure what was worse: the idea that the house was falling down around her, or that tiny beetles that looked like cockroaches were tunneling under the floors, laying eggs, hatching larvae, and crawling about at will. Overhead, the beam was peppered with shotgun holes, as though the cellar was being used as rifle range. She did not like being in the cellar to begin with, and it was only when Dale insisted that she hurried down the rickety stairs ahead of him to kick a certain manila envelope under a box and out of sight.

"Well? What can you do? We can't have bugs in the house." She hugged her sweater closer to her. It was surprisingly cold down here.

"These beams need to be replaced. Whole house should be jacked up, really, and new sills put in. Roof, gutters need doing. Ma, the house is a mess." He shook his head, as though somehow it were her fault, she had let things get to this point. She asked him how much it would cost. For that was what it all came down to, and wasn't that why things had gotten to this point? When Jim was alive they did things themselves. She had even helped him shingle the roof, if standing on a ladder passing shingles counted as helping. Since his death she had let things get away from her. She'd had no other choice. Every penny she earned, when she was working, had gone into the taxes, paying bills, keeping the car running. This recent flurry of work with Loretta, the papering and painting, had made her feel good, as though she was finally doing something. But when he quoted her a figure, she couldn't even begin to imagine it. Jacking up the house. They might as well burn it down and start over.

"There's nothing I can do about it now," she said, and headed up the stairs.

"Ma, look, I can do the work, but I'm too busy. You'd be better off hiring somebody. I can recommend – "

"I don't want anyone else in the house."

"Ma, even if I did it, I'd have to hire somebody to help me. I'd need equipment. It's not a one-man job."

They were in the kitchen. She slammed the bolt of the cellar door. She didn't want to think about those beetles anymore. Let them get at that envelope. A nice diet of paper and glue.

She went to see Dub Lillibridge. Ludlow's offer was her excuse. She wasn't sure if she hoped Dub would understand, thus giving her a sort of permission, or if she was looking for him to talk her out of what already seemed inevitable. He still lived in the tiny cottage, now surrounded on three sides by the raised ranches being built for Ludlow's development, and sitting in his kitchen with the smell of the morning's bacon and fried potatoes was a kind of visit to her future. The fall day was unseasonably warm, and the sound of hammering came through the windows, which were cracked to let in some of the Indian summer air.

On Dub's face was a mixture of absurd happiness at this improbable guest and a sort of generic sorrow he carried around now, the way some old men drape a sweater on their shoulders. His face was the color of boiled potatoes. When he walked to the metal cabinet for a store box of cookies, he shuffled, and his back was beginning to curve over.

He poured her coffee from a fresh pot and listened, moving slowly about the kitchen, as Helen told him about Ludlow's plans for another development in the cedar swamp. He sat down and said nothing for a long while. His spoon made a tinkling sound as he stirred his coffee, and he tucked into the cookies, one after another.

"I had a crazy idea once," he finally said, wiping his mouth with a napkin. "I had an idea that between the two of us we could fight son's a bitches like Ludlow Winter. But I guess that was an old man's fancy. Fact is Ludlow Winter and his ilk are inheriting the earth. Forget about the meek. We're the meek and we may be headed for heaven, but we sure as hell aren't inheriting the earth."

She wondered what he meant: *between the two of us*. She had treated him badly. All that time he had spent with her after the accident, the days when he leased her fields and would come into the house for his coffee break, she had treated him like a piece of the furniture. And the wedding. She had left him, alone, with all those strangers. Now he seemed old and bitter, and she wondered how much of that was Ludlow and how much of that was because of Helen Winter.

"I know I don't have any choice," she said. "It just feels like cutting off an arm. Pretty soon, I won't have any limbs left."

"What will this leave you?"

"The house, the barn, and ten acres."

"A damn sight more'n I have."

"And the pond." She had not realized it until now, but that always seemed to stay in the equation, no matter what. The damned pond.

"What about your children? What do they think?"

She did not want to admit she hadn't revealed a word of Ludlow's offer to Dale or Joyce. Dale only cared about money, and couldn't be trusted with it; she had learned that lesson. And Joyce – well, it seemed any conversation they had that went deeper than the weather was bound to end up in an argument. "They have a lot of big ideas unsupported by money or ambition."

He considered that, and choked out a dry, cackling laugh. "In other words, they'd take the farm now if you gave it to them, but their mother could die in the poorhouse for all they cared."

"I suppose that's harsh, but it's not too far from the truth."

"If I was a younger man, Helen Winter, I would have a more attractive offer to make you."

"Dub, I didn't mean – "

"I know you didn't. But I did. As I see it, though, any arrangement we made now would be just that, an arrangement. It wouldn't be all you wanted or all I wanted, for that matter. Getting married for purely economic reasons strikes me as a little un-Christian."

"Just a little." She smiled. She did love him, in a way. Just not that way.

"Well, if Ludlow Winter wants to pay you decent money for that old swamp, maybe you should take it." He paused, as though expecting her to protest, but she regarded him carefully, weighing his words. "Your kids'll probably end up selling the whole kit 'n' caboodle when they get it anyway."

Helen scraped her chair on the linoleum and rose to go. She was afraid Dub Lillibridge was right: It was all going to go eventually.

CHAPTER TWENTY

J oyce Winter, in her third year of teaching seventh- and eighth-grade American history, dreaded snow days. The other faculty members of the regional high school looked forward to them with the glee of a 13-year-old, but not Joyce. She lay awake in the pre-dawn dark when the wind keened and the snow scratched at the window. Her entire being was consumed in anxiety over the early-morning phone call or the bulletin on TV, while Althea, calling from her new apartment in Westerly, would all but sing out the news: "No school!" Part of the reason for her dread was Michael, who did not believe in snow days. Even when the Bay Campus was closed for the day, he would drive into work, putting in a good four or five hours at the office before coming home for an early dinner – if he didn't, that is, stop on the way home for a quick drink. He had bought a four-wheel-drive Jeep, but on the rare day he couldn't navigate it to Narragansett, he would hole up in his home office all day, refusing to be disturbed. This was not how Joyce had imagined such days when they were first married. She saw them as everyone else did, a sudden gift of Sunday in the middle of the week, a lazy day of reading, languid sex, and a stew simmering on the stove.

Alone, she was left to her thoughts. And in the cold, white desolation of a winter's day, those thoughts too often turned to the father. Sitting in Michael Avery's living room – she wondered when, if ever, she would think of this house as hers – the world intruded on all sides. Michael loved to sit here, surrounded by glass that let in water and light, but she did not. Looking out to the white stubble of the salt marsh, soon she began seeing things. A man's footprints, or a brackish weed of brown coloring that might carry a touch of blood. A coyote's tracks. Tire marks threading a pattern of white, creating a trail to somewhere she didn't want to go.

How did a man go out into the white of a winter's morning and never come back?

That was the question she wanted to ask Jim Winter, but the answer would eternally be denied her. What possibly could have been so bad that he had to take his life rather than come back in for breakfast? These thoughts always led to her mother. Never mind her. *What about me,* Joyce thought. *How could you leave me. And Dale. You could have divorced her, for God sake. Sent her back to New York for all I care.*

With the questions came memories. All the smells that Jim Winter carried in the house, from sawdust to cow balm to motor oil. His hands, big, rough and chapped, but gentle hands, that tousled her hair even when she was a teen and too old to be his little girl anymore; his reading glasses, thin, wire glasses that were so improbable in that reddened, expansive farmer's face, but perched there nonetheless every night as he read books that were even more improbable in a farmer's hands: thick histories, Barbara Tuchman and the like, and popular novelists like John Updike and James Michener. "I like to learn something when I read," he used to say. He knew more than anybody about any-thing. Wars, from the Trojan to the Civil; geography, from the remotest outpost of the Antarctic to tropical islands and archi-pelagos; theories of physics and geology.

He had an indoor smell, too, a mixture of hair tonic and Old Spice and soft flannel, his Sunday smell she called it; for those times when he had cleaned up and was getting ready to go out. Even when she was a teenager, she would sometimes beg to go with him. Anything to get away from her mother, who seemed perpetually in an unhappy motion of stomping and slamming and pacing and banging around. Sometimes her father would say yes, and take her out to a Grange meeting or a visit to the kitchen of some old Swamp Yankee friend or on a drive to check out a piece of machinery he wanted to buy or a plot of land he had been hired to clear. As time went on, just as often he said no, he didn't think so. Not this time.

Michael Avery's profession was to plumb the depths of the soil and extract the core, like a sandworm digging beneath the ocean with sharp jaws and its long, undulating body. What he brought up in these cores carried a secret code, revealing everything from climate change to storm patterns. That was about all Joyce understood of her husband's work. He was, she had thought, more of a historian than she was. While she stumbled about reading diaries and Colonial newspapers and musty old books, Michael was out there getting his hands into the only thing that was really left of the past – dirt. When he was so disposed, he would talk about his research with the sort of awe exhibited only by geniuses and the truly possessed. "The deeper we go, the more we'll find out," he liked to say. "It's limitless, and it's all there for the taking."

Clark had finished his dissertation, which Joyce had proofread, but the work that had earned him a Ph.D. was far from over. He and Michael were still analyzing the core sediments they had withdrawn from the South County coastline, and Michael was taking the model of experimentation they had developed and farming it out to universities all over the country, which meant more travel. Then there was the hurricane book. Michael Avery was writing something based on his research, but whenever Joyce brought it up, he grew testy. Once she had seen a pile of notes on his desk, but it had all been indecipherable, a jumble of phrases and mathematical formulas and freehand maps.

When she probed, his answers were flippant and unsatisfying.

"Some day we'll get another storm and you'll find out," he liked to say.

Unlike Michael Avery, Joyce had no jury-rigged contraption to probe into the depths of her past, and there was no developer's backhoe to spill it onto the surface, like the Indian bones Eric Robinson was finding all over South County. She had only her instincts and her imagination. She could not section out the years, divide them up like slices of cookie dough and watch each re-emerge, fresh baked, into the open air. Memory was fallible and finite; hers only went back so far, and everything important seemed to have happened before she existed. It had all turned to dust. How could she divine anything out of a clod of dirt? Her father was dead. Dale was too damaged, or too afraid, to give up what he knew. Her mother, who was the key to it all, was like the shifting sands – never revealing anything, never staying on a subject long enough to be found out. Although she knew her mother could tell her everything, Joyce saw no point in bringing her doubts into the air. Like the wind to the dunes, her mother would take them, grain by grain, and blow them away.

Trapped in the house by winter, Joyce reached for the phone, calling everyone she could think of, spinning her favorite armchair away from the outdoor view while she talked. But everyone else seemed to have something pressing indoors to attend to. For Camille, it was the children, their high-pitched squeals and shrieks like a Greek chorus in the background, and Camille's words interspersed with asides to them like the stage whisper of a leading lady. And even though Camille insisted Joyce was not interrupting, the children were fine really, she did want to talk, Joyce would eventually give up, tired of repeating herself, wondering what Camille had to say to her anyway. With Dale, his girlfriend was the bird chirping in the background; when Joyce could get through to him, that is. Too often Monica insisted her brother wasn't home, though Joyce wondered if it was true. Althea always seemed glad to hear from her, but Joyce could tell she was cooking, the phone pressed between shoulder and jawbone while she shook spices and stirred pots. Inevitably a timer would ring or a sauce would begin to bubble and Althea would be gone, her apologies ringing in Joyce's ears along with the dial tone.

On days like this she sometimes called Aunt Loretta and invited her for a walk. Even if the snow was knee deep or still blowing down, Loretta was always game to go out. She hated being cooped up as much as Joyce did, although for different reasons. Storms kept the birds from her feeders and the deep snow covered her usual trek through the Audubon land. Afraid of a broken hip and easily winded, however, she didn't like to push her way through snow and she didn't like to go alone; so she and Joyce would hike along the beach, from Matunuck to the Winter Farm and back, tramping on the hardened white shingle of sand.

Years ago, Joyce could remember Loretta striding through the drifts, pushing her way through with her walking stick. Time and age had hobbled her. She was bigger than ever, and she huffed now when she walked, occasionally dragging her left foot. Her man's clothes served her well in the cold – layers of flannel shirts and trousers of indeterminate gender – but she seemed to suffer it more, her cheeks quickly blazing up like a wood fire catching creosote.

On one of these snow days, when Joyce would have been content to plow on clear to Westerly to avoid returning home, they had to stop so Loretta could rest on a ship's timber that had washed up. Her chest rose and fell like the prow of the ferry making for Block Island. Sitting on the driftwood, her butt and feet numb, Joyce put her arm around Aunt Loretta's bulky green parka and tried not to complain.

Loretta pointed out birds in the marsh, oystercatchers and greater yellowlegs, funny names that so aptly described their purpose in the scheme of things. They talked this way for a while, companionably, over the wind that had roared in with an Arctic clipper the night before. Loretta asked her about Dale and Michael. In between her answers and her evasions she knew that Loretta's eyes read what Joyce could not say: that Dale was lost no matter how sober he was, and her husband was absent even when he was there. She confessed she wanted children but Michael did not. She hinted at grief. Slowly, like an unraveling sweater, she pulled apart the problems in her life and laid them out, hoping Loretta would help her wind up the yarn. When she was done talking Joyce had the sort of thought that comes to mind later, when one remembers a sweet moment in time: Loretta had become her mother because Helen no longer could do the job.

"Sometimes I wonder if my life will ever be what it would have been," Joyce said finally, gazing away from Loretta at the sea.

"Of course it will. You have to have faith." Loretta planted her cane in the sand and leaned on it with both hands. "Your spring will come, and it will be all the things you hoped it would be."

Joyce could not remember hopes and dreams. It seemed everything had stopped on January 23, 1978, and she was still back there, watching out the window for a father who would never come home.

"I thought it would get better, and it did for a while. But whenever I think something is changing my outlook, the feeling doesn't last. It's only a distraction." School, marriage, teaching. "I want to have a baby, but sometimes I wonder if that's just another way of avoiding dealing with what's really the matter. At least, that's what Michael thinks."

Loretta grunted. "Humph. That's easy for him to say. There's nothing unusual about wanting a baby at your age. What are you? Thirty?" Joyce nodded. "I was younger than you when Ludlow came along."

Joyce wondered at Loretta's careful wording. She had heard all the stories about Ludlow's questionable parentage, mostly from Helen, but she found it hard to cast her matronly, bird-watching aunt in the role of an unwed mother. She felt an aversion to asking her outright, the same paralysis that overcame her whenever she thought of her mother and the sister she had never known. But after all, what difference did it make? Loretta was so fully Ludlow's mother that the circumstances of his birth were immaterial.

"Michael hears Camille complain about her kids, and it freaks him out," she offered. That was one explanation, but the truth was probably that Michael was too selfish to imagine children in his life. She was covering for him. It was as though she were still trying to sell her family on the idea of Michael Avery: that, yes, he did love her and they did belong together. Of course he wants children. He's just . . . cautious. "I just feel like something's missing, that's all, and I can't explain it. I know part of it's because someone really is missing – Dad."

"I miss your father, too." Loretta traced a circle in the hardened sand with her left foot, like a child embarrassed to be talking to grownups. "So much loss in the family. Russell. I can hardly say his name without choking up, and it's been over forty years."

Joyce's uncle had been killed in the war, caught by a sniper in Belgium outside his tank, while he was trying to fix the gun turret. The baby of the family. His Purple Heart was embedded in the gravestone in the farm's cemetery, and her mother kept his obituary, ragged and yellowed by time, in the 'W' volume of the Encyclopedia Brittanica. For World War II, Joyce supposed.

They were quiet for a moment, and Joyce wondered if Loretta was thinking of the other loss, of Susan, the sister who had come before her. But Loretta continued on, her mind apparently still focused on Russell Winter. "Senseless, both of them. Russell. Eighteen, dying in that stupid, bloody war at the hand of some German boy who was probably no older than he was. And your father, blowing his head off, leaving you and your brother and Helen – your poor old helpless mother."

Joyce let that comment blow away on the sea wind. She was tired of people always making excuses for her mother – poor old helpless Helen. It made her want to gag.

"He must have known what it would do to everybody," Loretta went on, almost talking to herself. "God! He saw how I suffered when Russell died. And you weren't even out of high school when he did it . . . and Dale was not right, either. Then your mother making a perfect mess of things, selling off half the farm, giving Dale all that money to throw away on a boat . . ."

"But why did Dad do it, Aunt Loretta? Why? I can't get that question out of my head. Until I can answer it, I feel like my life is dead, stopped, over."

"There is no answer, at least not one I can give you," Loretta said, and she hoisted herself off the driftwood with a groan. "I wonder sometimes if even he knew why."

If Joyce saw change all around the coast, if she winced each time she passed a for sale sign or spotted a perc test pipe rising out of the woods like a periscope, she still recognized that the most alarming development was happening not along the shore but in once-sleepy downtown Wakefield.

She and Michael had developed the habit, as couples do, of going out on a particular night of the week, in their case Wednesdays. They had tried Fridays but, especially in summer, would find themselves circling throughout South County, vainly trying to find a restaurant without a line stretching out the door. Thursdays Michael always had some excuse – it was when he went out drinking with Chip and the gang, although he always pretended it was a sudden idea they had had, not a plan

– so Wednesdays were hers by default. Usually they ended up in Wakefield, at one of the newer restaurants that had cropped up – Alexander's or Casey's or the 108 House, new American dining they billed themselves as, with the same identical forest green paint and wooden beadboard trim, deep vinyl booths and oversized menus.

The roads that bisected the village, Main Street and Route 108 and Old Tower Hill Road, seemed to have a new curb cut every time they drove into town. Another mini-mall, each one a long, narrow concrete shoebox fronted by lines of stunted arbor vitae passed off as landscaping. Hardware, auto parts, vacuum cleaners; sandwiches, ice cream, pizza. It had gotten so bad that the newspaper had done a story about the last available commercial lot in town being for sale, at the unheard-of asking price of $200,000. In the sixties the town had stretched out from its 19th-century Main Street, with its impressive brick buildings, the stone columns of its bank, the old Victorian houses already converted to funky shops and a bookstore, to fill up its farmland outskirts with supermarkets and drugstores and fast-food restaurants. Now that land, that overflow land big enough to contain miles of asphalt and concrete, was almost gone.

Joyce would stir her drink, a diminutive sweet concoction with Kahlua or Amaretto. Outside the window she would catch a view of flashing neon, the car dealer's balloons shaking under the streetlights like oversized jellybeans. Michael never seemed to notice the changes when they went into town; he liked to say that Wakefield already was ugly, what did it matter if it got more so? He had grown up in New York, and it was as though nothing Rhode Island did could come close to the abominations he had seen.

"If you want to see development, go to Long Island," he would say. "When I was a kid it was all potato fields. Now it's nothing but car lots and malls. At least," he would add, ending the discussion, "they aren't building this crap near the water."

It bothered her nonetheless. She remembered when the village had a heart that beat each Friday night: blinking street lights and the glow of the Rexall pharmacy sign, ladies in high heels and dresses and gloves shopping in department stores like Kenyon's and Fleming's, fathers roaming through the Chevy lot, their fingers skimming over the apple red paint of new Chevelles and Impalas. They had a routine, the Winters; Dale would head off with their mother to Fleming's, where he could look at the toy trains while she hunted for some necessity, like dish towels or underwear. Joyce took her father's hand as they walked through the imposing entry of the Industrial National Bank, her mary janes clicking on the marble floor. The tellers stood behind grated windows, like jail cells Joyce thought, and in the echoing, cavernous room she felt tiny, awestruck. The tellers all knew Jim Winter, and they made small talk while he carefully pulled out his black savings book and unfolded the checks for deposit. This ritual, depositing the checks from the old ladies who bought his firewood, the markets and restaurants that stocked his bags of potatoes, was the culmination of his work week. Once a month in the pile somewhere would be a light blue payroll draft from the Chronicle Publishing Co., her mother's pay for her weekly column. Her father would deposit money and take some back in cash, neatly tucking the bills into his cracked black leather wallet. When their chores were complete, the family would meet at the drugstore for ice cream sodas before the long, dark ride home.

Now Friday night was any other night downtown. The bank had moved to the burgeoning commercial outskirts, and people drove up to it to do their business. Fleming's had left long ago and Kenyon's was barely hanging on; the malls in Warwick had taken their trade. The brick-front shops on Main Street hosted a rotating cast of businesses, small, struggling shops and restaurants that changed hands so quickly it was difficult to keep track of their names. And Joyce Winter wondered what had happened to the father who held her hand every Friday night and the older brother with his slicked-back hair and his polo shirt tucked into dress pants. Even her mother, who had looked so pretty in her belted cotton dresses and high heels, seemed to have disappeared, leaving only a haggard phantom in her wake.

Even though Dale had stopped drinking, Joyce met him once a week for fish and chips at the Salty Dog. There were so few nights they could connect: On Thursdays, he was at AA, on Wednesdays, Joyce was busy with Michael, and Tuesday Dale played hi-lo-jack in the bar's backroom. On Friday nights Monica was working the floor as a cocktail waitress and Michael was off with his friends, so she and her brother had drifted into this ritual, even if Joyce wasn't thrilled to find him still hanging out with the same old drunks in the same old dump.

Carpentry agreed with him more than fishing. He had lost some of the gaunt, ashen look of his drinking days, and he was in shape, his arms stained a tobacco tan even in winter. But Joyce couldn't help thinking his sobriety was the eye of the hurricane. Something edgy in the way he looked at her and still evaded her direct questions . . . and the nervous way he smoked Kent after Kent, lighting up one before the other was half gone. After their meal the ashtray would be filled with bent cigarettes at odd angles, like a mass grave of mixed-up bones.

"I walked with Loretta the day it snowed," Joyce said, a week after the talk with her aunt. "We had quite a discussion."

Dale wiped a moustache of sweat from his upper lip. "I'm thinking about getting the custard pie. How about you?"

"I told her I still couldn't figure out why Dad did what he did," she soldiered on. "And I told her I just wish I could get past it."

"Two pieces of custard pie it is," he said, snapping his fingers at Monica, who was balancing a tray of dirty dinner plates.

"She said something about you 'not being right' around the time Dad died. Do you know what she meant by that?"

"Oh, you know Aunt Loretta, she always thinks the worst about me."

"That's not what she meant." Joyce, who had planned this conversation while driving down the Drift Road, had tried to imagine what Dale's response would be, rehearsed what she would say against any eventuality, now had the odd sense she was talking to her mother. That casual way the two of them had of deflecting your questions. Passive-aggressive, Camille would call it.

When Monica brought the pie, topped with a double dollop of whipped cream that Joyce didn't need (and which Monica, with her skin-tight jeans and clinging top, probably had piled on with a sort of grim satisfaction), Joyce asked for more coffee. Stalling for time. If Dale wanted to linger over dessert and coffee, well, by God, she'd take advantage of it.

"I want you to tell me what was going on with you that Aunt Loretta would think you were in trouble."

"I got arrested a couple of times . . ."

"That's not what she was talking about."

"Look, Joycie, I don't want to talk about what happened back then . . . I'm sick of being the fucking scapegoat for everybody's problems, you know?" His hand, shaking, was stubbing out a cigarette that refused to be extinguished. "It's ancient fucking history."

The custard pie slipped into her mouth, smooth and cold. "No one's blaming you. Why would you think that? Aunt Loretta was suggesting you were . . .*troubled*."

"Yeah, I'm fucking troubled. You want to know how troubled I am? Growing up with that lunatic of a mother . . . you think she didn't blame me for everything? She blamed me for all of it. ALL OF IT. Why didn't I see her? Why didn't I stop her? Wasn't I old enough to watch my sister for a few fucking minutes? Maybe I followed her to the pond! Maybe I accidentally pushed her in! It's OK, you can tell Mother! We'll understand!"

Even over the jukebox blaring Cheap Trick and the raucous, drunken voices at the bar and in the booths, Dale's shouting was starting to draw attention. It was like poking an animal in the middle of the road, to see if it's alive, and all of a sudden it jumps up and bites you. Joyce sat back, the custard curdling in her mouth before one last, difficult swallow. All that time, she realized, she and Dale had been talking about two different things.

Dr. Michael Avery, professor of oceanography, expert on sedimentation analysis, had clocked more miles in travel in the previous year than any of his colleagues at the Graduate School. Joyce knew this intuitively, but it was reinforced by an article in the in-house publication the university published for Bay Campus faculty. It was right there in a one-column brief in The Wheelhouse, along with a picture of her husband, looking professorial and smug on the deck of the research vessel that had transported him on many of those jaunts. "The peripatetic Dr. Avery," the story said, "has traveled to 20 foreign countries and four continents in the last five years." It went on to describe his research in laymen's terms and added, ominously, "He already has been invited to visit countries in both Africa and Europe in the coming year."

Joyce was beyond the point of missing her husband when he was gone; some days his frequent absences were a relief from the tension that pervaded when he was home. She got used to having the house, such as it was, to herself. She invited Camille and Althea over for takeout; closed the curtains right at sunset; and, on the nights she was alone, ate Chef Boyardee heated up on the stove. She let the house gradually slide, when Michael was not around to complain that he had found a clump of hair in the tub and could she, would she mind, could she just *clean* once in a while? . . . When Michael was not around to notice that she had let her magazines pile up on the coffee table, his precious coffee table that had to be dusted frequently, along with its wooden duck and picture books of seashells and Audubon's stuffed birds and Impressionist paintings. When Michael was not present to complain that the mail was piling up on the kitchen table and the garbage needed to be emptied.

She missed him; of course she missed him. It was just that life was so much easier when he wasn't around. She hated the trips for the leave-taking and the homecoming, both points of tension, and she hated him for leaving her, time and time again, but if she were brutally honest with herself she did enjoy being alone. Even if she was miserable with missing him, she was more herself when he wasn't around.

But this was no way to build a marriage, and it was no way to start a family. Michael's frequent absences had all but precluded having a baby. Sometimes she thought it was intentional: He didn't want a family, and traveling so much, when so much of it seemed voluntary, was his way of keeping her off-kilter. If he wasn't around, they couldn't fight about whether to have a baby, could they? If he wasn't around, it proved his point, didn't it, that it was just too difficult for a serious academic to settle down and have children?

Of course, none of the other male professors seemed to subscribe to that philosophy. It was the poor graduate students and post-docs, people like Clark, who hesitated to take the next step, who were still saddled with debt and an uncertain future. Most of Michael's colleagues had not only wives but children, many of them two or three children. They found time for Little League games and PTO meetings and summer vacations. In fact, they seemed to lead quite balanced lives. They weren't out drinking beer every Friday night with the teaching assistants; they were taking their wives out to dinner or the movies. They threw barbecues every summer, and Joyce saw how they lived: in pleasant houses with big backyards, where their children cavorted on swing sets and black Labs chased after them. Their careers did not seem to be suffering for the normalcy, either. They might not be clocking as many miles as Michael Avery, but they were publishing in peer-reviewed journals and delivering lectures and getting press for their theories and findings. Joyce knew this because not the slightest achievement escaped Michael's notice. He could, in fact, brood for weeks over another professor's appointment to a national board or a feature story about a colleague in the statewide daily newspaper.

This craziness he had was rubbing off on her. Sometimes she looked at the other faculty wives, searching their faces – the laugh lines around their mouths, the hair casually combed back in a coarse flip, the eyes with no makeup – wondering what it was they had that she didn't. If Michael Avery did not want her to have his children, there must be a reason why.

Joyce still kept in touch with Lydia Franklin, the old woman who lived in the stone-ender in Richmond. Her visits were seldom and unpredictable, but she always made sure to bring her a paper – sometimes the woman seemed starved for news – and after a storm she would drive over to check on her. If the woman fell ill she would freeze to death in the drafty old house, and she had no way to keep her driveway clear except for a shovel and her own muscle power. Joyce had tried unsuccessfully to get Michael to accompany her, to help chop wood or shovel out her car, but he was never interested. "You barely know that old woman. She isn't your responsibility," he would say, or, "Can't she hire someone to plow her out?" At these times the difference in their backgrounds became glaring to Joyce. She had grown up on a farm where people solved their own problems through pure grit, and neighbors pitched in to help the helpless. But Michael had little understanding of self-reliance or poverty. To him, every problem could be solved by money. If he didn't want to do something and he couldn't manipulate Joyce into doing it, he hired somebody. This was true for plowing, landscaping, even minor household repairs that he was certainly capable of doing. Work for its own sake – as opposed to the pursuit of knowledge or recognition – was beneath him.

But Joyce understood Lydia Franklin all too well. She was a woman who had learned to take care of herself, and that self-reliance brought her a freedom that money never could. She wouldn't dream of parting with a nickel to pay someone to do something if she could do it herself. At the same time, she had a finely wrought sense of what was charity and what was generosity. If Joyce came over and helped her get in wood or start a fire, she would leave with a brick of hand-churned butter or a dozen homemade muffins, and the exchange was in the spirit of friendship, not pity. Conversely, if Joyce had ever tried to give her money or had paid someone to plow out her driveway, Lydia would have been furious. She was not a charity case.

She was getting frailer, though, and Joyce worried about her. She had dropped a tea kettle one day and burned her left leg, which oozed with red ulcers for weeks afterward, wounds she treated with poultices of lard. She hated doctors and refused to "trade" with them, as she put it. She also had had a bad year with the garden – Joyce wondered how much of that was weather and woodchucks and how much of it was her inability to keep up with the outdoor chores – and she had canned half as much as the previous year. Bringing her food was dicey, though; too much and Lydia would get her hackles up; if the gift was store bought, she would be insulted.

Lydia Franklin treated Joyce like an equal and listened to her, giving out bits of advice cut with the sweetness of honey in lemon. It was an odd friendship Joyce was at a loss to explain. Lydia had never been to her house, was not invited to her wedding (at Michael's insistence) and probably wouldn't have come to either if asked. Yet even when weeks passed and Joyce did not find time to drive out to Lydia's crooked old house, the woman was still in her mind, part of the running commentary in her head that narrated her every move.

It was natural, then, that Joyce would tell Lydia Franklin – a woman more than twice her age, and, some would say, an eccentric crone who shunned people and society and was probably touched in the head – about the thoughts and questions that haunted her. The suicide of her father, the sister she had never known, her brother's descent into uselessness, the long catalog of her mother's odd behaviors. Sometimes she brought up what was on her mind in mid-thought, as though Lydia had heard all about it before, as though she knew exactly what Joyce was thinking.

"I was telling Aunt Loretta it's like I'm stopped, I can't seem to go on with my life not knowing why he did it," Joyce told Lydia, a few days after the walk on the beach. "Time seems suspended. I haven't been able to do anything that I otherwise would have done."

Lydia, furiously banging in her rocking chair next to the old Gibson stove, considered this. She was chewing on a bobby pin pulled from the tangle of gray hair nesting on top of her head. "There was always talk about your father. But I imagine it was just talk."

Joyce leaned forward. She could feel her left eye twitching, a habit it had lately developed.

"Would have been – how old are you?" Joyce told her, quickly, not wanting to interrupt the flow of thought, which in Lydia sometimes veered in many directions. "About then. '59 or so. My mother was still alive. She heard about it down to the mill. He was shacking up with somebody, that was the story. But I wouldn't put much stock in it."

A spark suddenly flew out of the stove grate, and Lydia jumped up, stomping it out with her foot. "No, there was more," she said, standing there with her hands on her tiny hips, looking past Joyce with a frown. "Not just that he was shacking up, you know all men do that, I hope you know it, but who he was shacking up with. Crap! I can't remember a thing these days."

The conversation was over; they had tea, they walked outside (where Joyce helped her widen a path to the outhouse and clear off the clothesline), they brought in wood; and then, as Lydia folded up newspapers for kindling, she slapped one against the kitchen counter, her face tense like an animal that catches the stealthy approach of its prey. A line of newspaper type caught her eye: *Narragansett Indian remains found on farmland.* The neurons fired, and a mental image was formed, of a comely black woman living in a shack even smaller than hers, a woman who had found it more difficult than Lydia Franklin to live without a man in her life. What could explain why all those brain cells, formed to retain long-term memory, would hold on to an image like that and the stray piece of gossip that was attached to it; like everything about Lydia, those cells were old and creaky and frail but they functioned, by God, they functioned independent of any outside interference, medical or otherwise. No one would ever accuse Lydia Franklin of losing her mind.

But the image formed with no words attached to it, and Lydia Franklin turned her attention to the freshly baked apple pie on her counter. She would not send Joyce home empty-handed.

CHAPTER TWENTY-ONE

*The tree swallows are darting around the pond,
zipping in and out . . . eating mosquitoes and gnats . .
. getting ready to fly south to Florida, Mexico, Central
America . . . They come so close to my head I can almost
touch their white underbellies, if they only weren't
so fast. They feel like my thoughts, darting around,
never landing anywhere. I wish they would stop.*
– Helen Winter, private journal, Friday, Oct. 5, 1990

For Helen life had became a matter of doing the same thing, religiously, and writing it down so she knew that she had passed one milestone and could move on to the next. This was how she got through each day. It was a system of control and, like most systems, it worked if you followed it. But so many things could trip her up: interruptions, mostly. A phone call. The mail coming late; getting to the box, she would find it empty, and her walk would have been for naught, and she would wonder, *Now what do I do? Go home and come back later? What if I forget?* Also, the simple digression of a task, when she would become absorbed in what she was doing and lose all track of time, and then her goose was cooked, because she could not remember where she was or what she was supposed to be doing. Writing did this to her. No more column now, but she had her journal, the black and white composition notebook, and she wrote letters to her mother (who was alone now; her father had died late last year, collapsed in the barn of a stroke, and his passing seemed to have mellowed her mother, almost cheered her up). She wrote long letters and Helen replied in kind. From such a distance, she did not need to worry about her mother's sharp tongue.

Morning was Helen's best time. She rose earlier than ever before – 6:30, most days – and took a brisk shower, enveloped her steaming body in a chenille robe, dressed (clothes laid out the night before, another routine that had become necessary in the past year, otherwise she would waste half the morning debating what to wear), then fixed breakfast. Toast, an egg, black coffee. That woke her up. In another notebook on the kitchen table, she wrote down: the temperature outside; anything interesting out the window; tasks she needed to remember today.

This October morning, the list was short but important: Call Dale about the gutters. They were not working; it had rained yesterday and water had come streaming down in sheets out the living room windows. Dale would know what to do; he was off the fishing boat, doing only carpentry now, and as long as he was sober, he would get to the gutters right away. But it was a crapshoot these days, with Dale. He had been sober for 18 months and then gone on a three-day binge and disappeared; she suspected that tattooed girlfriend of his had something to do with it. Monica. But he had been good lately. She would have to see.

That was No. 1. She underlined it in black pen. She would call him before 8, when he left the house. No. 2 was to mail the taxes. She had enough money to live on these days, thanks to Ludlow; but the price he'd paid for the cedar lot seemed to be going at an alarming rate. (She had missed the last tax payment, forgotten about it completely, and now the town was sending her threatening letters, talking about putting a lien on the property.) What would she do when the money ran out? How they expected her to live on Social Security . . . She had so many expenses these days. It was ridiculous.

But there she was. Drifting. No. 3? Had there been a No. 3? Her notebook was blank after the taxes entry, although she would be damned if she hadn't thought of another item and then forgotten to write it down. Even the notebook was only as good as her mind, which wasn't saying much these days. No. 3 would come to her when it was too late. Lord, she prayed, let it be something that doesn't involve anyone else. Let me be the only one who knows how forgetful I've become.

Quarter to eight already. She picked up the phone and found Dale's number on the bulletin board. That chippy girlfriend of his was probably still in bed, but that was too bad. She had to catch him before he left for the day.

"Mother, I'm tied up on a job for at least a month." Dale sounded alert and, she was relieved to note, not in the least hung over. "That barn I was telling you about in Hopkinton. But after that I can probably squeeze you in."

"Dale. The rain is washing down the sides of the house."

"Mother, it's been doing that for years." There was a pause as he inhaled. "What you need is not just gutters but a whole new roof. And the floor joists are going too."

This was what exasperated her about Dale; he could never stay on the subject. "The gutters are an emergency. There's nothing wrong with the roof. It's not leaking, so far as I know. This house is tight as a drum. Just get some gutters up there and it'll be fine."

Dale sighed. "Listen, Mom. Listen. I've explained this to you. It's not that simple. Those are wooden gutters. I'm going to have to custom-make them, unless you want to go aluminum, which I know you don't want to do. But right now I have to go to work. I'll stop by after I get out and take another look at them."

She hung up and walked immediately to her chair, writing in her notebook: *Dale will stop by this afternoon, Oct. 5, 1990.* She thought a moment and then added: *Wooden gutters. Custom made.* Although she could not remember for the life of her having had that conversation with him before. When had the gutters overflowed as they had yesterday? Yet he talked like this was a long-standing problem.

The minute hand was inching toward the 12: 8 o'clock. She roused herself, did the dishes (carefully, methodically, so as not to get too lost in what was happening outdoors . . . the other day she had forgotten to rinse and left everything, all soapy, in the drainer) and ticked off her early morning chores: Make bed. Bring down the dirty clothes and put them in the washer. Dust her desk. She was moving the dust cloth quickly over the bookshelves when she remembered the third item, which she had never written down: the library. She had meant to go to the library today, when she paid the taxes. There was more: a particular book she was looking for. But what was it? Damn! Why didn't her mind work anymore, or rather, why did it work in such serpentine, twisted, confounding ways? Connecting randomly, only when it wanted to, not when she needed it to. She should have written the library down. Thinking that, she immediately went to her notebook and wrote: Library, this afternoon, Oct. 5, 1990. She had to date everything, because otherwise she would open to the wrong page and read some instruction from months ago and think it was meant for today.

Every day at 10 o'clock, Fran Kennedy came over for coffee. They had long ago arranged this schedule, and it seemed to work for both of them. By then Fran's kids were off to school and she had finished her early morning chores, too. Helen looked forward to Fran's visits so much that they had become the highlight of her day. Funny, there had been a time when she thought of Fran as a nuisance. Now she depended on her more than she did her own children. Fran did not judge her; Fran listened and asked only to be listened to in return. All of Fran's childish enthusiasms for the house and the property had endured, proving to Helen that they were sincere and unaffected. And Fran helped her so much. She would ask questions, gently, that prompted Helen to remember things she obviously had forgotten. Did she want to button up her cardigan? Was it time to turn on the heat? Was her oil tank full? Would she like her coffee heated up? Helen only had to say yes or no, and she no longer felt embarrassed when Fran pointed out, again gently, that her shirt had a slight stain and perhaps it needed to be washed, or the bread should be discarded because it was moldy.

At first Fran had been rather insistent about her going to the doctor. She thought perhaps Helen's eyesight was failing, but when Helen pointed to a black-capped chickadee perched in the bush by the barn, a speck of dust that Fran could barely see, she gave up on that idea. Routinely Fran suggested she visit a doctor, and just as routinely Helen brushed her off, until Fran apparently realized that their continued harmony was dependent on avoidance of the subject.

It was 10:05, and Fran had not appeared. Helen was growing agitated. She stood up, walked to the kitchen clock, checked the plug, sat down again, looked out the window (no Fran yet), rifled through her notebook (had Fran told her she wouldn't be over today? Had she forgotten to write it down?), fiddled with the place mat. The phone did not ring. The clock ticked loudly. The refrigerator droned; its motor seemed to run all the time; like everything else in the house, it needed replacing, but who could afford a new one? She got up and went into the bathroom to look in the mirror; her hair, which she had not combed after her shower, was matted all over her head. Perhaps she had even forgotten to shampoo it. She ran her fingers through the locks, and that improved matters a little. She must start wearing makeup or something. She was 63 years old and she looked like her mother – wrinkled, weary, spent.

Someone was knocking. Odd; Fran never knocked. What was the matter with her? She opened the door, annoyed, and there was Dub Lillibridge, carrying a bouquet of dahlias.

Then it came back to her.

The third item on her list: not the library. Her brain, which could not remember anything, had not lost its ability to invent, and the library was made up out of whole cloth. It was Mr. Lillibridge. He was coming to visit her, and she had told Fran not to come over today, because she was having company. All this had transpired yesterday over the phone, when the rain was streaking down the windows and she had been unable to walk to get the mail. Why hadn't she written any of this down? Maybe she had, but in the wrong place.

This was terrible.

"Oh, Dub, come in." She smiled, as though she had been expecting him. Which she had, she just didn't know it. Her hair. God, she looked awful. And what was she wearing? She looked down. That blue sweater with the missing button. Her khaki pants, though, were fairly new and pressed.

She took the dahlias and found a vase for them. How she loved dahlias. They were the year's last present; so full and rich, they came in sumptuous autumn colors, like butterscotch and burgundy and golden yellow. She could no longer grow flowers. That was the first, and most severe, symptom of what she had come to think of as her mind disorder: She could not tend the garden anymore. Not only could she not remember what to do, she could not do it; each task had too many steps, and she ended up frustrated, her hands limp in the dirt, all those automatic motions forgotten.

"Let me help you with that." Dub took the vase to the tap,

filled it with water and returned the flowers to it. She had forgotten the water. It was that daydreaming again. Thinking of all those beautiful gardens in her past.

She looked at Dub hopefully. Sooner or later he would explain his presence. She remembered to offer him coffee, and he accepted eagerly, sitting in Fran's seat at the table.

"Helen, what chores would you like to do today?"

Chores? Why was he asking her about chores? She smiled again, gamely. "Whatever you think is best." She had never talked like that in her life, but it was a phrase that did wonders to prompt a conversation along.

"You mentioned something about Town Hall on the phone," he said. There. She sighed visibly. He had offered to drive her today; but how had he known she needed driving? And why couldn't she drive herself? But the car did not seem to be out in the yard. Was it in the garage again?

"I need to pay my taxes," she said, fingering her notebook, "and . . . go to the library." For surely it was true after all. What she would do there, she wasn't sure, but she could always find something to take out, if the specifics of the library errand never surfaced.

"How about some lunch afterwards? My treat." He was dressed nicely, she noticed for the first time. Green-checked chamois shirt, pressed dark green trousers; and his face was pink from shaving. Seeing him across from her at the tiny kitchen table, consciously keeping her knees from knocking against his, she remembered vividly that day in his kitchen, when he had told her he was giving up his land. She had thought something might be blossoming between them, but it never had, at least nothing more than friendship.

"That sounds nice. But I need to be home by four. Dale is coming by to look at the gutters." She grinned at him like a star pupil. He could not know how good it felt to remember something.

The library was in a rambling granite building. Although it was much bigger and grander than the cottage library she had grown up with in Cooperstown, it gave her the same feeling: of being about to discover something. It had that familiar musty smell in the stacks, and an aroma of something else, perhaps a floor disinfectant, in the basement where the periodicals were kept. It was a scent she associated with old wooden schools and tiled hospital wards. It hit her sharply as they walked in the door, and she turned to Dub and said (without quite knowing why): "When I was 12 I played in the band at school. The clarinet. But my mother wouldn't let me march in the parade they held each Memorial Day. First she said it was unladylike. Then she said we couldn't afford the uniform. I spent the afternoon of the parade upstairs in the library, watching my classmates march by. The librarian, Miss Douglas her name was, gave me a piece of butterscotch candy."

Dub seemed astounded by this outburst, but before he could reply, she hurried forward to the fiction stacks, hoping something would catch her eye.

They had lunch in a diner in Narragansett, where they sat in a red vinyl booth and tried to make conversation over BLT sandwiches. Helen rarely went to restaurants. The waitress, a brassy looking redhead with a pencil stuck in her hair, made Helen nervous, as though she were testing her. How was everything? Did she want ketchup with her fries? Would she like to take anything home? Implying, of course, that she should have eaten more. She was a bad customer. She was grateful Dub was with her, that he would pay and leave the tip. She had no idea how much to leave.

"Have you given any more thought to what we talked about, Helen?"

She scrambled around in her mind. What had they talked about? But he looked so serious, almost mournful, that she got the gist of what he was saying. It had to do with them.

"I'm not myself, Dub." He was so kind. She wished she could love him. "I'm not any good to you like this."

"I could take care of you, Helen." He put a rough but cleanly manicured hand over hers. It was surprisingly warm. "You just need someone to look after you, that's all."

"Someone to look after me." She had developed this habit, which she longed to break, of repeating what people said. It made it easier somehow, kept the conversation going when she didn't know what to say. "That's why I had children. But I guess it didn't work out that way."

"Is that really why you had children? I don't think none of us can count on our children taking care of us. They've got their own lives, don't they?"

"Their own lives." Such as they were. Dale, climbing out of whatever black pit he had lately fallen into . . . Joyce, who seemed so miserable all the time, and her husband never around. "I guess I thought the odds were that at least one of them would be around if I needed them."

The sentence hung there, over the dirty plates and salt and pepper shakers and paper place mats with the cartoonish maps of Narragansett Pier. She did not know how much Dub Lillibridge knew about her family, but she was certain he knew about Susan, for he had lived here all his life. He read the newspapers. He drank coffee every morning at the luncheonette in Charlestown. He had worked around Jim Winter for years. They helped each other at haying time, traded tractor parts. He would know she had lost a daughter.

"I'm not just talking about a financial arrangement, you know. I would marry you in every sense of the word." He lowered his voice to ride below the clatter of plates being cleared. "I would cherish you, Helen Winter."

After lunch, they took a walk along the Pier sea wall. Built to keep the ocean out of Ocean Road, the wall had developed into a favorite promenade for joggers, mothers with strollers, casual walkers like themselves and, of course, lovers. Workers ranging from plumbers and electricians to lawyers and secretaries took their lunch here, and signs every 50 feet warned the many dog walkers to clean up after their pets. The wall stretched from South Pier Road to Narragansett's town beach, winding under a stone archway called the Towers, which once had been part of an exclusive casino in Narragansett's golden days. From the wall unfolded a sweeping view of the ocean entering Narragansett Bay, with Newport and Beavertail Light to the east and, closer to shore, the remnants of a lighthouse that had been blown away in the Hurricane of 1938. Dub pointed out many of these landmarks to Helen as though she had never been here before, as though she would not remember the familiar arch of the Newport Bridge in the distance or recognize the coal and oil freighters that drifted occasionally into view.

He was holding her hand, lightly, as they walked. Helen let herself be led, rather like a child. Finally, about half way between the Towers and the wall's southern end, she stopped, balking like a cow at a stile. The waves had caught her attention. How funny that where they stood, the tide sucked out, yet a few hundred feet to the south, waves were roaring in, over the scattered boulders that separated the wall from the water. It was like watching the past, the present and future all at once; she could not tell if the tide was coming in more quickly ahead of them, or if it already was retreating where they stood. What lay ahead might be the future, and it might be the past. The present, where they stood, gave no clue.

In January 1948 she had returned to Cornell University, the second semester of her junior year, days after tossing her ring into Lake Otsego. It was not, technically, an engagement ring. The truth was she had bought the tiny diamond herself at a jeweler's in Ithaca, and, each time she saw Professor Ericson, she slipped it quickly into her pocket and out of view. She had never examined, even years later, why she had spent half her savings on a ring that she knew David (for that was what she called him, when they were truly alone and there was no chance of a TA or fellow undergraduate walking in on them) would never have purchased for her. Although she hoped. Wasn't that the essence of the ring? She hoped. And she fretted, sick with guilt. The ring made everything all right somehow.

That was what she had been doing, that bleak day in December, right before Christmas break: stopping in the hallway next to the last clanking radiator before his office, and taking off her ring. She had stopped in mid-stride, looking up to make sure no one had seen her, and there across from her the office door was ajar. She could see on his lap the shapely, crossed legs of Etta Heathman, blonde, Phi Beta Kappa Etta, who despite the difficult post-war market always seemed to have new, perfect nylon stockings on those gams of hers.

That was pretty much the end of it. Of course, there had been remonstrations and hysterics; anguished phone calls to his apartment at late hours; but very shortly she had to go home for Christmas, packing her misery up with the one good wool suit and silk blouse that made her otherwise shabby wardrobe of sweaters and skirts acceptable.

So then she had dumped the ring overboard from the Otsego ferry and briefly thought of following it. What did you do when you had imagined your life, down to the last detail, when you had made a downpayment on a day that wasn't to come, and then discovered it was gone, another wisp of ferry exhaust exhaled into the sky? What did you do with the reality you'd carried around in your head for so long? The beliefs you'd held so firmly about yourself and someone else, which turned out to be just another cheap volume of fiction, worth no more than the 15-cent Pocket Books you bought at the drugstore?

The answer was inside her, spoiling like a rotten melon, making her sick and helpless. She imagined the whole world could see the wasted heart she carried around, which beat for no purpose, pumping drop after drop of blood around in a lackluster rhythm. But the truth was no one noticed. If her mother thought it odd she slept so late on Christmas vacation, if her father saw how little she ate at every meal, they did not remark on it; if her brother, busy sneaking drinks with his friends and chasing girls down at the textile mill where he worked second shift, sensed any change in his big sister, he shrugged it off. Women could be moody, after all.

It was not until three weeks later, at the first class meeting of American Poetry Since 1900, that her friend Jim Winter sat down next to her and saw the misery in her face.

"Crackerjack, you look like you lost your best friend." That was what he always called her: Crackerjack, or Crackers for short, because she was always snacking on it in the student union. He didn't know it was her lunch most days, all she could afford; she was on a limited meal plan. She always kidded him back: She called him Peanuts, because he took the peanuts out when she offered him a handful.

Otherwise, she didn't think about Jim Winter very much. An English major, he was in most of her classes. He was just another of those post-war veterans, older than she, in school on the GI bill. She wondered if he might even be as old as Professor Ericson, who seemed daringly sophisticated at 28.

She smiled at him wanly and, when he followed her to the bookstore to buy the class text and then invited her for a coffee, decided, Why not? He was so easy to talk to. Soon she had told him her whole sad story. Part of it, anyway. He did not have to know how far it had gone or why she really thought it prudent to be making her own engagement plans.

"Etta Heathman! Good God!" He seemed so astounded that they both laughed out loud. All of Etta's excesses, from the bleached blonde hair to the perfect seam in the back of her stockings, seemed wrapped up in his outburst.

And he was handsome when he laughed. Despite his stocky, tall, square build, he had a soft face, bland and boyish, with green eyes that darkened in a certain light. A pleasant and open face. Professor Ericson, who had tempted her with all sorts of sweet talk, had brown eyes that were striking but cold.

Soon Jim was taking her to dinner, at a small restaurant downtown called the Crystal Palace, where they served more food than she was used to eating in a day. They went roller skating at a large old rink on the outskirts of town, and when the weather moderated they began to take drives upstate in his '38 Plymouth, the windows cracked to tousle her hair. They stopped at picnic groves and scenic gorges to hike or eat lunch. When he kissed her for the first time, wrapping his bear-like arms around her in a firm grip, she felt the softness of his mouth like a lightning strike riving her body. She had forgotten the professor; she had forgotten the childhood on the Cooperstown farm and her mother's sharp, critical voice. She was looking firmly ahead, into the future. She was so sure she had imagined it correctly this time.

"Did I ever tell you how your father proposed?"

Helen was sitting in her favorite armchair, watching Joyce dust. She never came over without a reason, it seemed. Today that unstated purpose was like a serpent jerking around inside her. Helen could see it as Joyce moved about the room, picking up objects and putting them down, dragging a piece of Helen's old flannel nightgown over bric-a-brac, books, table lamps. Joyce was always complaining about how dusty the house was: How did her mother stand it? But Helen didn't notice. Perhaps her eyes were going, Joyce would say. Everybody had some medical theory as to what might be wrong with Helen Winter.

"It was 1949, right before I visited the farm for the first time." Helen plunged ahead, although her inquiry had received only a grunt from Joyce, who was giving careful attention to the spine of each book she picked up. "It was March. Still winter up in Ithaca; I remember being holed up in my tiny dorm room, writing a paper on Emily Dickinson, and I really felt a kinship with her, in that bedroom in Amherst. Except my room was always hot. The dorms had this awful steam heat – "

Joyce had stopped wiping down encyclopedias and was staring at her. "How Daddy proposed," she prompted.

"Yes." Damn, she hated interruptions. She had been working out this story in her mind all day, savoring the details, until she could smell the wool of her mittens baking on the radiator and see the snow-sugared spruce out the window. And Jim's face, smiling, reddened from the cold, when he appeared at her door. His boots dripped on the rug; his muffler was askew.

Let's make a snowman, he had said. It's probably the last big snow of the year.

"Your father had a real fun-loving streak in him. I know you probably didn't see much of it, but he was a great practical joker, and he always loved to play in the snow." Helen picked up the story where her mind had left it. "And he dragged me outside, even though I should have been finishing my paper."

"Outside where?" Joyce was carefully polishing the brass letter opener on Helen's desk. She held it pointed toward her mother like a dagger.

"Outside my dorm. Stop interrupting." Helen realized she had to get through the story in one breath or Joyce would ruin it with her puzzled looks and questions. "So he took me outside. And we made a snowman – it was great snow for it, wet and packable – and when we were done we put a carrot on for its nose and two black rocks for its eyes and some tiny pebbles all in a row for its mouth. And then he reached in his pocket and said, 'Here, what do you think he should do with this,' and it was a box. With a ring inside."

"I never saw you wear an engagement ring."

"Oh, I don't know what happened to it." Helen looked down at her finger, at the simple platinum band she had worn for more than 40 years, not taking it off even after Jim died. What had happened to her diamond? She could see the box it came in now, a square of black velvet Jim Winter had shoved into her hand as they approached the farm that spring weekend of 1948.

Of course, he had to get her to say yes before she knew what she was walking into, before she met Martha and saw the farm in all its flat, sere, forsaken glory. But that wasn't a story worth telling. She liked her version much better.

"Mother, I want to ask you something, and I want you to give me a straight answer."

Joyce had stopped dusting but still held the rag of flannel, now gray with filth. "I want to know why Dad killed himself. And I want to hear it from you."

Ah, that was the reason for the girl's nervous energy, why she was darting around the room like a dragonfly. That was the motive for coming over today to visit her mother. An interrogation.

"I don't know." She liked that answer. Simple, elegant, true as far as it went. Joyce didn't know she was asking the wrong question. Ultimately it wasn't Jim's suicide that was that important; the story lay in everything that had come before. More days of the past to ruminate over, rewrite as she saw fit. But confronted thus, without the luxury of turning the years over in her mind, Helen had nothing to offer.

"I think you do. I heard that Dad was having an affair." Chin up. Defiant. She enjoys this, Helen thought; she enjoys throwing all this in my face.

"Who told you that? Somebody who enjoys repeating ugly rumors? About a man who's been dead for 12 years now? And you believe it, of course." Helen wondered how this day, which had started with a rather pleasant reverie about Jim, the old Jim, the Jim who'd loved her, had turned into this, leapt so quickly into another part of the past. But that was her life these days: moving, inexorably, from memory to memory, from heartache to heartache. When you lived in the present you had enough sorrows to bear; but when you lived in any time, all time, the grief of the past kept getting compounded, until it was unbearable, inescapable.

"He did it on purpose, you know," she continued, Joyce's keen eyes on her. "Gave me that ring when he did. He knew I'd never have married him if I'd known the truth of what I was walking into."

The new year came, a time of fresh starts, and they sat around the television watching their new governor, hatless and cold, make a grim announcement on the steps of the State House.

The state's credit unions, all of them, had been closed. Failed.

"I remember when Roosevelt closed the banks." Helen was glad she could grasp this, had a way to relate to what was happening. Dale and Joyce, who had come over to wish her a happy new year (was it her imagination, or did they visit more often now? Keeping an eye on her?), sat on either arm of her chair, stunned. "It was panic. Pandemonium. Lines down the street. My father was a Republican. How he hated Roosevelt. After that, kept all his money under his mattress."

"I wish I'd kept my money under the mattress." Joyce buried her head in her hands.

"I've got two weeks pay at home, thank God." This from Dale, who, Helen knew, was paid strictly on a cash basis, under the table. She had always worried about it – what if the IRS caught up with him? – but now it seemed a blessing.

The kids wanted to know where she kept her money, and she had to think about it. Her mind, as it did so often these days, was an empty canvas. She imagined neurons stretching to reach each other, like arms to a drowning child, but never extending far enough, never quite making it.

"My bank book's over there, on the desk somewhere." She pointed vaguely and Joyce began rifling through drawers, shuffling papers, coming up with nothing. "Maybe in my purse."

The missing bank book became an incident, with Joyce tearing through the house, muttering under her breath. Dale just kept watching TV, as the newscasters regurgitated the governor's startling announcement. Helen tried to picture her bank, its square, cinderblock construction, its glowing neon sign high on a pedestal. It was a bank, wasn't it? And not a credit union?

"Industrial National," she finally said, triumphant.

"Mother, nobody calls it that anymore. It's Fleet." Joyce seemed almost disappointed. Her mother had not lost any funds after all.

"It fell out of the setting. That's what happened to it."

Helen was walking on the hard, rutted driveway with Fran Kennedy. They walked every day now, until it snowed or rained, in a circle: east toward the Audubon land, south to Fran's house, along the beach, and then back the way they had come.

Fran stopped, squeezed Helen's elbow. Fran was a toucher, what Joyce would call touchy-feely: She was always putting a hand on Helen's forearm, grasping her wrist, hugging her hard. At first Helen had recoiled from it; neither her family, the stoic Richmonds, nor any of the Winters – save perhaps Loretta – had been big on physical expressions of sentiment. In fact they were not big on emotional expressions of any sort. But she had gotten used to it.

"Fell out of the setting? What are you talking about, Hel?"

"My engagement ring. It got loose somehow, that's what happened to it." She had finally remembered. Walking along, looking at her feet, she had thought of things dropping, getting lost – the children's mittens, coins through pocket holes. And that was when the image had come to her of the empty prongs. Somehow her diamond had gotten loose, fallen out – in the garbage or down the sink, perhaps – and she had never seen it again. It was all a long time ago. The fifties at least. She was not sure that Joyce had even been born yet.

Helen tried to explain this to Fran, but she looked nonplussed, and they resumed walking. The air carried a chill. Helen thought of hot chocolate, with bulbous, melting marshmallows.

"Will you look at that."

Fran had stopped again and grabbed her, pointing this time. Off toward Ludlow's land, the cedar swamp Helen had sold him. He had cleared most of it, put roads in, and she could spot foundations through the trees. But that was nothing new. They had been there for months. She was sure of it.

"What? I don't see anything."

"That's right. There hasn't been a backhoe in there for weeks, or a pickup truck, or anything."

"It is winter."

"So? They've got the foundations in. The weather is clear. They should be framing. When we built our house – "

Helen started walking again, impatient for hot chocolate. She didn't want to linger near the swamp, where Jim had spent so much time. Bad enough they walked by the cemetery every morning.

But Fran had other ideas. She wanted to go over there, into

the woods, to check out the situation. Helen was appalled. On the west, blackberry briars and small hardwoods ringed the property like a barbed-wire fence, discouraging investigation. On the east, Helen knew, the land was wetter and sloped down precipitously. She argued against it. She was still spry, and Fran was certainly in shape, but they would be crazy to try to climb through there.

Instead, they walked to Fran's house and climbed into her new car. Audi, the nameplate said. When Helen sat in the passenger seat, it began to heat up, making her legs sweaty. A tiny thermometer above the rearview mirror showed the temperature inside and out.

They drove down the Post Road, until they reached the entrance of Ludlow's new subdivision. Winter Acres, a wooden sign read. Helen had never seen that before. At first, she felt a flash of umbrage, until she realized that Ludlow wasn't using her name. It was his name too.

They entered the development at Cedar Swamp Drive, which led to two cul-de-sacs – Blackberry Hill Road and Audubon Lane. Most of the lots, though still wooded, had been cleared enough to put in a foundation. Some had for-sale signs. The roads were paved, but a sidewalk on Cedar Swamp Drive stopped abruptly and became a dirt shoulder. A mound of dirt stood beside the road, covered with a tarp.

Fran circled through and then drove back, until they came to the only completed house, where a sign, "Model Open," was nailed to a tree. No one was in sight.

"I bet he's got all his money tied up in a credit union." Fran stopped the car next to the model home. Her eyes were wide. "It's been in all the papers. That's how these credit unions got into trouble, loaning too much money to real estate developers."

Helen tried to follow what she was saying. "You mean he's broke?"

"Let's go check it out." Fran had already unbuckled her seatbelt and opened her door.

Helen was aghast. "Isn't that trespassing?"

"Hey. It says 'Model Open.' "

Helen dragged along while Fran peeked in windows. The house was a step above the raised ranches Ludlow was famous for. It was Colonial in design, with a center chimney and a two-car garage. The clapboards painted a bright yellow, Helen realized when they got closer, were really vinyl siding. The yard was still a hard, rutted mess of frozen earth and ice, but a brick walkway led to the front door.

Fran tried the door, and it gave with a slight push. To Helen's horror, she walked right in.

"It's only breaking in if you have intent. There's no intent here. We're just two buyers, checking out a model home."

The foyer was brightly wallpapered, with a carpeted staircase and hardwood floors. Dark mahogany furnishings – a Queen Anne side table, a matching maroon chair – were positioned in the entry, which opened to the left onto an expansive living room. This, too, was furnished elegantly. The south wall featured a fireplace with a marble mantel.

Beyond the living room, however, the illusion ended. They walked into an empty kitchen, where maple cabinets had been built but no appliances installed. The downstairs lavette contained only pipes leading up from the floor. Up the carpeted stairs were similarly roughed-out rooms, separated only by wall studs.

"They didn't even finish the model." Fran ran her fingers along an unpainted windowsill, tracing a line in the dust. A strip of paper with paint colors printed on it – from Baby Blue Eyes to Mediterranean Sea – lay on the floor. Helen picked it up and then quickly threw it down again. It, too, was thick with dirt.

"Let's go home, Fran. We shouldn't be here."

"I hope that bastard paid you. Because you'll never get your money out of him now."

He had paid her. Hadn't he? Like the missing bank book, her arrangement with Ludlow was gone from her mind, another thread missing from the warp of her past.

"I wonder what that is," Fran said, pointing outside to the hole in the ground, covered in plastic.

To Helen it looked like only one thing: a fresh grave, waiting for a body.

CHAPTER TWENTY-TWO

▲

When the phone rang, Joyce had to answer it. This was one of the conditions that Michael had placed upon their marriage, to the point where she wondered how he had coped before she moved in. Hadn't he answered the phone when she called him, years before? But he was insistent. He hated the telephone; at work, he had a secretary to screen his calls, but at home the phone would interrupt whatever he was doing – working, usually, in his den, or less frequently eating or making love - and he detested interruptions.

Sometimes the phone rang while they were asleep, and even then Michael didn't stir. Whenever Camille complained about having to get up in the middle of the night to nurse the baby, Joyce thought of the telephone. Its jangle was Joyce's crying baby. You especially had to answer it then, because even though it was mostly wrong numbers or cranks – their number was one digit off from the Seashore Motel, and they were forever getting late calls – the possibility existed that it could be Dale, off the wagon and in a drunk tank somewhere.

In 1991, they began getting a different sort of telephone call. The first one came on a rainy night in March, at nearly 2 a.m. Michael had just returned from a two-week trip to Washington state and their night had started with a bottle of wine and ended with urgent, drunken sex, and he snored now next to her as the phone exploded from the other room. As she stumbled out to answer it the moon through the window reminded her of searchlights. She had been dreaming something, the same pattern, over and over, and her tongue felt like a slab of ham in her mouth.

It was her mother, screaming.

"Joyce! They're outside! I can see them. They're going to cut the wires and come in here. Joyce, come over here, please, they're going to break in!"

Helen's hysteria was like a sharp smell of ammonia under Joyce's nostrils. She ran back into the bedroom, violently shook Michael awake, threw on her dirty jeans and sweater, and called the police.

The cruisers arrived at the farm just as they did, lights cut and sirens off.

While two officers outside searched the "perimeter of the house," as they called it, the sergeant interviewed her mother in the kitchen. Helen's hair was flying in tatters about her head, and she wore a ratty red chenille bathrobe over her pajamas. The lapels were stained with food. The pupils of her eyes, Joyce noticed, were bulging, like those of a cat that's walked into a darkened room. Her hands shook as she talked.

Mrs. Winter might consider buying some exterior lighting for the house, the officer suggested. His uniform included a heavy blue mackinaw, and the plastic cover of his hat dripped like a shower cap. Mrs. Winter was off the road and the property was very dark at night. Her locks also needed replacing. A deadbolt, at the very least, and locks on the windows. He did not, however, think an alarm system necessary. They were expensive and touchy, often going off when there was no danger.

"It would just upset her more," the police officer, Sergeant Charles Antrim according to his name tag, said in an undertone to Joyce. "How long has your mother had Alzheimer's?"

"Alzheimer's?" She repeated, dazed. She looked at Helen, who in her nightwear looked older and thinner than she remembered, and realized she was going to turn 64 next month. But Alzheimer's? It was true Helen had displayed some disturbing symptoms lately. She sometimes – often – forgot details about dates, names, the itinerary of her day; she seemed less capable of taking care of herself. But Joyce had never before seen her so helpless and unkempt. She tried to brush the idea away, like a spider web on the cellar stairs. "I think she just woke up in the middle of the night, and was confused," she told the officer. "But she doesn't have Alzheimer's."

But Helen Winter's nightmares soon became a disturbing nightly pattern. At least once a week the phone would ring in the middle of the night, with Helen screaming on the other end that someone was trying to break in, and Joyce and Michael would rush over to the farmhouse to find her mother raving about burglars sneaking around in the yard. She seemed particularly distressed about a hole in the woods; she described it in great detail, the vanilla-colored tarp that covered it, the bones that lay just underneath. If Joyce entertained the idea even for a moment that a real threat existed at the farm, Helen's story about the freshly dug grave erased it.

After awhile they stopped calling the police, and eventually, like his refusal to answer the phone, Michael stopped driving over to the farm with her. Calming her crazy mother had become Joyce's job.

"You should get her to a doctor." Camille was breaking apart a bran muffin. She had suggested they meet at the doughnut shop. She had listened to Joyce's story, but she seemed rushed, distracted, even though it was her day off.

"She won't go. We've all suggested it. I can't even get her to go to the optometrist."

"Typical." Camille dumped a tumbler of cream in her coffee and stirred it absently. "The resistance, I mean. Alzheimer's patients have some clue there's something wrong, but they keep writing it off. And they have less and less ability to recognize their own symptoms as time goes on."

Did she have to use that word? Alzheimer's. It didn't seem possible. "But in some ways she's sharp as a tack. You should hear her tell stories about the past. Like it was yesterday."

"I don't want to scare you, but that's common. The old memories, the ones that are firmest in their minds, are always the last to go. It's the short-term memory that's giving her trouble. She'll continue to be able to interact with people – the social skills are more resilient. And she might never lose her long-term memories. But the cognitive stuff will become increasingly difficult. Is she still writing?"

Joyce hesitated. Her mother kept a notebook on the kitchen table, although it was obvious from the dust that she hadn't used the typewriter in some time. And when Joyce borrowed the newspaper, the crossword was only half done or sometimes not attempted at all. "I don't know. I'd have to snoop around."

"Don't feel guilty about it. You're snooping for a good reason." Camille brushed muffin crumbs off her sweater and the gesture seemed to put an end to that topic. "Listen. I have to talk to you about something."

Joyce pushed aside her irritation. Camille had listened to her and offered her good advice, yet . . . she always felt cheated, somehow, when they talked, as though her life was only a warm-up act to the more important topic, namely Camille. She never felt that way with Althea: If anything, Althea subsumed her life to everyone else's.

"Eric and I are having . . . trouble." Joyce let out an involuntary exclamation but Camille kept going. "I don't know what's going to happen. He just refuses to see my point about his job. He's spending all this time with the tribe, he's at meetings every night, and meanwhile I'm working my butt off taking extra shifts. He could be making big money at a Providence firm if he wanted to. But no. He's got to save the world."

At least your husband's around, Joyce thought. "Do you think you're going to get a divorce?" She hated to admit it, but the idea shocked her. No one in her family had ever divorced. She knew, intellectually, that divorce was commonplace, but the idea was repugnant to her, especially when she thought of Forrest and Skye.

"I don't know. And do what? Where would we live? What about the kids? It's a goddamn mess. All I know is, I can't stand all this fighting. When we're not fighting, it's like a Mexican standoff."

"What about your mother? Could you stay with her?"

"In the old shack? I don't think so." Camille looked back at her coldly. "There's more involved in this than having a place to stay. You have to prepare. If I walked out today he'd get everything, the house, maybe even the kids. Eric's a lawyer. I'm sure he knows all the tricks. You have to beat them at their own game."

When had Camille become so cynical? But maybe she had always been that way and Joyce had never realized it. "There's got to be a better way, Camille. God, you don't want to leave the kids behind."

"No shit. He's not getting a penny of mine, either. I already opened my own account, out of town. If this happens I'm not going to end up one of those poor single mothers collecting WIC every week."

Joyce did not know what WIC was, but she could guess. "I thought you loved Eric. I know he loves you."

"Don't be naïve, Joyce. Marriage is an economic arrangement. And when one partner isn't pulling his weight, you have to choose between carrying him or getting the hell out."

The coffee had soured in the back of Joyce's mouth. She didn't know what to say to Camille. She certainly wasn't qualified to give advice on marriage.

Joyce wanted to see Lydia, but there was never any time. Unlike Helen, Lydia had no children to visit her, no neighbors to check on her. Joyce imagined her in all sorts of predicaments: lying sick abed, with no one to tend to her; collapsed on the floor, the stove gone cold, her breath weak; fallen outside, her ankle twisted on a root, her ribs broken. In each image the life was leaking out of Lydia, dissipating on the wind. On her seldom visits Joyce noticed a difference: She was failing. Walking slower, rubbing her hands as though in pain. And her memory was slipping away. "I had something to tell you," she would say, "but I can't remember what it was."

Joyce worried about this almost as much as she worried about her mother, but it was a different sort of anxiety. She felt not guilt but a pang of loneliness when she imagined Lydia gone. What was it that made Joyce care more about this cantankerous woman than her own mother? Not caring more, but in a lighter, simpler way. With no bitter entanglements to spoil their bond.

Maybe it was because Lydia had lived her life on her terms but no one else's. Maybe it was because when she asked Joyce a question, she listened with her whole body in a suspended attention. Maybe it was because she had so little yet gave so much.

Whatever it was, beneath Lydia Franklin's stubborn, Yankee-proud, cussed exterior Joyce saw through to a thin flame of tenderness that burned pure and true.

This was what family trouble did: It brought everybody together. Helen's condition became a source of consternation and speculation: What to do? How to handle her? What's wrong with her? How to get her to the doctor? Should she really be left alone? The questions were endless and kept Joyce and Dale on the phone for hours. By some mutual agreement, unspoken, they had stopped meeting at the Salty Dog. Ostensibly because they didn't want to talk about Helen in public, but more, Joyce liked to think, because Dale had finally concluded that hanging out in a barroom was not the best way to support his sobriety. He had ditched the girlfriend, too, when she showed more interest in drinking after work with the bartenders and wait staff than in coming home to him.

"I'm OK with it," was all he said. "She was getting on my nerves anyway."

So Dale came to Joyce's house and they sat over dinner, many a night, trying to sort through the mess five miles to the east: the farmhouse falling apart, their mother coming unglued. Just when it seemed they had talked the problem every way but sideways, a new angle came up, a new problem.

There was the matter of the car. Helen had already had a minor accident, a fender-bender in the parking lot of the small grocery down the road. They suspected she might have had other, minor mishaps: the side panel was marred with two large scrapes, too deep to have come from the brush lining the driveway. She had also told Dale, but not Joyce, that one day she'd come out of the post office and for one terrifying minute could not decide whether to turn left or right out of the parking lot.

So one day, without saying a word, Dale took the keys and brought them home. Joyce wondered if that were too cruel to do to someone who was always misplacing things, but then they discovered that their mother had simply called the garage, which came and installed a new ignition. So her mother's cunning had foiled their attempt anyway. That required more drastic measures; Dale persuaded the mechanic, who had been doing business with the Winters for years, to come and take the car away, as though it were being serviced.

Her mother had more friends, more allies than they realized. That Fran Kennedy, for example. Joyce didn't like her, never had, but Dale finally convinced her Fran could undo everything they were trying to accomplish if they didn't take her into their confidence. And the result was that she was checking up on their mother every day now, not just when the spirit moved her, and more than once she reported some near calamity: a stove burner left on, a faucet running. It was Fran who realized that Helen needed structure. She told Joyce to call her at the same time every day, and she timed her own visits to the minute; now when Joyce left school every day, her first stop was the farm, and if she were delayed in the slightest – by a student who needed extra help, a traffic jam in the parking lot – Helen was nearly frantic when she arrived.

But the nightmares, they had intensified to the point where Dale and Joyce wondered how Helen could continue to live alone. They were wearing Joyce down, never knowing when the phone might ring, when her mother would have a bad night. When Michael was out of town she found herself staying overnight at the farm, figuring it was easier than getting up in a terrible scramble and tearing over there in the middle of the night. But even though he was sometimes thousands of miles away, Michael didn't like it. His tone was more weary than angry. "It's not that I don't understand, Joyce. But this is crazy. You can't take care of her 24 hours a day. It's not good for you."

And when he said it, he sounded more like the man she had married, or the man she had thought she married. He was right: She could not take care of her mother all the time, not and work and have a marriage. They would have to figure something out. Dale sometimes stayed over, but he, too, found the constant worry made for fitful sleep.

"She won't leave that place. You know that," Dale said. It was a Saturday, and he and Joyce were raking the last of the leaves before the snow flew. Michael was on his last trip of the year, to Sri Lanka. He had promised to be home for Christmas – and if all went well, to stay home for a while. The dean was retiring. Michael hoped at least to be appointed acting dean during the search, which could take a year.

"But suppose she did. What about those new apartments in town? For the elderly? We should put her name in. We don't have to tell her. There's probably a waiting list. By the time her name comes up, she may not even know what's what."

"Whoa." Dale huffed a pile of oak and maple leaves into a bag and then looked over at the farmhouse, as though Helen might be listening. "She would kill us. There is no way I'm doing that. Go ahead. I'll blame you when the time comes."

"Dale, you're not helping." Joyce was kneeling on the ground, already hard with early frost, and ripping out the stalks of daisies and foxglove and lilies, her mother's hardy perennials that came back every year even though she had not ventured into the garden all summer. "What would you suggest? We can't hire someone to come take care of her, not in this house. What nurse is going to want to live like this?"

It was true that, despite their best efforts, the house was getting worse. Dale had finally found time to replace the gutters and shingle the roof, with help from a couple of his carpenter friends, and Loretta's wallpapering had brightened the upstairs; but the rooms suffered so from Helen's inability to keep house that Joyce could barely prepare a sandwich or use the bathroom without stopping to clean first. The kitchen cabinets were thick with grease, the counters dusty; the refrigerator often was crowded with spoiled food, its shelves stained with spills; the kitchen and bathroom floors were gray and sticky. To add to the problem, Helen had begun accumulating stuff in the way old people will, leaving stacks of newspapers on chairs and filling up cupboards with empty plastic containers.

Dale had bagged the last pile of leaves and leaned his rake against the barn. "If I had time I'd take down that old tree," he said, pointing to the silver maple listing toward the barn's roof. "That's where most of the leaves come from. Listen," and he moved back into their conversation as though he had never left it. "For the time being, we get that Fran woman to stay with her during the day. We can pay her. Ma's got money, I know she has. I think she'd do it. At night, you and I and Aunt Loretta switch off. We haven't asked her to do much, and she'd help out."

Joyce was skeptical. Fran did seem to be crazy about their mother, why Joyce could not fathom, but she also had the schedule rich men's wives seem to adopt, full of yoga classes and club meetings. "Loretta's too old to be watching Ma. I don't think she's up to it," she added.

But they decided to ask them both. It was the only plan they could come up with.

Camille had put her in touch with a woman at the hospital, a senior advocate who worked with families and local senior centers. She was crisply dressed, in her fifties, and sat behind a desk totally devoid of papers, files, even pens or pencils. Only a computer monitor and a picture frame – its back to Joyce – sullied the empty perfection.

"What assets does your mother have?"

"She owns her house. And land."

"Worth? Estimated? If you put it on the market today."

Joyce was blank. "I don't know . . . it's a farm and about 50 acres . . . on the water. The house is in poor condition." She wanted to defend it, make it sound greater than it was, but she knew that was a bad tactic. Assets would mean her mother wasn't eligible for help. Camille had explained this to her.

"On the water? What do you mean? A pond?"

"Well, there is a pond, but that's not what I meant." She was rambling. The woman clicked her red fingernails on the computer keys, lightly, impatiently. "The ocean," Joyce added. "It's on the Atlantic Ocean. Near Green Hill."

"Your mother owns fifty acres on the ocean? Has she tried selling any of it?"

"She's sold it off, in bits and pieces. She sold a lot recently to my cousin. The farm was once a couple of hundred acres, but over the years it's dwindled."

The woman, whose name tag read only SAWYER, seized on this bit of information. "She recently sold a lot? For how much? She must have money from the sale?"

"I don't know." And that was true. Joyce had no idea how much money her mother had from selling the cedar lot to Ludlow. That was one area she and Dale had yet to penetrate. Her bank book never seemed to be in sight. Fran was driving her to the bank these days. Any mention of money usually provoked an argument.

The woman asked more questions. Did her mother get Social Security? How much? Did she have any interest income? Did Joyce have a copy of her tax return? Again and again Joyce had to say, "I don't know," until Sawyer gave up typing and looked at her with her gray-shadowed, finely lined eyes.

"It would be better if you came back when you have more information," Sawyer said. "I can't really help you if you don't know anything about your mother's finances." She opened a drawer and pulled out two documents.

"This can be a good way to start a discussion," she said. Patronizing. "These forms are meant to be filled out together, caregiver and patient. One is called Durable Power of Attorney. It assigns someone to make financial decisions for your mother if you determine she is no longer capable of making them herself. This form is Durable Power of Health Care. It empowers someone else to make medical decisions if," and she paused to clear her throat, "your mother has a medical event that keeps her from communicating intelligently with her doctors."

A medical event. Like when her mother fell on Dale's boat. Joyce wondered how many of Helen's problems were linked to that episode.

"This might be a good way to introduce some of these difficult topics," Sawyer concluded, passing the two pieces of paper into Joyce's hands.

Trying to be agreeable, she took the forms and muttered that she would be back. But she knew she wouldn't.

There was the delicate matter of Mr. Lillibridge. He had been squiring Helen around town since they took the car away. It was obvious he was sweet on her, as Helen would have put it, but Joyce felt uncomfortable talking to him. He was a typical farmer: He barely said two words to her, and blushed crimson whenever someone other than Helen addressed him. "Maybe you can talk to him," she suggested to Dale. "You know. Go over there and kick a couple of tractor tires with him."

"And say what? Are you trying to hump my mother?"

"Jesus, Dale!" He could be so crude sometimes. Even sober, he was a challenge. "NO. Talk to him about her. See what he thinks about her memory. Ask him if he would mind looking out for her."

"And when does the tractor-tire kicking come in? Before or after we chew a plug of tobacco?"

She sighed. She might as well do it herself.

To Joyce's surprise, both Fran and Loretta agreed to their plan. Fran said she could not work weekends, when her children were out of school, but otherwise she could stay with Helen every weekday – as long as they didn't mind if she brought Helen along on an occasional errand. Joyce, who imagined her mother sitting idly in a chair while Fran practiced a yoga pose, was not crazy about the idea, but even she had to admit that Fran sounded sincere. They would just have to give it a try. And Fran wouldn't accept a dime for her work – she didn't want the money and she didn't need it.

Loretta, when brought up to speed on how much Helen's memory loss had deteriorated, volunteered to help without hesitation. She would stay all weekend, Friday night to Monday morning, if she and Dale could manage the weeknights. Joyce was overjoyed.

Mr. Lillibridge surprised her even more. She called him on the phone, which seemed to get around the tire-kicking problem. He probably thought her abrupt – she had never been good at the long, prefatory conversation all the Swamp Yankees loved. She was a generation removed from her father, who would pontificate on the weather, the size of deer herds, the price of diesel fuel, the fate of last year's corn crop, and so on, before getting to the point of a visit or phone call. But when Lillibridge realized why Joyce was calling, he grew expansive. Yes, he had noticed that her mother seemed to be confused sometimes, as he put it. Yes, he would definitely check on her more often, maybe give Fran or Loretta a spell whenever possible. And he would be happy to continue to be her taxi wherever she needed to go.

"I would do more, you know, if she would let me," he said, cryptically, but then he simply thanked her for calling and hung up.

Joyce put aside the brochure Camille had given her about senior services. Meals on Wheels, rides to appointments, senior day care. They didn't need to worry about powers of attorney or income tax returns or CNAs coming into the old farmhouse; she wouldn't have to go back to the spare and cold office at the hospital. They had it covered.

"Do you think Fran Kennedy is too close to Mom?"

It was Dale, not Joyce, who first made this observation. Joyce was so happy she didn't have to worry about her mother all day while she was teaching that she hadn't given much thought to Fran. Joyce relieved her at 3 p.m. every day, stopping on her way home from work. Some days she stayed all night; others, Dale came by at 5 p.m. to take his turn. Her encounters with Fran were like chatting with a babysitter after a long day at work. Perfunctory, quick, their conversations dealt with essentials, sometimes whispered out of Helen's earshot. "She didn't eat much at lunch," Fran might say, or, "She was talking about the past again today. She seems depressed."

Fran's summation of the day was like a warning clarion: A sign of how well Joyce's next few hours, or overnight, were going to go. Some days her mother seemed perfectly normal. If you quizzed Helen about her day, she might draw a blank, but she could converse intelligently with Joyce about all manner of subjects, from the cardinals she had seen in the quince bush to the meaning of some arcane phrase that had just popped into her mind. Talking with her was like reading a dictionary, flipping arbitrarily from page to page: You never knew what the next subject would be or how interesting you might find it. Time had no meaning; she could flit from an episode in Joyce's childhood (which she herself had long forgotten) to a trivial piece of 14th-century Italian Renaissance history. It was like she was purging her mind, reading aloud each memory or fact before tossing it into the dustbin, never to be retrieved again.

Then there were the difficult days. Helen would be agitated, nervous. Pacing about the house. Fearful, even paranoid. Did Joyce lock the door? Did Joyce lock the door? Did Joyce lock the door? Repeated exactly, over and over, no matter how many times Joyce answered her or dragged her over the back door to prove it. More talk about the bones and the grave in the woods. Or she would grow obstinate, angry. No, she didn't want to eat now, at this hour, what ever made her think such a thing? No, she would not go to bed! Try to make her. Go ahead.

But Fran Kennedy – Joyce no longer felt animosity toward Fran, and she didn't see any reason to. If Fran was close to her mother, well, God bless her and good luck. Let them spend all the time they wanted to together.

"I just think there's something about it we ought to keep an eye on, that's all," Dale said. "She's been taking her to the bank, helping her pay bills. I offered but Ma said no, and then Fran chimed in and said it was all set. I'm not sure that's such a good idea."

Joyce scoffed. What, did he think that Fran Kennedy was stealing from Helen? The woman was practically a millionaire. Fran liked Helen, for some crazy reason. That was all.

Joyce did not have the emotional energy to worry about Fran Kennedy, just as she no longer had the energy to obsess about her husband's whereabouts, moods, or demands. Michael seemed to have sensed this change in her. Now that she no longer had time to lie around the house waiting for him, he was home all the time. He had received the appointment as acting dean and, although he continued to bring volumes of work home, he was out of work at a reasonable hour, wanting to go out to dinner or talk to her about her day. Joyce had been alone so long she could not get used to his sudden interest in her. And, because she was only home every other weeknight, she longed to have some time to herself. The truth was she just wanted to wash her hair and read a magazine, but she tried to humor him. On the good days she unburdened herself – recounted the hellish night she'd had with her mother, or complained that she was behind in correcting papers. On the bad days she bickered with him, usually over nothing. She didn't know how to tell him she was too exhausted to be wife and daughter at the same time.

"We should take a vacation this summer," he suggested one evening, as they sat over the remnants of a quick dinner picked up at the supermarket. "I don't have any trips planned. Tell me where you want to go. Anywhere."

She stretched her stocking feet and swallowed the last drop of her wine. "I hear summer in Maine is nice," she said, thinking aloud. "Somewhere up north, where it's cooler."

"How about Canada? The Maritimes? One place I've never been. I hear Nova Scotia is beautiful."

A few days later he visited a travel agency and brought home some brochures. Joyce didn't have the heart to say aloud what she was thinking: What about her mother? Who would take care of her mother while she was gone?

Dale was the thoughtful one. It shocked Joyce to realize this, but it was true. Stripped of his alcoholism and anxieties, he was the one who worried about other people, came up with ideas that never would have occurred to her. She was taking care of her mother out of duty. But Dale was motivated by love. After reading a book on Alzheimer's, he started bringing Helen toys and gifts to keep her mind active: Large-print, less challenging crosswords. Jigsaw puzzles designed to prod her sense of spatial relations. When Helen complained to him she could never remember the day of the week, he bought a large, wooden calendar of rotating numbers and days that could be kept current, usually by Fran, so Helen could refer to it as often as she wished.

These signs of Dale's caring were all over the house, but Joyce knew it wasn't the material goods that bothered her so much. Dale still had a great affection for their mother. Despite his outburst that day at the Salty Dog, despite his bitterness over various childhood hurts, Dale treated Helen tenderly. He worried about her. In short, he loved her.

Joyce wondered: What's wrong with me? Why can't I summon any affection for my own mother? She recalled that night by the hospital bed, after the fall, when she feared Helen would die. Joyce remembered the suffering, the fear of loss. But now her mother, gray and shrunken and not quite herself, still inspired a muted annoyance, even anger. She couldn't understand Fran's affection for Helen. Fran wasn't a relative, she was a neighbor, Fran didn't have to help Helen. Yet she did. And Dale loved her mother the way she should but could not: Unconditionally.

The phone rang on a May evening, when the breeze carried lilac scent and a fetid mix of mud and marsh grass. Still light out, too, enough to think about barbecues and late-evening walks on the beach.

"Did you see the paper?" It was Althea. "That woman you used to visit. She died."

Of course, Althea would have seen it; she read the Westerly paper, which would have carried Lydia's obituary. Joyce sat down on the sofa, sank into the cushions. This time of year? After making it through the winter?

"It's a pretty short obituary," Althea said. Apologizing. "It doesn't say much about her life at all."

CHAPTER TWENTY-THREE

*If I could never grow another flower again, I would
pick what nature gave me: the Queen Anne's lace
and black-eyed Susan in the fields, the tiger lily by
the roadside, the wild pink roses that ramble over the
stone wall. And if I could never walk again, I would sit
by my window, and wait for the goldfinch and the cardinal to flash their colors in the sun. And when I can
never rise again, I will close my eyes and remember
these things that made up the bounty of my summer.*
– A Country Woman's Diary, July 22, 1971; from a
newspaper clipping stuck with yellow tape on Helen's
desk

Helen's world was now divided into the familiar, and the
strange. What a comfort it was to catch a scent of something she recognized. The smell would race to her brain,
and it was like a jolt of electricity: She would remember. The pe-
culiar mix of steam and hot cotton brought to mind her mother,
ironing her father's shirts before church. Cinnamon conjured
up the applesauce they used to make in the home economics
building at Cornell. The smell would waft up from the basement
while she sat taking notes in tiny script in a history survey class
that had been forced into the building by the campus's crowded,
post-war conditions. The professor – she could see him now, 45
years later, although she could not remember his name – had a
hook nose, glasses that didn't stay put, and a sarcastic drawl that
seemed to say, "Why am I wasting my brilliance on a bunch of
freshmen? Especially women?" Wet earth – was there anything
more pungent, more elemental than rain mixing with dirt? –

aroused in her not a memory, but a feeling, almost an ache in her gut that could be homesickness but might be nothing at all, a biological reaction to a stimulus, a physical reflex that stayed on, a vestige, long after reason for its existence had passed. And the new leather of Fran's car seats . . . it always made her think of not cars but gloves, new leather gloves in Jim's Christmas stocking, supple and dark and smooth.

Each day had its points of familiarity. Fran coming over in the morning, making her breakfast. Saying goodbye to Joyce or Dale. Then, on the weekend, Loretta came. That was how she knew it was the weekend. Otherwise, her routine varied little. Breakfast at the same time. A walk in the morning. The mail, the newspaper, stuffed like a sausage in its red box by the roadside. Although she found the newsprint difficult to read, and asked Fran to read it to her. Her eyes, she would explain. They weren't as good as they used to be. And Fran would oblige, as she always did. Loretta, though, read too quickly, so Helen had trouble following, and she never wanted to read the same stories Helen did. She was always drifting over to the business page, checking her stocks. Then, after the newspaper, came lunch and a nap; then a little TV, or maybe a game with Fran (Helen liked Pictionary: Fran drew such detailed pictures that she didn't mind when the sand timer ran out). Finally, it was time for dinner, more TV, a bath – and this was not her favorite time of day, because Fran was gone and Joyce was so impatient; and Dale couldn't help her in the tub, he would stand outside the bathroom door and yell: "How are you doing, Ma? Are you OK? Is the water warm enough?" And then bed.

She hated bed. Always the same nightmare: walking in the woods, falling in the hole with the bones, the skeletons chasing her, the dead coming after her. It was part of her routine now, this dream. It was part of the life she had to live.

But too much, these days, too often, was unfamiliar.

She still recognized everyone. Or thought she did. How would she know when she had begun to fail? Would she see someone, Dale or Joyce, even Fran, as a stranger? She already had mixed up famous people, stumbled over the President's name, mistaken geography. It pained her that places, for someone who had always prided herself on a good sense of direction, had been the first to go. Now she just let Fran or Dub do the driving and trusted them to get there. She suppressed the impulse to ask: *Where are we? I never saw that house before. Is this the right turn? Are you sure?*

At least, she did most of the time. Sometimes she could not help herself. They would pass by something so startling, so unusual, that she would almost cry out: What a lovely house! Why, look at the view! It's a pond! And whoever was with her would have to explain patiently (and kindly), Yes, Helen. That's Point Judith Pond. Or: Yes, Helen, that's the Newport Bridge, remember? And she would remember. Of course! And be deeply embarrassed.

When everything was unfamiliar, you were constantly relearning. On Helen's bad days she felt as though she had forgotten how to do everything. Her blouse would not button. The TV remote control, a device she detested, became even more onerous, a bank of letters and arrows that made no sense and would not activate, no matter how vigorously she pointed it at the screen. Even the telephone, the old wall model that had hung in the kitchen for so many years, seemed to shrink into itself, unwilling to give up the voice on the other end. She would hang up, disgusted.

Eating was a chore. Nothing tasted the way she remembered – sometimes it seemed like she couldn't taste anything at all. Fran was patient, taking away what Fran didn't like, making her something else. Fran knew (and knew why) Helen could not stand grilled cheese sandwiches. These days it had extended to the smell of anything frying. Bacon, hamburgers, they were all out. She most liked little white bread sandwiches with something zesty between the slices, like pimento cheese or what they called sandwich spread, a sort of glorified tartar sauce, with a cup of soup. Tomato was her favorite, but some days she would settle for chicken noodle. The kind the kids ate, nothing gourmet or stuffed with vegetables. And Fran knew to take off the crusts.

The best times were in the afternoon. Helen would get up from her nap, a little tired and confused, but Fran was there, and had brewed her fresh tea. They would go downstairs and talk. Sometimes, if her nap was long, Helen would have a dream to relate. During the day she had her dreams of old – good, interesting dreams with crazy situations. Fran liked to hear her dreams, although she never offered to interpret them, the way that friend of Joyce's did. What was her name? Altoona? . . . No, that was a place . . . Sometimes Helen just started talking about the past, and Fran listened, so attentively, never interrupting with questions. She was a good listener, that Fran.

When Loretta was over, they would look at old pictures. Loretta was always bringing things for her to pore through: snapshots, her scrapbooks, magazines that must have been 20 years old, old wallpaper sample books, boxes of buttons and ribbon, once, even, a stereopticon. Helen liked them all. They were still in the familiar category, not the strange, and like a randomly caught scent on the wind, they gave her sudden flashbacks, reliable memories.

Still, it was Fran who got her to talk.

"Tell me about when you met Jim," she would say, or, "Tell me about Martha. It must have been awful for you."

"She was a tyrannical old witch." That was how she started. She had three stories about Martha: the baked beans story, in which Helen – young, silly bride – had mistakenly served baked beans on a Friday, and Martha had gone on for hours about how she thought it was Saturday, on account of the baked beans. The nosebleed story, how Martha would pick her nose until it bled, and then scream that she was hemorrhaging. And the worst of all, the one she could recite, second by second, but rarely told: the day Susan died.

"Do you know, Martha blamed me," she said one afternoon, the realization just hitting her. "She told Jim it was my fault, I never watched the kids. She said I was watching a soap opera on TV. 'The Edge of Night.'"

And if there were any parallels between Martha Winter and Helen, who had suffered through nursing a difficult old woman for 21 years, Helen neither spoke of, nor had any conscious thoughts about, what they might be.

One subject Helen knew she should think about, but could not: what would happen when she was gone.

It was hard to imagine the house without her. Helen's conscious apprehension of it seemed inextricably linked to its existence. Without her there, to trod on the worn stairs, to shuffle down the hall, to part the curtain when a car came in the drive, who would? But, of course, someone would do those things. The old house, which she now so thoroughly inhabited it seemed like an extension of her bones, would be occupied by other people, other families. Walls would be painted, new wallpaper put up, new furniture moved in to take the place of the worn antiques. Or – who knows – someone might decide it was better to start over, to tear the house down to the ground and build a new one.

It had happened before, this transition, many times. This had been Martha's house, and now it was hers. And before Martha Naylor it had belonged to another Winter wife, another woman who had been brought here to bake bread and scrub clothes and, perhaps, take care of an elderly relative who wouldn't get out of bed. And it would be ever thus. She had had her turn, and it was about to come to an end.

"I hate to leave the house," she would tell Fran, and Fran would misunderstand, try to convince her that it would be there when they got back.

"I mean forever. I hate to leave the house, not knowing what's going to happen to it. What if Ludlow gets his hands on it? I couldn't bear it. He's taken so much else.

"And Dale. I don't know." He certainly had affection for the old place, understood its inner workings, knew its weak points like any good carpenter. He would take care of its frame, but what about its soul? She loved him, but she mistrusted him still. At any moment he could stumble and fall. At any moment he could go back to his old ways, and that would be the end.

About Joyce, she said nothing. Her daughter seemed to love the farm, but every time she came over she surveyed the house in disgust, as though it were a dotty relative who had forgotten to bathe. She would clean it up – or maybe she would just tear it down, too, and build another house like Fran's down by water. She had always loved the water.

"This house has a lot of secrets, and they'll die with me." Helen liked to say that. It was a challenge, almost. Ask me if you dare.

But all Fran would say was, "We all have secrets, Helen. Some just aren't worth keeping."

Helen had gotten the idea of telling Fran her life story. Fran would tape record it, then type out a transcript. In her house, Fran had a home computer, a mysterious, humming object she kept on a desk in her mammoth kitchen. Helen had seen her use it. She operated it with a small device that fit in her palm, with a whip-like cord. She called it a mouse, which amused Helen to no end. She commented on it every time she was in Fran's house. Does it squeak? she would say. And Fran would laugh, as though Helen had said the funniest thing she'd ever heard.

Helen talked, the tape recorder whirred, and soon she had forgotten Fran was there at all. Sorting through her memories was like welcoming old friends into the house – although each time she opened the door, they said the exact same thing, stayed the same amount of time, looked the same, acted the same. Fran would ask her questions she couldn't answer. The story was the story; she had no hidden subplots, no elaboration.

A man came to see her one afternoon. He looked familiar but she could not place who he was. This was the purgatory between remembering and forgetting: Knowing you should remember, or remembering faintly, but not being able to nail it down. He was dressed like a farmer. He had pressed his blue jeans. He wore them low on his hips, belted, underneath a slight roll of belly – as Jim always had. But he was not Jim. His face was craggy, older than Jim's, and he looked at her so earnestly she had to look away. He turned his hat in his hands, bill, cap, bill, cap, like the rotation of the earth, the spinning of a cyclone. Fran seemed to know who he was, and even suggested that this man, this Mr. Lillibridge, would sit with her awhile so Fran could go out. The notion seized Helen with panic. What on earth would she say to him? But, finally, he suggested that they watch TV together, and he handed her a box of ginger snaps, which he somehow knew were her favorite. With a game show on, women cheering and jumping up and down, answers to be divined and puzzles to be solved, she settled into companionable silence with this Mr. Lillibridge. He turned his head away and seemed to be watching TV, too.

"It was my mother who drowned them." She and Fran were settling in, the tape recorder spinning. Helen was picking at the afghan in her lap, wishing she had a cat to pet. Peppermint – ah, she remembered him! His sweet, devoted nature – but he had been gone for many years now. And that's when it hit her.

"The barn cats were always having kittens, but I never saw them grow up to be cats," she continued. "My father always said, 'The coyotes must have got 'em.' But one day I saw my mother out by the creek that ran behind the farm. Fast in the summer. The current, that is. Dropping in a potato sack. She was drowning those kittens. I must have been young, not in school yet, maybe five. I think I knew what she was doing, but I just blocked it out."

"Oh, Helen." Fran tried not to interrupt, but sometimes she could not help herself.

"She was a cold woman, my mother. I hardly ever saw her smile. Oh, she had a bitter, triumphant sort of smirk, that she would use when she'd won a game of Parcheesi or cheated the butcher. I don't know how my father abided her. He was the salt of the earth. What I would give to see him again."

The funny thing was, since they had started this ritual of recording her memories, Helen's speech had improved. She sometimes muttered, deep in her throat, especially when she was tired and cantankerous. But when Helen began weaving tales from the past, she spoke in her old, mannered, articulate voice, straight out of a Boston finishing school. Fran had asked her about it one day: Where had she learned to talk that way? And Helen had laughed, throwing her head back.

"We took diction lessons at Cornell. All the young women. I was an ignorant farm girl. Smart, yes. I was there on a scholarship. But Miss Minerva Archer, oh, she was a funny one, big, buxom, very proper – she taught us to sit, stand, eat with the right fork and, most of all, speak correctly."

Fran, as she often did, remarked on her education. What had she planned to do with it? Hadn't she regretted ending up back on a farm, with another difficult woman? But Helen shook her head absently. She could not remember what was in her head back then. It was as though the events that happened to her were still there, preserved on celluloid, ready to be rewound and viewed again; but the soundtrack, the narration, was gone, and she could only guess at the rich inner life of the woman she had been.

Even the visions were fading away. Strips of film left out to bleed in the rain. One frame would be intact, but the next one would be liquefied, exaggerated, running off the border. "I just don't know," Helen would say then. "I just don't know." And Fran Kennedy would quietly press the tape recorder's stop button and tuck the afghan more tightly around Helen's matchstick-thin legs.

"If something happened, Helen, would you trust me to make the right decisions for you?"

Of course. That went without saying.

"If something happened, Helen, and you were very sick, would you want to be kept alive by extraordinary measures?"

No. That seemed like the right answer.

"If something happened, Helen, and you could no longer sign checks or manage your money, would you trust me to do it for you?"

Yes. She would trust Fran with her life.

Fran was taking her back. What did they call it, the psychiatrists? Hypnosis? It felt like that, a spooling backward, an unraveling, coming back to something long buried, forgotten.

It's January, 1978, she would say, and what was going on then? How were things between you and Jim? What was his mood?

The date stuck in her throat like a fishbone. She couldn't remember. It meant something, but she just wasn't sure.

"The aspirin," Fran prompted. "Remember, you found the receipt for the aspirin under the bed? Recently? From that time?"

"I should have been the one taking aspirin," Helen replied darkly. "He was over there. I told him, No more! I wouldn't have him over there. For one thing, he'd get himself killed, and where would I be? Hamilton wasn't going to mess around with some white farmer sniffing around his woman."

"Marian? He was at Marian's?"

"Of course. Can't trust any of them." At moments like these her voice would become guttural, hard to understand, as though it came from somewhere dark and savage. "Stupid daughter of his, told him no, couldn't be a father to her. Had his own daughter. Told 'im I'd leave I would. Leaving. Divorcing him, that's what I'll do."

"You threatened to divorce Jim?"

"I'll tell! I'll tell her, by God, I'll tell her! Tell her the truth!"

And Fran would have to stop the tape recorder, stop the interrogation. Helen was back there, somewhere, reliving it all.

Joyce was nagging her again. Why wouldn't she eat? She was skin and bones. Just a few bites. Why did she have to be so difficult?

Helen did not feel like eating. The very act of chewing and swallowing was painful, almost. It used up all her energy. Plus, she couldn't taste much these days. That was why she liked those ginger snaps: They were so pungent, a little of their bite always broke through on her tongue.

"Your grandmother used to make me eat oatmeal every morning. The oatmeal was warm when George and your grandfather got up to feed the cows, but by the time I came downstairs, it was a cold lump." Why had she thought of that, just now? The memory was so strong she could taste the gray, gelatinous form of it, cool and sticky on her tongue.

Joyce was asking her questions. That was nothing new: She was always pestering her, asking What had Fran done with the bank book? Where were Helen's reading glasses? Why wasn't the mail on the table? But these were different questions, deep, probing, dark questions. It was as though she were dragging Helen out of the everyday world and into some black forest, where she could see only a few steps ahead, but tree branches and roots and briars were everywhere, ready to trip her up, snag her, make her bleed.

"Mother, you know that I love you." This was how Joyce started.

She couldn't remember. Couldn't Joyce see that? She didn't want to remember. It was like eating: It made her tired.

"I need to know about Daddy. You're the only one who knows. Please tell me everything you remember."

Daddy? "He was a good man. The salt of the earth. What I would give to see him again."

"Yes, Mother, I know." Joyce was biting her lip, leaning forward in the chair across from her. "Tell me why he left the way he did. I know you know."

"I don't know. Where did he go?"

"Daddy! Why did he kill himself? Now I know this is difficult, but please! Mother! Tell me why, I just want to know why."

"Daddy didn't kill himself. He just dropped dead. He had gone to milk the cows one morning. My mother found him in the sawdust, keeled over. I think he went the way he wanted to go. He was the salt of the earth, you know. What I would give to see him again."

Joyce sighed heavily.

The tape recorder was whirring again, cycling around like a storm. Its buzz felt like a cattle prod. Helen heard it and emotions washed over her.

"I'm a bad person, you ought not to bother with me. I had a premonition, you know."

"About Jim's death?"

"Nooo." One wrong question and Helen was dislodged. How to get back there? The thread in her mind was so tenuous.

"About Susan."

There. "Just before I walked upstairs, I had a clutch in my chest. Should I leave her alone for a minute? I thought it would be all right. Just this once."

Fran put a hand over hers. "It wasn't your fault, Helen."

"Do you think I'll go to hell?"

"No, Helen. I don't."

"What about Susan? Why didn't you tell me about Susan? Did you think I wouldn't find out I had a sister? Why didn't you buy a gravestone for her?"

Helen took another sip of her coffee. It was steaming hot. She wrapped her fingers around the mug. She never seemed to be able to get warm.

"Susan was my daughter," she said finally. She was staring off, away from Joyce. A cardinal had come to the bird feeder. A male. So brilliantly red. "Susan Winter was my daughter. She was a blonde. She was the most beautiful child who ever lived. I don't remember much about how she died. Fran has all my information."

That became her standard answer. It seemed like a good one. No matter what Joyce was looking for, she referred her to Fran. She would take care of things, because she had promised to; Fran had promised to take care of everything, right until the end.

CHAPTER TWENTY-FOUR

It wasn't a big storm by any means. They warned it would carry salt spray to kill the dahlias and other blooms of late summer; they spoke of wind and lashing rain, of high tides and a storm surge. All we could do was wait and see how things turned out. We are born, and we die, and in between, Nature has her way with us.
– Helen Winter, A Country Woman's Diary, Aug. 12, 1976

Everybody made a big deal out of Hurricane Belle. The wind picked up last night around 9:30. When I went to bed at midnight the windows were rattling. "Queen Helen" was in a tizzy. This morning I woke up to find the old oak crashed against the barn. There were leaves and little branches all over the place. Dad and Dale sawed up the tree, then we walked down to the beach, where some driftwood and lobster pots had washed up. I went back to the house to get ready to go to the fair with Camille. The storm had passed, like it always does.
– Joyce Winter, diary, Aug. 10, 1976

It had been a typical summer weekend. Saturday, August 18, 1991, was perfect: a beach day, sunburn weather even, hot enough for the iced tea glasses to break a sweat. Sunday continued hot, with some fog in the morning that quickly burned off. While Michael golfed with Clark, Joyce spent the afternoon packing. She didn't know what to bring with her – she had heard it could be cool in Canada, even at the height of summer – but she didn't want to go without a bathing suit or shorts.

Layers, Camille had suggested. She had been to Nova Scotia a few years ago with the kids. So Joyce brought out linen blazers and long-sleeved T-shirts. She was ironing a pair of chinos, her hair hanging damp against her face, when the phone rang.

"Have you seen the news?" Loretta's throaty voice, hoarser than usual. She was huffing and puffing.

The coup in the Soviet Union. She had caught some of it on the radio that morning: The KGB was trying to overthrow Gorbachev, reassert its Communist muscle. Just when it seemed like the Iron Curtain was finally gone...

"Not that," Loretta said, interrupting her. "There's a hurricane coming, for God's sake."

It would be a week before Joyce would stumble on her suitcase, half filled, where she had left it in the middle of the bedroom floor.

Michael told her not to panic. True, the storm, born southeast of Bermuda two days before, had turned northward and was starting to intensify; but the New England waters would quickly cool it down. If it got that far; most Atlantic hurricanes veered out to sea before making landfall anywhere near New England. It was also a compact storm. However powerful it was, the bad weather wouldn't last long.

He saw no reason why they should change their plans. At the worst, they might have a rollicking ferry ride from Portland to Nova Scotia. If the storm was bad they could always leave a day later.

Joyce was torn. Her first impulse was to keep packing and forget about the hurricane. After all, Fran and Dale could stay with her mother. There were plenty of people around to take care of her. And she and Michael had been getting along so well. This was to be their first trip together since their honeymoon. And it was no weekend away – they were staying 14 days. She was sure, once in the remote cottage in Nova Scotia, Michael would begin to relent on the baby question.

On the other hand, she had waited a lifetime to see a good hurricane. That was an awful way to look at it, but it was true. Belle in 1976 had been no more than a brief gale, and Gloria in 1985 shook the trees around and that was all. She had heard all the stories about 1938 from Aunt Loretta. Now, with one headed straight for Rhode Island, she was getting ready to leave town.

And there was the matter of her mother. It nagged at her, though she tried to talk it away: Didn't she sleep at the farm three nights a week? Wasn't she doing her mother's grocery shopping, buying her clothes, cleaning the house? And for what? So her mother could stymie her at every turn? Joyce wasn't blind. She saw how Helen reacted to Fran, meekly followed her every gentle direction, then the minute Fran left refusing to eat dinner, take a bath, go to bed. It was like steering a mule.

She had done her time. All those years of being alone while Michael traveled, staying home in her private misery, while everyone else's world spun busily around. This was her turn. She deserved this vacation.

Loretta was staying at the farm Sunday night, but Joyce decided to go over there anyway. Her aunt sounded like she needed a break.

Helen and Loretta were watching the news. The hurricane, called Bob, was supposed to brush the Outer Banks of North Carolina before heading back out to sea. Landfall was expected on Block Island tomorrow afternoon. Winds already were approaching 100 mph.

The newscasters were talking about stocking up on food, water, batteries. Shelters were being opened. A reporter stood, microphone in hand, in a supermarket, where long lines snaked to the registers. Then another reporter appeared, standing at the sea wall in Narragansett Pier, a breeze ruffling her yellow mackinaw. Behind her, the Coast Guard House restaurant was being boarded up.

"Good heavens. I'm so glad you're here, Joyce."

She had never seen her aunt in such a state. Helen sat like a Buddha, plucking away at the skeins of her afghan, but Loretta was pacing around the room, shaking her head.

"They're going to evacuate us, you know. Everybody south of Route 1. What will we do? I can't take her to one of those shelters," and she dropped her voice, but Helen didn't seem to be paying attention anyway.

Joyce felt as dazed as Helen looked. How could this have happened so suddenly? The newspaper had had a brief story about the storm yesterday, but it seemed no threat to Rhode

Island. Now people were boarding up buildings, pulling boats out of the water, heading for higher ground.

There was so much to do Joyce had no idea where to begin. But she quickly realized that she could not leave Loretta, her 76-year-old aunt who had a coastal home of her own to worry about, in charge of her mother. And she would not ask Fran to come over, even if Helen would have preferred it. She was the daughter. Helen was her mother. She would have to take charge.

She called Michael, left him a message on the answering machine: There's a hurricane coming, I'm staying overnight at the farm to help my mother get ready. She called Dale, who said he was already on his way out the door. She called Camille but the phone rang and rang with no answer, no machine picking up. She called Althea, who volunteered to bring her groceries (bless her, thought Joyce: she never even had to ask); she even called cousin Ludlow. She hated to do it; she could almost see him sneering on the other end of the line. Would he go board up his mother's house?

Loretta seemed frozen to the spot, unable to decide where to go or what to do. "You might as well stay here. We should be safe enough," Joyce convinced her. "If they try to get us to evacuate, I'll explain that Mom can't be moved."

"Don't do that! They'll send an ambulance."

"That's ridiculous. They won't have time to worry about us. They'll be too busy at the beach shacks down at East Matunuck and Matunuck. Those are the people in danger."

"I just wish I knew what was the right thing to do!"

"What did you do in '38? You stayed put right here, and the house survived it. This can't be anywhere near that bad."

"We lost the corncrib, you know. It collapsed about a second after my father walked out of it. It's a wonder he wasn't killed."

Joyce, who had heard the story a hundred times, decided to put Loretta to work. "Run some water. Fill up the bathtub and any container you can find. If we lose power we won't be able to flush the toilet without it."

She made a list (batteries, milk, bread . . . since the Blizzard of '78 they had become a Rhode Island cliche, the three hottest items when a storm threatened), called Althea back; remembered some more items, called her back again. By now Dale was over, and he already was tidying up the yard, picking up anything that could take flight in a high wind, and slapping up plywood over the windows on the barn. Dark was threatening, and he still had to gas up the cars.

Then Camille showed up with Forrest and Skye, announcing that she had left her husband, and all hell broke loose.

Looking back, months later, Joyce would try to remember that night and the next day in slow motion, as though each frame, each second needed to be rewound, reexamined, like a movie in which the climax passes too quickly to be understood. Because at the time she was living it all in ignorance, not knowing what was really going on, not divining the fine shades of meaning that were unfolding before her. Camille was in her kitchen with a suitcase, an infant and a two-year-old, looking as though she hadn't slept in days. Helen suddenly got out of her chair, insensible, yelling something about "that woman." Loretta was trudging around the kitchen with two plastic jugs of water, sweat forming on her brow; Dale was carrying in bags of groceries from Althea's car; and Fran Kennedy, looking serene in a blue polka dot sun dress, slipped in, walking over to calm Helen without missing a beat.

By the time the 11 o'clock news aired, when Fran had gone home and Joyce had made up beds for Camille and the kids, Althea and Dale; when Loretta had settled in on a day bed in Helen's room and Joyce had made up the couch for herself, Hurricane Bob had passed the Outer Banks with gusts of 123 mph. Landfall was expected at Virginia Beach, and then the storm would make aim for Block Island, most likely by 2 o'clock the next day.

Camille didn't want to talk. Joyce settled on the couch and turned the TV sound to low. She watched the meteorologist drone on about wind sheer and the Gulf Stream, and then she drifted into sleep, where she dreamed again of a tide high enough to wash away Winter Farm.

The sky was gray, almost yellow when the household began to stir. Dale was up first. He tiptoed past Joyce on the couch and walked outside to have a cigarette. She followed the trail of its glow and found him leaning against the barn, looking south to the ocean.

"It'll get a little hairy for a while, but things will be all right," he said, not looking at her. "The old house has stood through worse. Just get ready for some rockin' and rollin.'"

She looked at him, a sudden wave of something filling her – admiration, respect, love. "I'm glad you're here."

"I think you've had the worst of it."

She misunderstood him. "Oh, it wasn't so bad. Loretta was a little hysterical, but everybody came over and pitched in."

"No. With Ma. You've had the worst of it. She doesn't cut you much slack. I always thought I had it tough, but she mellowed on me over the years. I don't think she's ever given an inch to you."

Joyce looked out to the horizon, not trusting herself to keep it together. "I guess it works both ways. I guess maybe I haven't given her an inch, either."

"Don't beat yourself up. You did the best you could." He stubbed the cigarette out in the dirt. "It's a hard act to follow, a four-year-old girl who never grew up. You were never cute enough or young enough . . . you weren't Susan. She couldn't see Joyce, she could only see that you weren't Susan."

"Sometimes I think she really doesn't know who I am. Did you see that yesterday? She was bellowing like a banshee, and Fran Kennedy came in and she snapped out of it, just like that."

"I don't want that woman over here." Dale's mood shifted, from reflective to vehement. "I keep telling you, she's bad news. Ma's way too attached to her. What if she moves away? What if she gets bored playing nursemaid, and decides to take up bridge instead? We'll be left to pick up the pieces."

Maybe they had been taking the easy way out. Sometimes a parent doesn't care who quiets a crying child, she thought. "You're probably right, but I can't think about that now. There's too much going on."

"So what's the deal with Camille?"

Joyce hadn't had a chance to get her alone. Getting the kids settled, feeding everyone and making up the beds had taken up the evening. Camille didn't look like she wanted to talk about it anyway. "She and Eric have been at odds for a while. She's sick of supporting him, while he donates his time to all these causes."

"She's a little high strung, if you ask me. She picked a great time to leave her husband."

Joyce couldn't disagree with that, but she was surprised; Camille and Dale had always been tight. "She's working a lot of hours, and the kids take a lot out of her. I think she wants him to step up to the plate a little more so she doesn't have to push so hard at the hospital. . . . But that's her side of it. I'm sure he has a completely different version."

They were silent for a while. Joyce watched her brother in profile, as he lit another cigarette and gazed out toward Block Island. She wondered about him, his inner life, what demons he had to push down to keep away from the booze and the women who were no good for him. Now, working with his hands, planing wood and nailing boards and turning moldings on a lathe, he seemed closer to himself somehow, more at ease with the world. But the scars were still there: the voice, with its ironic turns, the marks on his face from bar fights and all those days out in the North Atlantic, and his fingernails, which he still bit to the quick.

He leaned toward her, as though somebody might be listening. "That friend of yours? Althea? Has she got, you know, a significant other?"

Joyce laughed. "You old dog. Did you dream last night?"

"What? Yeah, I dreamt all night, one damned crazy thing after another."

"Tell her your dreams. That's the only advice I can give you."

When she'd taken the last bag of garbage out the night before, into the barn where Dale had dragged the trash cans, she saw that the windows of the Kennedy house were covered in plywood, blinded to the coming storm. Then, around breakfast time, their Audi roared out of the driveway, and Joyce assumed they were heading for shelter, or maybe even home to New Jersey. The car was packed to the gills. But apparently it carried only Peter Kennedy and the two teenagers, because around 9:30 Fran walked in, dressed in a pair of jeans and an old white T-shirt from the Hartford Open.

"I told Peter I had to stay and take care of your mother," she explained, helping herself to a cup of coffee. "This is going to be upsetting for her. Any change in routine is very difficult."

"Everything's under control, Fran. We've got a full house: my brother, my friend Camille and her two children, my friend Althea, my aunt . . . " Just reciting the list was exhausting. "Thanks, but we really don't need you."

"Thanks, but I think I'll stay."

They stared each other down. Fran, tall, willowy, leaning on one leg as she lifted up the coffee pot (How often did she pour herself a cup? Did this kitchen feel like her own, the mug molding to her palm, exuding a familiar warmth?); Joyce, arms crossed, feeling awkward, suddenly, in her mother's own house, wondering when it had ceased to be home.

Helen's voice, querulous, weak, came from the next room, deciding it. "Is that you, Fran? Fran? Can you come help me? Fran?"

The rain came around noon. The sky turned smudgy, then black, as the first bands of precipitation began undulating in like the tide. These were no little drops or sprinkles; first, it was dry, then a second later all was wet, water pouring down. The wind was blowing the rain against the window panes, then suddenly it was seeping in, where the sashes, rotted, had separated ever so slightly from the frame. Just as quickly the leak became a torrent, running down the sills, staining the living room wallpaper, pooling on the old maple floor.

Joyce ran to get rags, towels, anything she could think of, and they rolled them up like bolsters, wedged against the windowsills. As quickly as they plugged the leaks, the rain soaked through.

The wind picked up, and the house seemed to be responding, emitting eerie sounds. The glass in the windowpanes rattled. The floors and walls moaned, creaked, strained. Every so often a strong gust would come along, punctuated by a bang outside. Something outdoors had worked loose. By 12:30 the power was out. The wobbly pedestal lamp and the droning refrigerator kicked off, and a grayness descended over the house.

The household, which had been a cacophony of voices all morning, had been reduced to whispers. They congregated in the living room, not because it was the safest place – on the contrary, one wall of its windows faced south, with a view to the sea – but because it was the largest. Here they could huddle and get some measure of security from their numbers.

Miraculously, baby Forrest slept in his mother's arms, the nipple of a plastic baby bottle still in his mouth, a tiny bubble forming at his lip. Camille rocked so vigorously that even above the wind they could hear the chair's wood rubbing against the floor. Her face, pale brown like cement, was a mask.

Skye lay at her feet on a blanket, where she rolled around and occasionally whimpered. She played with a toe of Camille's stocking and sucked her thumb.

Helen was talking to Skye, trying to play pat-a-cake, but she shrank away. No one could fool the little girl: The old woman's voice had gone all high and scratchy, but yesterday, when they came to this place, she hadn't wanted them there. Still, Helen was undeterred, squatting on the floor next to her. "Oh, she's a shy thing. Do you want me to pick you up? Do you want to come to Grandma Helen? Oh, come to Grandma Helen. I'll read you a story. Do you want to hear a story?"

"She's a little shy," Camille said. "Maybe you should leave her alone." There was an edge to her voice, like the store clerk who's trying hard to be polite to an irritating customer.

"Perhaps she's tired," Fran suggested.

"My, she's a sweet thing," Helen continued, ignoring both of them. "Funny, she looks like her grandfather."

"She doesn't have a grandfather," Camille snapped. She was looking at Helen, furious, as though the old woman should know better.

The gathering lapsed back into an embarrassed silence. Sometimes my mother seems so normal, Joyce thought, that we forget she isn't.

Suddenly, a roar came from the south side of the house. Through the rain Joyce could see the trees in the orchard bending toward the ground. A metal garbage can, probably from one of the Salt Marsh Acres houses, flew by the window. The roar, like a tornado, brought a shrieking wind. Then the old silver maple, the one Dale had wanted to cut down, gave a final creak and crashed onto the barn roof.

Loretta was covering her head, rocking on the sofa, mumbling something. Joyce read her lips: She was praying.

"Maybe we better move into the kitchen," Dale suggested, but nobody moved. It was as though, planted in whatever chair or perch they had found, each member of the assemblage did not want to risk exchanging it for another. Joyce had thought about bringing out some of the snacks Althea had brought, but she didn't want to get up, either. Moving would break the spell, bring bad luck. No sooner would she walk into the kitchen, she thought, than something would crash onto the house. Althea, perhaps sensing her thoughts, leaned over, pressed her knee for encouragement.

Then, as quickly as the terrifying gust had blown through, the winds seemed to dissipate. The rains still lashed the windows, but the storm had blown out. The gray sky was brightening.

Loretta got up and without a word walked to the back door. Joyce followed her. Loretta stood in the driveway, her eyes trained above, where large, black-winged birds were tossing about in the wind.

Joyce walked over and together they stood there, the rain soaking their clothes, the wind kicking up stones and twigs at their feet.

"Black skimmers. All the way from the Carolinas. They get sucked into the storm, sometimes get carried hundreds of miles. The last time I saw one this far north was in the hurricane of '44."

Even above the keening wind Joyce could hear the birds' high-pitched auw, auw. "I'm glad the worst is over."

"It's not over, honey. This is just the eye of the storm. It's coming back at us, harder than ever."

While they were outside, the household had taken advantage of the lull and scattered. Althea was dumping wet towels into a bucket, wringing them out, mopping up the floor. Dale, on his hands and knees, helped her, stuffing the window edges with fresh rags he'd found under the sink. Camille put the baby down on the couch, a rolled blanket at his back, and covered Skye, who somehow had managed to fall asleep on the floor. Fran, Dale said, had taken Helen upstairs for a nap.

"I don't know why everybody thinks they can go to sleep."

Joyce felt grouchy. She wondered where Michael was. He had told her he was going to the Bay Campus. He had already spent most of Sunday there, supervising the dry-docking of the boats, tying down the bigger vessels, securing the buildings. Now he felt compelled to watch over the campus, although he had made a lame promise about coming over later. Obviously he hadn't made it, and she wondered if he intended to spend the night there. And who was watching their house? If they even had a house left.

She wandered upstairs. Her mother, indeed, was lying down; not only napping, but snoring. Fran was in Joyce's old room – where Camille had slept the night before – changing the sheets.

Joyce stood in the doorway, arms folded. "Camille's sleeping here. You don't have to change the sheets."

Fran piled the used sheets into a loose bundle and tossed them into a corner. "I think it would be best if she didn't stay another night. It upsets and confuses your mother."

"Everything upsets and confuses her." She's nuts, Joyce wanted to add, but restrained herself. "Besides, she really warmed up to the children. I think it's good for her. And I'm not turning Camille out."

Fran tucked in a fresh bottom sheet, smoothing the corners, not looking up. "Joyce, think about your mother." *For once*, seemed to be the implication. "Just imagine what it must do to her to see Camille, and then Camille's children. Help me with this, will you?"

Joyce, confused, wondered if she meant the bed-making or managing Helen. But she walked to the opposite end of the mattress, grabbed the top sheet, and together they snapped it into place and began bending and tucking. "I don't know why it should upset her to see Camille, any more than it ever has."

"Joyce." Fran straightened up. She was really quite tall: Joyce wouldn't have been surprised if she came close to six feet. She was doing that pose again, one foot on top of another. "Your mother has had a tough life. She doesn't need to be reminded of it at every turn."

"No one ever said she's had it easy. But it hasn't been easy for us, either." She started to say more but checked herself. She didn't want to air the family laundry with Fran Kennedy of all people. "I don't need you telling me how to handle my mother."

Fran was stuffing a pillow into its case, holding it by the corners. "I'm not telling you how to handle your mother. I'm telling you she has feelings, and they should be regarded. Seeing Camille upsets her, and the children confuse her even more."

"I know she made that comment about their grandfather, but she doesn't know what she's talking about."

"Maybe she does." Camille had walked into the room. "I think she knows exactly what she's talking about."

Fran, caught in the act of unfolding a pink cotton blanket, slowly raised her head. "I think you've done enough, Camille."

Joyce, trying to catch up with the conversation, looked from one to the other. Fran and Camille were exchanging looks of such enmity that it was almost as if Helen, and not Fran, were in the room.

"Maybe you don't think I belong here." Camille took a step forward, toward Fran, who stood there, the blanket limp in her hands. "Is that it? Am I not good enough to be in this house?"

"It upsets her. She's confused enough as it is, without you bringing those kids here."

Joyce felt like Helen suddenly, unmoored, hearing words but not understanding them. "Will you two stop it? If my mother's upset it's because she's ill! She has dementia! She doesn't know what she's talking about. Of course she wasn't making some comment about Camille's father. And Fran, I think you should mind your own business. This isn't your house, as much as you like to act that it is. I know my mother seems to like you, but I'm her daughter and Camille's my friend and you don't know anything about this family."

Fran shook out the blanket on the bed, and static electricity crackled.

"I know more about your mother than anyone. I know about your sister, who drowned in the pond. And your father blamed your mother. She was taking care of that witch of a grandmother of yours."

"Please, Fran, don't." Joyce stood there, arms at her sides. She didn't want to hear this, not from Fran. Not from some outsider.

"Your father was unfaithful to your mother, and finally left her when she was pregnant with you. She went back to New York, to her parents'. But at the last minute he relented and came to get her."

"My father loved us, all of us. You don't know what you're talking about." Joyce looked over at Camille, but her head was bowed and she wouldn't meet Joyce's eyes.

Fran Kennedy shook out the bedspread. "At first, she believed him when he said it was over. But then the talk started. The other woman was a Narragansett Indian, and now she had a little baby of her own."

That day at Lydia Franklin's, when the old woman had talked of infidelity, it seemed too crazy to believe. Ugly gossip from years ago, from before Joyce was born. She hadn't wanted to face it. But this was too much – Fran's regurgitating everything her mother said, whether it was real or not, still might add up to the truth. Faces flashed through her head: her mother, her father, Marian Evans.

"No." A baby . . .

"It's true." It had seemed hours since Camille had last uttered a word and now her voice was rough and low, that old voice Joyce remembered from years ago. "Yeah, it's true. My mother finally told me, but you know, I think I had guessed it anyway. She always tried to put a good face on it. To me, what did it matter? He was dead by the time I found out. He was always your father. He was never mine."

"Imagine what your mother goes through, when she sees Camille." The wind was picking up again, and Fran gave the bed a shove with her leg, pushing it back against the wall. "Even now, some part of her knows."

Joyce walked over to the window, where she could see the Atlantic boiling in a frenzy, sending waves crashing over the dunes and against the porch of Fran Kennedy's house. Why hadn't they told her? Why had Helen let it go on, all these years?

Fran's voice, which had been angry and triumphant, now had a strain of regret. "She was angry," Fran continued, as though she could hear the questions pounding in Joyce's head. "I don't think she ever really would have told you. But she threatened to. She was trying to control him, I think: She thought he was back with Marian. She threatened to tell you and to divorce your father. He couldn't bear it."

Joyce felt the blood draining from her head. She had never fainted, but she imagined this is what you felt right before going down: a sudden loss of warmth, your head going light and floaty like a balloon bouncing around in the wind.

"And you knew." She turned toward Camille. "You knew."

"What of it?" The voice hard. "Would it have made a difference? Would you have taken a new family portrait? Would your mother have welcomed me into the fold?"

Joyce felt Fran step behind her, grasp her shoulders as though bucking her up. "I'm sorry, Joyce," Fran said.

The hurricane shifted, and the counter-clockwise winds roared in, from the west this time. Somewhere in the house, a door slammed shut, a sudden vacuum filled.

Helen lay in bed, her eyes closed, her hands folded on her chest. She could hear the sounds of the house breaking up. Rain slapping at the windows, glass shattering, vines creeping in, cellar flooding, floorboards buckling, beams crashing, shingles flying, boards exploding outward in mid-air, until she floated, alone, in her double bed, half on Jim's side, half on her own.

She heard voices. Singing, or maybe animals chattering – scurrying in, taking over, reclaiming the land the house had held for three hundred years. Nonsense sounds.

Her chest rose and fell. Inhale, exhale.

Behind her eyelids the water came. It was murky green. Fronds and weeds waved gently in a bubbly broth of salt water and fresh. All around her was water, the air was gone, the atmosphere was viridian, cloudy; yet her chest rose and fell. Inhale, exhale.

She opened her eyes, and there was her son, Dale, his skin smooth and young again, his face caught in surprise, wonderment. Or was it Jim, just as he had looked that day so many years ago at Cornell, when he walked into class and lifted her out of misery? His mouth was moving, he was talking or singing, but she could not hear what he said, all was waves, undulation, rings in a circle. The green was gone, and all about her room was a golden luster.

Next to him was her daughter, her blonde hair falling about her shoulders in crimps and ringlets, her smile glowing like candle fire. Susan. All grown up at last, and a beauty – with the glow of life so strong you had to shade your eyes from it, as though you, a mere mortal, were not equipped to receive it, were too weak to appreciate the strands of beauty woven into the whole.

Yes, they were at the foot of her bed, smiling down at her, talking a new language of love and forgiveness, sounding like a gentle wind, like birdsong. Heaven's language. The language of all time.

She sighed, took one last inhalation, and closed her eyes.

Joyce, lying down in Martha's old musty featherbed, a pillow over her ears to block out the branches scratching at the window, did not hear Camille bustling out with the two children. She did not hear any footsteps, no matter how insubstantial, pass by the door. She slept the sleep of the drunk or sedated: dreamless, a hollow that's fallen into, a nothingness. When she finally woke, her mouth tasting like old socks, and padded downstairs, she felt the joviality of the room blowing out the door with the departing storm.

The men showed up, just as the storm was winding down. Ludlow arrived for his mother. Eric Robinson came looking for his wife, and was told she had left with the kids for Marian's house. (This was news to Joyce.) He looked quite distressed: "There's wires down everywhere. Why couldn't she have stayed put?" Michael Avery, his hair wet from rain, burst in, his face florid, his voice too loud. He was expressive, hugging her, making a show of tramping about the house, checking for damage. She could smell a few beers on his breath. When he could find nothing to do, nothing to criticize, he sank into a chair, dejected. Joyce looked at him and thought how superfluous he had become. She had made it through everything – the preparations, the storm, the incredible scene with Fran and Camille – and here she was, on the other side of the storm, and here he was, having weathered nothing more than a few hours on a barstool and a marriage that served his needs completely.

She did not sit down, though he patted the cushion next to him, his twisted smile just shy of belligerent. There must be something she should be doing. The house, after her nap, had regained its chaotic feel: Eric pacing about, trying to call Marian's, then deciding to go up there again; Ludlow and Loretta arguing about what to do about the cottages that were damaged; Althea and Dale in the kitchen, making sandwiches, Althea singing a Cher song. She wished, suddenly, they would all go home, and she wondered how it was that all these people had crammed into this house, this house she had always thought of as home.

Fran came downstairs. She was walking fast but in her stocking feet no one noticed until she was upon them.

"Has anyone seen Helen?"

Joyce would remember later exactly what she was doing when she heard Fran's voice: For she was turned away, her back to Fran, rifling through the desk drawer for the extra batteries she had stowed away that morning. They would need the flashlights tonight, she had thought, to get around the house.

"I thought she was napping." She turned to see Fran; her face was ashen. The chatter of the room quieted. The last one to speak was Loretta: "I told you to cut down that tree last year," but then her voice, too, drifted away, as Fran's question sunk in.

"She can't have gone anywhere. Did you check the bathroom?" Loretta said.

The rest of them stood there, frozen.

"I checked the entire upstairs. I was right there! I was sleeping on the cot!" Fran was dissolving in hysterics.

They ran about, searching the downstairs. Closets, cupboards, as though she were a child or a kitten seeking a new hiding place. They looked under beds. They threw back shower curtains, hoping against hope to find her there, in the tub, and to scold her: "Helen! How did you do this, all by yourself?" Until finally the truth sank in: Helen was not in the house. Somehow, when no one was looking, when the tide was still roaring over the dunes and the wind was pummeling the house, she had slipped out, unnoticed.

Dale, Ludlow and Michael Avery searched the farm for hours. By the time they called the police it had grown too dark to continue. Besides, there was only one place they had not looked.

In the morning Michael called Clark, and he arrived with two friends from the graduate school and their diving equipment. The pond was murky and turbid from the hurricane, and it was running a mean current, like water sloshing in a bowl. It could take hours to find anything, if there was anything to find.

As it happened, the grim job took no time at all. Helen Winter was just under the pond's lip, one leg trapped in marsh grass, her body facing the muddy bottom.

CHAPTER TWENTY-FIVE

▲

The lawyer had an office in the old bank where Joyce used to accompany her father. Like many of Main Street's historic buildings, it had been chopped into offices in the '70s when the bank moved to a new concrete box on the outskirts of town. It made her sad to step into its anteroom and be confronted with a plywood wall. It was as though someone had taken her memory of the place and boarded it up, so she never again could see the little girl holding her father's hand. The marble floor, which she had clicked across in her mary janes, was covered in thin, rust-colored carpet.

She had spent many hours in the lawyer's office. He was a familiar figure in town, a man named Rush whose demeanor was anything but: Sometimes five minutes would go by as he rifled through papers and folders, looking for the matter that brought her there. He had a leisurely way of talking, too, and liked to lean back in his chair and gaze at the ceiling. If Joyce didn't particularly like him, if she sometimes mistrusted his ways of doing business, she couldn't imagine whom else to retain. In Wakefield he was the man you visited to have your will done, your estate planned, your zoning issue resolved, and it had been that way since Joyce was a child.

This was her last day in Mr. Rush's office. All the matters that concerned them were resolved. Her mother's will had been probated and, if its contents still distressed her, if she felt in her heart she should have fought it, it was too late now. Mr. Rush had offered her practical advice, and she had taken it. Challenging Helen's will would have been a long, costly, and potentially fruitless exercise, especially when the other party involved had offered a tidy settlement to make the whole matter go away. She tried to believe that she and Dale had done the right thing.

Certainly there were worse alternatives: Cousin Ludlow, for example. The way he talked to Joyce, his oily persistence, made her shudder. She knew now what her mother had been up against, all those years. None of his setbacks seemed to affect him. First the Indians had stopped his cedar swamp development when they found ancient remains there, and then the credit unions had closed. He took such a loss Loretta convinced him to sell some of the land dirt cheap to the Audubon Society. Perhaps the biggest blow was when Loretta announced she also was leaving her entire estate – house, fields, woods – to Audubon. But the real estate market would come back, Ludlow was telling everybody. Just you wait.

She wasn't sure why Mr. Rush had called her in today. The paperwork had been signed. His fee had been paid. There was the matter of the house she was buying in town, but the closing had already taken place. It was a small cottage on a side street, a fixer-upper with great potential, the real estate agent had told her. But it was perfect for one person. And Dale would help her with the carpentry. He already had offered. There was the matter, too, of her divorce, but only one court appearance remained. Yes, she had been seeing a lot of Mr. Rush these days. She no longer grew impatient as he sorted through the papers on his desk, emitting a heavy sigh. She no longer wondered why he had only a part-time secretary. This was just his style: The dusty floors, the stacks of manila folders betrayed an outward disorganization, but they also represented his refusal to give in to the big-city lawyers who were moving down here. No fancy new office or full-time secretary for him.

"Here it is." Mr. Rush grabbed a stack of papers, lifted one off the top. It was tri-folded, heavy. He passed it to Joyce.

"Forgot about this. It's yours. Yours and your brother's. Had to write it up separately, was waiting for my secretary to type it up."

He handed it to her and she held it, feeling its weight.

"Deed to the cemetery. Broke that out, your mother did, wanted to make sure it was taken care of."

If she sometimes imagined the scene of her mother, sitting in this very office, giving Mr. Rush instructions, perched on the edge of the hard walnut chair, if she wondered who else was in the room – along just in case she was needed, of course – Joyce tried not to let it bother her. She had accepted the way things were. She had settled the case. It was over.

She unfolded the deed, glanced at it, refolded it, slipped it into her purse. She stood up and offered her hand to Mr. Rush.

He rose, the chair creaking. "Got the right-of-way in there, of course. You've got the right to pass and repass, in perpetuity. It's all in the deed. Your mother wanted that in there."

She thanked him and left. As she passed through the glass door to the outside, the sun emerged from a patch of cloud. It was going to be a nice day, for April.

It was school vacation, and she had a lot to do around her new house; scraping, painting, cleaning, organizing. But this one afternoon, all that could wait. She packed up the car with her tools and drove out of town, along the winding Route 1 that divided the hills from the sea, down old Post Road with its ruts and dented mailboxes, to the driveway that wound through the pines.

Next to the old house, the muddy lane was jammed with vehicles: a white panel van with a lightning bolt painted on the side, a pickup truck with ladders hanging off it, Dale's rusty blue Ford Tempo. Men were working in the yard, sawing two-by-fours, carrying in lumber, swaggering around in toolbelts. She didn't see her brother, but there was Fran Kennedy, in a pair of black stretch capris and a sweatshirt, talking to one of the men and pointing to the roof.

Joyce hoped she didn't notice her, but there she was waving, putting up one finger, signaling her to wait. Fran was trying so hard to make things right but, just for today, Joyce didn't want to talk to her and smile. She didn't want to nod approvingly at her plans, her choices of paint and wallpaper. Most of all, she didn't want a tour of the house in progress.

Joyce rolled down the window. Fran was waving something at her.

"I found this, in the cellar. I thought you should have it." Fran passed her a manila envelope, streaked with dirt and covered with pen markings. "Don't open it now. If you don't want to. Later, when you're alone."

At the cemetery Joyce stopped the car, got out and stretched. It felt good to be on Winter ground. From here, across fields starting to green up with spring, she could see the thin, blue strip of ocean. The Kennedy house was freshly shingled and painted. They were selling it to some relatives from New Jersey, who were going to use it as a summer place. "It will be just like a family compound," Fran had told her.

She took her tools out of the trunk and then, as she tossed her coat into the car, she saw the envelope, waiting there on the seat.

She picked it up. It smelled like unwashed potatoes. The flap was dull with dried mucilage.

She sighed and threw it back on the seat.

Joyce swung open the cemetery's metal gate. It hung limp on one hinge. She would have to ask Dale to fix that, when he could. His services were much in demand these days.

She knelt at the grave of her grandmother, Martha Winter, and with a wire brush began scrubbing away mildew from the stone. It was such an annoyance: green patches of fungus that spread out in all directions. Her mother had performed this chore, every year, but she had ignored Martha's stone to the point you could barely read its inscription:

| Martha Naylor Winter |
| 1903-1971 |
| Called home to Jesus |

Her father had come up with that. "Your grandmother loved to go to church. Sang in the choir," he had explained to her the day the granite maker brought the stone, which took three men to heave into place. "It broke her heart when she was too sick to attend services."

Joyce wondered about Martha, whom she had seen only through the lens of her mother's hatred. She remembered her as gruff and demanding too, but Jim Winter had adored his mother. He must have had a reason.

She moved to the next one and the next, cleaning the stone faces of generations of Winters – sea captains and farmers and housewives, children who died too young of typhus and diphtheria and scarlet fever, women who went to the grave with them, dead of childbed fever or contagious disease. So many shortened, sad lives; so much hard work, so much struggle.

Not ready for the last stones, that most recent corner, she went to her car for lunch and ate it sitting in the grass. She and Dale had known struggle too, but maybe a different kind. Their hearts had suffered if their bodies hadn't. Now life seemed to be turning around. Dale was in love with Althea. What an accident of happiness, her brother finding romance with her quirky, sincere, spiritual, wonderful friend. She was just what he needed. Someday, Joyce thought, she might find a love like that. And she might not. She knew now that searching for love was different from searching for a lost father, or a sister you never knew. Those sorts of aches could not be appeased by another person.

And if she had one regret, one secret agony, it was Camille. She had barely spoken to Joyce since the hurricane. Joyce had tried to reach out to her, but the truth was still too raw, too painful. "Do you hate looking at me?" Camille had said to her. And if there was some truth in that – if Joyce could not look upon her friend without a twisting pain in the gut – she tried to hide it. (She could not call her sister, not yet.) She had talked to Eric and tried to enlist his help, but he and his wife were in a tentative rapprochement and he didn't want to upset it. He understood Camille less than Joyce did, sometimes.

Dale, he had tried as well, his effort fueled by a sort of guilt that he had never recognized the truth when it was right in front of him. But she had repulsed him as well.

Joyce had one last crazy impulse today, when she left Mr. Rush's office, but it appeared that she had been rebuffed again.

She walked back to her car. There was the envelope, staring up at her. She didn't have to open it. But until she did, she would never be free of what was inside.

Joyce picked up the envelope. She weighed it one more time on her palm before opening the flap and reaching in for the thin piece of paper inside.

She recognized her father's cramped, busy hand. He always wrote as though it were a struggle to get his callused fingers to use a pen.

Jan. 19, 1978

Dear Joyce and Camille,

After I am gone, you will receive this letter. Camille, your mother is holding it for me, so I know she will give it to you when you are ready. Joyce, I hope you see this letter before your mother tells you the truth.

Years ago, before you were born, the farm was a place of grief. Your sister Susan had fallen into the pond and drowned. After that, my marriage was never the same. Camille, your mother helped me survive when I thought I would never be able to go on. I'm not saying it was right, but when people are grieving they do things they might not otherwise do. Marian and I both knew it was wrong but, Camille, we both loved you very much. I just couldn't be a father to you. I hope you can understand.

Joyce, I have tried to be a good father to you and Dale, but I have failed you. I don't think I could ever look you in the eye once you know the truth.

Somehow you girls have found each other. Don't let this split you apart. You are sisters. Half, step, I don't care what they want to call it, you are sisters. You are my daughters.

I know this is the coward's way out. I only hope that you both will forgive me.

It was signed James Winter, the signature flourishing, as though it were some legal document, and in parentheses: "*your father.*"

Only a few stones remained.

The new graves were in the northwest corner of the plot. One, a tiny rectangle of pink granite, had finally replaced the quartz Helen had dragged there years before. Its inscription read:

> Susan Elaine Winter
> Born July 15, 1951
> Died April 10, 1956
>
> *Full many a flower is born to blush unseen*
> *And waste its sweetness on the desert air.*

The quotation, from Gray's "Elegy Written in a Country Churchyard," had been Joyce's idea. Dale was not sure if he liked it, but he said poetry had never been his strong suit. And when she picked out one for their mother's grave, he warmed to the idea:

> Helen Richmond Winter
> Born Sept. 9, 1923
> Died Aug. 19, 1991
>
> *Ars longa, vita brevis.*

She felt her mother would have liked it: Art is long, life is short. Her mother always thought of herself as an artist. A writer. And the Latin was a nice touch. Her mother was a scholar above all. It was one last tribute to the best of who she was, and it said what Joyce truly believed, that her mother had been taken from them too soon, too cruelly.

For Fran Kennedy was right, after all. Her mother had had a hard life, one she wasn't prepared for. How much better off she would have been if she hadn't met their father . . . yet she did, and she bore Joyce, and Dale, and Susan, and she fell in love with this place. It was as much a part of her as flesh and bone. They had never given one thought to burying her in Cooperstown, though Uncle George had made some noise about it. No, she would not have been better off without James Winter; for who could change all the good and bad that had happened? It was all mixed up together.

Joyce, her knees aching, stood up, and looked back toward the house, stretching her arms to the sky.

Someone was coming, had parked behind the electrician's van and was sidestepping through the mud. A tall woman, with dark hair that swung around her face, and a long, free gait, like her father's.

Camille was out of breath when she reached Joyce, but she walked through the gate casually, as though she had stumbled on this place by accident. She smiled a little crookedly at Joyce standing there, a wire brush in her hand, as though she were about to style someone's hair. But Camille's eyes were wet and she couldn't seem to get the joke out.

"I heard you needed some help," she said finally.

There was only one grave left. Joyce and Camille knelt. After a while they began, together, to wipe clean the stone that was their father's.

The End

ABOUT THE AUTHOR

Betty J. Cotter holds an MFA in writing from the Vermont College of Fine Arts. Her first novel, Roberta's Woods, was published by Five Star in 2008. Publisher's Weekly praised its "strong character development, sensual writing and absorbing plot." An excerpt from The Winters earned her a fiction fellowship from the R.I. State Council on the Arts in 2006. She teaches writing at the University of Rhode Island and works as a newspaper editor.

Also by Betty J. Cotter

Roberta's Woods, A Novel
- Published by Five Star Expressions, March 2008

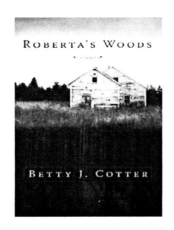